## PRAISE FOR *BENEATH THE VEIL OF SMOKE AND ASH*



"*Beneath the Veil of Smoke and Ash* exudes atmosphere and intrigue and gripped me from the very first page. . . . The storytelling in this novel is second to none, telling a gripping story of the struggle immigrants faced, whilst keeping twists and turns you won't see coming that serve to keep the story engaging throughout."

—*READERS' FAVORITE*, 5-star review

"A gripping, immersive story of immigrant grit in early-twentieth-century America. Set against the grim backdrop of Western Pennsylvania's steel mills and coal mines, this is an engrossing tale of poverty, desperation, and betrayal. Above all, *Beneath the Veil of Smoke and Ash* is a tale of overcoming tragedy and the transformative power of love. Pasterick's deftly wrought prose is nothing short of sublime."

—TONYA MITCHELL, award-winning author of *A Feigned Madness*

"Drawn from the author's family archives, this richly wrought family saga invites readers inside immigrant coal mining communities in early-twentieth-century Western Pennsylvania. Gritty and riveting, Pasterick's debut novel exposes the depths and lengths humans go to protect honor, family, and love."

—ASHLEY E. SWEENEY, award-winning author of *Answer Creek*

"*Beneath the Veil of Smoke and Ash* is a riveting, graphic etching of the impossible choices and unthinkable consequences forced upon early-twentieth-century immigrant workers by a bigoted society bent on ensuring they had no other options. Pasterick's vividly empathetic page-turner brings together an ensemble cast by turns relatable and reprehensible, drawn from a family history that could belong to countless American families. Heart-wrenching, yes, but don't turn away from this one. We have to read stories like this to truly know who we are as a nation."

—Ellen Notbohm, award-winning author of *The River by Starlight*

"At the turn into the twentieth century, immigrants were forced to accept the most dangerous jobs to sustain their families. This is the unforgettable story of one such family, struggling to survive against unimaginable odds and heartbreaking challenges in the cruel mines of Pennsylvania."

—Kathryn Johnson, award-winning author of *The Gentleman Poet*

"The novel's structure presents many short chapters from different points of view, giving energy to the complex exposition, which addresses topics such as mental illness, infertility, rape, and postpartum depression."

—*Kirkus Reviews*

"A striking portrait of the constant danger and risks associated with immigrants working in the mines and factories of early-twentieth-century industrial America."

—Michael Kopanic, Jr., Professor, University of Maryland Global Campus

"*Beneath the Veil of Smoke and Ash* tells the compelling and very human story of working-class immigrants in early-twentieth-century America. Meticulously researched, the author's compelling account captivates the reader while providing insight into the harsh and harrowing experience of immigrants coming to this country. In doing so, the book highlights the enormous strength and sacrifice required of those who came before us."

—Paul F. Clark, Director and Professor, School of Labor and Employment Relations, Penn State University

# Beneath the Veil of Smoke and Ash

*A Novel*

# Beneath the Veil of Smoke and Ash

TAMMY PASTERICK

SHE WRITES PRESS

Published 2021
Printed in the United States of America
Print ISBN: 978-1-64742-191-5
E-ISBN: 978-1-64742-192-2
Library of Congress Control Number: 2021908159

For information, address:
She Writes Press
1569 Solano Ave #546
Berkeley, CA 94707

Interior design by Tabitha Lahr

She Writes Press is a division of SparkPoint Studio, LLC.

Map of Pittsburgh created by Rick Antolic

For the countless immigrants who lost their lives in the steel mills and coal mines of Western Pennsylvania.

For Ethan and Morgan, my *zlatíčka.*

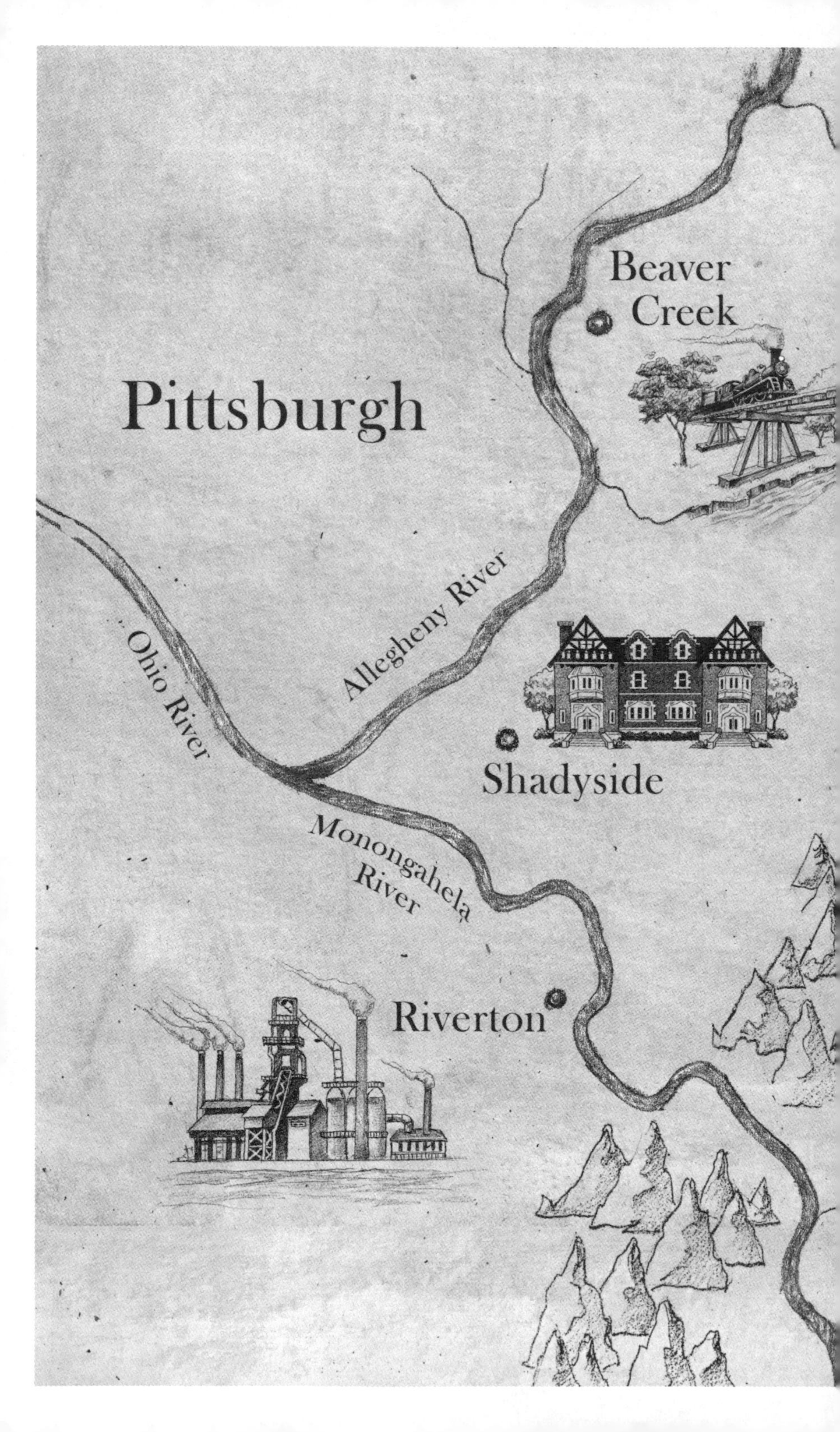
Beaver
Creek
Pittsburgh
Allegheny River
Ohio River
Shadyside
Monongahela
River
Riverton

N
W
E
S
Abbott's Hollow
Portage
Johnstown

*. . . we visited Mount Washington and took a bird's eye view of your city by moonlight. With the moon soft and mellow floating in the heavens we sauntered about the mount, and looked down on the lake of fire and flame. It looked like a miniature hell with the lid off.*

—Mark Twain, as quoted in the *Pittsburgh Daily Post*, December 31, 1884

# June 1910

"Is Lukas going to die, Papa?"

Janos swallowed hard as he forced himself not to look away from his daughter. Sofie's eyes were red and swollen, her dress caked in the dried blood of her little brother. The horrors of the day had followed them home.

"The doctors have done all they can for him," Janos said as he touched Sofie's shoulder. "It's in God's hands now."

"Will Mama come with us to the hospital tomorrow? Lukas will want her there when he wakes up."

Another wave of nausea hit Janos as he wiped a bead of sweat from his temple. Where was Karina? Her son was barely clinging to life, and she was nowhere to be found. He wasn't sure whether to be worried or angered by her absence. "Of course, *zlatíčko,*" he stammered. "I know she'd want to be at your brother's side."

Suddenly, Janos heard urgent footsteps climbing the steps to the back porch. As he sprang to his feet to open the door, his sister, Anna, burst into the room, her face ashen.

"The police are coming," she said breathlessly. "There's been a murder in the Heights. They're looking for the woman who works for Henry Archer."

Janos gasped. "A murder?"

"Was it Mr. Archer?" Sofie clutched her chest.

"I don't know. The neighbors are speaking to the detectives now. I didn't hang around long enough to get the details." Anna scanned the room. "Has Karina come home yet?"

Janos shook his head. "Still haven't seen her since last night."

Anna's eyes grew wide.

And then it struck him. Janos stumbled backwards onto the kitchen table, gripping its edge for support. *Lukas hadn't been confused. He was telling the truth.*

"I'm going back down the street to see what I can find out," Anna said as she rushed toward the door. "Maybe I can stall the police."

"Sofie," Janos whispered to his daughter. "Go up to bed and stay there."

"Yes, Papa," she replied, her lip quivering.

"And one more thing . . . don't tell anyone what Lukas saw at the train station this morning."

# *One Month Earlier*

# *One*

## KARINA

### RIVERTON, MAY 27, 1910

Karina Kovac heard the harsh caw of a crow passing overhead as she began her walk to work. She looked up at the early morning sky and frowned. The gray cloud of soot greeted her as it did every morning. No matter the time of day or season, the eerie mass hung, thick and heavy, casting its dismal shadow over her, darkening her mood.

She imagined the town along the river had once been beautiful—before industry and progress had blanketed the valley in a veil of smoke. But the Riverton she knew was ugly and depressing. The buildings were covered in a dingy layer of grime, and the air was an assault on her senses. It was only slightly less suffocating than that of Pittsburgh, which was ten miles downstream. The steel capital of the world was famous for its perpetually dark sky, which often necessitated the use of street lamps during the day. Karina's neighbors, most of them newly arrived from Eastern Europe, were unbothered by the smoky haze smothering the region. To them, it signaled opportunity and the promise of a better future. Jobs and prosperity.

Karina hated that gloomy sky, cursing it daily. It followed her everywhere, mocking her and laughing at her lack of success. She had failed to acquire the comfortable lifestyle she'd envisioned when she left Austria-Hungary over a decade earlier, and that sky wouldn't let her forget it.

Karina had known it would take time for her and Janos to build a new life, but she'd never expected it to take so long. Working as a housekeeper in the town's wealthiest neighborhood gave her a glimpse of what she and her family had not yet achieved. Her current employer owned every modern convenience she craved. Electricity. Indoor plumbing. A spacious kitchen with the latest Garland gas cookstove and McCray refrigerator. All had been installed in the mill manager's new Foursquare home.

Karina stood in awe before the door of that refrigerator every morning, marveling at how fresh the food stayed. Her family's ancient ice chest smelled of souring milk and had to be scrubbed constantly with Old Dutch Cleanser.

As Karina endured her daily coughing fit near the steel mill's towering smokestacks, she heard a sharp whistle coming from a worker in the rail yard. She rolled her eyes. Though her housekeeper's uniform was boring and drab, she still managed to attract unwanted attention. Perhaps her elaborate hairstyle had caught the man's eye. She'd spent a ridiculous amount of time fussing with her hair that morning in the hopes that the executives coming from US Steel's Pittsburgh offices would take notice of her. While she was grateful for the position in Henry Archer's home, she longed to work at one of the grand estates in Shadyside or Squirrel Hill. What a relief it would be to get lost among an entire staff of servants.

Karina sighed as she thought of the first weeks in her employer's home. She had wandered dreamily through the rooms, fingering the fine linens and switching the lights off and on, for fun. She'd soaked in the bathtub and napped beneath an expensive, snowy white Marseilles quilt. She thought she'd found the perfect escape from her dreary neighborhood and her job at the boarding house, but little did she know, the luxury of working in that home would come with a price.

A gust of wind suddenly hit Karina from behind and interrupted her brooding. She patted the mound of curls at the back of her head to make sure her garnet hair comb was still in place. She froze when her fingertips failed to locate it. Her heart pounding, she scanned the unpaved street and then shook her dress, hoping the comb would fall out of one of its folds. *Where could it be?* Her mind began to race.

Karina turned and rushed back down the street toward the shabby rows of homes erected by the steel company. Her eyes darted in every direction, hoping to find the only valuable piece of jewelry she owned. When she arrived home breathless, she burst through the front door and began searching the sitting room.

"Karina? I thought you'd left for work," Janos said, peeking through the kitchen doorway.

"My hair comb is missing. I got the whole way to the mill before I realized it was gone. I retraced my steps, but can't find it anywhere." Karina inspected the floor and every nearby surface, her eyes welling with tears. "It's the only thing I own of value."

"Was it the comb with the tiny garnets?" Janos touched her on the shoulder, his face full of concern.

"Do I have another worth fretting over?" Karina glared at her husband as she brushed his hand away and hurried toward the staircase. "Maybe it's in the bedroom," she murmured.

"Mama!" Sofie shouted. "Did you bother to look in your brown pocketbook? That's the one you came home with yesterday."

Startled, Karina paused at the foot of the stairs as her ten-year-old daughter stomped out of the kitchen. "Shouldn't you be in bed, Sofie? The sun's barely up."

"Where's the pocketbook?" Janos asked his wife.

"It's on the bookcase," Karina said, dabbing her wet eyes with the sleeve of her dress. "But I'm sure I put the comb in my hair this morning. I know I did."

"You need to calm down," Janos said coolly as he picked up the worn pocketbook and peered inside. It took him just seconds to pull out the tortoise shell comb adorned with garnets.

Karina grabbed the hair comb and dashed toward the front door. "How could I forget?" she groaned, turning the doorknob.

"Wait," Janos said. "Don't you have something to say to Sofie?"

Karina sighed as she looked at her daughter for the first time that morning. "Thank you, honey. You were very helpful."

Sofie ran to her mother and hugged her. "Good luck today, Mama. I know those important men from Pittsburgh will be impressed with your cooking."

"Let's hope so."

"Is that why you're so agitated this morning?" Janos asked.

"I guess," Karina said, smoothing Sofie's unruly hair. "I want to make a good impression today. Meeting these executives could lead to something . . . maybe a better position."

Janos raised an eyebrow.

"I need to go. I'm running late. And, Sofie, please do something with your hair before you leave for school. You can't go out in public with that mess on your head." Her poor daughter's thick blonde hair often looked like a bird's nest when she woke in the morning.

Sofie nodded politely, despite the wounded look on her face.

"Maybe we could all go to the Radovics' tonight to listen to Mihal play the accordion," Janos said as Karina stepped onto the front porch. "An evening with friends will help you relax after such a big day at work."

"The new Sears Roebuck catalog is out. Maybe another time," Karina said, trying to disguise her guilt. She knew her family was tired of her excuses, but she did not enjoy socializing with the neighbors. Besides, she really did want to see the latest spring fashions.

As Karina hurried down the street toward the mill, she tucked her hair comb into her pocketbook, figuring there was no way to place it perfectly on her head without a mirror. And she dared not risk losing it on the street. Poverty had made her desperate. Her neighbors, too. They all clung fiercely to the few valuable items they owned, because they couldn't afford to replace them.

When Karina finally reached Riverton Heights, she inhaled the cool morning air. The neighborhood sat high on the hill above town and escaped much of the smoke in the valley below. Fresh air was her reward for her twenty-minute climb uphill. The streets were lined with new Craftsman and Foursquare homes as well as some older Victorians. Graceful oak trees shaded the streets, and the sweet scent of pansies permeated the air.

Karina's stomach quivered as she stepped onto Henry Archer's front porch and unlocked the mahogany door. If one of the Pittsburgh executives failed to take notice of her, she planned to ask Henry for a raise. She had been working very long hours since she'd accepted the position with him six months earlier and had only received a slight increase in pay when her duties were expanded in March. Karina was certain she had proven her worth many times over in recent weeks, especially since her new responsibilities had little to do with keeping a house.

She closed the front door behind her and made her way to the kitchen at the back of the house. The sun was now up, but there were no sounds from upstairs to indicate Henry had risen. Not wanting to wake him, she quietly gathered ingredients for a pot roast from the refrigerator and pantry. As Karina washed vegetables in the farmhouse sink, she heard footsteps in the hall. She turned around to find Henry standing in the doorway of the kitchen with a smirk on his face.

"There's no need to make lunch today," he announced. "I got a call from Pittsburgh last night. The meeting has been cancelled."

Karina gasped. "But I thought those men were coming to discuss your promotion."

She tried to her hide her disappointment as she studied the face of her employer. She had never found him attractive. The college-educated bachelor was several inches shorter than her husband and lacked the brawn she was accustomed to seeing in the men around her neighborhood. He wore a permanent frown on his face, and his thin, charcoal-colored hair was receding. But today, he looked surprisingly pleasant, grinning like a school boy. How could he not be disappointed by their change in fortune?

"They were, but I'm no longer being considered for the position here in Riverton. I'm being transferred to headquarters in New York City." Henry clapped his hands with excitement. "I'm going home."

Paralyzed by the news, Karina stood motionless, trying to control the panic welling inside her. She leaned back against the porcelain sink for support, suddenly unable to breathe, her chest tightening.

Still grinning, Henry crossed the kitchen in three long strides. He grabbed Karina's left breast and shoved his tongue into her mouth. His free hand moved greedily down the front of her dress. Even after three months of enduring his touch, Karina still had to remind herself not to recoil. But this morning, she was completely unaffected by Henry's groping. Her singular focus was her uncertain future.

She gently pulled away from his eager kisses and took a deep breath. "When do you leave?"

"Not until the end of June. I need to train my replacement and tie up some loose ends at the mill. But I need you to start packing right away."

Suddenly, memories of a run-down boarding house full of drunks flooded Karina's mind. She flinched as a filthy immigrant squeezed her buttocks, the stench of his sweaty, unwashed body burning her nose. Shouts for more moonshine drowned out an old man's complaint that the tripe was too chewy. A newcomer griped that someone had taken prostitutes into his room and soiled his mattress. He demanded that Karina clean the mess immediately. She groaned as she tried to shake the chaos from her head. *I can't go back.*

A slight pinch transported Karina back to Henry's kitchen. His teeth were on her earlobe.

"Shall we go into the bedroom to celebrate?" he whispered.

## Two

# SOFIE

### RIVERTON, MAY 27, 1910

*Work in the mill makes a man old before his time.* That was what the grown-ups in Sofie Kovac's neighborhood always said. She thought of this tired expression as she studied the figure of a man hobbling across the courtyard behind her house. He was barely visible in the early morning fog, but seemed to be headed for the communal privy just steps from her back porch. He was a steelworker, like her father, but looked much older. He shuffled along slowly, clutching his knee with each labored step. Sofie crossed herself, praying her father wouldn't suffer the same fate.

She refocused her attention from the window back to the bacon grease. It flowed, like liquid gold, from the cast iron frying pan into the Mason jar she struggled to keep steady on the kitchen counter. She had dropped Aunt Anna's grease jar once before and watched the precious drippings from a week's worth of meals slide between the cracks in the floorboards. She shuddered at the thought of repeating that mistake.

Aunt Anna had lectured her for days about the value of all those flavorings now resting permanently in the dirt beneath the kitchen floor. "Like tossing coins into the river," her aunt had scolded.

Sofie held her breath and tightened her grip on the jar as the last few drops of grease plopped from the frying pan onto the hardening pile of sludge—the key ingredient in all her aunt's recipes. The pan now empty, she let out a sigh of relief.

"Do you need some help, *zlatíčko*?" Papa asked, his footsteps growing louder as he neared the kitchen counter.

Sofie shook her head. "The bacon's a little crispy. I left it on the stove too long. If Mama hadn't distracted me—"

"You never told me why you're making breakfast this morning instead of your aunt," Papa said, changing the subject.

"I had a nightmare. I couldn't get back to sleep, so I told Aunt Anna I'd do the cooking today."

"You're so thoughtful," Papa said as he bent to kiss Sofie on the forehead. "Do you want to tell me about the nightmare? Sometimes it helps to talk about it."

"No, not really." Suddenly, a haunting image flashed before Sofie's eyes. Her father's lifeless body lay on the ground in front of a furnace, blistered and burnt. It was the same disturbing vision that appeared in her sleep every few weeks. Why was it now tormenting her in the light of day?

"So what's for lunch?"

"Bacon sandwiches, leftover fried cabbage, and an apple," Sofie said as she fidgeted with the items in her father's beat-up tin lunch bucket. It was badly dented and covered in grime, but one of her favorite things. Seeing that bucket on the kitchen counter always made her happy. It was proof that her father was home safe from the mill.

Once Papa's lunch was packed, Sofie filled two plates with eggs and bacon and placed them on the wobbly kitchen table. She sat down across from her father, who was extinguishing the oil lamp. He looked tired, his eyes still heavy with sleep. A ray of sunlight pouring through the kitchen window accentuated the gray in his freshly combed hair, making him look older.

Sofie stared at the tattered brown shirt her father wore. He'd ripped off its sleeves since his work in front of the furnace was so terribly hot. In fact, anytime Aunt Anna bought him a new shirt at the second-hand store, Papa promptly tore off the sleeves and gave them back to her for use as cleaning rags. How Sofie wished Papa could wear a suit to work every day. He'd be so much safer in an office job. She slammed her glass of water onto the table, startling herself.

"Are you all right?" Papa asked. "What's got you so upset? The nightmare?"

Sofie nodded. "Mama, too," she grumbled as she shoved a fork full of eggs into her mouth. She wasn't even hungry. She was still angry about her mother's lame excuse for not joining them at the neighbors' that evening. *The Sears Catalog?* Sofie never understood why her mother spent so much time staring at clothing she couldn't afford.

"I'm sorry your mother hurt your feelings." Papa patted Sofie's hand. "That happens too often."

Sofie wondered whether Mama had hurt his feelings, too. She'd angrily brushed Papa's hand away when he'd laid it on her shoulder. Mama always ignored his affections. Sofie couldn't remember the last time she saw her parents share an embrace. They were so different from the other couples in the neighborhood. The Lithuanians across the street acted like they might never see each other again when the husband left for the mill each morning.

"Why don't you tell me about your dream," Papa said, stroking Sofie's hair.

She laid down her fork and studied her father's concerned face. She hated bothering him with her troubles. He had a fair amount of his own.

"I'm listening."

Sofie could no longer resist the urge to confide in her father. "It was the same one I always have—you're at work in the mill, in front of your furnace. And there's an accident . . ." Sofie's eyes filled with tears. "It's a little different every time, but the ending is always the same." She began to cry.

Papa reached across the table and pulled Sofie into his arms. He rubbed her back as she buried her face in his chest. "You need to stop worrying about me. The mill is dangerous, but I'm careful. I have years of experience."

"Will you please quit?" Sofie pleaded, looking up at her father. "Can't you find a safer job?"

"I wish I could, but only the mills and mines will hire immigrants," he said, shaking his head.

"But your English is perfect. Doesn't that make a difference?"

"Don't worry your pretty little head about me. You need to focus on school and getting into trouble with your friends," Papa said with a wink. "Now finish your breakfast before it's cold."

Sofie trudged back to her chair, wiping her eyes with the hem of her dress and feeling no more at ease with her father's work at the mill. As she nibbled on a piece of bacon, she forced her mind to switch gears. "How did Lukas end up on the floor again last night? I nearly tripped over him this morning. He was curled up in a ball near the door."

"He can't seem to lie still anymore. I put him back on the mattress and covered him with a blanket before I came downstairs."

"I guess he doesn't have enough space on the mattress with you anymore, Papa. He's getting too big."

Sofie watched as her father pushed the remains of his eggs around on his plate, scratching his graying temple. He looked up at his daughter and sighed.

"That's not the problem. I fear your brother is becoming more like your mother. Restless. And in search of a better position."

# *Three*

## JANOS

### RIVERTON, MAY 27, 1910

At the Riverton mill, Janos Kovac stood before an open-hearth furnace filled with molten steel heated to over 2500°F. He wiped his sweaty brow with his forearm as he held a heavy crowbar in his hands. A dull, persistent ache plagued his lower back, making his thirty-three-year-old body feel like it belonged to a much older man. The mill's excessive heat, persistent noise, and stifling air filled with mineral dust and furnace exhaust were taking a terrible toll on his health. Janos had survived a decade of twelve-hour shifts, often seven days per week, but wondered how much more his body could endure. Massaging his lower back, he was sorry he had sacrificed his youth to the mill.

Janos thought about how naive he'd been when he arrived in America with his pregnant wife in the winter of 1900. Work at the mill was to be temporary, a means of survival until he became fluent in English. Once he achieved that goal, he would fulfill his lifelong dream of becoming a writer or teacher.

Sadly, Janos had not expected that advancement would be next to impossible for an immigrant. While he mastered the English language within a year of his arrival in America—nearly unheard of for an immigrant—his linguistic talent did not liberate him from the mill. He couldn't even manage to escape his position as a melter at one of the mill's sixty open-hearth furnaces.

Janos tried not to lose hope, but was constantly reminded of his place in American society. Whether strolling through town or working at his furnace, native-born citizens ridiculed his nationality and accent. His foreignness was offensive to them. Frightening, even. After several failed interviews with newspapers and schools and no hopes of a promotion in sight, Janos's hopes faded. Life in the mill provided him with a daily dose of seething reality. Blazing hot, fiery, glowing, molten steel would be his life's work.

"Janos! Wake up! You tappin' that furnace or not?" barked Patrick O'Boyle, the Irish crane operator whose job it was to maneuver a hundred-ton ladle of molten metal away from the furnace and over to the molds where the ingots were formed.

"Sorry, Pat. I was lost in thought."

"Now's not the time to be ponderin'," muttered the crane operator. He spat a wad of chewing tobacco over his shoulder. The brown juice dribbled down the side of the crane.

As Janos prepared to knock the hole out in the furnace door, his thoughts turned to his conversation with Sofie at breakfast. He hadn't realized his daughter was so deeply troubled by his work at the mill. He hoped she was simply going through another phase and that this most recent fear would pass as quickly as had her dread of spiders. He sighed, wondering if Sofie's anxiety was something she might outgrow. It seemed to be worsening as of late.

But weighing more heavily on Janos's mind than his nervous daughter was his capricious wife. In describing Lukas's fitful sleep to Sofie, he had inadvertently stumbled upon an insightful truth about Karina. *She is restless and in search of something better.*

Janos felt a familiar ache and sense of unease. Karina's unpredictable mood swings and long periods of sadness had been a strain on him for as long as he could remember. After the birth of Sofie and then Lukas, Karina had been especially melancholy. She'd seemed detached from her babies and showed little interest in them. It still puzzled Janos. He could not comprehend how a woman who had given birth to a healthy baby could feel anything but joy.

Janos often wished his wife would be more like the other Slovak women in the neighborhood—like the women he'd known all his life. His own mother and sister were such devoted wives and mothers. Family and faith were at the center of their lives. Unfortunately, the same could not be said of Karina. She was always indifferent when her children entered the room or when she begrudgingly attended mass at St. Michael's Roman Catholic Church. Her mind always seemed to be somewhere else. Janos had struggled for years to make his wife happy—or at least something short of miserable—but she was constantly out of his reach.

Fortunately, Karina's mood had improved since she'd left the boarding house, and Janos was grateful. His wife took great pride in working for Mr. Archer, as positions in a house such as his were usually reserved for native-born Americans or Irish immigrants. Certainly not a Slovak. Janos suspected Karina's beauty was the reason Mr. Archer had hired someone from the lowest class of immigrants. The man's motivations made no difference to Janos as long as his wife was treated well and paid a fair wage.

Karina's long-awaited escape from the boarding house should have put Janos's mind at ease, but he could not shake the feeling that something was still amiss. He had fully expected his wife's contentment with her new position to lead to more intimacy in their marriage. He'd always believed that the rift between them was a result of her bitterness about working at the boarding house. Janos had clearly been mistaken because Karina still wouldn't let him touch her. She hadn't in months.

"Kovac! Stop starin' at that crowbar!" the crane operator yelled. "Tap the goddamned furnace already."

Janos flinched. He'd almost forgotten where he was. He quickly raised his bar and knocked the hole out in the furnace door. He watched as glowing red fluid gushed from the door into the ladle waiting in the eight-foot-deep pit below the furnace. The heat was so intense that his already damp work shirt was soon drenched and clinging to his body. Sparks flew, singeing the hair on his arms. Janos imagined this was probably what hell looked like, glowing red flames all around. He half expected to see the devil crawl out of that raging pit.

Once the ladle was brimming with molten steel, Janos backed far away from the path it would take to the molds. "Ready, Pat?" he shouted.

The crane operator nodded his head and waved his arm. He began to lift the massive ladle out of the pit. Janos continually surveyed the ladle's progress and scanned the area to make sure everyone was at a safe distance.

And then the unthinkable happened.

Just as the crane was about to swing toward the molds, Janos heard a loud *crack*. It was sharp and quick and reminded him of a firecracker his neighbor had set off the last 4th of July. He watched in terror as the ladle carrying a hundred tons of molten metal crashed to the ground. It exploded on impact, sending splatters of fiery liquid twenty-five feet in every direction. Janos's blood ran cold as he witnessed a worker being struck by the blast.

Horrified, he ran to the far side of the furnace where Tomas Tomicek was lying on the ground, much of the left side of his body burnt beyond recognition. Janos fought the urge to retch.

The scent of the man's burning flesh was pungent, like meat frying in a pan.

Trembling and blinded by tears, Janos knelt beside his co-worker and grabbed his right hand, which had been untouched by the molten metal. Poor Tomas now looked like half a man. The skin on the left side of his face had been melted by the scorching steel, revealing his cheekbone and jawbone. The other side of his face remained completely intact, looking just as young and healthy as it had moments before. Tomas's left arm, shoulder, and upper chest had also melted. The brown work shirt he'd been wearing had disintegrated, revealing a grisly mixture of flesh and blood. Janos had never seen a more gruesome accident at the mill. He knew there was no hope.

He leaned closer, positioning his face inches from Tomas's. Praying to the Holy Spirit for guidance, Janos struggled to find the words that might comfort a dying man. Through quivering lips, he whispered in Slovak, "Lie still, Tomas. Stay calm." He squeezed the man's hand. "Your brother will be here soon." Janos glanced up at the chaos surrounding him. Men ran frantically in every direction, desperate to find Tomas's twin brother.

At the sound of a guttural moan, Janos turned his attention back to the young man. He was trembling now, coughing up blood. Tears streaming down his face, Janos tried to reassure him. "God is with you, Tomas. His healing hands are upon you. He is cradling you in his arms."

Janos could no longer maintain his composure. He began to weep.

Suddenly, Pavol Tomicek appeared, panic-stricken, hands outstretched. "Tomas! Tomas!" he screamed. "No!"

Pavol reached his brother's side and, seeing what was left of his charred and blistered body, dropped to his knees in violent sobs. He reached for his brother's hand, but it was too late.

Janos had felt the dying man's hand go limp in his own just seconds earlier. Tomas Tomicek was already gone.

## *Four*

# HENRY

### RIVERTON, MAY 27, 1910

Henry Archer was having a splendid morning. He knew he would be late for work, but that didn't matter. He only had a little over a month left in this hellhole. He had worked hard over the past five years to impress his superiors and had proven himself to be a competent manager. He knew that some thought him arrogant, but even he had not predicted a promotion to US Steel Headquarters in New York City. It was too good to be true. He was giddy with the possibilities.

Also too good to be true was the blue-eyed, blonde beauty lying next to him. Henry had bedded plenty of women over the years—many of whom were paid generously for their services—but no one compared to Karina. She had the most flawless skin he'd ever seen and perfectly round breasts. Her tiny waist gave them a more ample look than they deserved, but the effect was breathtaking. Henry had never met a woman with such an incredible body and face to match.

Henry hated to admit it, but his lust for Karina was becoming uncontrollable. Images of her naked body flashed before his eyes at the most inconvenient moments. The previous week, he had been forced to excuse himself from an important meeting at the mill so he could relieve himself in the men's bathroom. Since the start of his affair with Karina a few months earlier, his focus at work had steadily declined.

Staring at her lying on her back with a sheet covering only her lower body, Henry was becoming aroused yet again. He rolled over toward his petite lover and squeezed her breast.

Karina opened her eyes. "The first time wasn't enough?"

"I'm insatiable," Henry said, chuckling. "I'm not sure I'll ever get enough."

"What will you do when you move to New York?"

The question nearly knocked the wind out of Henry. He hadn't considered his arrangement with Karina since receiving word of his promotion. He'd been too excited about his career prospects to think of anything else. What would he do without her? Could he find a replacement for her in New York? Surely his prestigious position at US Steel headquarters would make him more attractive to the society women he hadn't dared approach years earlier. He knew they valued wealth and influence above all else.

"Looks like you've got a problem." Karina pushed Henry away from her chest and started to get up from the bed.

"Where are you going? I wasn't finished." He sat up and grabbed her by the elbow. "We only have a month left together."

Karina turned around, her eyes narrowed. "In a month, I'll be out of work, and you'll be in New York City at your cushy new job. Why should I crawl back into bed with you?"

"Shouldn't we enjoy the time we have left? Are you ready to go back to that disgusting boarding house already? Because I can hire someone else to pack my things." Henry was certain his threat would scare Karina back into bed.

"I can't think of anything worse," she grumbled.

Henry studied Karina as she sat on the edge of the bed, eyes closed, hands clutching her knees. She sat motionless for several minutes. He could only assume she was thinking about the boarding house and her lack of options. Suddenly, she opened her eyes and turned to face him.

"Take me with you, Henry. Take me to New York."

He raised an eyebrow. "You're joking, right?"

Karina shook her head sheepishly.

Henry's eyes widened. "Have you lost your mind?"

"Probably. The idea of going back to that wretched boarding house is driving me mad. I can't do it," she said, her voice breaking.

Henry watched as a tear rolled down Karina's cheek. She quickly brushed it away and pulled the sheet over her chest. She stared blankly toward the foot of the bed. Henry suspected his chances of dipping his wick one more time before work were slipping away. He needed to act fast.

"Maybe I can give you a reference. Surely there's another family who'd be willing to hire you." Henry doubted his words the instant they'd left his lips. No woman in her right mind would want a looker like Karina under the same roof as her husband. And few would hire a Hunky housekeeper anyway. Henry was the exception. His hiring decisions were driven by his weakness for gorgeous women.

Karina looked up. "I'm not sure that's what I want. I've had enough of this filthy town."

"But your family . . ."

"I know. I know," Karina whined. She pulled at her hair, dropping the sheet that was covering her chest.

Henry trembled with excitement. Karina looked so alluring with her hands above her head, her breasts on full display. Maybe he couldn't live without her. Perhaps taking his housekeeper to New York wasn't so absurd. If she lived with him, he would have access to her both day and night. He imagined waking up from an erotic dream in the dark of night and rolling over toward Karina to satisfy himself.

"Why are you grinning like that?" she asked, interrupting Henry's fantasy.

"I'm considering your request. It could be mutually beneficial."

"You are?" Karina's jaw dropped.

"But I need to figure out what role you would play. Your beauty is wasted in a housekeeper's uniform. I wonder if my society friends might be accepting of you as my mistress. You'd look stunning in proper evening attire." Henry did not mention that he had yet to make any society friends. But he was sure his promotion would open many doors for him. Perhaps he could procure a spot on the board of a prestigious charity.

"A mistress?" Karina asked, sounding surprised.

"You can't go as my wife." Henry shook his head. "Someone of my stature would never marry a Hunky immigrant."

Karina glared at him. "I suppose we could tell your friends I'm Russian or German. No one in your circles would be able to identify my accent. It's so faint anyway."

"You look Russian. I haven't had much experience with foreigners, but I once met a girl from Moscow who had cheekbones like yours." Henry did not dare mention that the girl was a prostitute he had paid to pleasure him. "Tell me again why your English is so good. Don't you Hunkies all live together in the same neighborhood speaking Slovak and eating cabbage and noodles?"

Another glare. "My husband took the English classes offered by the mill when we first arrived in America. He taught me everything he learned," she said, straightening her back.

"Do you think you can lose the accent?"

Karina shrugged. "Maybe."

Henry cleared his throat. "If I allow you to accompany me to New York, I expect you to make some changes. I need a mistress fit for high society." He smirked as he offered his terms, certain he sounded like a man of power and influence.

Karina frowned as she stood up and went to the window facing the smoky valley occupied by the mill. She muttered to herself in Slovak for several minutes while staring at the town she loathed. In the midst of her apparent deliberating, she turned around twice to give Henry a long, hard look.

Was she sizing him up? Was it really so difficult to make a choice between him and Riverton? Henry was insulted, but reminded himself that she did have a husband and children to think of. Still, as the clock ticked, his irritation grew. He considered rescinding his offer.

Suddenly, Karina went silent. She turned around slowly and climbed back into bed, a determined look on her face. She planted herself on top of Henry and leered at him like an animal about to pounce on its prey. He wasn't sure whether to be aroused or scared.

"Who do you want me to be, Henry?" Karina asked, clutching his face.

"I don't know. I can't concentrate when you look like you're about to hurt me." Henry couldn't decide if Karina was angry or merely playing a new erotic game. The look in her eyes was menacing.

She mumbled something in Slovak—a curse perhaps—and then loosened her grip on Henry's face. "This is insane. I should leave," she said, shaking her head and turning away from him.

"If that's what you want," he said, trying to sound resigned. "Those drunks at the boarding house sure will be surprised to see your pretty face in the morning."

Karina scowled.

Henry reached up to stroke her hair. "Don't you want to go to New York? Don't you want to get away from this miserable town?" He stared at Karina's twisted face, watching the potency of his words take effect. As her chin moved in an almost imperceptible nod, he gently pushed her head toward his midsection.

Karina closed her eyes and let out a deep sigh. She then inched her way down the length of Henry's chest, pausing just below his abdomen. He thought he heard her whimper, but was soon too caught up in his own pleasure to wonder why.

# Five

## SOFIE

### RIVERTON, MAY 27, 1910

As Sofie headed down the steep hill from St. Michael's Catholic School toward the river, she could barely contain her excitement. She loved escaping the noisy commotion of her town—the screeching trains heading to and from the mill, the overwhelming chatter of a half-dozen languages being spoken in the town's market district, the squeals of children playing in her run-down Slavic neighborhood. Fishing along the banks of the Monongahela River was her favorite Friday afternoon pastime.

Sofie had begun exploring the river's banks with her father as soon as she'd learned to walk. He had shown her all the best places to fish, far away from the center of town and upstream from the mill where the water ran clear. He'd warned her not to fish anywhere near where the mill dumped its waste into the river. The scent of it was rank, and it sickened the fish if it didn't kill them.

With the help of her father and her best friend, Pole, Sofie had become an expert fisherman. She was proud of her skills and grateful she could provide for her family in her own small way. Fresh fish from the river meant less of Papa's paycheck had to be spent at the market.

As Sofie followed the narrow trail at the edge of town that led to her favorite fishing spot, she heard the roar of an angry river. The morning's thunderstorm had left the river swollen and had strengthened its already swiftly moving currents. She immediately spotted Pole leaning against a hazelnut tree with three carp on his stringer. Though he was a few months shy of his thirteenth birthday, he looked older due to his height and muscular build. His wavy, brown hair was disheveled, and his flannel shirt was covered in dirt.

"How did you catch three fish already?"

"I skipped my Slovak lesson. Couldn't really see the point," Pole said in his most rebellious tone.

"The point is to preserve our heritage. I like learning about our culture and language."

"Your parents may be Slovak, but you're American, Sofie. You were born here. Besides, I'm only half Slovak, and that's not my favorite side. I like bein' Polish better."

"I know, *Pole*," Sofie said sarcastically.

Pole's defiant nature sometimes irritated her, but he had good reason to be bitter. His mother died two years earlier, and all he had left was a drunken father. John Stofanik worked at the mill and made Sofie's father uneasy. He worried that Stofanik would fall into a pot of molten steel, or worse, he would be responsible for someone else's death.

Pole was currently wearing a nasty shiner, and Sofie didn't need to ask where it came from. Even if she did, Pole would invent a ridiculous story. He was ashamed of his father, and who could blame him? That drunk was the reason Pole rejected his Slovak heritage and embraced his mother's Polish one.

"I saw your mama on her way to work this morning. Does she always leave that early?"

"Sometimes. She doesn't seem to mind though," Sofie said, trying not to sound angry. She resented the fact that her mother was more devoted to her job than her family. Mama had practically sprinted out the door that morning to impress the men from Pittsburgh. Sofie was still upset about the comment her mother had made about her hair. Suddenly, a disturbing thought popped into her head. *Mama doesn't think I'm pretty.* Was that the reason she never paid her any attention?

"Must be paradise cookin' and cleanin' for Mr. Archer all day in a house like that. How'd she get so lucky?" Pole picked up his tin can full of worms and handed it to Sofie.

She grabbed the can and gave him a dirty look.

"I guess that was a stupid question. Who wouldn't prefer a pretty lady washin' their drawers over an ugly one? Your mama's a looker." Pole brushed some dirt off his knee and gazed across the river. "You know, you have her blonde hair and blue eyes."

"I'd rather have a fat, ugly mother who loves me." Sofie bit her lip and angrily baited her hook with a worm. The poor creature bore the brunt of her frustration.

"At least you've got your papa. He's a good man. I'd trade my pop in any day for yours." Pole sighed and stared at his fishing rod.

The two sat quietly for several minutes, tending their fishing poles. The top of her head growing warm, Sofie looked up to see an exceptionally bright sun beating down upon her. The sky over Riverton was usually filled with too much smoke to see the sun, but the morning's thunderstorm had cut down the haze.

Sofie turned her attention to the river and watched the afternoon sunlight sparkle on its ever-changing surface. It was mesmerizing. The little twinkles of light danced among the currents, carrying her upsetting thoughts away with them downstream. Sofie inhaled deeply as she caught the scent of wild lilacs in the gentle breeze. She leaned toward the ground to smell the earthworms and wet grass. She was suddenly calm and content.

A strong tug at the end of Sofie's fishing line interrupted her reverie. She tightened her grip on her rod and began to reel in what she imagined was an enormous beast. Beads of sweat formed on her forehead as she jerked her rod while fighting her way backwards up the riverbank. The fish was tenacious, yanking so hard on Sofie's line she feared it might snap. She was encouraged when her adversary's head emerged from the water several minutes into the battle, but it quickly fought its way back to its murky domain. Sofie cursed under her breath.

"Need a hand?" Pole asked from behind her.

"No, I've got him," she said, grunting. Determined to conquer her dinner, Sofie gritted her teeth and gave her rod one last forceful jerk. She squealed as the fish sailed through the air and landed in the grass at Pole's feet.

"That's a monster!" he shouted.

Sofie leapt with joy at the sight of the carp. It was nearly as long as her arm. She rushed over to Pole to retrieve her prize.

"Let me put it on the stringer for you, Sof," he said, holding the fish. "You catch your breath."

As Pole busied himself with the stringer, Sofie found herself staring at her best friend instead of her fish. "How lucky would we be if we lived together in a house with my father and your mother?" she wondered aloud. "If she were still alive, of course. We'd have the perfect family." Sofie had always wished for a mother as sweet and thoughtful as Pole's. She often had freshly baked cookies waiting for them when they returned from fishing. And she gave the best hugs.

"Sounds nice, but there's no use daydreamin' about things that can never be."

Sofie frowned, disappointed in Pole's lack of imagination.

"Aww, come on." He laid a hand on her shoulder. "I'm not tryin' to be mean. I just think you're better off keeping your head out of the clouds. You gotta deal with the reality you've got."

Sofie thought about her awkward interaction with her mother that morning and her poor excuse for not wanting to visit the neighbors. It was nothing out of the ordinary. Mama was always looking for ways to avoid her family. Sofie doubted it would ever change.

"Wipe that frown off your face and look at the size of this fish you caught," Pole said, holding up the stringer. "Wait until your papa sees it. He won't believe his eyes."

Sofie glanced at the enormous carp and then studied Pole's face. "Why do *you* look so proud? You didn't catch that fish."

"No, but I wish I did." Pole chuckled. "I'm proud of you, Sof. Now let's hurry up and catch a few more. I can't wait to get back to town to show off this beast."

Sofie blushed as she shoved a hook through a worm. She suddenly couldn't remember what had been troubling her minutes earlier.

*Six*

# POLE

## RIVERTON, MAY 27, 1910

When Pole Stofanik returned just before sunset to the Hunky boarding house he and his father called home, he quickly noticed the somber mood of his fellow residents. On the bowed wooden front porch of the crumbling hotel sat three young steelworkers speaking Slovak in hushed tones, each with a whiskey in hand. Two of the boarding house's maids sat on the porch steps, arms entwined and heads hung low. Something must have happened at the mill. Friday nights at the boarding house were usually anything but quiet.

Pole and his father had come to live at the Janosik family's dilapidated hotel just months after his mother's death. Without the additional income from her job at the bakery, his father couldn't afford to continue renting the two-room shack the family shared on Railroad Street. John Stofanik's penchant for booze would ensure that they stayed broke forever.

Life at the boarding house had required adjustments for Pole, but he was resilient and resourceful. He seized the opportunity to make money and quickly befriended the immigrants fresh off the boat. He often sold them fish or accompanied them on their errands in town, translating for them at the market or bank. He knew enough Slovak and Polish to be able to sell his services, but he had to refer the Russians and Lithuanians to his friend Dmitri, who lived down the street.

The boarding house was rather run-down, but it was a fascinating place to live. It was a three-story hotel built into the side of a hill. Years earlier, an ingenious—or possibly thrifty—builder attached three walls of pine siding and a shake roof to a limestone rock face. It was a novel but imperfect idea. During heavy rains, water seeped into the building at the seams near the rock face and created a thick layer of green mold on every nearby surface. The one benefit, however, was that the limestone wall at the back of the boarding house stayed cool in the summer, while the rest of the house did not.

Because Pole's father spent most of his paycheck from the mill on whiskey, all they could afford was a tiny third-floor bedroom at the back of the house. It was probably less habitable than a dog box. Pole and his father had to share an old, sour-smelling mattress stained yellow with the sweat and oil of working men. Pole shuddered when he imagined the sorts of things that might have occurred on such a mattress. Prostitutes were always hanging around the town's boarding houses. After first moving into the room, Pole had slept on the cold, filthy floor for almost a week while trying to locate a cheap sheet or blanket to cover Mrs. Janosik's poor excuse for a bed.

Pole's week of sleep on the floor proved to be an uncomfortable yet eye-opening experience. Because the gaps between the wooden floorboards were so wide, he could see, hear, and smell everything that occurred in the room below him. His neighbors' drunken laughter and shouting interrupted his sleep several times each night while clouds of acrid cigarette smoke constantly wafted upward, threatening to suffocate him. Perhaps the only benefit to those gaps in the floor was the education he received on the relations between men and women.

At first, Pole was rather fascinated by all the belly bumping taking place below him—the soft curves of the young women, their round breasts, and plump bottoms. Even their moans and groans during the act were intriguing. It was all so new and exciting for a boy on the verge of manhood. But after several nights of poor sleep and a sore throat from the cigarette smoke, Pole grew tired of the antics of his neighbors below. It wasn't just that he desperately needed a good night's sleep, he lost interest mostly because the participants in all that tail-tickling were often not very attractive. Some of them were quite hideous, in fact.

His boyish curiosity satisfied, Pole was relieved when he finally found a tired-looking Indian wool blanket at a second-hand store across town. It was exactly what he needed to provide a barrier between himself and his mattress.

Since his mother's death, Pole's life had become a series of unusual events—some calamitous and some downright amusing. He never knew what the day would bring when he woke up each morning, but he was now confident in his ability to survive.

Glancing at the young girls comforting each other on the front steps, Pole wondered what misfortune had befallen the boarding house on this occasion. He cautiously approached the one steelworker on the porch whose English was better than Pole's Slovak. His name was Josef, but people called him "Sef."

"What's wrong?" Pole asked, trying to speak clearly so the immigrant could understand.

"Accident at mill. Tomas Tomicek die."

Pole gasped. Injury and death were a fact of life at the mill, but he was deeply affected by this news. He'd considered Tomas Tomicek a good friend. He had lost at cards to him and his brother, Pavol, more times than he could count. Fighting back tears, Pole whispered, "What happened?"

"He burned. Very bad." Sef stared at his whiskey momentarily before lifting the glass and downing the remainder of the clear liquid in one quick gulp. He faced Pole with an intent look in his red, watery eyes. He spoke slowly, struggling to find the words in English. "Don't end up in mill. It kill you. You die quick and ugly like Tomicek boy, or you die like rest of us . . . slow." Sef shook his head. "Not sure who got it worse." A tear fell down his dirty, pockmarked cheek as he got up and went into the house to refill his moonshine.

Mrs. Janosik suddenly appeared, carrying a plate of food. As if sensing Pole's need for comfort, she put her arm around his waist. She had grown rather fond of him in the past couple of years and tried to mother him when she had spare time, which wasn't often. And she always did her best to speak English for Pole.

"Sit on steps. I have dinner for you."

"Thanks, Mrs. Janosik."

"You hear about accident?"

"A little. Sef told me Tomas was burned real bad. Didn't seem like he wanted to say more. He's pretty upset."

"*Áno.* Everyone is. Janos Kovac bring Pavol back to house after accident. He tell me something go wrong with crane. It drop pot of hot steel near Tomas. He die quick. *Vďaka Bohu.*"

"How is Pavol?"

"He pass out drunk in bed. Best place for him now."

Mrs. Janosik sniffled and then wiped her nose on the sleeve of her dress. She was a hard-looking woman with a weathered face full of wrinkles and a round figure. Pole supposed running a boarding house full of drunken immigrants for the last fifteen years was to blame.

"Tomicek boys were twins. You know?" Mrs. Janosik asked while watching Pole devour his plate of *halušky*.

"Yeah. Pavol told me his mother died givin' birth to them," Pole said, brushing a noodle off his chin. "Their father died a few years ago. That's why they came to America. They had no one left in the old country."

"Now Pavol is all alone. It so sad. And now he must tell Tomas bride."

"Tomas isn't married," Pole said.

"His sweetheart is on ship to America. She suppose to marry Tomas next week."

Pole stopped chewing his *halušky*. He bowed his head, overcome by the unfairness of the world in which he lived. He opened his mouth to speak, but no words came.

# *Seven*

## JANOS

### RIVERTON, MAY 27, 1910

Janos had never been so thankful to stand in front of his modest little house with the clapboard siding weathered in various shades of gray. He looked up at the lonely window above the front porch, noticing the little fingerprints and smudges covering the bottom half of the glass. The evening sun was unkind and illuminated all the house's imperfections. Janos smiled. In this humble structure were the people responsible for those little prints—the people he loved most in this world. He wondered whether they were in that upstairs bedroom at that very moment playing marbles or jacks.

Overwhelmed by the need to see his family, Janos climbed the two steps on the front porch in one stride and burst through the door. He immediately caught the scent of frying fish wafting from the back of the house. He hurried through the narrow sitting room and into the kitchen where he found Sofie and his older sister, Anna, busy at the cookstove. As soon as he saw his little girl, Janos scooped her up in his arms.

"We're so glad you're home, Papa," Sofie whispered into her father's ear.

"Me, too," he said, gasping for air. Sofie's arms were wrapped so tightly around his neck, he could barely breathe. "I guess you heard about the accident," he said, placing his daughter back on her feet, noting her worried expression.

"Marie's father stopped by on his way home. He said the accident happened at your furnace."

"It did. It was the worst I've seen. Tomas was standing far from the crane. Anyone would have thought him safe in that spot." Janos sighed as he sat down at the kitchen table and rested his head in his hands. He immediately feared he'd said too much. Maybe he had given Sofie yet another reason to be anxious about the mill.

"We poured you some whiskey," Anna said, gesturing to the glass of clear liquid on the table. "It doesn't seem to get any better with time, does it? Ten years . . . and the mill isn't any safer."

Sofie gave her father a confused look.

"It's been ten years since your uncle died," he whispered to her.

Sofie nodded somberly.

Anna suddenly put down her metal spatula and left the front of the wood-fired cookstove. She took a seat at the kitchen table, one eye still focused on the fish frying in the pan. Janos was surprised by the move, as his sister rarely ventured far from her cookstove. She often leaned against it with a newspaper or novel even when she wasn't cooking. Janos suspected the day's tragic events were stirring up painful memories.

"I always thought Stefan would be safe in the rail yard, far away from the furnaces. I never imagined . . ." Anna said, casting her gaze downward and picking a crumb out of a deep crack in the table's surface.

Janos studied his sister's face. With her dull brown hair, green eyes, and tall, thin frame, she could have been his twin. And though twelve years his senior, she shared his temperament, too. She was thoughtful and emotional, a combination of traits that often compelled her to reexamine old wounds.

"What happened?" Sofie asked as she sat down in the empty chair next to her aunt. "I never heard the whole story."

"You were too young," Janos replied.

"Well, I'm not anymore."

Janos could not deny that Sofie was a mature ten-year-old, but the details of his brother-in-law's tragic death would only give her more nightmares. "It's already been an emotional day. Another time," he said, patting Sofie's hand.

"Remember how odd the weather was the day Stefan died," Anna said, as if to herself. "It was so cold and rainy for late October. And that wind . . ."

A chill went down Janos's spine. Anna was going to recount that horrific day, despite his protests. He had hoped to spare Sofie the details of Stefan's death, but knew his sister's demons would not go away until she confronted them. Janos reached for her hand.

"Did he die in a storm?" Sofie asked innocently.

"No, sweetheart—though I've always believed the weather was a factor. Stefan was crushed by a load of steel pipe. As he was passing by a railcar, the bottom of the load shifted, and the whole pile gave way." Anna closed her eyes.

Janos squeezed his sister's hand as tears streamed down her face.

Sofie pulled a handkerchief out of her pocket and offered it to her aunt. "I'm so sorry, Aunt Anna."

"The men who dug Stefan out told me he didn't suffer. There were several tons of pipe on that railcar. He was probably killed instantly," Anna said, wiping at her eyes.

"Your mother and I came to Riverton as soon as we received word of your uncle's death," Janos told Sofie. "We were newly married and planning a move to America, but once we learned of Stefan's passing, we hastened our plans. Anna and her boys needed us."

"What a terrible accident," Sofie whispered.

Anna winced.

"Sofie, your aunt doesn't like that word. She believes her husband's death was the result of negligence."

"What do you mean?"

"Your aunt and I—as well as many others at the mill—believe that the load of pipe wasn't properly secured. The men loading the railcar that day were probably in a hurry due to the wind and rain. They may have forgotten to tie a portion of the load down."

"Or just decided not to do it," Anna snapped. "If the union had still been around, there might have inspections."

"Sofie, take the fish off the stove before it burns. Put it on some plates with the potatoes," Janos said, trying to change the subject.

"I know talk of the union makes you uncomfortable, but there are no company spies hiding under the bed," Anna said, glaring at her brother. "Maybe it's time for the workers to try organizing again."

"And get fired? Or worse?" Janos asked. Since the Homestead strike of 1892 when nine steelworkers were killed, few dared mention the word "union." A visit from the steel company's thugs never ended well.

Suddenly, the front door opened, and Lukas blasted into the room. "I found Mama at the bakery. She bought a cake!" he squealed with delight.

Karina walked through the door, carrying a pink box wrapped with a white ribbon. Her blonde hair was down around her shoulders in curls. Janos thought it odd, as she normally wore her hair pulled back at work. But he couldn't deny that she looked lovely.

"I guess the lunch with the mill executives went well," he said.

"Not exactly. Mr. Archer didn't get the promotion he was expecting." Karina frowned. "The cake is for you, Janos. I heard you had a rough day."

"A bit extravagant, don't you think?" Anna chided. "That's not exactly the kind of comfort your husband needs."

Janos felt the tension in the room grow thick. He resented the fact that he always had to play peacekeeper with his wife and sister, but it was a role he had grown accustomed to. In fact, he excelled at it these days, most likely due to the frequency with which he was forced to intervene.

"At least you won't need to do any baking tomorrow, Anna. Maybe you could use the extra time to stop by the library and get a new novel," Janos said as he got up from the table and took the cake from his wife. "Thank you, Karina. That was very thoughtful."

Much to his surprise, Karina pulled Janos's face to hers and kissed him on the lips. It had been so long since she'd shown him any warmth or tenderness, he did not know how to react. He took the cake over to the stove and lingered there for a moment, hoping his flushed face would soon calm down.

"Mama, sit by me," Lukas pleaded.

"Of course, honey," Karina said, rubbing her son's back.

Janos returned to his chair as Sofie passed out plates of fish and potatoes. She gave her father a puzzled look as she placed his dinner in front of him. He knew exactly what she was thinking. Who was this thoughtful, affectionate person who had replaced his wife?

Normally, if Karina made it home in time to eat dinner with her family, she was too consumed with her own troubles to ask about anyone else's. And she certainly didn't show any affection. The only exception was the perfunctory kiss she gave to each of her children on her way to bed immediately following dinner. The rest of the family spent their evenings around the kitchen table playing word games or reading children's books and Bible stories. Karina slept above them, oblivious to all the joy she was missing below.

"You look very pretty today," Karina told Sofie as she joined the others at the table. "You're getting so tall. We should go shopping tomorrow for some new dresses."

"But Aunt Anna always takes me shopping."

"Maybe it's time you and I go together." Karina smiled sweetly.

Janos looked around the table, studying his family as they ate burnt fish and potatoes. The day had been unspeakably awful and had stirred in him serious concerns about his safety at the mill. However, at the moment, he was more concerned about the unexpected change in his wife's behavior.

# Eight

## KARINA

### RIVERTON, MAY 27, 1910

Karina gazed at Janos as he returned a collection of children's stories to the bookcase that stood along the wall in the sitting room. She had forgotten how attractive he was. Working at the mill for over a decade had grayed his hair only slightly, and his body was still in good shape. His skin looked young and healthy, unlike so many of the mill's men who had leathery complexions. Heavy drinking and long hours in front of a blazing furnace were the likely culprits, but her husband wasn't suffering the same fate. Janos only drank during the most stressful of times, today being one of them.

Karina took another sip of whiskey in an attempt to drown her feelings. Since her humiliation at the home of her employer, she had been suffering alternating fits of guilt and rage. She had bent to Henry's will yet again and surrendered her dignity in order to avoid returning to the boarding house. She'd convinced herself that tolerating his advances was more bearable than cleaning up after the filthy drunks who used to grope her. The fact that Karina's life was a series of unfair tradeoffs made her want to scream.

Her indecent arrangement with Henry had been tormenting her conscience for months, but she had experienced a frightening new level of shame that morning. She had pleasured Henry in the hopes that he would take her far away from Riverton—and her family. Karina tasted bile in her throat. Her latest betrayal of her husband was indefensible. She downed the remainder of her whiskey in one gulp.

"The children were so happy you stayed up to read with them," Janos said, returning to the table and refilling her empty glass.

"We had a lovely evening, didn't we?" She grasped the drink with both hands.

He nodded. "Tonight, I saw more of the woman I married so long ago. I'm grateful, but I wonder what has changed."

Karina bit her lip. Was the guilt written all over her face? She rushed to find a response. "I suppose it was the accident at the mill. You could've died today. It made me realize I've been taking you and our family for granted." Karina was surprised by the sincerity of her words. She had made an unusual effort to spend time with her family that evening, and now she was left battling pangs of regret. She rarely showed her children or husband the affection they deserved.

"I hope that's true," Janos said, touching Karina's arm. "I know you feel cheated. Working in that house of Mr. Archer's is a cruel reminder of the things we don't have."

It certainly is, Karina thought. It was no wonder she had been intrigued by Henry's talk of life among New York City's social elite. All she ever did was fantasize about a life outside Riverton. Whether admiring the fashions in *Vogue* magazine—which she purchased with Henry's grocery money—or strolling through Riverton Heights at dusk to peek into the windows of the mansions, Karina constantly wished for a more glamorous life. Try as she might, she could not stifle the longing Henry had stirred within her when he'd offered her a chance to go to New

York. It was that powerful yearning that had compelled her to crawl back into his bed. But could she leave her family behind?

"Karina, are you all right?" Janos interrupted her deliberating. "Did you hear what I said?"

"Sorry." She tried to focus on her husband's face.

"You are blessed in more important ways. You have the love of two healthy children and a devoted husband. Life's most precious gifts are the things you cannot see." Janos's face turned sullen. "You often forget that."

Karina felt a twinge of anger. Janos doubted her newfound appreciation of her family. He expected her to resume her complaining at any moment, and she could not blame him. She had a history of wild mood swings, and Janos was all too familiar with her vicious cycle. She'd lost all credibility with him. She looked into his bright green eyes and saw pity. Maybe even condescension.

Feeling brave from the whiskey, she blurted, "Do you still love me, Janos? I know you'd never leave me—you're so dutiful and righteous. But I wonder if you'd be happier without me."

"What kind of question is that?" he snapped.

"A simple one. I feel like an outsider in this house—like I don't belong."

"Maybe it's because you make so little effort to connect with your children. You're always avoiding them. Never mind your aversion to me." Janos looked away.

"That's unfair."

"Is it? You're too consumed with your own suffering to notice anyone around you."

Karina exploded. "Why is it so wrong to want things? Why is it selfish to want a house with electricity? And a bath tub?" Her eyes bored into her husband's. "Aren't you tired of working so hard and having little to show for it?"

Janos's face softened. "Of course, I am. I never imagined things would be so difficult here. I wish I didn't have to work in a steel mill, but I've made peace with it. I've learned to accept the things I cannot change." He reached for his wife's hand. "I focus on what brings me joy . . . the love of family and friends, my faith."

Karina envied her husband. She wished she could find the peace he had. Maybe it was his faith or the inexplicable bond he shared with his children, but she knew she didn't have his rare gift of finding light in the darkest of places.

"That's the difference between you and me. I can't calm the anger boiling inside me. I can't accept the unfairness in this country." Karina crossed her arms. "It doesn't matter how long or how hard we work." She began to cry.

Karina suddenly felt Janos's strong arms around her. His touch was warm and comforting. He planted soft kisses on top of her head and whispered softly, "I still love you, Karina. I do. But we can't go on like this." He stroked her hair. "Forget what you thought your life was going to be. Forget about all the *things* you think you've been denied. See the gifts that are right here under this roof."

Karina looked up at Janos. He smiled at her as he brushed a curl away from her face. His dimples were showing. In that moment, she remembered why she'd fallen in love with him over a decade ago. He was such a good man.

"What if I can't find peace? What if I can't find happiness in this town?"

Janos stiffened. "You need to find a way and you need to do it soon. Your self-inflicted suffering is destroying our family. I won't allow it to continue."

Karina was struck by the harshness of his tone. Was he threatening her? It was very uncharacteristic of him. Filled with remorse and a desperate need to make amends, she leaned into her husband's face and kissed him. His lips were soft and tasted faintly of cake and frosting. She ran her fingers through his hair.

Soon Janos's mouth trailed the length of Karina's jaw, neck, and collarbone, stirring in her a deep and long forgotten wave of passion. He picked her up and carried her over to the worn sofa in the tiny sitting room at the front of the house.

Janos slowly unbuttoned Karina's blouse and gently removed her skirt, appearing to savor the act of undressing her. She was surprised at how much she was enjoying his touch. She didn't know if it was the whiskey or the fact that it had been so long since they'd been intimate, but she was suddenly overcome with emotion.

Janos made love to Karina slowly and tenderly, with concern for only her pleasure. He was the exact opposite of Henry Archer. Karina connected with her husband in a way she hadn't in years, his touch reminding her of the passion he'd ignited within her when she was a girl of seventeen. Karina went to bed that night confused, her head spinning wildly. For the first time in a long time, she wished she could find contentment as the wife of a steelworker.

# Nine

## HENRY

### RIVERTON, JUNE 2, 1910

*The pungent smells in a steel mill take some getting used to.* That was what a US Steel executive told Henry Archer during an interview for a position with the company over five years earlier. Henry had been in Riverton for 1,834 days, and he still wanted to retch every time he caught the scent of furnace exhaust and sulfur on his way to work in the morning. He would never get used to the foul smells in a steel mill, but luckily, he wouldn't have to.

His promotion to headquarters in New York City was unexpected. Few details had been revealed to him. He had only been told that he would be working with the company's new central safety committee, developing standards and protocols. It was a relatively new campaign within the company to ensure workers' health and safety and to study new methods of accident prevention.

Henry had made some improvements at the Riverton mill over the last few years and had overseen equipment inspections. His contact in New York had informed him that his hands-on knowledge at the plant would be beneficial to the committee. Henry didn't care what headquarters wanted him to do. He would be happy scrubbing toilets at their offices as long as he was rescued from the blight of Riverton. And, of course, there was the issue of compensation. He had been assured he would receive a substantial increase in pay.

As he strolled into the mill's offices, Henry spied the superintendent, Herbert Blackwood Davies III, hovering over his desk, his dark brows furrowed. Within minutes of meeting his new boss a year earlier, Henry had known he would suffer at the hands of the aristocratic prick. His name practically said it all—he was an over-privileged jackass born with a silver spoon in his mouth, a hefty trust fund, and ties to influential people. He was younger than Henry by a few years and more attractive, though Henry hated to admit it. Tall and muscular with dark hair and piercing blue eyes, he was the kind of man women loved and men hated. He'd played football at Harvard and had been his fraternity's president. Henry loathed him.

Everyone at the mill knew Davies's stay in Riverton was temporary. His Harvard education and family name ensured he would rise to the highest levels of the company. Henry feared, with good reason, that his boss would eventually make his way to New York headquarters to resume his daily torment of him. His only hope was that he might be safe from Davies on the company's new safety committee. Surely the United States Steel Corporation had more important pursuits planned for a man like Herbert Blackwood Davies III.

Henry approached Davies cautiously, bracing himself for his daily berating. "Can I help you with something, Mr. Davies?"

Davies didn't even bother to glance up as he continued to shuffle noisily through the paperwork on Henry's desk. He clearly had no problem invading his subordinates' work space and exerting his authority. Henry felt his face grow hot.

"I need to see your inspection data for the past few months. We may have a problem. Quickly, Archer."

"Is something wrong?"

"There have been some unpleasant rumblings among the workers about the death of the laborer at Furnace #9 last week. There are concerns that the crane was not inspected. Perhaps some routine maintenance or repairs were overlooked." Davies narrowed his eyes. "I will feel much better about the situation once I see the proof on paper. I already assured Bill Jennings that the necessary inspections and repairs were being conducted under your purview."

Henry swallowed hard. "It may take me a few minutes to locate the documents, Mr. Davies. I'll bring them to you shortly."

"I am catching a train for Pittsburgh in twenty minutes. I have important meetings to attend. Make sure you have that paperwork in order. I do not expect anything will come of the grumblings of immigrants, but I need to ensure my record here at the mill is impeccable. Do you understand?" Davies asked, derision in his voice.

"Of course. I'll take care of it right away."

"And one more thing . . . I need you to attend a company function in Shadyside next weekend in my stead. It's a dinner party at the house of William Rankin. I will be in Chicago for a cousin's wedding—she's marrying a Rockefeller." Davies smiled smugly. "Anyway, Mr. Rankin would merely like to bring some of the region's mill managers together to exchange ideas over cocktails and cigars."

"I would be honored to attend," Henry stammered.

Davies nodded his head and swiftly exited the room, heading down the corridor toward his own office. Henry sank into his chair and began shuffling through stacks of papers on his desk. He sifted through piles of memoranda, work orders, and inspection reports for over ten minutes, pulling out all the safety data from the last three months. However, he was unable to locate the inspection report for the crane in question.

As he glanced at the clock on the wall, he broke into a cold sweat. Davies would be leaving for the train station in less than five minutes. Henry could not let him leave empty-handed. He wondered if he had forgotten to complete a report for the crane. He'd been having a hard time keeping track of all the safety data he'd been falsifying in recent months. It was possible he had missed that piece of equipment.

Suddenly, Henry remembered he'd taken some blank inspection reports home a few weeks earlier. His office had been particularly busy that day, and he hadn't had enough privacy to complete his reports. He rushed over to his briefcase and began digging through its compartments. He immediately found three inspection reports, one of which was for the crane at Furnace #9. Henry almost jumped for joy as he ran down the corridor and caught up with Davies as he was exiting the building.

"Here is the safety data for the past three months, Mr. Davies. You will be pleased to see that everything is in order."

"It took you long enough, Archer," Davies said as he snatched the documents from him. "I advise you to find a better system for organizing your paperwork. The condition of your desk is unacceptable."

"I'm terribly sorry, sir. I will take care of it immediately," Henry replied pleasantly as he imagined what Herbert Blackwood Davies III would look like with a missing tooth and a black eye.

After watching Davies head down the street toward the train station, Henry glided back to his office and collapsed into his chair. He wiped the sweat from his brow and pulled a snack out of his briefcase. As he happily nibbled on a banana Karina had packed for him, he fantasized about the dinner party he would attend the following week.

He had only met William Rankin a few times and was rather intimidated by him. He was US Steel's Western Pennsylvania Area President and was filthy rich. Henry knew a large portion of his wealth was inherited, but US Steel stock had also fattened his wallet. Henry was nervous about attending the party, but figured he should probably get used to fraternizing with the social elite. Who knew what lay in store for him in New York City?

Still weighing heavily on Henry's mind was Karina. He wasn't entirely convinced he should take her to New York, but he saw no reason to make a final decision about the matter until a day or two before his departure. It would be foolish to reject her any sooner when he still had weeks to enjoy the pleasure of her company.

Henry had noticed over the past week that Karina seemed hopeful she would soon be leaving Riverton. He'd given it tremendous thought and could not deny that he was leaning toward taking her. Karina had become his addiction, and he wasn't quite sure he could live without her. He just needed to calculate the risks a bit further. Henry wondered how difficult it would be to ditch her in New York City if he caught a glimpse of a more suitable mistress.

Henry threw his banana peel in the trash and glanced at the desks of the other two managers with whom he shared a workspace. He supposed they were out on the mill floor dispensing new orders for steel, specifying tensile strength and tonnage. It was probably time he made an appearance on the floor. Even though he'd already checked out mentally from his position at the Riverton mill, he needed to crush any suspicion among the workers that he was shirking his responsibilities. Or that he was incompetent.

No one need know that he had failed to have the mill's mechanics complete maintenance on over a dozen pieces of equipment during the past few months. Henry knew the crane at Furnace #9 was in need of general maintenance, but sometimes there wasn't enough manpower or time to accomplish everything that was required.

Davies had been on Henry's back for months about squeezing more work out of the mechanics they already had instead of hiring additional help. Lacking the energy to battle with the overworked mechanics for longer hours and more efficiency, Henry had started falsifying safety data. The paperwork he'd completed on the faulty crane at Furnace #9 stated that Dickie Jones had conducted an inspection and performed routine repairs in late April. Henry just needed to take care of one minor detail. He needed to *remind* Dickie that he did, in fact, inspect that crane.

# *Ten*

## SOFIE

### RIVERTON, JUNE 2, 1910

Sofie sat with her friend Marie on the steps of her back porch on an unusually cool June evening. She shivered as she buttoned up her sweater while waiting for her turn at the water pump. Her family shared the pump, as well as a communal privy, with seven other families who lived on the same court. It was a busy place, especially at supper time.

Sofie watched as her neighbors rushed to retrieve water from the well after they'd dumped soapy waste water from their laundry tubs. The women were always in a hurry at this time of day. They had to finish their chores and put a hot meal on the table by the time their men arrived home from the mill. Aunt Anna always said the neighborhood women would have plenty of time for housework if they didn't waste so much of it exchanging gossip in the courtyard.

Sofie glanced at the privy and counted the number of people waiting in line. There were three, which wasn't bad. The crooked little structure always had someone standing in front of it, as it serviced more than thirty people. Luckily, it had multiple compartments, so waiting for access to a toilet was not nearly as time consuming as waiting for fresh water at the pump.

Chilly as it was, Sofie was grateful she didn't have to endure the unbearable smell that usually came from the privy during the summer months. A whiff of it in mid-July could knock a grown man out. When there was a drought and no storm runoff to flush the toilets, the odors became especially foul. Misbehaving kids were forced to connect a hose to the water pump and flush the toilets manually. It was a punishment no neighborhood ruffian wanted to receive.

Sofie glanced at her little brother, Lukas, who was jumping into a pool of dirty water from a neighbor's laundry tub. The back of his pants was splattered with mud. She thought about the river and the long summer days she would spend along its banks. She had only one week of school left and was growing excited. She turned to face Marie, who was unbraiding her curly brown hair.

"Are you cleaning houses with your mama again this summer?"

Marie bobbed her head. "Just until Papa quits the mill."

Sofie eyed her friend. "What are you talking about? Your family can't survive on what your mother brings home." Sofie had asked her father less than a week earlier if he would quit the mill, and he'd made it sound impossible.

Marie looked down at her lap. "We're moving at the end of the summer. Mama wants Papa to find work in a glass factory."

Sofie gasped. "Where?"

"Somewhere north of the city. The pay isn't as good, but it's safer. My brothers will have to work, too."

"But what about school?"

"Paul will be finished after next week, and Peter wants to quit."

"Peter's only twelve!" cried Sofie. "He needs to finish the seventh grade, at least."

"Why? All the neighborhood boys end up in the mills and factories whether they finish school or not. Mama just wants her boys to be safe. That's all she cares about."

Sofie thought about Mrs. Radovic and how sad she'd been since Marie's little sister died of the fever the previous fall. She was only four years old. Since the loss of her youngest, Mrs. Radovic had become nervous, constantly worrying that something terrible was going to happen to her husband at the mill.

"How is your mama doing? Is she getting any better?"

Marie dropped her braid and stared into the court filled with children running about. "She's still sad all the time. She has terrible nightmares and wakes up crying."

Sofie knew quite a bit about nightmares. She put her arm around her friend and rested her head on her shoulder. "Losing a child must be awful. Aunt Anna says you never get over it. I understand why your mother is worried about your father and brothers. She doesn't want to lose them, too."

"Your Aunt Anna lost a child, didn't she?"

"Her daughter died when she was only a few weeks old. My cousins Walter and Daniel work in the mines, and Aunt Anna worries about them constantly."

"Just like you worry about your papa."

Sofie closed her eyes. Marie knew her too well. "I do worry about Papa. I go to bed every night wishing he didn't have to work in that stupid mill. He's been saving money and looking through the newspapers for a new job for as long as I can remember."

"Your mother must make good money working for Mr. Archer. He's rich!"

"She doesn't bring home as much money as Papa thought she would. I think she saves some of it for herself."

"That's a horrible thing to say."

"Marie . . ." Sofie turned around and peeked through the back door of her house to make sure Aunt Anna was still in the kitchen. She could see her pouring the grease from her frying pan into a Mason jar. Sofie scanned the court to make sure Lukas wasn't eavesdropping nearby. Thankfully, he was on the opposite side of the yard playing kickball with a toddler. Sofie lowered her voice. "My mother is selfish. Sometimes I think she only cares about herself."

"I know she's not the best mother, but do you really think she would keep money for herself? Doesn't she want to help your father get out of the mill?"

"I don't know. She never seems to worry about Papa. I'm not even sure she loves him." Sofie remembered the argument she had overheard between her parents a couple of months earlier. She had crept downstairs after bedtime to get a drink of water. Papa was complaining that Mama was working too many evenings at Mr. Archer's and missing out on time with her family. He told her how much he missed her. When Sofie peeked around the corner of the staircase to get a glimpse of what was happening, she saw her father try to kiss her mother. But Mama turned her head and said she wanted to go to bed. Sofie would never forget the expression on Papa's face.

"Your father would never marry someone who didn't love him. He's a smart man."

"I know he is," Sofie replied. Knowing that fact only deepened the mystery of why her parents were together.

"He speaks better English than anyone I know," said Marie. "Even better than Sister Agnes."

Sofie saw it was finally her turn at the water pump. She walked over to it and began to fill her empty metal buckets. She motioned for Marie to move closer so she could tell her the latest news about her mother.

"Mama took me shopping for dresses last weekend."

"That's nice, isn't it?"

"I'm not sure. It was strange. I used to beg her to take me shopping when my clothes were too small. When Mama never made time, Aunt Anna started taking me."

"So why does she suddenly want to go shopping with you now?"

"I'm still trying to figure that out. Something's different about Mama lately. She's being a lot nicer. You know, she took me to Kaufmann's department store on the other side of town."

Marie's jaw dropped. "Is that where she bought you dresses?"

"Of course not! We got a couple at Bernie's second-hand shop. But you should've seen her looking at the clothing in that department store. She said she just wanted to see what rich people were wearing these days, but she seemed pretty serious about those fabrics and patterns. Studying them almost."

"What do you think that means?"

"I don't know. Maybe she saved up enough money to buy some fabric for a new dress. But where would she wear it? She's acting stranger than usual."

Sofie finished her work at the pump and called over her shoulder for Lukas. She and Marie put the buckets down on the porch steps.

"Marie!" a voice shouted from a few doors down.

"That's Mama. I have to go home and help with dinner. You never told me what you're doing this summer, Sofie."

"I'll be fishing with Pole. He makes good money selling fish to Mrs. Janosik and the men at the boarding house."

"You two spend an awful lot of time together." Marie smirked.

Sofie tilted her head. "Why are you making that face?"

"You like him, don't you? And I can see why." Marie giggled. "That wavy hair … those green eyes."

"What? Pole's my best friend. He's practically my brother."

Marie raised an eyebrow.

Suddenly, Lukas came sprinting across the court at full speed with an older boy trailing him. "Help!" he shouted. "Help!"

Sofie assumed he had gotten himself into some sort of trouble again. A fight, perhaps. She watched her brother run toward her, eyes wide, arms flailing. He must have been terrified because he didn't see the puddle of soapy water in front of her and Marie. He ran right through it, slipping and falling face first into a heap of mud at Marie's feet. Realizing his fortuitous position, Lukas lifted the hem of her skirt.

Marie stomped on his head as she turned to face Sofie. "Looks like your little brother is curious about the opposite sex. You must be a late bloomer."

## *Eleven*

# JANOS

## RIVERTON, JUNE 8, 1910

"Kovac! Janos Kovac!" shouted a voice.

Exhausted and eager to get home, Janos reluctantly turned around to see who had called his name. A fellow mill worker ran toward him, breathless, with sweat dripping from his ruddy cheeks. Janos recognized the man, but did not know his name. He was a laborer and new to town. Struggling to be patient, Janos waited for him to catch up in the stifling summer heat. Though it was early evening, the air was unusually muggy, as an unexpected heat wave had set in. The poor man looked spent.

Taking a deep breath, he offered his hand. "I'm Josef Balog. I'm new at the mill. Can I buy you a drink?" he asked in Slovak.

"Thank you, but I'm in a hurry to get home," Janos replied politely.

"I hear you're a well-respected member of the community. A wise man. You were there when Tomas Tomicek died a couple weeks back, weren't you?"

Janos nodded.

"I have something to tell you."

Janos raised an eyebrow. He didn't frequent the saloons very often. Spending his hard-earned money on whiskey was a waste, but his curiosity had been piqued. "I guess I have time for a drink. Dalibor's is around the corner."

Janos walked in silence with Josef Balog as they approached the most popular Slavic saloon in town. At the end of each day turn at the mill, a line of dirty, foul-mouthed men of Slovak, Polish, Hungarian, and Lithuanian descent formed out the door. It was a popular establishment mainly because it was the first pub the men passed on their way home from work. It also had an entertaining proprietor named Dalibor, who told disgusting jokes.

Most of the mill workers bought only one whiskey or two, desperate to wash the mineral dust out of their throats after a long, hot day's work. However, a few men, known as Dalibor's gang, sometimes spent as much as twenty dollars in a single night. They were a rough group, and Janos tried to avoid them whenever possible.

Janos had only been to Dalibor's a few times since he had settled in Riverton over a decade ago, the last time being about five years earlier. Upon entering, he noticed that the saloon's atmosphere had not improved. The place actually looked more run-down. The tables were covered with cigarette burns and carved with profanity in a half-dozen languages. The chairs looked like they were about to collapse under the weight of the men sitting in them. Janos coughed and rubbed at his eyes as he and Josef made a path through the smoky room toward the bar.

"Two Irish whiskies," Josef demanded as he neared the bartender.

A fat, disheveled-looking man, whom Janos didn't recognize, filled two glasses to the brim. The armpits of his shirt were soaked, and he smelled sour with sweat. "I guess Dalibor hired some help," Janos said casually as the man handed him his whiskey. "Business must be good if he can afford a break."

"I'm Dalibor," the heavy man shouted bitterly, pointing to his chest. "And I haven't had a goddamned day off in years!"

Janos was shocked. The person he'd known as Dalibor looked nothing like the slovenly creature standing in front of him. Janos felt sorry for him. Apparently, the saloon's proprietor liked his whiskey as much as his gang did. He looked in worse shape than the ramshackle furniture around the bar.

"Thank you, sir," Janos said, leaving a tip on the bar even though Josef had already paid. He sensed he needed to smooth things over with the easily angered man.

Once they were seated at a table in the back corner of the saloon, Janos said, "I appreciate the drink, Mr. Balog. What you have to say must be important."

"I think it is. But I won't take too much of your time. I can tell you're not used to this sort of place." Josef winked. "I've only been at the Riverton mill a few months. I worked in Homestead for a few years until I heard things were better up-river in the smaller towns." Josef paused to take a gulp of his amber-colored whiskey. "This tastes much better than the moonshine I'm used to drinking at the boarding house. A lot more expensive, though."

"Which boarding house do you live in?"

"The Janosik's. It's smaller than the one in Homestead, but it's cheap. You get to know your neighbors. Sometimes that's good and sometimes . . . well, you know how that goes," Josef said with a chuckle. "I've seen my fair share of fights. Been in a few."

Sensing that Josef liked to blather, Janos tried to hurry him along. "What kind of information do you have for me?"

The man cleared his throat. "I'm a laborer at the mill. I spend my days loading coal, so I don't have much need to speak English, even though I can. Everyone assumes I'm just another dumb Hunky." Josef took a sip of his whiskey and laughed.

"That's where that cocky son of a bitch Henry Archer made his mistake."

"What do you mean?" Janos leaned forward.

"Archer pulled that mechanic Dickie Jones aside last week to talk to him about the accident at your furnace. He saw me working ten feet away, but paid me no mind. Must've assumed I couldn't understand a word he was saying."

"And?" Janos was on the edge of his seat.

"He told Dickie that if anyone asks him about the crane, he'd better tell them he inspected it and found nothing wrong. Dickie said he hadn't gone near that crane in months. None of the other mechanics had either. That's when Archer shoved him. Hard. He told Dickie if he wanted to keep his job, he'd better remember working on that crane."

"The incompetent jackass!"

"Archer also said something about his paperwork being in order—all they had to do was stick to the story. He's being promoted at the end of the month and doesn't want anything screwing it up."

"A promotion?"

"Yeah. He's leaving the mill and going to work in New York City. No one knows about it yet. Just the managers and Dickie. And now you and me." Josef sneered.

Janos shuddered. Karina would soon be without a job and have little chance of finding another one as lucrative. His wife would have no choice but to return to work at one of the town's boarding houses.

He thought about the evening almost two weeks earlier when Karina had come home with a cake after hearing about the accident at his furnace. She'd been surprisingly affectionate and had shown a genuine interest in her family. She even seemed to enjoy making love to him. Janos went to bed that night elated and feeling more hopeful about his marriage than he had in years.

However, within a few days, it became clear that Karina's affections were fleeting. She resumed her routine of working late and heading to bed early. She ignored her children and rejected Janos's advances. He wondered what his wife would be like without her daily escape to the comfort of Archer's home. He knew the answer. He would never forget the sad state she was in before she had found work in an upper-class neighborhood.

Janos considered what Archer's promotion meant for him. Since the accident at his furnace, all he could think about was quitting the mill. He had contemplated it for years, but was always afraid no other job would provide him with enough money to support his family. But witnessing Tomas Tomicek's death had traumatized him. Janos was now constantly tortured by thoughts of being killed in an accident and leaving Sofie and Lukas behind. And with a mother like Karina, he knew his children needed him.

In the past few days, he had decided that, with his savings, the family could get by for a while with only Karina's income. Janos would get out of the mill and find safer work. But now? Everything was about to change.

"Janos? What do you think?"

Shaking the unpleasant thoughts from his head, he met Josef's gaze. "I'm not surprised Archer isn't conducting inspections. Men like him don't care about people like us." Janos took a swig of his whiskey and slammed the glass down on the table. "There's not much we can do."

"Are you sure?"

"There's no union to speak for us. Even if there were, no one could prove that an inspection would've prevented that accident. Steel mills are dangerous places. Accidents happen every day." Janos finished his whiskey. "Did you tell anyone else what you know?"

Josef shook his head. "I wanted to get some advice first. I thought about approaching my foreman, but I'm not sure he'd believe me. I'm afraid I'll be known as a grouser, or worse yet, I'll lose my job."

"You can't tell anyone. Nothing would come of it even if you could prove you were telling the truth. Management is more worried about tonnage and profits than workers' safety." Janos sighed. "Archer is leaving soon anyway."

"I was leaning towards keeping my mouth shut," Josef said, sounding resigned.

"It's best to keep quiet. It's a shame what happened to Tomas, but damn it, there's nothing we can do." Janos pounded the table with his fist. "We've got mouths to feed."

"I don't think I should tell Pavol Tomicek what I know. If he knew Archer had anything to do with that accident, he'd kill him for sure."

# *Twelve*

## KARINA

### RIVERTON, JUNE 8, 1910

Why on Earth was it so hot? The summer heat and humidity had set in early this year. Little beads of sweat trickled down Karina's neck as she made her way down the hill from Henry's peaceful neighborhood toward the mill. It was long after sunset and approaching ten o'clock. Surely her family would be asleep when she got home. At least that was what she hoped.

Karina had stayed unusually late at Henry's, repaying him for the unexpected kindness he had shown her earlier in the day. Much to her surprise, he had come home with a department store dressmaker bearing loads of fabrics and patterns. Henry wanted Karina to have a wardrobe of expensive clothing that would befit her new position among New York society. He took a keen interest in the fabric samples, choosing a green satin and a red chiffon for her. Karina could barely contain her excitement when she fingered the luxurious textiles.

Though conflicted and plagued with guilt, Karina had decided within a few days of Henry's proposition that it would be wise to keep her options open. She'd continued to satisfy his needs and had even stopped by the library to read the *New York Times* society pages. She familiarized herself with the names of the city's most prominent families and read about their interesting affairs. She grew both anxious and excited every time she imagined herself fashionably dressed at a social gathering on Park Avenue.

As Karina tiptoed through the front door, she was surprised to find Janos reading at the kitchen table by candlelight. The house had looked dark from the outside. "Why aren't you using the oil lamp?" she whispered.

"Wax is cheaper," Janos mumbled. "Karina, sit down. We need to talk."

Her husband sounded frighteningly serious. Karina sank into a chair as he took her hand and squeezed it gently. She grew nervous as she studied his troubled face.

"I got some disturbing news today. I'm not supposed to know this, but secrets have a way of getting out." Janos swallowed hard. "Henry Archer is being promoted and moving to New York City. You're going to lose your job."

Karina gasped. "How did you find out? It was supposed to be a secret."

"You knew about this?" Janos let go of her hand and gave her a sideways look.

"I've known for about a week." Karina had bent the truth only slightly.

"Why didn't you tell me? We can't survive long on my paycheck. You need to start looking for a new job right away."

Karina groaned. That was exactly why she had kept her mouth shut. Why go to the trouble of scouring the town in search of a new job when there was a chance she wouldn't need one? If she left for New York with Henry, those humiliating efforts would have been wasted.

"Are you going to answer me?"

"I didn't want to worry you, Janos. I was trying to figure things out on my own. I'm sorry." She stroked her husband's arm, ashamed of the lies that came so easily. "How did you find out about the promotion?"

"One of the workers at the mill overheard Archer talking to a mechanic. He didn't say when he was leaving, but I'm sure it's soon."

"End of June."

Janos nodded. "I wish you'd told me. I've been sitting here all evening trying to think of a solution. I don't want you back at the boarding house."

Karina studied Janos as he scraped some dried wax off the table. His fingers were cracked and callused, the nails badly chipped and discolored. He had the hands of a working man. A laborer.

After a minute of silence, he looked up. "I've also been thinking that it's time for me to get out of the mill."

Karina's eyes widened. "How? You'd never find a job that pays as good."

"Maybe not, but it's time to look at other options. Maybe ten years in Riverton is long enough. We came here to take care of Anna and the boys after Stefan died, and now Walter and Daniel are grown." Janos leaned back in his chair, crossing his arms. "I have some money saved. I think it's time to leave."

"Where would we go?"

"Sofie told me Marie's family is thinking of heading up north to work in a glass factory. Maybe we could go, too. I could get a job as a laborer—it would be safer than the mill. The pay wouldn't be as good, but we could rent a bigger house with my savings and take in some boarders."

"I suggested renting to boarders years ago, but you refused. You were too worried about the safety of the children."

"I know. But Sofie and Lukas are older now. I'll make sure the boarders are good people. There will be no drinking or cursing in our home."

"And the extra housework?"

"You and Anna can take care of the cooking and washing. Sofie and Lukas can help after school. It could work."

Karina was speechless. She did want a safer job for Janos and a better life for her family. But she couldn't imagine going back to cooking and cleaning all day for strangers, much less sharing a house with them. If she decided not to leave town with Henry, she would have no choice but to go along with Janos's plan.

"Karina? What do you think?"

"What makes you so sure Anna will leave? She's lived in this town for twenty-five years."

"I've already spoken to her. Her boys are in Connellsville and have their own lives now. She loves Sofie and Lukas as if they were her own. She wants what's best for our family."

Karina shook her head. "But why now? I thought you'd made peace with working in the mill."

"I thought I did, too, but I can't stop thinking about what happened to Tomas Tomicek—and several others who've been injured or killed over the years. What would happen to all of you if I died? How would you survive? It's all I can think about."

"I don't know what to say. I'm surprised you'd take such a huge risk."

"Staying at the mill is an even bigger risk. And if the glass factory doesn't work out, I'll try something else." Janos scratched his head. "Maybe one of the Heinz plants. Or farming. I have enough saved to rent some land and a small house."

"You're beginning to sound desperate."

"I just want to be here for my children."

"And what about your wife?" Karina crossed her arms.

"I want to be here for you, too, but would you even notice? I'm invisible to you."

Karina winced. The guilt struck her like lightning. She looked into her husband's sad eyes and felt genuine remorse for neglecting him. "I'm sorry that's how you feel." She reached for his hand.

Janos pulled his chair closer to Karina and wrapped an arm around her. He rubbed her back gently. "Maybe getting out of this town will change everything for us. Maybe we can find our way back to each other." He kissed his wife's neck as he slipped a hand under the waistband of her skirt.

Karina pushed his hand away. "I'm sorry. I'm too tired tonight."

Janos let go of her and straightened. "Then why did you work so late this evening?" he asked with a hint of sarcasm.

Karina's mind rushed to invent an excuse. "Henry's tailor was at the house with fabric samples and patterns for new suits. They drank cocktails all evening and wanted a late dinner. I had to feed them, of course."

"Since when do you address your employer as 'Henry'?" Janos narrowed his eyes.

Realizing her slip, Karina tried to make light of her mistake. "Is that what I said? Must be because I heard the tailor calling him that all evening. Drunken fools."

"I wonder if those suits are for his new job. That would certainly make sense. There's something else I need to tell you about your employer."

"What now?"

"Archer's partly to blame for that crane accident. He's in charge of equipment inspections at the mill. He somehow forgot—or didn't care—to have someone work on the crane at my furnace."

"Why am I not surprised?" Karina sighed.

"He threatened a mechanic. He's forcing the guy to tell anyone who asks that he inspected the crane and found nothing wrong with it. Archer even falsified his inspection reports."

"Does it matter, Janos? He's leaving for New York."

"It would matter to Pavol Tomicek. His brother is dead, and from what I hear, he's out for blood."

"It's sad, but these stories are not new."

"No, they're not. Too many immigrants have been sacrificed in the mills in the name of progress. We're so easily replaced. At least now you know what kind of man you've been working for."

"You don't need to tell me. I know him all too well." Karina winced as an image of Henry's naked body flashed before her eyes. She shook it from her head. "Let's go to bed. I really am tired."

When Karina laid down next to Sofie that night, she struggled to fall asleep. Her eyes remained fixed on the cracks in the ceiling as she thought about Janos's plan to quit the mill. She wondered whether he would still be able to do it if she decided to leave with Henry.

He'd said that he'd saved some money—that would pay for the family's move to a new town and maybe the first few months' rent. Anna would just have to manage the boarders by herself. And Sofie could quit school, if necessary. She wouldn't be the first Slovak girl to give up her education to earn a living. With all Janos's efforts to educate his children, she was probably already smarter than most girls who made it through the eighth grade anyway.

The idea of leaving Janos and the children made Karina feel awful, but the more she deliberated, the more convinced she was that they would be happier without her. She had often noticed how the laughter around the dinner table increased the minute she climbed the stairs to bed. She knew her family was more at ease in her absence—and she was more at ease alone in her room. She often wondered why being surrounded by happy people always made her feel miserable. Perhaps her departure would be a welcome change for everyone. That's what Karina told herself as she fought to fall asleep.

# *Thirteen*

## HENRY

### SHADYSIDE, JUNE 11, 1910

Henry Archer stood before William Rankin's mansion in the Pittsburgh neighborhood of Shadyside, mouth agape. He was no stranger to upscale neighborhoods. He had strolled through plenty of them in New York City. However, nothing had prepared him for the splendor of the steel magnate's home.

He had heard that it was an impressive example of Italianate architecture, but standing just feet from the portico, he felt dwarfed by the massive four-story brick structure. It was breathtaking. The house's two imposing turrets cast their shadows over him as the evening sun set behind them. They reminded Henry of his insignificance in this elite locale.

Scanning the facade and side of the house closest to him, he counted five balconies and porches. He wondered how many were on the back and opposite sides of the house. As he watched a couple of squirrels race across the neatly manicured lawn, he caught the scent of roses and peonies. Lovely. What might it cost to landscape such a place and keep it so perfectly trimmed? It looked like an arboretum with its wide variety of trees, shrubs, and exotic-looking flowers.

Excited and terribly nervous, Henry forced himself to climb the stairs under the portico where a male servant awaited his arrival. Though a series of violent thunderstorms had moved through the area the previous night, ending the week's heat wave, Henry was still perspiring beneath his clothes. He quickly wiped a bead of sweat from his temple.

"Good evening, sir. Welcome to Shetland House. Mr. and Mrs. Rankin will be delighted to receive you," the man said as he opened the door.

Henry fought to suppress a frown as he noticed the servant's black dress coat was of a higher quality than his own. Feeling self-conscious, he adjusted his bow tie as he passed the valet and stepped into the entrance hall.

The two-story foyer was paneled in cherry, while colorful stained-glass windows lined the staircase. A plush red carpet runner lay beneath Henry's feet, and a massive antique grandfather clock stood to his left. Trapped in a state of awe over the home's expensive-looking furnishings, Henry barely noticed when Mr. Rankin and a plump lady approached him at the foot of the stairs.

"Mr. Archer, we are honored you could join us. Permit me to present my lovely wife, Mrs. Rankin," said the gray-haired gentleman.

"It is an honor," Henry said as he bowed and kissed the woman's white-gloved hand. "Your home is stunning."

"Thank you, Mr. Archer. Restoring this house is one of my many passions."

"Please join us for cocktails in the parlor." Mr. Rankin motioned to Henry. "What is your drink of choice? A martini?"

"Yes, please," Henry answered in his most gracious tone.

"I am sure you will recognize a few of my guests. They are all superintendents at area mills." Mr. Rankin led Henry over to the piano where several couples were sipping martinis and conversing quietly. "Allow me to introduce you to Mr.

and Mrs. Robert Wells of Homestead, Mr. and Mrs. George Baldwin of Braddock, and Mr. and Mrs. Francis McGowan of Vandergrift."

Henry shook hands with each of the men and bowed politely to the ladies dressed in elegant gowns. Jewels dangled from their ears and sparkled around their throats. A servant handed Henry an exquisite blue crystal martini glass with a red swan at the base. He took a sip of his cocktail, pleasantly surprised at its smoothness. Expensive gin, to be sure.

"Mr. Archer, I must introduce you to my wife's cousin Miss Covington Girard. She has been staying with us this spring. Such a lovely girl . . . but where the devil is she?" Mr. Rankin asked, scanning the room.

"I believe she had to retrieve something from upstairs." Mrs. Rankin peered through the parlor entrance and then clasped her hands in delight. "Here she comes now. Edith, darling, our final guest has arrived. He is waiting to meet you."

As the young woman entered the room, Mrs. Rankin proudly announced, "Mr. Archer, this is my dear cousin Miss Covington Girard of the New York Covingtons and the Philadelphia Girards."

Henry's eyes immediately caught the shimmer of dark red silk. Mrs. Rankin's cousin wore the most beautiful dress he had ever seen. It was a ruby-toned, tiered gown covered with an intricate pattern of rhinestones and black beads. Enormous diamond earrings and a heavy-looking necklace completed the striking costume. As Henry focused on the sparkling jewels dangling from the woman's ears, he caught a glimpse of her face.

*How unfortunate.*

Miss Covington Girard's face was rather displeasing, a stark contrast to the magnificence of her attire. While her individual features were all very normal-looking, perhaps even slightly pretty, she was unfortunately plagued by excessive hair growth on her upper lip and jaw. Even her pretty blue eyes could not divert one's attention from the dark shadows defiling her lower face.

Aware that he was staring, Henry quickly turned on the charm so as not to offend his hosts. "Forgive me, Miss Covington Girard, I did not intend to stare. It's just . . . I have never seen anyone so lovely. I am honored to meet you." Henry bowed.

"Please call me Miss Girard. My name can be cumbersome, I know. I apologize if I have delayed dinner."

Henry immediately noticed how deep the woman's voice was. It was unsettling.

"We are getting ready to take our places in the dining room. Mr. Archer, perhaps you would like to sit next to my cousin this evening. She is unaccompanied," Mrs. Rankin said with a sly smile.

Henry didn't need to be a genius to figure out his host's intentions. He wished he could skip the charades and tell Mrs. Rankin that her cousin had little chance of winning his affections, but instead he replied, "Of course. I would be delighted."

Henry followed the other guests into the dining room, which was paneled in the same cherry wood as the adjoining parlor and entrance hall. In the center of the room hung a grand crystal chandelier that sparkled and glistened, casting amusing reflections all around. A bevy of servants directed each of the guests to their seats at the elaborately set table, each place setting complete with five different drinking glasses and three different forks, knives, and spoons. Henry was intimidated.

He suddenly wondered how Karina would fare at such a sophisticated gathering. Would she be able to grasp the rules of etiquette—or at least manage to fake it? He surveyed the female guests and tried to picture Karina in each of their stylish gowns. Her beauty would outshine them all. Of that he was certain.

As the first course of Oysters Rockefeller was being served, Henry made polite conversation with Miss Girard, who was seated to his right, and Mr. and Mrs. McGowan, who were seated to his left. The discussion was light in nature and centered on everyone's plans for the upcoming summer vacations. The McGowans were traveling to Chicago and the Great Lakes, while Miss Girard would spend the months of July and August with her parents in Newport, Rhode Island. Henry explained that he was starting a new job and would be in New York City.

"The city is so dreadfully hot in the summer months," Miss Girard remarked. "You really should try to get away on the weekends. Glen Cove on the North Shore has the most wonderful yachting and country clubs. The Hamptons are becoming quite popular, too."

"Yes, I've heard," Henry lied. "I spent a lot of time on Coney Island as a child, but I haven't been to any of the other resort towns on Long Island. I must do more traveling," he said, embarrassed he could not comment any further on these exclusive destinations.

As dinner progressed, Henry became acquainted with his hosts and their well-to-do guests over an extravagant eleven-course meal. Following the oysters, he was served a cream of barley soup, salmon with mousseline sauce and cucumber—which he did not care for—and the most tender cut of filet mignon he had ever eaten. He almost cried when he swallowed his last bite of beef, wishing he could ask the server for another helping. Over the fifth course of lamb with mint sauce and creamed carrots, he learned more than he ever wanted to know about Shetland sheepdogs.

"Shelties are wonderful dogs. They are extremely intelligent and learn commands with remarkable ease," Mrs. Rankin said.

"I am not familiar with this breed," said Mrs. Baldwin, an eyebrow raised.

"They are from the Shetland Islands of Scotland and have been used to herd sheep for years. They resemble a collie, but are much smaller in size."

"Fascinating." Mrs. Baldwin's attempt at feigning interest was feeble at best.

"My English cousins have several at their country home in North Yorkshire. I had one as a child at my family's estate near Philadelphia. Lady was her name. She was a lovely creature," Mrs. Rankin mused.

"How many Shelties do you have now?" Mr. Wells asked.

"Five. They are in the stable now, of course, but you must return another time to see them. I have taught them the most adorable tricks."

"That's why your home is named Shetland House!" Mrs. Wells exclaimed.

"Darling, you really are quite the genius," Mr. Wells said with a hint of sarcasm as he turned to face his wife.

"Mrs. Rankin and I were never blessed with a house full of children, so we take great pride in our dogs and horses. We find it fulfilling. And, of course, my wife is well known around Pittsburgh and Philadelphia for her charity work." Mr. Rankin smiled proudly at his spouse.

"Enough about me. Miss Girard, do tell our guests about your grand tour of Europe last autumn," Mrs. Rankin suggested. "You are practically an expert now on France and Italy."

"I do not want to boast," Miss Girard said shyly.

"I would love to hear about Europe," Henry said. He was genuinely curious about the woman sitting next to him. He could tell by her jewels and knowledge of resort towns that she was of the privileged upper class, but he was dying to know exactly how wealthy she was. Could she possibly be related to the same New York Covingtons who had made a fortune in railroads?

As servants served the sixth course of sorbet and the seventh course of roast squab, Henry sat hypnotized as Miss Girard recounted her tour through Europe. She spoke of the paintings in the Louvre, the beauty of Notre Dame, and the splendor of

Versailles. She described the vineyards in the south of France and how stunning the hillsides looked as the grape leaves slowly changed colors in the warm autumn sun.

Long after the other dinner guests fell into conversations of their own, Henry continued to listen intently to Miss Girard's stories.

"Mr. Archer, I feel as though I have monopolized the conversation. Surely you do not want to hear about me all night. It is rather rude on my part."

"On the contrary, Miss Girard, I find the tales of your travels captivating. And how did you find Italy?"

"I loved it. There is simply no place on Earth more romantic than Tuscany. The food is heavenly."

"What was your favorite?"

"The cannoli. Mother and I could not stop eating them."

"So you traveled with family?"

"Yes. In fact, the trip was rather spontaneous. I had other plans for the fall, but sometimes, life does not turn out quite the way you planned. My mother thought Europe would be a wonderful consolation."

Sensing a painful story behind Miss Girard's sad eyes, Henry decided it would be rude to ask about the circumstances that necessitated an escape to Europe. He wished he could flee the country at a moment's notice. The rich. They had no idea how lucky they were.

"I hope your trip provided you with whatever it was you sought," Henry replied in an encouraging tone.

"It certainly helped," Miss Girard said, looking down at her lap and readjusting her napkin.

The dinner progressed with more talk of travel and hobbies as well as gossip about prominent families around Pittsburgh and even Philadelphia and New York. Politics were discussed only briefly near the end of dinner when multiple courses of salads and sweets were served. Henry especially enjoyed the chocolate eclairs and the fruit and cheese plate. He could have skipped the asparagus vinaigrette, but Mrs. Rankin was especially proud of that course as it came from her very own garden. Henry complimented her vegetables vigorously, knowing full well that the gardener deserved all the credit. He couldn't imagine the plump society woman on her hands and knees in the hot sun raking and pulling weeds.

At the end of dinner, Mr. Rankin declared that the men would have their discussion about the mills in his study over port and cigars. Henry's eyes grew wide as he entered the mahogany-paneled room adorned with animal trophies. The heads of a moose, a bear, an elk, and three different deer hovered over him, their glass eyes staring down at him creepily. A fully stuffed wolf and cougar lounged comfortably at the far end of the room near the window.

"That's quite a collection you have, Mr. Rankin," Henry said. "I've never seen anything like it."

"It is an extraordinary display of beasts, isn't it?" Mr. Rankin replied proudly. "I hope to add a lion and a Cape buffalo after my trip to Africa next year. Hunting deer and moose isn't as thrilling as it used to be. It will be fun to go after something that wants to eat me."

Henry's jaw dropped.

"Come now, Mr. Archer. Don't look so shocked. Surely you've experienced the thrill of the hunt," Mr. Rankin teased.

"I can't say that I have."

"It certainly is exciting," Mr. McGowan said. "I think it will be Mr. Rankin's full-time occupation once he retires in a few years. Isn't that right, William?"

"I hope so. Now gentlemen, I have some very fine Cuban cigars for you. Have a seat, and we'll get started with business."

Mr. Rankin gave each of the men a cigar and a glass of port. Once they were seated comfortably on the leather sofa and armchairs, they proceeded to discuss matters at the mill—increasing productivity with new technologies, cutting costs, improving safety. The conversation went on for at least an hour. Henry tried not to look bored.

"Now, Mr. Archer, be sure to relay this information to Mr. Davies. I know some of it does not apply to you, as you will soon be in New York working on safety protocols, but Davies will certainly be interested in what we have discussed. The last thing I would like to mention pertains to the workers. More specifically, their lack of representation." Mr. Rankin cleared his throat.

"US Steel has been very successful over the past two decades at quashing any union activity, and the powers above me would like to keep it that way. I must admit that I sympathize with our workers and can understand their desire to organize. The work they perform in the mills is strenuous, and at times, dangerous. However, the company's main objective is to maximize profits and tonnage. Having a union interfere with the manner in which we conduct business could prove disastrous to our bottom line. As such, the company is instituting new policies that may quiet dissent and ensure the workers do not attempt to organize."

"We're not going to have the Pinkertons take care of them? Intimidate 'em and beat 'em up every once in a while?" Mr. Wells chuckled as an audible belch escaped him.

Mr. Rankin glared at the inebriated, heavyset man. "I know that is how things have traditionally been done in Homestead, Mr. Wells, but I would like to think US Steel is better than that. I am referring to a new relief plan for workers who are injured or killed in the mills. Many leave behind wives and children who cannot afford to support themselves. The company is introducing this plan on a trial basis and will compensate widows and their families with eighteen months to three years' worth of lost wages."

"Is it not enough to help with the funeral expenses?" Mr. Baldwin asked.

"We have done that for some time, but the company believes providing death benefits and pensions will help increase workers' satisfaction and trust in the company. This relief plan could help us avoid unionization."

"At least for a time," Mr. McGowan said. "I think it's a step in the right direction."

Mr. Rankin continued, "My time at US Steel is winding down, but gentlemen, as relatively young managers, you need to realize that talk of collective bargaining among the workers will not go away anytime soon. If we are to keep the unions out, we must do some things to appease our workforce. Compromises must be made. We have to show the workers that the company has a conscience."

Henry watched as his host stood up and walked over to the window. "It's getting late, gentlemen. We should join the ladies in the parlor. Mr. Archer, the last train back to Riverton will be leaving soon. Can my valet give you a ride to the station?"

"I'll take him," Mr. McGowan said. "I love driving my new automobile."

"You're still staying the night, aren't you, Francis? We can shoot squirrels after breakfast," Mr. Rankin said, winking at his friend. "Maybe even during breakfast if we eat outside on the patio."

"That's an offer I cannot refuse." Mr. McGowan chuckled.

In the parlor, the guests thanked Mr. and Mrs. Rankin for a wonderful evening before departing. Henry noticed that Miss Girard was no longer present. As he started for the front door with Mr. McGowan, Mrs. Rankin called after him.

"Mr. Archer, my cousin was sorry she could not stay up to say goodbye, but she did want you to know that she enjoyed your company. Perhaps you would like to join us next weekend for a picnic."

Henry was surprised by the invitation, but wondered if a closer acquaintance with Miss Girard and the Rankins could prove advantageous. Perhaps they would provide him with new social connections in New York. "That would be lovely, Mrs. Rankin," Henry said with a smile.

"Splendid. We'll see you next Saturday at noon."

As Henry fingered the black leather upholstery in Mr. McGowan's brand-new Ford Model T, he felt a twinge of jealousy. "I had hoped to purchase an automobile soon, but I guess there's no need now that I'll be returning to New York."

"In what part of the city will you be living, Mr. Archer?"

"I'm hoping to find an apartment in Lower Manhattan near the Empire Building. I'll be staying with my aunt in Brooklyn while I'm conducting my search."

"So you're a Brooklyn boy!"

"I am. My parents died when I was very young. My aunt and uncle raised me not far from Prospect Park."

"I'm sorry to hear that," the older man said sympathetically.

Henry studied Mr. McGowan, who looked very content in the driver's seat of his new car. He was a thin, athletic-looking man with a kind face and a pleasant demeanor. Henry liked him.

"Mr. McGowan, what can you tell me about Miss Girard? I have a feeling she hasn't met too many men from Brooklyn."

"I doubt it." He chuckled. "She's an heiress. I'm sure you've heard of the Covington railroad empire."

Henry was astonished that his hunch had been correct. He had never been in the same room with anyone so wealthy. "What's she doing in Pittsburgh?"

"I think she's trying to find a husband. Mrs. Rankin has been playing matchmaker for her all spring."

"Surely someone of her background would have men lined up outside the door." Henry immediately thought of her unsightly facial hair and deep voice, both likely deterrents.

"You would think. I believe she's had a rather difficult year. There were some unpleasant circumstances."

"Such as?"

Mr. McGowan hesitated. He seemed to be considering something, or just focusing on the road ahead, which was difficult to see in the dark even with the headlamps. "I don't know all the details, Mr. Archer. What I do know is that she seemed quite taken with *you*."

"I enjoyed our conversation, but . . ."

Mr. McGowan smirked. "I know what you're thinking. Her face is . . . disappointing. No matter. With a fortune like hers, someone will be willing to overlook it. She simply hasn't found him yet."

*Fourteen*

## SOFIE

### RIVERTON, JUNE 11, 1910

"Papa! You finally made it!" Sofie shouted joyfully as she ran toward her father in the musty basement of St. Michael's Roman Catholic Church. He had just completed his Saturday shift at the mill, but had gone home to wash up and change clothing. His black suit, reserved for Sundays and special occasions, was freshly pressed and made him look rather distinguished. A passerby on the street would never guess he was a mill worker.

"I wish you could've seen the wedding ceremony. Jenny looked lovely. She wore the most beautiful wreath, and her veil trailed down to the floor."

"Aren't the bride and groom still here?" Papa asked, sounding confused.

"They are, but the old ladies already did the *čepčenie* ceremony." Sofie had watched in awe as they'd removed the fragile veil and replaced it with a white kerchief. "Jenny still looks beautiful, but that veil . . ."

"One day you will wear such a veil at your own wedding, *zlatíčko*."

Sofie blushed as her father kissed her on the forehead.

"Your new blue dress brings out the color in your eyes," he added. "You look very pretty."

"Thanks, Papa. Did you see the elm tree across the street? Father Figlar said it was struck by lightning during last night's storm."

"How could I miss it? That storm was a little frightening, wasn't it? Lukas was tossing and turning all night."

"At least it's not so hot now. The church basement is still damp from all that rain though. Father Figlar had a bunch of the boys mop up the puddles near the walls."

"A little rainwater won't ruin the celebration. Why don't you take me to your mother and aunt? Where are they sitting?"

"They're in that corner with the Radovics." Sofie pointed to a poorly lit area on the other side of the room. "The *babas* saved some *holubky* and *pirohy* for you and the others coming from the mill. There are still lots of cookies left, but you'd better hurry. Pole and Lukas have been playing cards near the cookie table all night. They're filling their pockets with them."

"Why am I not surprised?"

"And Mama . . . she's had a good bit of whiskey."

A sly smile formed on Papa's lips. "She should be in the mood for a dance then."

Sofie gave her father a confused look.

Papa laughed. "Weddings and whiskey always put people in the mood for romance."

Sofie led her father over to the table where her mother and aunt were seated with her friend Marie's parents. She watched as her father greeted everyone in Slovak and complimented the ladies on how beautifully they were dressed. Sofie was struck yet again by her mother's elegant appearance. Next to the bride, she was the loveliest woman in the room in her ivory lace gown. Mama had claimed she'd borrowed the delicate dress from a woman who lived in Mr. Archer's neighborhood, but Sofie was skeptical. She could not imagine why anyone would part with such an expensive garment even for just one evening. Nevertheless, Mama looked stunning with her curled blonde hair arranged at the nape of her neck in a loose chignon. Sofie was surprised by how proud she was of her mother's beauty. She wondered if she would ever look as pretty.

Sofie sat down next to her father and watched him devour a half-dozen *holubky* while listening to Mihal Radovic detail his plans to relocate his family somewhere up north. Sofie tried hard to follow the conversation, but unfortunately, her Slovak wasn't good enough to follow such rapid speech. Growing bored, she got up and ventured over to the cookie table. It was tradition for the neighborhood *babas* to bake cookies for all the church's weddings since no one could afford the luxury of a wedding cake. As Sofie surveyed what was left of the delicious treats, she tripped over her brother and Pole, who were playing Hearts on the floor.

"Hey, Sof! Wanna play?" Pole asked.

"I'm getting Papa some cookies. I can't believe the *babas* haven't kicked you two out of here." She narrowed her eyes. "Of all the places to play cards! You couldn't be more obvious."

Pole laughed as Lukas shoved a few apricot *koláče* into his mouth.

"Where did Peter and Paul go?" Sofie asked.

"They're outside with Marie catchin' lightning bugs. I'm going soon. You wanna come?" Pole looked up hopefully.

"Maybe in a few minutes. I want Papa to have some of these walnut *koláče* before they're all gone."

Sofie went back to the table where her parents were sitting with Aunt Anna. Mr. and Mrs. Radovic were dancing a polka to a lively tune played by a small group of musicians on accordions and violins. Just as Sofie placed the plate of desserts in front of her father, he stood up and took her hand.

"May I have a dance with the prettiest girl in the room?"

Sofie smiled as her father whisked her over to the dance floor. They joined the ring of cheerful dancers who were stepping and hopping in circles with their partners. Sofie let her father lead and tried not to get dizzy as he whirled her around the room. She was surprised he still had so much energy at the end of a workday. The tempo of the music was fast, and Sofie struggled to keep up.

As the polka changed over to a waltz, Papa led Sofie back to the table. "May I have a dance with the most beautiful woman in the room?" he asked Mama.

"Of course," she replied with a wink.

Sofie watched her mother and father waltz to a slow tune played by a violin. She studied them closely, admiring how lovely they looked together. As they gazed affectionately at each other, Sofie tried to remember the last time she had seen them look so happy. They were acting like a married couple. She suddenly felt confused and turned to Aunt Anna, who was the only person left at the table.

"What's gotten into them?" Sofie asked.

"People always get sentimental at weddings. It reminds them of when they were young and in love. And there's also the whiskey."

"Must be powerful stuff. I've never seen Mama look at Papa like that."

Aunt Anna laughed. "You know, Sofie, when your parents first came to Riverton, they were the couple everyone envied. They were so devoted to each other."

"What changed?"

"Life. Living in the shadow of the mill. Your parents have worked too hard for too long and have little to show for it. They're exhausted." Aunt Anna sighed. "Maybe even disappointed."

"I know Mama's disappointed. She doesn't like having a family."

"That's not true. She loves you and Lukas. She's just not very good at showing it." Sofie's aunt bit into a cookie, chewing slowly. "She's too consumed with her own troubles."

"Mama's been sad for as long as I can remember. She's been better lately, but sometimes she barely says a word to me for days." Sofie's lip quivered.

Aunt Anna pulled her niece close and kissed her on the forehead. She tilted Sofie's chin and looked into her eyes. "You are a wonderful little girl. Anyone would be lucky to have you as a daughter. But your mama's suffering is so great that she can't see the good in her life." Aunt Anna shook her head. "Sometimes I'm not sure it's entirely her fault."

"What do you mean?"

"I've never seen a person struggle the way your mama does. Her dark moods are always getting in the way of her happiness. It was especially difficult after you and Lukas were born."

"How so?"

"She was gloomy and somber when she should've been overjoyed."

"I knew she didn't want us." Sofie huffed, crossing her arms.

"Of course, she did. I'm simply making the point that your mother's sadness might be more complicated than we realize."

"They're almost ready to do the bridal dance," Papa said, startling Sofie. "Why don't you find Pole and the other boys and see if they'd like to dance with Jenny?"

"Pole doesn't dance."

"He'd better learn if he wants to impress the girls."

Just as Sofie was about to head outside to find Pole, he snuck up behind her and tickled her ear with a feather.

"You're just in time for the bridal dance," Papa said to him. "The line is long, but you can dance with Sofie while you're waiting."

"We'll be the only kids on the dance floor," Sofie whined. "And Pole doesn't even know any steps."

"Sure, I do!" he said defensively.

Sofie crossed her arms. "Really? When did you learn how to dance?"

"There's always an accordion playin' at the boarding house on the weekends. I might've picked up a few steps."

"There you go," Papa said, pushing Sofie and Pole onto the dance floor. "Have fun. It's not every weekend you get to attend a wedding."

Sofie rolled her eyes as Pole took her hand and led her to the other side of the dance floor, away from the bridal dance. The band was playing a fast polka. She tried to hide her embarrassment as Pole put one hand across her back and suspended the other in the air. Her cheeks were growing hot.

"You goin' to take my hand or not?" he asked, smirking. "I won't bite."

"I might." Sofie growled in the lowest voice she could muster, but she and Pole wound up laughing at her pitiful attempt at sounding like a mountain lion. "Don't even think of stepping on my toes," she warned him.

"I wouldn't dare."

Pole grabbed Sofie's hand and whirled her around the dance floor at a dizzying pace. She was pleasantly surprised that he had a good sense of rhythm. He knew quite a few steps, but she helped him add more to his repertoire. They danced through two fast polkas, joking and laughing when they tripped over each other's feet.

"See, Sof. I'm not that bad."

"You're not that great either. I think my big toe is broken," she teased.

"Well, I'm pretty sure I'm goin' to have a nasty bruise on my shin tomorrow. You kicked me. More than once."

Suddenly, the tempo of the music changed. Sofie and Pole stopped moving and stared at each other, unsure of what to do.

"This is a waltz," she said. "Let's get something to drink."

As she and Pole left the dance floor, Sofie caught a glimpse of her father, who was handing a few coins to a groomsman in exchange for a shot of whiskey and a dance with the bride.

He winked at her and motioned for her to start dancing again. Sofie shook her head vigorously. She wasn't about to make a fool of herself during a waltz.

"Why didn't you tell me that Marie and her family are moving at the end of the summer?" Pole asked Sofie as they arrived at the punch bowl. "Peter and Paul told me while we were playin' cards. They seem excited."

"I'm not. And neither is Marie. We're pretending it's not happening." Hot tears burned Sofie's eyes.

"Now, don't cry." Pole patted her back. "I know you're going to miss Marie, but you can visit her, write letters."

"It's not the same," Sofie said, sniffling.

"I know." Pole brushed a strand of hair away from her face. "But it's not the end of the world. You still have me," he said, pointing to his chest. "What more could you ask for?"

Sofie studied Pole, who was grinning proudly, apparently satisfied with himself. He was her best friend in the entire world. As much as she would miss Marie, losing Pole would be far worse. She couldn't explain why, but her heart was certain of that truth.

"We can spend more time at the fishin' hole. And maybe you can help get me caught up with my Slovak. Sister Agnes will have to find someone else to smack with her ruler."

Sofie nodded, feeling her mood begin to lighten. "I'd like that. But you have to promise me that you're not going to leave town, too."

"Now why would I leave a paradise like Riverton?" Pole chuckled. "We've got the biggest mill around with more smoke than we know what to do with."

Sofie giggled as she popped another cookie into her mouth.

"First fishing pals and now dance partners. What next?" Papa asked as he approached from the dance floor.

"I'm going to help Pole with his Slovak," Sofie announced.

"That's a noble endeavor, *zlatíčko*, but it'll have to wait," Papa said. "We need to get home. I start the long turn in the morning."

"My pop does, too. I don't know how anyone makes it through a twenty-four-hour shift at the mill."

"I pray you'll never have to find out," Papa said, ruffling Pole's hair.

As Sofie turned to leave with her father, she called over her shoulder, "See you tomorrow at the fishing hole."

Pole smiled and winked at her.

As Sofie walked home with her family, gazing at the stars shining faintly through the smoky haze, she felt beyond content. She had never imagined the wedding would be so special. Seeing her parents look so happy on the dance floor had given her a newfound feeling of hope. Mama and Papa still cared for each other. It was such a relief.

And as much as she dreaded losing Marie, she was looking forward to spending more time with Pole. Fishing along the banks of the river *and* playing Slovak teacher sounded like the perfect way to pass the summer, even if her student wouldn't be the most enthusiastic. Sofie suddenly wondered whether her fishing pole would be a good substitute for Sister Agnes's ruler.

# *Fifteen*

## HENRY

### PITTSBURGH, JUNE 18, 1910

Orchids, lily pads, liriope. Henry had never seen so many exotic flowers and plants in all his life. Instead of returning to Shetland House for a picnic as Mrs. Rankin had suggested the previous week, she had sent him a telegram requesting that he meet her and Miss Girard at Phipps Conservatory in Schenley Park.

He and Miss Girard had spent the entire Saturday morning shuffling through various themed exhibit rooms showcasing rare species of plants while Mrs. Rankin and her friend Mrs. Potter followed closely behind, serving as chaperones.

Annuals, biennials, perennials—Henry had never given these terms any thought. What did he need to know about gardening? He had listened politely as Miss Girard led him through the conservatory, pointing out plant species she recognized. Henry feigned interest and complimented her on her impressive knowledge of the natural world. His performance must have been convincing because they'd spent almost an hour in the Cacti House staring at scorpion weed and southwestern prickly poppy.

Sitting comfortably with Miss Girard on a woolen picnic blanket next to Panther Hollow Lake, Henry felt more relaxed with an egg sandwich and lemonade in hand. Mrs. Rankin and Mrs. Potter were seated on a bench several yards away. Henry hadn't meant this outing to be the start of a courtship, but it seemed that was what the women had intended all along. He had hoped Mr. Rankin would be part of the group visiting the conservatory, but unfortunately, he was on a hunting trip in the Allegheny Mountains.

"Did you enjoy the conservatory, Mr. Archer?" Miss Girard asked after finishing her sandwich.

"Yes. It was rather interesting," Henry replied as he inconspicuously eyed her cleavage. Her green dress was cut low, so he figured he might as well steal a peek. Compensation for staring at plants all day. "Those are lovely earrings you're wearing, Miss Girard. Are they emeralds?"

"Yes. They were a gift from my parents. A present for my eighteenth birthday."

"You mentioned your knowledge of plants came from your mother."

Miss Girard nodded. "She helped design the Italian garden at our summer home in Newport." She paused to take a sip of lemonade. "It's so beautiful there. The house sits on a bluff overlooking the Atlantic and has ocean views from every room."

"You must find Pittsburgh so dismal with all its mills and factories."

"Shadyside is nice. It's away from much of the industry. And I do enjoy my cousin's company."

"How long have you been staying with Mr. and Mrs. Rankin?" Henry asked, hoping to finally uncover the mystery of Miss Girard's escape to Europe the previous autumn.

"Since April."

"That long? You and Mrs. Rankin must be incredibly close. Like sisters, perhaps."

"I wouldn't say that. It's just . . ." Miss Girard nervously swept a curl of hair away from her face and took another sip of lemonade.

Henry stared at her emeralds. Her jewelry and clothing exuded so much wealth. And status. It was a shame that her face was so unattractive. However, if it weren't, she wouldn't be picnicking in a Pittsburgh park with a lowly steel mill manager.

"Perhaps I should be honest, Mr. Archer."

"Please, Miss Girard. You can trust me with anything." Henry felt a rush of excitement. Maybe now he would get the real story.

"I was to be married last autumn, but . . ." She inhaled deeply. "A few days before the wedding, my fiancé broke the engagement. There were unforeseen circumstances."

"I am sorry to hear that. That's terrible."

"Thank you. Yes, it was awful. And embarrassing. My fiancé was from a prominent family of bankers and we—meaning my parents and I—thought he was a smart match. We could not have been more mistaken."

"I assume that is what prompted the trip to Europe."

"Yes. My mother hoped it would lift my spirits. And it did."

Henry wondered what could have motivated Miss Girard's fiancé to break the engagement. Perhaps another woman was involved? With a prettier face? He analyzed Miss Girard's facial features as she unpacked jam tartlets from the picnic basket. Her nose was pointy, her lips thin, but her blue eyes were pretty, almost the color of the sky. And while Henry usually preferred blondes, he didn't mind Miss Girard's dark brown hair. There was just too much of it, in the wrong places. He immediately wondered if she could shave it off. Or perhaps pluck it. Didn't women do that to their eyebrows?

"Mr. Archer, would you like a strawberry or blueberry tartlet?"

"Strawberry, please." Henry accepted the dessert and took a bite. It was delicious. "You haven't quite explained the long stay in Pittsburgh." He hoped he wasn't lingering too long on the same topic.

"I guess I haven't. I simply wanted to broaden my social circles and meet new people. Everyone in New York society knows of my disastrous engagement last fall, and I'm tired of my friends looking at me with pity and whispering behind my back. After my return from Europe, I realized things in New York would never be the same."

"I see," Henry replied. "May I ask why you shared such a personal story with me? I thought you wanted a fresh start."

"I honestly do not know, Henry. May I call you 'Henry'?"

"Yes, of course."

"You seem different from the pretentious men I've been surrounded by my entire life. Perhaps it's your modest background and profession. You don't seem obsessed with money and status like so many men I know. You're approachable and friendly."

Henry was astounded. The poor girl was so naive. Because he worked at a steel mill and didn't own an automobile, she assumed he didn't care about money. How absurd! Money was all he ever thought about. Besides sex with Karina, of course. Obviously, his performance for Miss Girard had been successful, although in ways he hadn't expected. He had never intended for her to think of him as ordinary and humble, although his lack of travel experience and knowledge of horticulture spoke for itself. However, much to his surprise, Miss Girard found those traits endearing. And she trusted him as well. Life was so unpredictable.

"I'm flattered that you think so highly of me, Edith. I assume we are now on a first name basis." Henry winked.

"Yes, I would like that."

"I'm glad you shared your story with me, and I want you to know I will protect it. I'm terribly sorry you had to endure such a misfortune, but I am confident that happier times are ahead."

"I think so, too."

"Edith, darling, did the cook pack any bread crumbs in your basket?" Mrs. Rankin had snuck up behind them. "I've run out, and there are more ducks to feed."

"I'll look, Clara."

As Henry watched Edith dig through the picnic basket in search of bread crumbs, he found himself staring at her cleavage again. He frowned. She was certainly no Karina. While Edith's bosom was ample, so was the rest of her. She was not overly fat—just thick and in need of a waistline.

"Here are two bags," Edith said, handing them to her cousin.

"Why don't you and Mr. Archer join us on the other side of the lake? The ducks have moved."

"That would be lovely," Edith replied.

Henry helped Edith up from the picnic blanket and offered to carry the empty baskets over to Mrs. Rankin's driver, who was napping under a tree nearer the conservatory. On his way back toward the lake, Henry noticed that his three female companions were huddled together and whispering excitedly. He approached them cautiously.

"Shall we feed the waterfowl, ladies?"

"Mr. Archer, Miss Girard and I were just discussing our plans for next weekend. Perhaps you could join us at my stable. I'd love to show you my Shelties."

"I'm afraid that won't be possible, Mrs. Rankin. I'm leaving for New York City next Saturday."

"So soon? That's only the twenty-fifth. I thought you weren't starting your new position until the beginning of July," Edith said, sounding disappointed.

"Headquarters now wants me to start work on the twenty-seventh."

"That's unfortunate," Mrs. Rankin said. "We are all growing rather fond of you. Perhaps you can join Miss Girard for a weekend in Newport."

"That would be delightful," Henry said.

Edith's face lit up as Mrs. Rankin clapped her hands with excitement. Henry thought he saw Mrs. Potter wink at him.

"Edith, darling, I will speak with your mother and have her send an invitation to Mr. Archer once he gets settled in New York. Come now, everyone, the ducks are waiting for us."

Henry extended an arm to Edith, who accepted it much too eagerly. She made no effort to disguise her girlish enthusiasm. He suddenly felt like a big fish being reeled in. Was he the great catch Miss Girard had been waiting for? As he strolled through the park with the uncomely railroad heiress on his arm, Henry wondered whether he would actually travel to Newport, Rhode Island to see her. To a bluff overlooking the Atlantic Ocean. Yet another attractive option to consider before making his departure from the scourge that was Riverton.

# Sixteen

## JANOS

### RIVERTON, JUNE 23, 1910

As Janos entered his kitchen after a long day in front of the furnace, he was greeted by the mouthwatering scent of roasted chicken. Sitting in a pan atop the cookstove was a golden-brown bird, rubbed with herbs and steaming hot. He wondered what the special occasion was. Surely he hadn't forgotten a birthday.

Noticing the kitchen door was open, Janos stepped onto the back porch where he found Karina reading *The Adventures of Huckleberry Finn* to Lukas. He stood silently for several minutes, listening to the sound of his wife's voice and watching his son snuggle close against his mother. It was a rare sight. Janos felt his hope renew. Maybe there was a way to go back to the beginning. Perhaps the prospect of leaving Riverton was lifting his wife's spirits.

When Karina finished the chapter, Janos said, "You're home early. There's a chicken on the stove, and you're reading. I guess it's been a good day."

She turned around and smiled. "I'm almost done packing

Mr. Archer's house, and he didn't need me to make dinner. He's celebrating his promotion at some fancy restaurant downtown."

"So tomorrow is his last day." Janos sighed. "Yours, too."

"It is."

"You seem to be handling it well. I expected you to be more . . ."

"Upset?"

Janos nodded as he sat down on the porch steps with his wife and son.

"I know I have a history of falling apart during difficult times. I understand why you'd expect the worst of me." Karina kissed Lukas on the head and gave him a nudge. "Go find Aunt Anna and Sofie. Tell them Papa is home."

As Lukas skipped across the courtyard, she continued, "I don't tell you enough, Janos, but I appreciate all you've done for our family over the years. I was not always the kind of wife you wanted or deserved. I put quite a strain on you, at times, and never helped enough with the children. I'm sorry."

Janos rubbed his wife's back. "There's no sense in dwelling on the past—it can't be changed. Let's focus on the future. I stopped by the Radovics' on my way home, and Mihal thinks he can get me a job at the glass factory. He'll know for sure in about a week."

"That's really good news."

"He also said that Iveta is willing to share her houses with you for the rest of the summer."

"Really?"

"With you, Iveta, and Marie cleaning together, you'll get the work done fast. You should have some free time."

"That's hard to imagine," Karina muttered.

"You get time to yourself at Mr. Archer's, don't you? How hard can it be keeping a bachelor's house in order? The man has no wife or kids."

"Oh, you'd be surprised," Karina said bitterly, shaking her head. "That man is never satisfied."

"I think it's best we don't tell the children about the possibility of moving until we know for certain." Janos patted his wife's knee. "Sofie will be relieved that she won't lose Marie after all, but Pole . . ." Janos stared at a toddler making mud pies in the courtyard and wiping the gooey mess on his shirt.

"What about him?"

"What will he do without Sofie? His mother's gone, and his father's a lousy drunk. Sofie means the world to him." Janos looked down at his lap and thought about the special bond his daughter shared with her best friend. "Maybe he could come with us," he said, turning to his wife.

"I know you want to solve all the world's problems, but you can't. Pole's a survivor. He'll be fine."

"I'm not so sure." Janos pulled Karina close and buried his face in her hair. It smelled sweet, like rose water. He kissed her neck softly.

"Do you really think we'll be moving by the end of summer?" she whispered.

Janos turned her face toward his. "I do. It's time for us to get out of Riverton and make a fresh start. Happier times are ahead."

Karina closed her eyes.

"We're going to build a new life, Karina. We're going to find our way back to each other."

She opened her eyes and caressed her husband's face. "Janos Kovac, you are such a good man—too good for the likes of me. No matter what damage I've caused our family, you've always found a way to repair it. Sofie and Lukas will always be safe in your care."

Before Janos could ask his wife what she meant by that strange comment, the children came racing back across the courtyard with Anna trailing behind them.

"Let's get that bird on the table before it's cold," Anna said once she'd caught up to her family on the porch.

Janos followed his wife, sister, and children into the house for a very special meal. Roast chicken was a rarity in the Kovac home, but rarer were the laughter and smiles shared around the dinner table.

Karina was in good spirits and seemed to be making an extra effort to get along with her children and, in particular, with Anna, with whom she was usually at odds. She had no trouble connecting with Lukas and winning him over with her charm. He was always desperate for his mother's attention. No matter how long she was lost to him in a torrent of sadness, he always welcomed her back with open arms. Sofie, however, was the more hesitant child, unsure of how to interpret her mother's increased attention. Janos had caught her eyeing her mother suspiciously a few times during dinner.

"I think you should read us a chapter from *The Wonderful Wizard of Oz*," Karina said to Sofie once the table was cleared. "I love hearing about all those fascinating creatures."

"Really?" Sofie asked, her tone skeptical. "You're interested in winged monkeys and Kalidahs?"

"Your mother is trying to take an interest in the things you enjoy. Go get the book," Janos suggested.

Sofie retrieved her favorite novel from the bookcase and began reading aloud the story of Dorothy's journey along the yellow-brick road. Lukas clutched his mother's arm during scary parts in the story and buried his head in her lap whenever the winged monkeys and the Wicked Witch of the West appeared. After Sofie completed the chapter, she closed the book and looked up.

"You're such a good reader. Maybe you'll be a teacher one day," Karina mused.

"Maybe," Sofie muttered.

"I'm going to bed early tonight," Anna said with a yawn. "I have lots of washing to do in the morning."

"We should put the kids to bed, too, Karina. They were up at the crack of dawn this morning," Janos said.

"I'm not going fishing anymore with Sofie and Pole. They get up too early," Lukas complained.

"You're the one who begged me to go," Sofie snapped.

"Come on, you two. Up to bed!" Janos grabbed Sofie's hand and led her up the crooked stairs to the family bedroom. Karina and Lukas followed closely behind. Once the children were neatly tucked under their blankets and had received goodnight kisses from each of their parents, Janos and Karina turned toward the door.

Suddenly, a soft voice whispered in the dark. "Mama, I'm sorry I wasn't very nice to you tonight. I didn't know you liked Oz so much. It's just . . ."

Karina turned around to face Sofie. "What is it?"

"You're so confusing. You normally don't stay up to read with us, but tonight, you seemed really interested in hearing the story. And you were so kind to everyone." Sofie sighed.

"And that upsets you?" Karina asked.

"No. It made me happy." Sofie went silent for a moment. "But confused. I never know what to expect from you."

Sensing his wife and daughter needed help communicating, Janos stepped in. "Sofie, your mother may be unpredictable at times, but she loves you very much."

Karina got down on her hands and knees so she could reach Sofie on the thin mattress on the floor. She kissed her forehead and stroked her hair. "You'll always be my little girl. I love you, Sofie. Don't ever forget that."

"I love you, too, Mama."

As Karina stood up from the floor, Janos wrapped his arm around her and led her back downstairs to the kitchen. He poured two glasses of whiskey and motioned for her to join him on the sofa in the sitting room.

"We had a lovely evening. I hope we have more like these

ahead. The children are growing up so fast, and I don't want you to miss any more precious time with them. I think, with a little work, you'll be able to win Sofie's trust back."

"I've really messed things up with her, haven't I?"

"You've spent a lot of time locked in the bedroom being sad. Lukas doesn't seem to hold it against you, but Sofie does. She feels cheated."

"I know how that feels." Karina drained her glass of whiskey and got up to pour herself another.

"Karina!" Janos scolded her.

"I'm sorry. Bad habit, I guess. I need to focus on the positive, right?" She returned to the sofa.

"You do. And there are a lot more positive things in your life than negative. You just need to change the way you see the world."

"That's easier said than done. How do you change your own nature?"

"I'm not sure, but we'll figure that out together. Once we get away from Riverton, we can forget about the past and wipe the slate clean. We'll build a new life for our family." Janos caressed his wife's cheek. "Say you'll help me. Say you want to start over."

Karina's expression softened as she met Janos's gaze. She stared at him for several seconds, then nodded slowly. A tear escaped down her cheek. "I do. I do want to start over."

Janos put his and Karina's drinks on the wobbly table beside the sofa. He moved closer to his wife, cupping her chin, pulling it towards him. When his mouth met hers, he was surprised that his kisses were met eagerly with soft, inviting lips. Karina wanted him! Suddenly, her hand slid down the front of Janos's pants. He broke into a wide, boyish grin, trying to remember the last time his wife had been so lascivious.

After Janos made love to Karina, she grew sentimental, reminiscing about the happy times they'd shared before coming to

America. She recalled her first impression of Janos when she saw him loading a wagon of lumber outside a sawmill in Bardejov.

"I had just arrived in town with my aunt, and you were the first person I saw. You were covered in sawdust, and all I could see were your bright green eyes and dimples. You were laughing and joking with another worker. I remember thinking that I had to get your attention."

"Is that why you dropped your suitcase in the middle of the road?"

"That was an accident. I was so embarrassed. But you came over and helped me pick up my clothes."

"I'd never seen eyes as blue as yours. Or hair so blonde and thick. I knew I'd never see a lovelier girl in all my life." Janos chuckled as he took a sip of whiskey. "Still haven't."

Karina blushed and climbed on top of her husband.

Janos was surprised by his wife's initiative, but he allowed her to take the lead as she kissed him hard on the mouth and rocked back and forth on his lap. He studied her pretty face and the way her long blonde hair fell across her shoulders. Her breasts were still perfect and round even after two children. Karina was simply stunning.

At that moment, Janos forgot about the years of his wife's unpredictable mood swings and infinite sadness. Her bitterness and lack of affection. He no longer cared about any of it. All that mattered was that his beautiful Karina—the young girl who had cast a spell on him over a decade ago—was on top of him, sending chills up and down his spine, gazing at him seductively.

Suddenly overcome with emotion, Janos rolled his wife over and wrapped his arms around her. He whispered softly in her ear, "What is this power you have over me? I love you too much."

## *Seventeen*

# KARINA

### RIVERTON, JUNE 24, 1910

Karina watched from Henry's front porch as a truck drove away with most of his clothing and household belongings. The transport company was taking the contents of his house to the train station to be loaded on a car and shipped to New York City. All that was left inside Henry's home was his bedroom furniture and a few suitcases filled with enough clothing to get him through the first week at his new job.

Also neatly packed in a suitcase were Karina's four new dresses along with hats and accessories Henry had allowed her to purchase from the department store. The few items she wanted to take with her from her former life would be easy to smuggle out of her house in a laundry bag before sunrise the following morning.

Karina had enjoyed a wonderful evening with her husband and children the night before, but it had left her confused. She'd convinced herself in the past week that leaving for New York with Henry was her best chance at happiness. She'd grown more comfortable with the idea of leaving her family and had persuaded herself that she could tolerate living with Henry. But with her departure less than twenty-four hours away, Karina found herself wavering. Was she making a huge mistake?

Her passionate night with Janos had left her wondering if anyone would ever touch her as tenderly or love her as completely as he had. She was certain Henry Archer never would. Her stomach twisted in knots. She wasn't sure the trade she was about to make was a fair one. Would her new social status and lavish lifestyle compensate for a loveless relationship? Would she feel guilty for the rest of her life that she'd abandoned the only man she had ever loved—and her children? A week earlier, she had been closer to the answers.

Further complicating matters was the fact that Janos had given her an unexpected glimmer of hope the previous evening. He really was determined to build a new life for his family far away from Riverton. Karina knew the move wouldn't solve all her family's problems—certainly not their financial ones—but leaving the steel town was a step in the right direction. She and Janos might still struggle to make ends meet, especially since he would be taking a lower-paying job at a glass factory. But taking in boarders could offset the loss in income. Karina closed her eyes, trying to calculate monthly expenses in her head. As she added multiple sets of figures, her headache intensified. She rubbed at her temples, wishing she could quiet her restless mind.

Sighing, Karina got up from the porch and went into the house to get a cold drink. As she poured herself a glass of iced tea, she glanced at the suicide note lying on the counter. If she continued on her current path, she would need a way to explain her disappearance to her family. They would hate her for sure if they knew her selfish reasons for abandoning them. Staging her own suicide was a viable option, but it was not one she was fond of. She wondered what would happen if she simply disappeared. Would her family believe she was the victim of a horrible accident or crime—perhaps a drowning or kidnapping?

"How'd it go with the transport company?"

Karina jumped at the sound of Henry's voice. She hadn't heard him slip into the house in the midst of her deliberating. "You're home early."

"There wasn't much left for me to do at the mill. I stopped by the bank to close my account. Had a few drinks at the saloon." Henry hiccupped.

"All that's left in the house are your suitcases and bedroom furniture. I made sandwiches for dinner," Karina said, approaching the refrigerator.

Suddenly, Henry was behind her, pushing her up against the chilly appliance, shoving a hand up her skirt. He kissed her roughly as he tugged at her blouse.

"Henry! How much have you had to drink?" Karina tasted alcohol on his tongue and turned her head to avoid his punishing kiss.

"Not nearly enough!" he said, laughing. "Don't you see, Karina? I'm finally done with Riverton. I wanna celebrate! I've got a pretty good stiffy we can use." He forced a finger inside her and bit her on the neck.

"Ouch! Why are you being so rough? Is this what I have to look forward to?"

"I thought you wanted to go to New York. This is part of the deal. I pay for your lifestyle and clothes. You keep me satisfied."

"You don't have to be so crude." Karina tried to wiggle her way out of Henry's grip. "This is no way to treat your mistress."

"I'll treat you any way I see fit."

Karina's stomach turned. She had always known Henry was no gentleman, but she never expected him to be abusive. Leaving Riverton and being entirely dependent on him could leave her in a vulnerable position. Was she surrendering all her freedom? Or perhaps it was just the alcohol making him act like such an ass.

Sensing he needed a reminder of what he had to lose if he didn't treat her well, she said, "We can go into the bedroom,

Henry, but you will be gentle. Remember, I can leave at any time. I have limits."

"Of course. I'm sorry. I'm a little excited, that's all."

Karina led Henry into the bedroom where she unbuttoned her blouse and removed her skirt. He stood motionless, gaping at her naked body as she took off her underclothes. "What's the matter? There's nothing here you haven't seen before."

"I'm just taking in the view. It sure is lovely."

Henry practically tore off his shirt and pants and then swaggered toward Karina, his eyes twinkling. He yanked on her hair and pulled it out of the bun she had arranged neatly at the back of her head. He threw her on the bed and climbed on top of her.

Karina closed her eyes as Henry planted sloppy kisses all over her face and groped her breasts clumsily. When he entered her a little too roughly, she winced and prayed it would not take him long to finish. Unfortunately, the amount of whiskey he'd consumed would make that an unlikely prospect. She could practically smell the booze seeping out of his pores. She held her breath, attempting to fend off the pungent odors coming from her employer.

As Henry's voracious lovemaking intensified, so did his grunting and groaning. The sounds were so vulgar, Karina had to cover her ears. She had never been more repulsed by another human being—until she felt something wet land on her cheek. She opened her eyes to find a line of drool hanging from the corner of Henry's mouth. Her irritation with his drunkenness was now bordering on outrage.

As she lay under the weight of Henry's body, forcing herself not to flee, thoughts of Janos drifted into her head. Her husband was everything Henry Archer would never be—gentle, loving, attractive. Karina so often dismissed the connection she had with her husband, choosing to focus only on the fact that he was a steelworker. Had she been a fool? She looked up at

Henry as a deafening moan escaped his lips and wondered how long she could endure his company.

"That was something, wasn't it?" he asked, rolling off her. He hit the bed with a loud thud.

"Unforgettable," she replied sarcastically. Karina hoped Henry's heavy drinking was an isolated incident brought on by his excitement about leaving the mill. He usually showed more restraint. For good measure, she added, "You drank too much. Don't make a habit of it."

Henry snickered. "Since when do I take orders from you? You're forgetting your place, woman," he slurred.

Karina did not like Henry's tone. She was wavering again, the path ahead becoming more unclear. Drunk or not, he was being too bold. She could not allow him to believe he was holding all the cards. "I know you're drunk and feeling like you can conquer the world, but we are equal partners in this arrangement. Don't act like I'm your inferior. I know how desperately you need me."

Karina thought of Henry's insatiable sexual appetite. She wondered if it would ever abate. It actually seemed to be growing as of late, probably because Henry had been forcing her to prove her value. Had she awakened a dangerous beast? "I will not tolerate drunkenness and repulsive lovemaking. That is the last time you will touch me in that state," she announced.

Henry rolled over to face her, wearing an exaggerated frown. "That's the last time I will touch you at all."

"What are you talking about?" Karina sat up.

"Circumstances have changed. I'm not taking you to New York."

"What do you mean?" Karina's heart began to race. "We made plans."

"Plans change, darling. I still don't know how I'll live without that body of yours, but my newfound fortune will be a consolation."

"What fortune?" Karina's anger rose so quickly she nearly choked on her words.

"I met a railroad heiress. She's quite enamored with me."

"What on Earth would an heiress want with *you*?" Karina sniggered. "You're so painfully ordinary."

"The situation's complicated, for sure. Edith will never win a beauty contest. But she has more money than you or I could ever dream of. We had a pleasant evening last night, and I'll be traveling to her family's home in Rhode Island this summer. It seems I've got a better offer."

"You selfish son of a bitch. You used me!" Karina threw a pillow at Henry. It was the closest thing within reach, but useless. She pounced on him, wanting to choke the life out of him. Unfortunately, he caught her in mid-air and grabbed her by the wrists. He shook her a few times before pinning her down on the bed.

"And you haven't been using me?" he sneered. "You and I are exactly the same. Don't pretend you wouldn't ditch me for the next best thing in New York. With a body and face like yours, you'd eventually find someone with a fatter wallet than mine. I know how that pretty little head of yours works."

Karina spat on Henry as she struggled beneath his grip. She kicked wildly, hoping to knee him between the legs. "You dirty bastard! You knew you weren't taking me to New York and you lured me into your bed anyway. I hate you!" Karina continued to fight under the weight of Henry's body, but her petite frame was no match for his. He outweighed her by at least seventy pounds.

"Sorry about that. But you know the effect you have on me," Henry nodded animatedly.

Karina scowled at him. "Who's going to satisfy you now if your heiress is so homely?"

"No need to worry about me. With my future wife's money, I'll have my pick of mistresses. You wouldn't believe how many gorgeous women walk the streets of New York. I'll miss you though. I have no doubt." Henry leaned over to kiss her.

Still pinned, Karina dodged Henry's kiss and bit his forearm until she drew blood. He yanked her up by her hair, slapped her across the face, and then threw her on the floor.

"Really? That's how you wanna say goodbye? Get your clothes and get outta my house!" Henry shouted, pointing forcefully at the bedroom door. "And gimme back my house key!"

"You're going to wish you'd never met me," Karina snarled, a venomous rage flowing like poison through her veins. She gathered her clothes and made her way to the door. She turned around to take one last look at Henry Archer as she pulled the key out of her skirt pocket and threw it on the bed. "You're going to regret this. Mark my words."

"What are you going to do, Karina? You're just a dirty immigrant whore."

A few blocks down the street from Henry's house, Karina sat on a bench in the town's only park, gazing at her reflection in a compact mirror. The sting and hot flush of her cheek from Henry's slap were subsiding, but she wondered if there would be a bruise. She combed out her disheveled hair and arranged it in a bun. She checked the mirror once again. She looked altogether normal, even pretty, except for the slight puffiness around her eyes from crying.

As she lingered on the park bench, watching an ominous cloud swallow the sun, she tried to quiet her fury and come to terms with Henry's betrayal. He was leaving Riverton without her and trading her in for some ugly heiress. And though Karina hated to admit it, she knew her beauty was no match for a colossal railroad fortune.

As she mulled over her limited options, the irony of the situation struck her. Only moments before Henry had ditched her, she was wondering whether she could run away with him after all. She was having serious doubts and considering the possibility of staying with Janos and her family. So why was she now so enraged?

Karina groaned and stared down at her lap. She caught a glimpse of the apple in her open pocketbook and realized she was hungry. She picked it up and rubbed it on her skirt, revealing its perfect, shiny red skin. She then rolled it around in her hands and considered her predicament. She fought hard to concentrate, but images of Henry's arrogant expression kept flashing before her eyes. His mocking words echoed in her ears.

Suddenly, Karina couldn't breathe. She felt dizzy and hot and vaguely aware that her fingers were tingling. The pace of her thoughts quickened.

*How dare he use me and toss me aside like a piece of garbage! I betrayed my husband for that man! I was going to leave my family for him!*

She put a hand to her chest. Her heart was beating eerily fast. She wrapped her arms around herself and rocked back and forth, hoping the motion might calm her, quell her rising panic. Her efforts had little effect.

Karina cursed her former employer and the railroad heiress who had stolen her future. She hoped they would have a miserable life together. The image of Henry on the arm of an overweight woman with a face full of pimples and an overbearing, screeching mother-in-law trailing behind them gave Karina a fleeting moment of comfort.

A soft thud interrupted her swirling thoughts. Karina's pristine apple had fallen to the ground. She picked it up and admired it for a second before angrily biting into it. The fruit was unusually sweet and tasted just as good as it looked. It was a welcome—albeit temporary—distraction from her troubles. Her search for a path forward would have to wait until after she finished her snack.

As Karina's hunger quieted, so did her racing mind. And then, during an improbable moment of stillness, it finally appeared—an idea as flawless as the apple in front of her face. Satisfied and feeling strangely calm, Karina got up from her bench and walked down the hill. She knew how to deal with Henry Archer.

As Karina neared the Janosik boarding house, she cringed. Judging by the sounds coming from the front porch, the house was still populated with unsavory characters. Though she shared a common ancestry and language with these people, Karina had never felt any kinship with them. The dirty, foul-mouthed drunks were degenerates, unworthy of her compassion. She shuddered as she thought of the many times one of them had shoved his tongue down her throat or grabbed her breasts or buttocks. On a few occasions, she'd even been pinned against the wall and groped between her legs. She dreaded setting foot in that dump again.

It was not long before sunset on a Friday night, and the porch was crowded with unattractive men sharing bottles of moonshine with young girls perched on their laps. One looked barely older than Sofie. Karina shook her head. She scanned the crowd to see if she knew anyone, but the only person she recognized was Pole's father. He was shirtless and passed out in the corner of the porch. Karina groaned as she made her way up the crooked steps and into the house to find Mrs. Janosik.

Once inside, Karina was hit by a wall of acrid cigarette smoke and stale, sour air. It was stiflingly hot. There weren't many people in the house—only a few men in the dining room emptying soup bowls filled with an unappetizing mixture of mystery meat, vegetables, and broth. Karina had often helped in the kitchen and grimly remembered the types of animal parts Mrs. Janosik had brought home from the butcher. She took just about anything as long as it was on sale. Pig feet and knuckles, chicken gizzards, tripe, and even beef tongue. Karina preferred the more expensive meats she had grown accustomed to preparing for Henry. As she made her way into the kitchen, she saw Mrs. Janosik leaning over the stove.

"I see some things never change," Karina said in Slovak.

The old woman nearly jumped. "Karina! I didn't think I'd ever see you here again. Are you looking for work?"

"No, no. I'm looking for someone. Does Pavol Tomicek live here?"

Mrs. Janosik nodded. "He lives on the second floor, but he's with his sweetheart right now. He doesn't want to be disturbed."

"I have something very important to tell him. Which room is he in?"

"The last one on the right, but I doubt he'll answer the door."

"Thank you," Karina said as she turned toward the hallway.

"Don't you have time for a drink with an old friend? I've been wondering what it's like in that fancy neighborhood where you work."

"Maybe in a bit, Luba. I need to talk to Pavol first."

Karina carefully made her way up the collapsing staircase that led to the second floor. The steps were narrow and steep and in desperate need of repair. The entire place seemed to be falling down and caving in. Once at the top of the stairs, she noticed the only door closed on the entire floor was Pavol's. All the others were open in an attempt to circulate the stale, humid air.

Karina put her head against Pavol's door. She could hear the faint sounds of moaning and groaning coming from inside the room. A bed squeaked loudly under the weight of bodies, presumably in the act of lovemaking. She rolled her eyes and knocked on the door.

"Go away!" a muffled voice shouted in Slovak.

"I need to talk to you, Pavol. It's important," Karina said.

"Come back later."

Karina heard the distinct giggle of a woman. "I think you'll want to hear what I have to say. It's about your brother, Tomas."

There was a pause that lasted almost a minute followed by

voices arguing in hushed tones. Finally, the sound of heavy footsteps and the creaking of floorboards. The door opened, and a man, half-naked and sweaty, appeared. He wore a bed sheet around his waist, shielding the lower half of his stocky frame. Karina glanced past him toward the bed where a woman was hiding under a blanket.

"What about him?"

"I have some disturbing information about his accident. Please let me come in, and we'll talk about it over a drink or two." Karina held up a bottle of whiskey she'd snatched from Luba Janosik's kitchen when the old lady had her head in the oven.

The young woman hiding in the bed peeked out from under the blanket and frowned.

"Don't worry," Karina said as she entered the room. "There's no need to be embarrassed."

"Put some clothes on, Milena," Pavol grumbled. "You'll want to hear this, too." Turning to face Karina, he said, "She was to be my brother's wife."

"I'm so sorry," Karina said. "At least you have found comfort in each other." As she watched the two young people scramble to cover themselves, Karina wondered how long they had waited to jump into bed together after poor Tomas was buried.

Still shirtless, but wearing a pair of ripped pants, Pavol pulled a rickety chair out of the corner. He placed it near the bed and motioned for Karina to sit down. He and his scantily clad lover sat on the edge of the mattress. The girl wore a thin nightgown that was practically transparent. Karina could see the outline of her nipples.

"You opening that whiskey, or not?" Pavol pointed to the bottle Karina had placed on the floor near her feet.

"I'm sorry. I nearly forgot. You and your sweetheart can have it." Karina picked up the moonshine and handed it to Pavol as she glanced at the skinny girl sitting next to him. "Milena, is it?" she asked in the sweetest tone she could muster.

The girl nodded shyly.

"What do you have to say? And who are you?" Pavol asked, eyeing Karina suspiciously as he took a swig from the bottle.

"It seems you and I share a common enemy. His name is Henry Archer. Your brother Tomas's death was the result of his negligence."

"Who?" Pavol asked, his eyes narrowing.

"Henry Archer," Karina repeated herself. "He's one of the managers at the mill. He oversees equipment inspections. He's the reason your brother died in that horrible accident. He lied about having the crane near your brother's furnace inspected."

Karina crossed her arms, waiting for the potency of her words to take effect.

Pavol's face went pale. He shook his head and clenched his fists. "There was talk—talk about inspections. Rumors that the crane needed repairs. The company men said it was an accident. It couldn't have been prevented."

"They lied. Henry wasn't having the equipment inspected. He falsified his reports. I heard it from a reliable source."

Pavol stared at Karina. She nodded her head slowly.

Suddenly, the bottle of whiskey sailed through the air, hitting the wall with a loud, shrill *crack*. Shards of glass rained down on the floor. The moonshine trickled down the wall and followed the sloped floor to its lowest point in the corner.

"I'm going to kill that son of a bitch!" Pavol got up from the bed and paced around the room.

A stream of tears flowed down Milena's cheeks.

Seizing her opportunity, Karina said, "I know you're angry. You have every right to be. But I have a plan for you to get revenge on Henry Archer."

"Why do you care?" Pavol turned around. "What's in it for you?"

"I have a reason to hate Archer, too." Karina seethed.

"You going to tell me?"

"No."

Pavol walked back over to the bed and sat down. He sighed. "What's your plan, then?"

"Milena, honey . . ." Karina said. "Why don't you go downstairs and get another bottle of whiskey from Luba? Here, I'll give you the money for it."

## *Eighteen*

# POLE

### RIVERTON, JUNE 25, 1910

Pole stood on Sofie's front porch, wiping a tear from his cheek with his dirty shirt sleeve. The sun would be up soon. He hoped Mr. Kovac had already left for work. He desperately needed to speak to Sofie and preferred to do it in private. She was the only person he could trust with a secret.

As he neared the front door, he caught the scent of fried eggs and bacon and heard the banging of pots and pans. Aunt Anna was awake and in the kitchen making breakfast. He smoothed his hair and knocked on the door.

"I'm coming, Iveta. I'm coming," Sofie's aunt grumbled in Slovak. The door opened abruptly, and Aunt Anna appeared, wielding a greasy spatula. "Pole! I wasn't expecting you," she said, switching over to English. "Mrs. Radovic usually shows up at this time of day to borrow eggs."

"Is Sofie up yet?"

"No. I thought you two weren't going fishing until mid-morning."

"Something came up. Can I talk to her?"

"Is everything okay? You look upset."

"Yes, ma'am." Pole tried not to cry.

Aunt Anna eyed him suspiciously. "She's still sleeping, but I'll get her up and tell her to put on her work clothes."

"We don't have to get to the fishin' hole now. We just need to chat a few minutes."

"Do you want to come in and have breakfast while you wait for Sofie?"

"No, thanks. I'm not hungry."

Pole waited for almost five minutes on the front stoop. He stared into the street and watched a crow peck at a banana peel someone had thrown on the ground. He bowed his head and examined the top of his left shoe where his big toe was peeking out through a hole.

Suddenly, he heard the squeak of a door hinge. He turned around to find Sofie standing in a pink nightgown, her long blonde hair in tangles around her face. Her eyes were sleepy, her cheeks the color of her cotton dress.

"What's the matter, Pole? Is someone using our fishing hole again? Is it the Russians?"

"No, Sof." He smiled weakly. "It's nothin' like that."

She sat down next to him, a concerned look on her face.

"I have something important to tell you, but you have to keep it a secret. You can't even tell your papa."

Sofie frowned. "But I tell him everything. What's going on?"

Pole took a deep breath. "My pop woke me up real early this morning. He told me to meet him at the train station at eight-thirty. We're leaving town."

"For how long?" Sofie leaned forward.

"He wouldn't tell me. I told him I wasn't goin' anywhere with him—he knows I can survive on my own. But he told me I'd better be at that station if I want to meet my baby sister."

Sofie's eyes grew to the size of saucers. "Has he lost his mind? He's been drinking too much!"

"No, I think he was serious. And sober." Pole looked down at his big toe again, trying to hide his watery eyes. "He said I have a five-year-old sister, and we're going to stay with her and her mama for a while."

"You can't!"

"I have to. Ever since Mama died, I've been having a hard time believing that the only family I have left in this world is my jackass father." He glanced up at Sofie. "Sorry for the cussin'."

"Are you sure about this?"

"Not really, but sometimes I feel so lonely. I miss Mama. And now I think . . ."

"It sure would be nice to have a sister."

Pole looked up and smiled.

"Where do these people live?"

"I can't say for sure. I looked at the train schedule Mrs. Janosik keeps on the front table in the boarding house. It says the eight-thirty train goes to Washington D.C."

"That doesn't make any sense. How would someone like your father get involved with a rich lady from the city?"

"Cities are full of poor folks, too. But I don't think that's where we're headed. That train to the capitol goes right through coal country—Connellsville, Pennsylvania. That's the kind of place you'd find a lady willing to . . . um," Pole stammered, his face turning red.

"Have a baby with your father?" Sofie smirked.

"That's one way to put it." Pole laughed nervously. "That's the part I need you to keep secret. I'm not sure exactly where we're going, but you can't tell anyone which train we took."

"Do you think your pop is in some kind of trouble?"

"Of course, he is. He owes a lot of people money. He probably wants to hide out for a bit."

"When do you think you'll be back? How will I know you're okay?" Sofie clutched Pole's arm.

"I don't know. I hope real soon. In the meantime, you keep

the fishin' going and sell to the guys at the boarding house. Deal with Sef. He's honest and won't let anyone take advantage of you."

Sofie buried her face in Pole's shoulder. She began to cry.

Fighting back the tears threatening to roll down his cheek, Pole wrapped his arms around her. "I won't be gone long. I'll be back before you know it." As soon as the words rolled off his tongue, Pole regretted them. He had no idea what was going on with his pop, but he was sure it was complicated and ugly. It could be a while before he got back to Riverton.

"Don't you remember?" Sofie asked, looking up, sniffling. "At the wedding, when we talked about Marie and her family moving?"

Pole closed his eyes as a wave of guilt struck him. "I told you I wasn't going anywhere."

Sofie pulled away from him. "First Marie and now you! My two best friends are leaving me. How could you? You're a liar!" she shouted.

The words stung. Pole felt the tear he'd been fighting for the last few minutes finally trickle down his cheek. He reached out to Sofie, but she swatted at him.

"I never saw this comin'. I didn't know I had a sister," he pleaded. "What if my father gets drunk and hits her? What if she has no one around to protect her?"

"She has a mother, doesn't she?"

Pole watched Sofie's face twist in pain. She seemed to catch her mistake almost instantly. He stroked her cheek and pulled her into his chest. "That doesn't always make a difference, does it?" he whispered.

"No." She sighed heavily.

Sofie snuggled tight against Pole's chest and seemed to relax as the minutes passed. He tried to savor every second he had left with her. He knew the clock was ticking and that his train would be leaving soon. He wondered gloomily when he might see her again. Sofie had been the one constant in his life since his mother had passed. She was his best friend and the person he cared most about in the entire world. Overcome with emotion, Pole gently placed his hand under her chin and tilted her head upward.

"I'll be back, Sof. I can't say when, but I promise I'll come back."

# *Nineteen*

## KARINA

### RIVERTON, JUNE 25, 1910

Just before sunrise, Karina crept around the side of Henry Archer's house toward the backyard. It was early on a Saturday morning, so all the houses in the neighborhood were dark, the inhabitants inside fast asleep. Including Henry. His train didn't leave until nine o'clock, so Karina felt confident she had plenty of time to execute her plan.

As she stood in the shadows near the back porch waiting for Pavol, she thought about the possible fallout from her scheme. She had analyzed the situation carefully and concluded that she could not go inside the house to watch Pavol beat up and rob Henry. While she desperately wanted to witness him get the thumping he so deserved, she could not risk him recognizing the outline of her body or her familiar scent. When he recovered, he might remember her presence and report her to the police.

Karina would have to trust that Pavol's vengeance would be forceful and swift. Only if Henry were knocked unconscious, would she sneak into the house to take a peek at his wounds. It was safer this way. He would never know who had attacked him in the dark. The beating and subsequent robbery would look random.

Suddenly, Karina heard footsteps approaching from behind her. She turned around to greet Pavol, but was surprised by a man of greater stature. He was carrying an axe handle.

"What are *you* doing here?" she asked sarcastically in Slovak. "Where's Pavol?"

"He's right behind me," the man replied in a gruff voice.

"I brought Stofanik, just in case," Pavol said as he emerged from the shadows with a club.

"In case what?" Karina asked.

"In case he needs extra muscle." Stofanik laughed as he held up his bicep and waved the axe handle in the air.

Karina stiffened. "I don't think it's going to take two of you to get the job done." She scowled as she looked at the implements her accomplices were carrying. "And take it easy with those weapons. You're just going to rough him up a little."

"Aww, come on. We want this to be fun," Stofanik whined.

"The real prize is the cash. But you'll have to pay him out of your share, Pavol," Karina said as she motioned toward Stofanik. "I'm not splitting Henry's money three ways."

"Whatever." Pavol huffed.

"A little greedy, aren't we, Mrs. Kovac? Why should you get half the money when we do all the work?" Stofanik asked.

"Neither one of you would have this opportunity if it weren't for me. Just get in there and get me the cash."

Karina's stomach lurched. John Stofanik was an unexpected wrinkle in her once brilliant plan. She was aware of his violent tendencies and hoped his presence wouldn't do more harm than good. She had seen him beat up quite a few men when she worked at the boarding house. He was also known for roughing up his son, too. Karina frowned as she thought of poor Pole. She disliked Stofanik, but maybe he'd come in handy if Pavol lost his nerve.

"I'd never pass up a chance to stick it to the boss man." Stofanik laughed wickedly. "I'd do this for free if I wasn't so damned broke."

"Shh! You're going to wake someone," Karina scolded Stofanik as she scanned the area. "Pavol, did you tell him the plan?"

"You'd better go over it again. I'm not sure he remembers much of our conversation from last night. He was pretty drunk."

"Why am I not surprised?" Karina groaned. "Now, listen up. Henry's bedroom is the second door on the left at the top of the stairs. Once you smack him around a few times, get his wallet out of the nightstand next to the bed. He went to the bank yesterday to close his account, so it should be full of cash."

"How much?" Stofanik asked.

"At least twenty dollars. I think he had most of his money transferred to his new bank, but he's got to have plenty of cash for traveling."

"That's a few months' rent," Pavol said, nodding. "Anything else of value?"

"Just his pocket watch. The transport company shipped everything else to New York. Henry's supposed to catch a nine o'clock train this morning. He's leaving Riverton for good."

"I'm not sure he'll be able to make that train. Might have to postpone his trip a few days." Stofanik sniggered.

Karina trembled. She wondered whether it was too late to call off her plan. She shook her head vigorously, trying to stave off her doubts. Her family needed the money, she reminded herself. *She* needed it. She'd earned it anyway—going to so much trouble to keep Henry satisfied.

"Let's get this over with," Pavol said as he climbed the porch steps and headed for the back door.

"Hold on." Karina rummaged through her pockets. "I've got to unlock the door. I need to find my extra key."

"Exactly how long have you been planning this?" Stofanik asked.

"Less than twelve hours. I had the extra key made months ago. You know, just in case."

"Uh huh," Stofanik said, eyeing Karina. "You're something else."

Karina quietly unlocked the back door and motioned Pavol and Stofanik to tiptoe down the hallway toward the staircase. She clasped her hands together to stop them from shaking. She then watched Pavol climb the steps while Stofanik hung back at the foot of the stairs.

She returned to the back porch and began to pace. She tried to keep calm and wait patiently for the return of her accomplices, but her curiosity grew more uncontrollable with each passing minute. Karina could not resist the temptation to go inside the house. Throwing caution to the wind, she slipped through the back door and hurried toward the staircase, pausing at the newel post. She listened for some sort of tussle or brawl coming from above. Had Pavol and Stofanik already confronted Henry? The house was eerily quiet.

Her heart pounding wildly, Karina climbed the steps to the second floor to have a look for herself. When she reached the top of the stairs, she saw the silhouette of a man standing in the doorway of Henry's bedroom. Was that Pavol? Why hadn't he gone in yet? And where was Stofanik?

Karina narrowed her eyes as she examined the man more carefully. Her heart sank. She heard the distinct *click* from the hammer of a gun.

"Who the hell are you?" Henry shouted, pointing a gun into his own bedroom.

Karina shuddered. *This can't be happening!*

"Sorry, sir. I in wrong house," Stofanik stammered in broken English from somewhere inside the bedroom. "I drunk. Had too much whiskey."

"Shut up! You think I can't hear your foul Hunky accent? Get on your knees. I'm calling the police. This is exactly the sort of thing I'd expect from that bitch."

Karina panicked. This was not the ending she had envisioned. And where was Pavol? She scanned the hallway. Dawn was approaching, and light was beginning to filter through the windows of the four bedrooms situated around the hall. Karina gasped. She saw a pair of feet peeking out of the doorway in the bedroom closest to her. She slipped inside and found Pavol lying on the floor, unconscious. Had Henry knocked him out?

Karina felt nauseous. She could still hear Stofanik pleading with Henry in his feigned drunken state. How had two strong steelworkers armed with a club and an axe handle managed to screw this up so badly?

As Karina bent over Pavol, her mind raced. Her eyes darted frantically around the room in search of a weapon. There was no way she was letting Henry Archer leave town without paying for his sins. At last, she spotted a cast iron doorstop in the shape of a cat on the floor of the open bedroom closet. The transport company missed it!

Without thinking, Karina grabbed the cat and charged toward Henry. She raised the heavy doorstop high into the air and struck the back of his head. Henry made no sound as he crumbled to the floor, blood gushing from his scalp. He lay motionless as a bright red puddle formed around his head, staining the expensive Persian rug that was to be sold with the house.

"My my, Mrs. Kovac! You *are* special."

"What the hell happened in here? Why is Pavol unconscious in the other room?"

"I was wondering what happened to him. He told me he wanted Archer all to himself for a few minutes so he could strike the first blows. He told me to wait downstairs for a bit. I guess your sweetheart was ready for him."

"And you didn't help him?"

"I didn't hear anything. I figured Pavol took the easy route and knocked the guy out in his sleep. I came up to the bedroom to get my share of the cash, and your sweetheart surprised me from behind—with a gun," Stofanik said, shaking his head.

"Stop calling him my sweetheart," Karina demanded.

"Isn't that what he is? Only a jilted lover would go to all this trouble for revenge."

"Just get his wallet, John."

"I think you should have the honor."

Karina bent down and dug through Henry's pants' pockets. It didn't take her long to locate the wallet. She pulled it out and admired its thickness.

"Open it up and count it out where I can see," Stofanik urged.

Karina began counting. "One, two, three . . ." Her eyes grew wide. "There's almost eight hundred dollars! Why on Earth?"

"Christ Almighty!" Stofanik slapped his leg. "That's more than I make in a year."

Karina looked at the money in her hands and then glanced down at Henry. Blood continued to pour out of his head. "Why is he bleeding so much?"

"You hit him good and hard."

"He's going to be all right, isn't he?"

"Aww . . . he'll be fine. Might be a little sore when he wakes up though. Or maybe not," Stofanik said, scratching his temple. "That's a pretty good bit of blood."

"Oh, my God!" Karina leaned over and put her ear to Henry's mouth. She couldn't tell if he was breathing.

"You need to check his wrist. See if you feel a pulse. Lemme do it," Stofanik said, pushing Karina out of the way. He knelt down and grabbed Henry's wrist. He felt around for half a minute and then looked up at her. "I hate to say it, but I think you killed the bastard."

Karina's hand flew to her mouth. "I didn't mean to. I just wanted . . ." she stammered.

"What did you do?" Pavol asked, stumbling into the bedroom. He stared at Henry's bloody head as he rubbed the back of his own. "That son of a bitch hit me from behind. He knocked me out."

"Mrs. Kovac took care of him for you. She killed him." Stofanik chuckled.

"I didn't kill him!" Karina whined, covering her face with her hands. "It was an accident."

"All right, come on. We've gotta get out of here while it's still dark. Get up." Stofanik dragged Karina to her feet and led her to the top of the stairs. She looked back over her shoulder at Henry lying on the floor in his own blood. She felt nauseous, dizzy. Suddenly, Stofanik turned around and walked back over to the body.

"I almost forgot the pocket watch."

Karina stared at the large man as he searched her employer's clothing. Henry's arm fell limply to the ground as Stofanik rolled him over to retrieve the watch from his back pocket.

"Now, hand me that wallet. Me and Pavol will take four hundred and the watch. You can have the rest."

Karina didn't object as Stofanik counted out his and Pavol's share and handed the wallet back to her. She stood motionless, stunned by what had transpired.

"Mrs. Kovac, pull yourself together. We got more cash now than we know what to do with. Of course, I'm sure I'll find a way to spend it," Stofanik said gleefully. "Pavol, are you okay? You're mighty quiet."

"My goddamned head hurts. I'm supposed to work today," he said, still clutching his head.

"Never mind that mill. You got enough money to live comfortably for months. Hurry up, now. Let's slip out the back door and get outta this neighborhood."

Still in a daze, Karina followed her accomplices down the stairs and past the parlor. "What am I going to do?" she moaned. "What if the police suspect me? I was his housekeeper."

"You're not going to hang around and find out, are you? You need to lie low for a while," Stofanik said. "Get out of town."

Panic welling inside her, Karina thought of her family. What would they think if she didn't come home? She had planned to stay. She was going to use Henry's money to help pay for their move up north. Suddenly, she didn't want to go anywhere but home. She didn't want to be with anyone but Janos. A series of slaps to her cheek interrupted her desperate thoughts.

"Wake up, honey. There's no time to think. We gotta go!"

Stofanik led Karina by the arm to the back of the house. As soon as they reached the door, her mind began to clear. "Wait, there's something I need from the parlor."

She rushed back down the hallway to the empty room at the front of the house. In the middle of the vast space sat her traveling suitcase filled with her new dresses, hats, and accessories. She grabbed it and ran to the back door.

"Can one of you help me carry this to the train station?"

# Twenty

## SOFIE

### RIVERTON, JUNE 25, 1910

Sofie pushed her half-eaten eggs around her plate with a fork and let out a huge sigh. She glanced at her brother, who was inhaling his breakfast. He looked like a miniature version of her father except that his green eyes were a shade darker, and his hair was blonde and messy. She envied his appetite and wondered if there would ever be a time or circumstance that would diminish his ravenous hunger. She doubted it.

Sensing that his sister was staring at him, or perhaps just needing to catch his breath in between bites, Lukas looked up for a split second. He noticed his sister's plate, her scrambled eggs and bacon slices untouched. He smiled and gave Sofie an expectant look. She dropped her fork and shoved the plate in her brother's direction. She then rested her head on her hand and closed her eyes.

"What's the matter, Sofie?" Aunt Anna asked. "What did Pole say that got you so upset?"

"I don't feel like talking about it."

"It's not like you to skip breakfast. Are you sure you don't want to tell me?"

Sofie looked down at her thumb and examined the puncture wound she had gotten from a fishing hook the day before. She didn't know what to say. She always told Aunt Anna her problems, but she didn't want to betray Pole's trust. She couldn't lie to her aunt either. She had always been so good to Sofie, more affectionate and loving than her own mother. Sofie sat for a few moments, watching her brother gorge himself while considering her choice of words.

"If you don't want to help Pole with the fishing anymore, I'm sure he'll understand. Sometimes when you turn a hobby into an occupation, you lose your love for it," Aunt Anna said.

"It's not that. Pole's leaving me on my own for a bit to manage the fishing. He's got some other business to take care of."

Sofie's aunt put down her teacup. "What sort?"

"Family stuff. He's not sure when he can help me again."

"He won't leave you on your own for long. I know how fond he is of you. You'd better be careful at that boarding house though. Maybe I should go with you when you sell your fish."

Sofie nodded.

"Why don't you get dressed and take Lukas with you to the fishing hole? He's not Pole, but he can help."

Sofie didn't want to take her brother, but she figured she had better follow her aunt's advice and get out the door before she asked any more questions. She had been able to get away with giving Aunt Anna a partial truth about Pole and hadn't been forced to lie. Hopefully, that would be the end of the discussion. She got up from the table and went to the bedroom to put on some clothes.

As Sofie made her way down the street toward the fishing hole, Lukas followed several steps behind. He was so easily distracted, stopping to pick up rocks or poke at a dead mouse lying in the dirt, half-eaten by stray cats. She glanced back at him and shook her head. It was probably after eight o'clock, and the best fishing would soon be behind them. Sofie froze in her tracks. She pulled her father's old pocket watch out of her dress pocket and saw that it was a quarter past eight. Could she make it to the train station in time to see Pole before he left?

She turned around and ran past her brother. "Lukas, I forgot that I need to take care of something downtown. I'll pick you up later. Wait at home with Aunt Anna."

Sofie ran back down the unpaved street toward her house, dropping her fishing pole and bucket on the front porch with a loud *clang*. She sprinted through the streets of her neighborhood and into the ethnic side of the town's market district where one of her Catholic school classmates was selling wild strawberries. She only had time to give the girl a quick wave.

The urge to see Pole growing stronger, Sofie crossed over Riverton Avenue, entering the affluent side of town. She passed the bank, the town hall, and Kaufmann's department store, trying not to bump into the well-dressed ladies lining the sidewalks. She ran hard, struggling to catch her breath in the smoky air. A side stitch started to irritate her a few hundred feet from the train station, but she ignored it and pushed on.

As she climbed the steps to the station and burst through the heavy front doors of the brick building, she heard a shrill train whistle and the rhythmic chug of an engine. Her heart sank.

Sofie ran through the station and out to the platform where she came to an abrupt stop. She watched in despair as a train pulled away from the station on the southern track. It was headed in the opposite direction of Pittsburgh. She glanced up at the clock and felt a wave of disappointment. It was 8:31 a.m. Pole was gone.

"Would you like a muffin?" a gruff voice came from behind her.

Sofie turned around to find an old man holding a basket full of muffins, bearing a toothless grin. She tried not to look frightened when she noticed the thick scar trailing from his left eye to his jaw. He wore a dark patch over that eye, making Sofie wonder what atrocity hid beneath it. She suspected the mill was to blame for the poor man's misfortune.

"I have banana and blueberry," he said.

Sofie felt guilty that she was penniless. She dug through her pockets, hoping a nickel might magically appear. "I'm sorry, sir, but I don't have any money."

"I'll take a dozen. Six blueberry and six banana," said a dark-haired woman in a shimmering green dress with matching stones dangling from her ears.

Sofie was spellbound by the dazzling green gems sparkling in the early morning sunlight. She couldn't remember what they were called, but she knew they were expensive. She was used to seeing fancy ladies around Kaufmann's department store, but none of them wore jewelry such as this. Sofie wondered what this woman was doing in Riverton.

"What kind of muffin would you like, young lady?" the woman asked.

Sofie looked around and, seeing no other young lady besides herself, said, "Who, me?"

The woman nodded and smiled.

"I'd like a blueberry one, but I don't have any money."

"No matter," the woman said, handing the old man a few coins. "It's my treat."

"Thank you, ma'am," Sofie said as the old man handed her a muffin. As he counted out six blueberry and six banana muffins and placed them in a brown paper bag, another well-dressed woman appeared. She was much plumper than the woman in green. Her pretty blue dress looked like it was about to burst at the seams.

"Edith, darling, you must come back inside the station. A man is playing an accordion. He is quite good."

"But Clara, Henry will be here at any minute."

"He will have to enter the building to reach the platform, will he not?" the woman in blue said, tilting her head.

"I suppose," the woman in green said, fingering her chin. "Very well then. Good day to you, sir, and to you, young lady," she said as she turned toward the building.

As the women walked away, Sofie overheard the plumper one say, "This is such a peculiar town. It's as if we have stepped into another country. I have never heard so many strange languages."

Sofie popped the last bite of muffin into her mouth, wondering what had brought such wealthy women to Riverton. She turned to the muffin man for an answer, but he just shrugged his shoulders and smiled.

Suddenly, Sofie heard someone shouting, "Mama! Mama!" She quickly turned to follow the voice, as it sounded a lot like her little brother. She could not believe her eyes.

Lukas was running wildly along the platform next to a slowly moving train. It was heading north, in the direction of Pittsburgh. He struggled to keep up as he made repeated attempts to jump to the height of one of its windows. He seemed to be trying to get the attention of someone inside. The squeal of the train's steel wheels combined with the hissing and chugging of the steam engine drowned out the eight-year-old's cries.

Struggling to make sense of the situation, Sofie stared at the car Lukas was trailing. She could see a woman inside dressed in an expensive red dress and hat, but Sofie was too far away to see the woman's face. She was certain her brother was confused.

Fearing for his safety, she raced after him. "Mama's not here, Lukas. Stop running before you get hurt. Stop!"

The train began to pick up speed as it pulled away from the station. Sofie ran hard, trying to cover thirty yards in seconds. She bumped into an old woman and knocked over a stack of suitcases. She rushed by a dozen people, none of whom seemed concerned by her panic. Her brother was nearing the end of the platform and didn't seem to notice the drop ahead of him.

Sofie cried out again from only a few feet away, "Stop, Lukas! Stop!"

The instant the words left her mouth, Lukas made a final heroic attempt to jump high enough to reach the train's window. He came close to hitting his target—his hand missing the glass by just inches. But when gravity forced his little body back to the ground, he lost his balance. His left foot landed firmly on the platform, while the other disappeared into the narrow space between the platform and the swiftly accelerating wheels of the train.

Sofie heard a blood-curdling scream, but wasn't sure if it was Lukas's or her own.

# SEPTEMBER 1917

## *Twenty-One*

# POLE

### ABBOTT'S HOLLOW,
### SEPTEMBER 24, 1917

Pole trudged down the muddy road through Abbott's Hollow toward the mine entrance, relieved the rain had finally stopped. All weekend long, strong winds had brought down tree limbs while drenching downpours had created a small stream through the middle of the patch village's main thoroughfare. The water was slowly drying up, but it would take days for the muck to harden. The little hollow nestled in the Allegheny Mountains always caught the runoff from the surrounding slopes, but this storm had been especially bad. The entire village appeared to have sunk several inches into the giant bowl of mud.

Pole looked down at the ground, a bizarre kaleidoscope of fall color. The storm had downed the autumn leaves prematurely, mixing them with layers of mud and rock. The yellows, oranges, and reds of the leaves were muted and partially covered in silt, but they were still sort of pretty. Pole loved the beauty of the fall season, but it was a bittersweet reminder that harsh winter weather was approaching.

He glanced at the ominous clouds overhead, hoping the sun would soon return. The dreary weather was ruining his mood. It was bad enough that the chimneys above Abbott's Hollow spat flurries of coal ash at him every time he went outside. The stoves in the village were almost as dusty as the miners coming home from a shift underground.

Ashes and dust. There was no escaping them. Miners breathed them in—bathed in them—both day and night. Unwittingly, they became part of a coal miner's soul. Darkening it. Suffocating it.

As Pole approached the boney pile a few hundred feet to the left of the mine entrance and tipple, he heard the squishing of muddy footsteps behind him. It was Monday morning, and soon the road would be filled with workers carrying picks, shovels, axes, and lunch buckets. He turned around, expecting to greet a fellow miner.

"Please don't be mad, Pole. I have to go to the boney pile."

"Why on Earth would you do that? I just left the house ten minutes ago. There was plenty of coal to get us through the next couple of days."

"There was, but . . ."

Pole looked at his little sister and sighed. Lily, with her curly red hair, fair skin, and freckles, was such a kind-hearted soul. She had more heart than common sense. It was becoming a detriment.

"Who did you give it to this time?"

"Mrs. Blazovich had her baby last night. She came early. They didn't have enough coal to keep the house warm."

"I thought the baby wasn't due until next month. That's too bad." Pole felt his anger dissipate. He looked down at the ground where his muddy work boots were buried. They had disappeared below the surface sometime in the last minute.

"She might survive. We need to be hopeful."

"Be hopeful, Lily, but be realistic. Babies born too soon have little chance of makin' it. 'Specially around here."

His sister shrugged. "We'll see. I'm going to pray for Mrs. Blazovich's baby. You should, too."

Trying to avoid another conversation about God and religion, Pole put a hand on Lily's shoulder. "I don't want you on that boney pile. It's too wet out. If it gives way, you'll get buried."

"We need coal for the stove. The weather's getting colder, and I need to make Mama's breakfast. She's not feeling well this morning."

"What's wrong with Bridget now?" Pole's sister's mother was sickly and always plagued by some type of ailment. Lily often had to skip school to take care of her mother's washing. Their house was too small to take in boarders, so Bridget did the laundry for her neighbors' boarders for a small fee.

"She woke up with a headache and cough. She has a fever, too."

"Go ahead and pick some coal out of that pile, but don't get caught. There's a rumor goin' around that the superintendent is hiring a guard."

Pole shook his head at the irony of the situation. He had been working in the mines for seven years, and his family still had to steal coal. For some poor families, it was the only way to get fuel for their stoves. Women and children climbed the boney pile in search of chunks of good coal that were thrown out with the rubble brought out of the mine. Usually, miners bought coal from the company at a discount, but some folks couldn't afford it after paying rent and buying supplies at the company store. The prices were exorbitant and sometimes inflated as much as two hundred percent.

"I promise I'll be quick. I won't go up very high either," Lily said.

Pole kissed his sister on the cheek. "Be careful. See you this evening."

"Since I'm not going to school today, I'll bake you something special. Maybe a pumpkin pie."

"Sounds good."

Pole watched Lily climb down over the bank toward the bottom of the boney pile. The seventy-foot-high mountain of waste rock from the mine had almost doubled in size since Pole had arrived in the hollow. It was filling in the gully that ran along the north edge of the village. The gray and black conical-shaped mound was an eyesore, a stark and dismal contrast to the colorful vegetation surrounding it. Barren and devoid of life, it scarred the mountain landscape and created a hazard. Pole had heard plenty of stories of people being buried by shifting boney piles. Luckily, incidents near the pile in Abbott's Hollow had always been minor. A middle-aged woman once suffered a heart attack while picking coal, and a cat was buried the previous spring while chasing after a bird. Nothing too tragic.

Pole marveled at his sister as she dashed almost twenty feet up the pile in only a few seconds. She was nimble, even though her body had recently begun to fill out. Lily was beginning to attract attention from the neighborhood boys, giving Pole yet another reason to worry. He groaned as he continued up the slope toward the mine.

As he waded through the muck, he wondered how much longer he would have to endure mountain living. It did not appeal to him. He felt cut off from the rest of the world and desperately missed the conveniences of town living. He had taken so many of Riverton's luxuries for granted—second-hand stores, butcher shops, bakeries. The only place to shop in Abbott's Hollow was the overpriced company store, and the mine's owners were intent on keeping it that way. Sometimes Pole made the hour's long walk to Portage or hitched a ride there with one of the few in town who owned a horse and wagon, but he rarely had time for such an excursion.

The only reason he remained in the hollow was to provide for his little sister. She was the only family he had left. For years,

Pole had tried to persuade Lily's mother to move with him and Lily to a more civilized place—Pittsburgh, to be exact. But Bridget refused to leave the patch village where her Irish family had lived for over a decade. Pole gritted his teeth and waited patiently for the time when Lily would be old enough to make her own decisions.

Pole entered the cage that would take him eight hundred feet below the ground. He stood with four other workers, all wearing carbide headlamps and carrying shovels and picks. Their faces were clean, their work clothes freshly washed. It was a futile exercise. Within minutes, they would all be covered in a fine layer of coal dust. Pole had recently noticed that his hands were now tinted a permanent black hue, as the dust had settled in the cracks and creases of his fingertips and palms. Yet another irritating feature of work in the mines.

As the cage elevator descended, a young mule driver nudged Pole. "Do you think the stables will be flooded? I was worried about Gus all weekend. I brought him some lumps of sugar."

"There's nothin' to worry about, Mickey," Pole said as he patted the boy's head. "The mine's far underground. There are hundreds of feet of bedrock between the stable and the surface. Floods can't get down here."

The kid looked up and smiled. "Haven't been in the mines long. Still workin' it out."

"No worries, laddie," said Hamish, a veteran miner, in his thick Scottish accent. "You stick with yer mule. He'll teach you everything you need to know about the mine. Mules know this place better'n us. Rats, too."

"I drove Gus when I was about your age. He's the best mule in the mine. Had to switch to Bessie though," Pole said, shaking his head. "No one else could handle her. She kept squeezin' all her drivers against the walls."

The cage landed on the floor of the mine, and all the workers got out. It was pitch black except for the streams of light beaming from their headlamps. "Do you want me to take your tag to the office so you can head straight to the mule barn?" Pole asked Mickey.

"Sure!" the boy said as he threw his tag in Pole's direction.

Pole watched the young kid skip down the passageway toward his mule. He followed the other three men into the office, which was well lit and warmer than the rest of the mine. He hung his and Mickey's tags on the pegboard and made his way over to the fire boss's slate to read his notes about mine conditions.

"Och, damn it!" Hamish turned to Pole. "Boss wants me and you to work that new section end of Ruthie Tunnel. We gotta reinforce the roof before we can get any real work done."

"Who's helping us?"

"Looks like them two new Russians—Blazovich and Petras," Hamish said as he read the slate. "They don't speak English."

"They're Rusyns, I think," Pole said, trying to remember what his sister had told him about their new neighbors. Lily had a habit of collecting all sorts of information about the families in the patch village.

Hamish glared at Pole. "That's what I said. Russians."

Pole chuckled. "You did. But I said *Rusyns*. There's a difference. These people come from the mountains of Eastern Europe—not the land of the czars." Pole was suddenly impressed that he'd recalled a little of what Lily had told him.

"Whatever," Hamish grumbled. "Makes no difference where they come from. I still can't understand 'em."

"Come on. Let's get to Ruthie," Pole said as he slapped the old-timer on the back and grabbed the canary. He studied the grouchy Scot for a few seconds and tried to guess his age. Could he be fifty? That was old for a miner. Most were dead or maimed by that age. But Hamish was tough—or maybe just lucky. Pole thought of the accident that had claimed so many in the summer he had arrived in Abbott's Hollow. Hamish was the only man who had made it out alive. Pole shuddered. He tried to think of something pleasant . . . pumpkin pie.

## *Twenty-Two*

## SOFIE

### BEAVER CREEK, SEPTEMBER 25, 1917

Sofie feverishly stroked the keys of her Underwood typewriter. The *Beaver Creek Dispatch's* weekly immigrant page would be issued the following morning, and she needed to have her article at the newspaper's office within a few hours. Unlike the feature articles she often wrote, this article wouldn't be proofread multiple times by her perfectionist editor before it went to the printer. It was written in Slovak.

America had been at war with the Germans for almost six months, and the United States government had recently passed the Lever Food and Fuel Control Act. Food shortages in war-torn Europe had placed a heavy demand on American farmers and had caused a sharp increase in prices. One of the initiatives under the new law was a voluntary rationing program, which encouraged people to eliminate waste and eat less meat, wheat, sugar, and fats. If America was to continue to feed itself, its growing army, and its allies in Europe, people on the home front would have to conserve food.

Sofie's article detailed the rationing program for the town's Slovak population and reminded everyone to participate in meatless Mondays and wheatless Wednesdays. She also advised her readers to harvest what was left of their victory gardens before the first frost. It was late September, and the growing season was nearly over. As Sofie finished typing canning instructions and a recipe for pumpkin butter, it occurred to her that it would be fitting to end her piece with the popular wartime slogan, *Food Will Win the War!* She smiled. She wondered if her colleagues' articles in Polish and Italian would be as inspiring.

"Supper's ready! Come and get some peanut butter soup," Aunt Anna shouted from below.

Sofie wrinkled her nose. Her aunt's efforts at wartime rationing were commendable, but soup with peanuts in any form did not sound appetizing. She got up from her desk and adjusted her skirt. She glanced at her reflection in the full-length mirror in her bedroom, smoothing her braided hair and tucking a loose strand behind her ear. Satisfied with her appearance, she headed downstairs to the kitchen where her aunt was hovering over the gas cookstove with a magazine in hand.

"You're becoming quite the patriot, Aunt Anna. President Wilson would be proud. Your victory garden is the envy of all the neighbors, and now you're making soup with peanuts. Where did you get the idea?"

"In the *Ladies' Home Journal*, of course," the gray-haired woman replied, holding up her magazine and grinning.

Sofie smirked. Aunt Anna was over the age of fifty, but still full of energy. Her garden was one of the nicest in town, even if it wasn't the largest. Her aunt grew tomatoes, cucumbers, squash, corn, snap beans, melons, and pumpkins. Every inch of space in their backyard was covered by some type of food-producing plant. Aunt Anna loved working in her garden almost as much as she loved cooking for her family and the house's two boarders.

Sofie took the magazine from her aunt and flipped through the pages. "It's funny. There's an article in here on fat and oil conservation. You've been doing this for years—pouring every bit of grease from the frying pan into jars. Labeling them and lining them up on a shelf above the stove. Are you sure you didn't write this?"

"I could have. I use leftover grease in almost all my recipes. You know, I sometimes put bacon grease in my apple pie crust." Aunt Anna winked.

Sofie laughed. "So that's why your crust is so flaky—and salty. Mrs. Radovic has been trying to get your secret recipe out of me for years. I swore to her that I didn't know it." Sofie turned to her aunt, suddenly concerned. "Why are you telling me now? You love to keep us guessing about your cooking."

"I'm an old lady now." Aunt Anna placed a hand on her niece's shoulder. "Who knows how much time I've got left? I'm counting on you to keep our family traditions alive."

"Stop it! You're in better shape than some of the young mothers I see chasing children around the neighborhood. But I would like to hear more about your secret recipes. I promise I won't tell the neighbors."

Aunt Anna grinned as she stirred her soup. "Pass them down to your children. You'll be chasing little ones around before you know it."

Sofie chuckled. "I don't graduate from high school until next spring. And I don't even have a sweetheart."

"It's not like you don't have options. I can name a half-dozen boys from church who would love to woo you."

"I'm not interested. I'm going to work for the newspaper full-time after I graduate."

"You might change your mind."

"I doubt it." Sofie sighed as she stared out the window at the bright orange pumpkins in the garden. She wondered why her aunt was so bothered by her lack of interest in boys. She was friendly with a few of the smarter ones in her class, but had no intention of making a fool of herself pining after them the way Marie did. Her best friend had a different love interest every week. Besides, Sofie found most boys her age immature and stupid. Hoping to change the subject, she said, "We should pick the rest of those pumpkins by the end of the week. We can make a few pies and use the rest for butter."

"We've never had so many canned fruits and vegetables in the cellar before," her aunt said. "We won't be starving this winter, that's for sure. If I could just get your father to buy a gun and start hunting, we'd have plenty of venison, too."

"I don't see that happening. Papa's perfectly content with fishing."

Aunt Anna filled two bowls with peanut butter soup and took them to the dining room. "Can you get the cucumber sandwiches out of the refrigerator?" she called over her shoulder.

"Sure." Sofie opened the refrigerator door to retrieve the sandwiches, pausing for a moment to admire the porcelain interior of the appliance. "I just love this new Leonard refrigerator. It's as pretty on the inside as it is on the outside." She wiped her finger across the door, amazed at how smooth and clean it was.

"Snap out of it, Sofie," Aunt Anna said as she reentered the kitchen. "The boys will be home soon, and I'd like to get dinner on the table. Maybe you should be selling appliances instead of writing for the newspaper. Did you finish the article you were working on?"

"I did. I'm going to drop it off at the *Dispatch* after dinner."

"Can you stop by the store and take some soup to your father? He's doing the books tonight."

"I thought it was Mrs. Moretti's turn."

"It is, but she's still learning how to do the accounting. Your father's helping her."

"Papa practically lives at the store these days," Sofie whined.

"How can we complain? He owns half of that store now. He's a business owner. We should be proud."

"I'm very proud of him. I just wish he spent as much time with us as he does with Mrs. Moretti."

"Take him the soup and you can spend the entire evening with him. I'm sure he can find you some shelves to stock. Or a floor to sweep." Aunt Anna laughed.

"I still have some reading to do for English class. Maybe I'll do it at the store and walk home with Papa. It was warm today. It should be a nice evening for a stroll."

Suddenly, the front door opened. Sofie heard the sound of two men joking in Slovak. Vilium and Marek were home from the glass factory. She rushed into the dining room with the cucumber sandwiches.

"Hello, Vilium. How was your day?" Sofie asked.

"Good. I'm hungry," said the stocky, blonde teenager as he sat down at the long oak table.

"Where's Marek?"

"He went to bathroom. Dirty hands," Vilium said as he held up his own, which were clean, but badly cracked and callused.

"Aunt Anna made something new tonight. Peanut butter soup."

"Peenit? I do not understand."

Sofie giggled. "I don't know how to translate it into Slovak. Aunt Anna!" she yelled into the kitchen. "How do you say peanut butter in Slovak?"

"It doesn't matter." Sofie's aunt huffed as she came into the dining room. "We're supposed to be teaching these boys English. Just try my soup."

Sofie sat down next to Vilium. "I've never had this soup before either. Just eat it and pretend that you like it," she whispered to him in Slovak.

"I heard that. I may be over fifty, but I'm not deaf."

Sofie and Vilium exchanged worried glances as they plunged their spoons into the caramel-colored liquid.

## *Twenty-Three*

### JANOS

### BEAVER CREEK, SEPTEMBER 25, 1917

"Janos, I can't tell whether this is a seven or a one. What do you think?"

Squinting his eyes, Janos tried to decipher the handwriting on the invoice his business partner had handed him. He adjusted his eyeglasses and leaned in under the desk lamp for a closer look. "That's a one. Is that the last invoice, Concetta?"

She nodded, tucking a strand of gray hair behind her ear.

Janos watched as she signed a check for twenty-one dollars, her lip bit in concentration. "I think you're ready to do the books by yourself now," he said. "But you might want to think about getting a pair of eyeglasses."

The tiny Italian woman looked up at Janos, narrowing her eyes. "I don't need eyeglasses. You squinted, too, when you tried to read this illegible handwriting." She pointed to a number on the invoice and asked, "Who writes a one like this?"

"Our German supplier. You'll get used to it." Janos chuckled.

"I'm not sure I want to. I wish Tony were still here to help with the store. I'm too old for this."

"You most certainly are not. You're not even forty yet."

"I'm forty-two." She sighed. "This store was Antonio's. When he died, I thought Tony would take it and pass it down to his sons. I never imagined he would leave me and move to Philadelphia."

Janos felt sorry for his business partner. It had been over three years since the sudden death of her husband, and she still seemed broken. And now her only son had moved to Philadelphia because his new wife was homesick and didn't want to live far from her sisters.

"Children grow up, Concetta. There's no guarantee they will stay close to home." Janos touched her hand. "Maybe in a few years, I will have enough money saved to buy your share of the store. You can move to Philadelphia then."

"I can't ask you to do that. You've done too much already. You managed the store all by yourself for an entire year after Antonio died. I still feel guilty about that."

"What else could I do? You were inconsolable, and having Tony quit school was not an option. I'm grateful you sold me half the business. Working with Tony these past two years has been a pleasure."

"He's a good boy, isn't he?" Concetta smiled proudly. "I just miss him so much." Her smile faded as her eyes welled with tears.

"Papa!" Janos heard Sofie's voice as the bell on the store's front door chimed. He squeezed Concetta's hand as he stood up from his desk. "Think about what I said. I'm willing to buy your share of the store. Maybe I can get a bank loan to expedite the process."

Concetta wiped at her eyes.

Janos left his partner in the office at the back of the store and found Sofie straightening a display of canned peaches.

"I brought you dinner, Papa. Aunt Anna made peanut butter soup."

"What kind of soup?" he asked, tilting his head.

"Peanut butter. It's not bad."

Janos fought to suppress a frown as he took the bowl from Sofie. "Marie stopped by the store this afternoon. We had an interesting conversation."

"Really?"

"She told me how disappointed she was that you weren't allowed to go to the school dances last year." Janos raised an eyebrow. "She was hoping to convince me to allow you to go to the dance this weekend. She assured me there would be plenty of chaperones."

Sofie groaned.

"Care to explain?"

"Oh, Papa. You know I have no interest in chasing after boys at school dances. Marie wouldn't stop pestering me about going last year, so I told her I wasn't allowed."

Janos glared at his daughter.

"It was an innocent lie."

"Don't you think it might be fun to go to a dance? You spend far too much time writing for the paper and obsessing over your schoolwork." Janos often worried that his daughter didn't share the interests of her friends. She always rolled her eyes whenever Marie Radovic gushed about a handsome boy and avoided going to after-school functions. He wondered what was wrong with her. Had the losses she'd suffered affected her ability to connect with people? Suddenly, Janos heard light footsteps behind him.

"Hello, Sofie," Concetta said softly. "I'm on my way to the kitchen to make a pot of tea. Would you and your father like to join me? I made biscotti this afternoon."

"That's very kind of you, Mrs. Moretti, but I have to get to the *Dispatch*. I have an article to drop off."

Janos studied his daughter. She wasn't carrying the black folder she normally used to submit her work to the paper. Was she lying again? Janos pulled out his pocket watch and groaned audibly when he saw the time. "It's not like you to miss a deadline, Sofie. It's after seven."

She looked down at her shoes. "Actually . . . I did drop off the article, but I think I made a mistake. I need to rush back to the paper and correct it before it gets printed." Sofie looked up at her father, a hint of remorse on her face.

"I see," Janos said, satisfied that his daughter knew she had been caught in another lie. He wondered why she didn't want to have tea with him and Concetta. Sofie had never turned down homemade biscotti before. Her behavior was becoming more unpredictable every day.

"Another time then, Sofie," Concetta said. "Will you be joining me, Janos?" She touched him lightly on the shoulder.

"Of course. You know how I feel about your biscotti. Maybe I'll even share my peanut butter soup with you." He winked at her. "See you at home, Sofie."

"Yes, Papa. Goodnight, Mrs. Moretti," Sofie said as she waved and slipped out the door.

Janos wondered why his daughter was in such a hurry. He didn't believe her story about the mistake in her article, but he would uncover the truth later. At the moment, he was more focused on Concetta's biscotti.

# *Twenty-Four*

## EDITH

### SHADYSIDE, SEPTEMBER 27, 1917

Edith Covington Girard Harford looked up from her novel and smiled. Her husband, James, had entered the parlor of their Shadyside mansion carrying a box of chocolates and a bouquet of orange chrysanthemums.

"Hello, darling. How was the appointment with your new doctor?"

"You didn't have to bring me sweets," Edith said as James kissed her on the cheek and handed her the yellow box. She lifted the lid and inhaled the scent of caramel and hazelnut. "Perhaps you suspected I might need some cheering up."

"I simply wanted to make my lovely wife smile." James's face fell. "Did the doctor have bad news?"

"Not really. It was more of the same. All my ailments seem to revolve around the same problem." Edith groaned. "Every doctor I see is deeply troubled by my irregular menses. This one said we need to provoke the flowers."

"Provoke the what?" James gave her a confused look.

"The flowers." Edith looked away, embarrassed. "We need to induce my monthly flow." James sat down next to his wife on the green velvet sofa and wrapped his arm around her. Edith was dwarfed by her husband's large frame, but welcomed the comfort of his touch. She loved how he always made her feel so protected.

"What exactly did the doctor say?"

"He told me to continue with the mugwort and pennyroyal. But instead of putting the herbs in my tea, he wants me to eat several leaves per day."

"How fortunate we are to have our own greenhouse. I'll be sure to tell the gardener to order more seeds. We can grow your herbs all winter long." James rubbed his wife's back. "Was there anything else?"

Edith looked down at her lap. Her husband leaned closer. She could feel his breath against her cheek. "He was not very encouraging. He told me that women with my symptoms rarely become pregnant."

"What about the pregnancy two years ago?"

"He didn't say pregnancy was impossible—just very unlikely. I haven't had my monthly flow in over six months. And my other symptoms . . . they all point to the same thing."

Edith caught herself fingering the stubble growing on her chin. She had shaved a few days before, but the hair was already coming back. Her mother had convinced her to start shaving her upper lip and jaw several years earlier when it had become clear that her excessive hair growth was hindering her efforts at finding a husband.

"Stop it, Edith. Obsessing about it won't do you any good."

"What are you talking about?"

"You're touching your face again. Stop fretting over it. No one notices it, except you."

"This is too embarrassing a subject to discuss with one's husband," Edith replied, her face flushing.

"When are you going to realize that I don't give a damn about what you look like? I care only about your health. The hair growth on your face and the absence of your menses point to a serious health problem. I don't care if we ever have a baby. I simply want you to be healthy."

"You don't really mean that. I know you would like a child of your own. And, besides . . . would you really want to attend social events at the university with a bearded lady? I could be a sideshow, for heaven's sake."

"It can't be that bad." James patted his wife's knee.

"How would I know? I've been shaving since before we met over six years ago. I'm terrified to see what would happen if I let it grow. And I've gained another five pounds," she added somberly.

"Now there's more of you to love." James tickled his wife's side as he planted kisses along her neck.

Edith couldn't contain her giggles. "I'm not sure I deserve you." She embraced her husband and rested her head on his shoulder.

She was so grateful to have found such a compassionate man, one who always seemed unfazed by her multitude of embarrassing health problems. He was a stark contrast to her ex-fiancé, Frederick Metzler Morgan. Frederick was so painfully superficial and concerned only with outward appearances. When Edith had suddenly gained weight in the months before their wedding, Frederick had thrown a massive fit and pressured her to skip meals. Edith was still haunted by the look on her former fiancé's face the first time he had noticed dark hair growing on her upper lip.

"What are you thinking about now?"

"How lucky I am to have found you. You've been so supportive these past few years. Trying to start a family hasn't been easy."

"Few things in life are." James stroked her cheek. "It's time to stop worrying. I have a plan for us."

"What's that, Mr. Harford?" Edith gazed into her husband's big blue eyes. They were a striking feature on an otherwise ordinary face. James was a bit of a walking contradiction. He was a massive man in both height and girth, but was blessed with a pleasant demeanor and an enormous heart. A gentle giant. And although he was a well-respected history professor with several published books to his credit, he was incredibly witty. His laughter was infectious and often spread through a room like wildfire. He was one of the most sought-after guests at dinner parties.

"I think you should try the herbs for a few more months. Maybe ingesting them whole will be more effective than putting them in your tea. However, if we still see no improvement in your health by spring, we should consider other alternatives."

Edith sighed. "You mean adoption?"

"Possibly. Or even a life without children. We've been trying to have a baby for six years. You're approaching thirty, and I'm thirty-seven. Maybe we need to accept that it might not happen. We can have a happy life with just the two of us. And we still have Lukas."

Edith laid her head on her husband's shoulder again. "I know," she whispered.

"Is he coming for a visit this weekend? We haven't seen him since the school year began."

"He is."

"I'm sure he'll be full of stories about his teachers and classmates. You should be very proud, Edith. That boy would never have had a chance at a first-class education if it weren't for you. Westmont Academy is one of the finest boarding schools in Pennsylvania—the country, even."

"It is. Lukas will be able to attend any Ivy League school he chooses." Edith lifted her head and met her husband's loving gaze. "It was a cruel twist of fate that brought Lukas into my life, but I am grateful all the same."

"Indeed," James said, kissing his wife's forehead. "And I'm thankful he brought *you* into *my* life. If you hadn't been so relentless in your pursuit of a perfect fit for Lukas's prosthetic leg, I might never have met you."

Edith chuckled. "I was determined, wasn't I?" She thought about the way she had stormed into a New Year's Eve party almost seven years ago in search of James's brother. It had been six months since Lukas's accident, and he had finally received a prosthetic leg from Dr. Samuel Harford a month earlier. But after almost a dozen fittings, the leg was still uncomfortable. Edith had promised to take Lukas to see a fireworks display that evening to celebrate the new year, but his prosthetic was causing him so much pain that he'd had to remove it. When Edith suggested that Lukas use his crutches that night, the poor boy had burst into tears. Angry and irritated, Edith had gone in search of Dr. Harford on New Year's Eve to demand that he adjust Lukas's prosthetic yet again.

"I still feel bad about embarrassing your brother in front of the mayor, but my sweet boy wanted to see the fireworks. I couldn't bear to make him go on those dreadful crutches."

"I was in awe of you that night," James said, smiling.

"You were?"

"I had never seen a woman with more resolve. Your devotion to that boy was—and still is—remarkable."

Edith blushed. "I never imagined that making a scene at a society party would help me attract the attention of a fine man like you. You are quite the catch, James Harford."

"Life is full of surprises, darling. You never know what's waiting around the corner."

*Twenty-Five*

# LUKAS

## JOHNSTOWN, SEPTEMBER 28, 1917

Lukas sat on the edge of his dormitory bed, adjusting the leather straps and laces on his Gillingham prosthetic leg. His train to Pittsburgh was leaving in less than an hour. He would have to hurry to make it to the station on time. He was very particular about the fit of his wood and leather leg, always taking great care in fastening it to his thigh. A good fit ensured a comfortable walk with little swelling or chafing on his stump.

Since the accident that took his right foot and a portion of his calf over seven years earlier, Lukas had tried several different types of prosthetics. Almost all of them had been uncomfortable and sometimes even painful. His stump was often left red and swollen from the leather straps rubbing against his skin, and the weight of the device was cumbersome. Maneuvering a wooden leg around all day left him exhausted. There were months when he refused to wear his leg at all.

And then Aunt Edith suggested they travel to Chard, England to meet James Gillingham. It wasn't easy convincing Janos Kovac to allow her to take his only son on a steamship across the Atlantic, but Edith Harford was determined and persistent. She had read that James Gillingham made the best prosthetics in the world with the most comfortable fit. He was a man of rare talent. Lukas's father eventually acquiesced and allowed his son to travel to Europe with the woman who had become his benefactor—and aunt, of sorts. At least, that's what she considered herself.

Lukas looked down at the leather straps on his prosthetic leg and nodded. He stood up and walked around the room, testing the fit. It had been a few years since his trip to England, and he would soon outgrow the longer leg Mr. Gillingham had created to replace the one Lukas had been fitted with in Chard. The doctor had warned that boys his age outgrew prosthetics rather quickly. Lukas suspected he would need a new one by the following summer, but the war in Europe was making overseas travel impossible. Aunt Edith would have to find a local doctor to fit him with a new leg.

"You'd better hurry up, Lukas. We're going to miss our train if you don't stop playing with that leg of yours."

Lukas turned around to find his roommate, Frankie, standing in the doorway. "I'm ready to go. You packed yet?"

"My suitcase is in the common room. You want me to carry your bag for you?"

Lukas appreciated his friend's constant attempts to ease his burdens, but he was determined to prove to the world that he was still normal and whole, even if the device under his pant leg indicated otherwise. "No, thanks. The walk to the incline is less than a mile."

As Lukas walked with Frankie down the tree-lined path from the dormitory to the edge of Westmont Academy's campus, he listened to the rustle of autumn leaves beneath his feet. It was a crisp afternoon, but the late day sun was bright and warmed his back. He was excited about the upcoming weekend and looking forward to a break from the scornful eyes of his teachers and the piles of homework accumulating on his desk.

The academic standards at his prestigious boarding school were becoming increasingly difficult to meet. Lukas was in his sophomore year and struggling to catch up with his peers. His public school education through the eighth grade had not prepared him to compete with wealthy classmates who had attended exclusive private primary schools all over Pennsylvania. Aunt Edith had tried for years to persuade Lukas's father to allow him to live with her in Shadyside during the school year so he could attend one of the private schools in her neighborhood. But for better or worse, Janos Kovac was a proud man. He had insisted that his son live with his family in Beaver Creek until high school, at the very least.

Aunt Edith had tried to compensate for Lukas's inadequate public school education by hiring a team of tutors every summer to help him catch up. Since the age of nine, Lukas had spent the entire month of July at Edith's Shadyside mansion. There he learned all the important math and science concepts the incompetent Beaver Creek school system had failed to teach him the previous year. He also received lessons in Latin and French and learned how to play the piano. Despite Edith's best efforts, Lukas was still behind his classmates.

"What's on your mind, Lukas? You're so quiet today. Aren't you excited about the football game tomorrow? We might meet some girls."

"Sure I am. I was just thinking about school."

"Cut it out. You can think about it Sunday night when we get back." Frankie gave Lukas a sympathetic look. "You're not still thinking about leaving, are you?"

"I don't know. I'm not sure I belong here. I was the smartest kid in my class in Beaver Creek and now I can't keep up."

Frankie laughed as he punched Lukas in the arm. "You're steps ahead of me. I've always been at the bottom of my class. Doesn't bother me one bit."

"But you have the Spencer family name. Your father will

make sure you get into the right university. I'm sure he already has a spot reserved for you at his firm."

"Maybe. But don't you think your aunt Edith will do the same for you?"

"That's different. She's not even my aunt."

"Who cares? She pays for your education, doesn't she? She took you to Europe and bought you the world's most expensive wooden leg. How much did that thing cost anyway?" Frankie asked with a smirk as he pointed to Lukas's right foot.

"I never asked. I'm sure it's an embarrassing amount."

"You may not have had the luck of being born into a wealthy family like I did, but at least you found Edith Harford Girard Cooperton." Frankie chuckled. "Or whatever her name is."

"It's Edith Covington Girard Harford. And she found me. You know the story."

Lukas cringed as he thought of his accident at the Riverton train station. He could still hear his sister's anguished cries for help as he lay on the ground with a mangled, bloody leg. He couldn't remember being in terrible pain, only that he was cold and shivering uncontrollably. Suddenly, a dark-haired woman dressed in green was kneeling over him, comforting him.

"You got lucky that day."

"Depends on how you look at it. I had to lose a leg to get hooked up with a rich lady who wants to mother me and finance my education."

Frankie shook his head. "I don't know. If you hadn't been in that accident, you wouldn't have met her. You'd be destined for work in a mill or factory." He shuddered. "Seems like a fair trade to me."

"We'll see."

"By the way, what was a woman like your aunt doing at a train station in a dirty steel town? Seems like an unlikely place for someone like her."

"She was there to say goodbye to a friend."

"She knew someone from Riverton?" Frankie asked, making no effort to hide his shock. "I thought that place was pretty rough."

"It was. Still is, I think. Her friend worked at the mill. He was leaving town to start a new job."

As Lukas and Frankie walked along Edgehill Drive toward the Johnstown Inclined Plane's hilltop station, they passed a row of relatively new mansions of various architectural styles—late Victorian, English Tudor, and even the newer Shingle style. The homes were much smaller than the grand estates of Shadyside, but they still deserved to be called mansions. Lukas held a particular interest in art and architecture, awakened only when he had begun to spend time at Aunt Edith's English Tudor estate. Westmont was not nearly as extravagant as Shadyside, but it was far more appealing to Lukas. It was less gaudy, and the people weren't as pretentious as his aunt Edith's neighbors.

"Looks like the car just went down the hill," Frankie said as they arrived at the station. "We'll have to wait another five minutes for the next one."

Lukas looked down at his wristwatch. Aunt Edith had purchased it for him in London a few summers ago, convinced that everyone would soon be wearing timepieces on their wrists. The gadgets had become increasingly popular in the last few years since the start of the Great War. Soldiers fighting in the trenches found glancing at a wristwatch far more convenient than digging through their trousers for a pocket watch during the heat of battle.

"Our train leaves in twenty minutes. We should have enough time to walk the few blocks to the station. You hungry?" Lukas asked Frankie as he pulled a Hershey bar out of his pocket.

"Sure. I'll take a few pieces."

"You know, this incline is the steepest in the world. The slope has a seventy percent grade," Lukas said.

"How do you know that?"

"Geometry class. Mr. Hansen mentioned it during his lesson on slopes and grades. Guess you weren't paying attention."

"No. I have a D in geometry at the moment." Frankie shrugged.

Lukas wondered if his friend's attitude toward school would ever change. He doubted it. Frankie's future was guaranteed by a hefty trust fund—his expensive education simply a formality. Lukas envied him. He wished he could be as carefree, secure in the knowledge that his life's course had already been charted, his position in society assured. He was still trying to figure out where he belonged.

Lukas left his friend's side and walked over to the observation deck beside the incline's station. He leaned over the railing and peered at the smoky valley containing the Conemaugh River and its many steel mills. He recalled his history lesson on the Johnstown Flood of 1889. The catastrophic flood killed two thousand people and wiped out most of the town. As a result, the inclined plane was constructed, and the hilltop on which he was standing was developed as a residential area for executives of the Cambria Iron Company. They wanted to live high above Johnstown, safe from the flooding in the valley below.

How ironic that Lukas, the son of a steelworker, had inadvertently become one of the privileged living at the top of the hill, looking down on the poor mill workers. Pitying them. He didn't have to worry about losing his home and valuables—or maybe even his life—to a swollen river. He was not suffocated both day and night by noxious fumes coming from the mills. Through no feat of his own, he'd escaped the plight of these people who were once his peers. He felt guilty, but not nearly as much as he should have.

"What are you looking at?" Frankie leaned over the rail. "I can't see anything through all that smoke."

"The mills. They remind me of Riverton."

"Bet you're glad you escaped that place."

"Truth is . . . I didn't know how miserable it was until I'd left. I had no idea people lived the way you do." Lukas gestured toward Frankie's expensive clothing, his eyes coming to rest on his friend's Italian leather shoes. "But I'm grateful I got out."

"And all you had to do was lose a leg."

"Jackass." Lukas shoved Frankie, knocking him against the railing.

"Sorry. I was just speaking the truth."

"Don't I know it." Lukas draped his arm over his friend's shoulder and led him toward the gate to the incline. "Our car's here."

As Lukas descended the steep hillside, the inclined plane's car breaking through the ceiling of smoke over town, he was keenly aware of his prosthetic leg. It was a constant source of bitterness for him. And anger. Lukas hated that his leg made him different from the other boys. But as his friend had pointed out, it had been his ticket out of the mills.

## Twenty-Six

# POLE

### ABBOTT'S HOLLOW, SEPTEMBER 28, 1917

Pole had spent half the week with Hamish and the two Rusyns reinforcing the roof in the new section at the end of Ruthie Tunnel. Over a dozen massive timbers now lined the walls of the ten-foot-wide tunnel. The oak tree trunks they had used were heavy and had been difficult to maneuver into place, but they were rock solid. Pole's back ached, but he didn't mind as long as the roof above him stayed put. When blasting had begun in the tunnel late in the day on Wednesday, he'd been pleasantly surprised when the timbers barely shifted. There hadn't been much creaking either.

As Pole drilled a hole in the face of the coal seam so Hamish could fill it with explosives, he felt a tap on his shoulder.

"Hey, Pole. Me and Gus are takin' over for Billy and Rosie."

Pole turned around to find Mickey standing behind him. "Where'd Billy go? It's almost quittin' time on a Friday. Makes no sense to switch him now."

"He got kicked in the mouth. Mule knocked out two of his teeth and cut his lip real good," the boy said, shaking his head.

"Which one was it? I know Rosie couldna done it. She's a sweetheart," Hamish said as he spat some chewing tobacco.

"It was one of them new mules. The big one, I think."

"Billy's lucky that mule didn't take his head off," Pole said.

"It wasn't a direct hit. He just got clipped in the side of the head." Mickey stroked Gus's muzzle and pulled a sugar cube out of his pocket.

Pole watched the muscular gray mule gently take the sugar cube out of Mickey's hand. He chewed it up quickly and nuzzled against the boy. "I've never seen that mule so attached to anyone," Pole said.

"It's all them sugar cubes the lad keeps feedin' him. Be careful now," Hamish said as he shoved a stick of black powder into the coal face. "That mule's not a pet. He's got a job to do down here, just like you and me."

"Go easy," said Pole. "A kid his age should be up top where the sun's shinin'. Going to school and playing with his pals. If he's gonna be stuck underground, he deserves at least one friend—even if he is a jackass."

Hamish roared. "All my friends are jackasses! Down here and up top." The old man laughed so hard he broke into a coughing fit. "Och, damn it! Where's my water jug?"

"We're getting ready to blast that wall in a few minutes, Mickey. You take Gus back down the tunnel and wait for me." Pole looked over at the Rusyns, who were stabilizing one of the timbers that had buckled in the previous blast. "Blazovich! You done yet?"

The tall, blonde man turned around at the sound of his name.

"You done?" Pole repeated.

The man held up one finger.

"Okay. Another minute." Pole pulled out his pocket watch. "It's almost four o'clock. Hopefully, the next blast will give us a couple more loads of coal, and we can get outta here. Hamish, how's that canary lookin'?"

Hamish walked over to where the yellow bird was sitting in her cage near the water jugs. "Still singin'. Methane must be all right. Let's get that fuse lit."

Pole glanced at Blazovich and Petras, who were driving a lag bolt into the wooden beam that was being squeezed under the weight of the roof. He pulled a handkerchief out of his pocket and wiped at the grime on his face. Pole hated the heavy black mask of coal dust, sweat, and grease that he wore after a long day in the mine. It made smiling cumbersome. Although he didn't have much reason to smile when he was mining almost a thousand feet underground.

"I'll light the fuse this time," Pole said. "The rest of you head back down the tunnel with Mickey and Gus. I'll be there in a minute."

As Hamish and the Rusyns left the area with their lunch buckets and water jugs, Pole approached the coal face. He took off his carbide headlamp and held its flame up to the end of the fuse hanging out of the hole packed with explosives. The fuse glowed faintly and let out a few puffs of smoke before it burst into a red-hot flame. As Pole backed up quickly, he admired the yellow and orange sparks flying in every direction. They reminded him of the sparklers he sometimes bought his sister at the five-and-dime in Portage. He could understand why she found them so mesmerizing.

As Pole turned around to head down the tunnel to where the others were waiting for him, his eye caught a flash of yellow along the wall, just eight or nine feet from where the blast would go off. It was the canary in her cage, agitated by the fireworks nearby. Pole had passed by the bird seconds earlier, but hadn't noticed her in the dark. He'd been too focused on the dancing fuse.

"Christ Almighty!" he yelled. "Who left the goddamned bird?" Pole hesitated for a second and then ran back in the direction of the lit fuse. He grabbed the cage as the bird squawked and flapped its wings in protest. Pole sprinted down the tunnel toward safety. He guessed only twenty seconds had gone by since he'd lit the fuse. He hoped, anyway.

"Damn it, Pole! Did you turn around for that bird?" Hamish scolded him as soon as he saw the cage.

"What was I supposed to do? Let the poor thing get blown to bits? Besides, those safety fuses burn at a rate of thirty seconds per foot. I had—"

*Boom.*

The explosion cut Pole off in mid-sentence. The thunderous clatter of rocks falling to the ground followed instantly. Within seconds, a dense cloud of dust blew up the tunnel, forcing everyone to bury their faces in their shirtsleeves. Pole was able to shield his eyes from the black dust, but there was no way to prevent it from entering his lungs. He was soon hacking and coughing, as was everyone else.

"Sit tight a few minutes until that dust clears," Pole said. "We'll go back in when the roof stops creakin'. Mickey, I forgot my water jug. Can I have a drink of yours?"

"Least you didn't forget the bird." Hamish sniggered through deep, violent coughs. "That's what's important."

After they had inspected the roof and timbers, Pole, Hamish, and the Rusyns loaded coal for over an hour. Pole's backache was worsening by the minute. Each time he lifted a shovel full of coal, he felt a sharp pain shoot down his leg.

"I don't care what the foreman says. I'm not workin' tomorrow. I deserve a Saturday off every once in a while," Pole said as he threw down his shovel and wiped his brow with his sleeve. He was hot and sweaty even though the temperature in the mine was no more than fifty degrees. He took a drink from his water jug.

"I think it's quittin' time. Them cars are full enough," Hamish said to the Rusyns.

Blazovich and Petras continued to shovel coal, oblivious to what Hamish had said.

"Are those lads deaf, or do they really not understand a lick of English?" He walked over to the Rusyns and tapped the shorter one on the shoulder. When the dark-haired man turned around, Hamish gave him a thumbs up. "We're done."

Petras smiled happily, his big yellow teeth lighting up his blackened face.

"Mickey, hook Gus up to that car," Pole said, pointing to the car he and Hamish had just loaded. "I'll help Blazovich and Petras push theirs down the track."

Pole walked over to the Rusyns and helped them line their car up with the one Mickey was chaining to his mule's harness. Each car weighed almost a thousand pounds, but luckily for both mule and miner, the cars were on rails. Pole and the two Rusyns put all their weight behind the car and pushed it several feet down the track. Pole winced as sharp, stabbing pains traveled down his right leg.

"All right, Gus," Pole said as he rubbed the back of his leg. "The rest is up to you." He turned to Hamish and the Rusyns. "You three go up ahead of the mule. I'm goin' to hang back with Mickey and Gus in case they get into trouble."

"Yer sure?" asked Hamish. "You don't look so good."

"I don't feel so good either. It's my goddamned back and leg."

"Kinda young, aren't you? To be so soft." Hamish chuckled.

"Just get outta here, old-timer." Pole slapped Hamish on the back. He nodded to Blazovich and Petras, who waved at him as they grabbed their tools and lunch buckets. Petras, with his yellow-toothed grin, grabbed the bird cage and winked.

"Thanks for offering to stay with me, Pole, but I got this. Me and Gus know what we're doin'," said Mickey.

"I know you've got the best mule in the mine. He's strong and sturdy."

"Never even used my whip on him. He just goes when I slap his ass," Mickey said, smacking the mule on the behind. The massive beast slowly pulled the cars down the tracks.

"I figured you might like some human company, too. It's creepy down here after all the miners clear out for the day," Pole said.

"Yeah, it's mighty dark. And the rats are the size of dogs."

Pole chuckled as he looked up the tunnel. His carbide headlamp threw a beam of light along the track, illuminating two rats running toward them.

"Aww, shit. Here come a couple now," said Mickey. "And two more behind 'em."

"Fuck." Pole was struck by a wave of panic. "That's not a good sign, Mickey. Stop Gus and keep quiet. We need to listen."

As the rats scurried by Pole's feet, he heard the ominous sound of creaking coming from somewhere up Ruthie Tunnel. He couldn't be sure how far it was. Maybe fifty or sixty yards? He stood completely still as the creaking got louder. He looked over at Mickey whose face had gone white.

"Take it easy there, kid. We need to stay put for a few minutes. Chances are . . . that roof will calm down."

Suddenly, Pole heard a shower of rocks. At first, it was only a few, but within seconds, it sounded like a violent hail storm. Only hundreds of times louder. It was getting closer. "Mickey! Unhook Gus! We need to get back to the other end of the tunnel!"

Pole grabbed the water jugs as the boy fussed with the mule's harness. The downpour was growing louder. "Forget the harness! Just unhook the chain on the car. He can drag it behind him." Pole's heart raced as a rush of adrenaline surged through him.

Mickey did as he was told and ran with Gus and Pole back down the tunnel to where they had been working.

"Run, lads, run!" Hamish screamed from somewhere behind. "The whole fuckin' tunnel's cavin' in!"

Pole turned around to see Hamish stumbling behind him, his headlamp casting an erratic beam of light in every direction. He was clutching a bloody shoulder and struggling to catch his breath. A massive cloud of dust was on his heels, pursuing him like a wild animal.

Pole ran the ten yards back to where Hamish was staggering along the tunnel wall and grabbed him by the arm. He pulled him through the darkness toward what he hoped was safety.

And then the most ghastly of sounds. An avalanche of earth and rock. An enormous cloud of dust.

Pole hit the ground and the world went dark.

# Twenty-Seven

## LUKAS

### SHADYSIDE, SEPTEMBER 28, 1917

Lukas stabbed an unusually large piece of romaine lettuce on his Meissen salad plate as he listened to his adopted aunt and uncle debate the menu for the following evening's dinner party. His stomach was nearly full, but he knew he'd never get any dessert if he didn't finish his salad. He wondered what sorts of sweets the chef had concocted in honor of his visit.

"I'm sorry, James, but I don't think it's appropriate to serve roast beef to a state senator when our country is in the middle of a war. How would that look? We're supposed to be rationing meat. The cook has plenty of salmon left for tomorrow night. It was delicious, wasn't it, Lukas?" Aunt Edith asked.

"Yes, it was. I especially liked the sauce. Very buttery." He tried to hide his smirk.

"I don't care how buttery the damn sauce was. I've known Harry Easton my entire life. It doesn't matter whether he's a state senator or President of the United States. The man likes beef." Uncle James wiped his mouth with a napkin. "Shannon!" he called after the lead kitchen maid.

A lovely redhead came running into the room. "Yes, Mr. Harford."

"Tell the chef we are having roast beef tomorrow evening. I don't care if he has to scour the countryside and butcher the cow himself."

"Yes, sir."

James leaned back, patting his midsection. "Do you think I can maintain this figure on fish alone?"

Aunt Edith burst into laughter. "I never had a chance, did I? I can't argue with both you and your appetite. But honestly, I'm tired of fish, too. Beef with mushroom sauce sounds heavenly. I hope the Eastons don't think we have no regard for the war effort."

"Write them a check to give to the American Red Cross. That should compensate for our failure to adhere to the rationing program."

"That's easy enough," Aunt Edith said happily. "Lukas, do tell us more about school."

Lukas looked across the polished walnut table at his aunt to begin a story about his grumpy English teacher when he spotted something unusual on the mural behind her. "Did you have a little girl and a dog added to your mural since I left for school? I thought Gustaf went back to Philadelphia."

Uncle James gave his wife, who was now blushing, a curious look.

"He did. But I thought the castle and herd of sheep needed a human element, so I added the girl and sheepdog. I know I'm no Gustaf, but I think my additions fit rather nicely. What do you think, Lukas? You have such a keen eye for art."

Lukas got up from the table and walked over to the mural that the promising young Swedish painter, Gustaf Karlsson, had worked on for several months the previous spring. He scanned the entire landscape, which covered the top half of the eighteen-foot-long wall. He examined the medieval stone castle, the sheep scattered throughout the hilly meadow, the clusters of lush, green trees, and the pond filled with snow-white geese. Finally, Lukas focused on the young girl running down the hill away from the castle, her sheepdog trailing playfully behind her. She wore a pretty blue dress with white petticoats and a straw hat.

Lukas felt Aunt Edith's hand on his back. "Do you like it?"

"I do. I think you did a remarkable job. The girl looks as though Gustaf painted her himself. You're very talented, Aunt Edith."

"I've been encouraging her to get more training. Some of the landscapes she has done recently are quite striking," Uncle James said.

"You're both too kind. Gustaf gave me a few lessons last spring when he wasn't working on the mural. I find painting relaxing."

"The girl . . ." said Uncle James. "I hadn't noticed her until Lukas said something. How long has she been there?"

"Only a few hours. I worked on her all day," Aunt Edith said. "I saw her in a dream last night."

Lukas took his aunt's arm and escorted her back to the table. It was no secret how badly she and her husband wanted a child. They didn't discuss the topic with him much, but he had heard whispers among the servants. Rumors of failed pregnancies. He had also noticed that Aunt Edith had begun spending an enormous amount of time in the greenhouse over the past couple of years. She grew all sorts of strange herbs meant to treat her mysterious ailments.

"Now this might fill me up," Uncle James joked as a chocolate eclair was placed in front of him. "You'd better get me another, Colleen. That salmon was merely an hors d'oeuvre. These eclairs will be my main course."

Lukas nodded emphatically at his uncle. The chef *had* made something special for his visit. "I'd like two as well," he said, looking to his aunt for permission.

"Why not?" she said, smiling. "You're a growing boy."

As Lukas took a bite of the tantalizingly sweet eclair, he suddenly didn't mind being spoiled by James and Edith Harford. He always enjoyed being in their company, even if they were vastly different from his own family. Sofie often complained that they were overprivileged and unaware of the struggles of the classes beneath them, but they were still such kind and generous people. Lukas wished he could say the same for some of their neighbors.

"Will you be back to visit next month, or will we need to wait until Thanksgiving to see you again?" Aunt Edith asked Lukas.

"I'm not sure yet. I'm overwhelmed with homework and tests. I'd like to see my family before the holidays, but getting to Beaver Creek from Westmont is difficult. I may have to wait until Christmas."

"That's a long time. Your father must miss you terribly. Why don't we invite him and your sister for Thanksgiving dinner here in Shadyside? Maybe your aunt could come, too."

"That's very thoughtful of you, but my father doesn't like to leave his store for long. And this neighborhood makes him uncomfortable."

"Me, too," Uncle James said, his mouth full of chocolate eclair.

"We don't have to decide anything now," Aunt Edith said. "We have time. Maybe your family can visit next summer."

"I've been wanting to talk to you about that. I was wondering if I could spend the entire summer break here in Shadyside."

"That would be lovely. But won't you miss your family and friends in Beaver Creek? And your father, especially? He'll be heartbroken if he doesn't get to spend at least part of the summer with you."

"I know. I don't want to hurt him, but . . ." Lukas looked down at his half-eaten eclair.

"Is something wrong at home?"

"No, my family is fine. I'm just not sure I belong in Beaver Creek anymore."

"You told us before dinner that you don't feel like you belong at Westmont Academy." Aunt Edith tilted her head. "Where do you belong then?"

"That's the problem. I'm not sure."

Uncle James put down his fork. "I was wondering when this would happen."

Aunt Edith gave her husband a quizzical look.

"Don't you see? The boy is trapped between two worlds. His friends in Beaver Creek shun him because he's the rich kid who attends boarding school. His classmates at Westmont Academy are unaccepting of him because he lacks a blue-blood pedigree. He's a bit stuck at the moment."

"Is that true, Lukas?" Aunt Edith asked.

"Yes, but there's more. I'm not always comfortable at school, but I feel even less so in Beaver Creek. I love seeing my family, but going back to that town is . . ." Lukas hesitated. He wasn't sure he could share what was on his mind.

"Go ahead. You can tell us anything," Aunt Edith urged.

"Being in Beaver Creek is difficult. I feel more at home in Shadyside. I know I don't fit in here with my Slovak last name, but at least I can be myself. I don't have to act dumb or pretend that school is stupid. I don't have to hide my interest in art and music."

"Surely there are a few people in Beaver Creek who value education—besides your family, of course. Not everyone in that town works at the glass factory," Aunt Edith said.

"There are some. Teachers, mostly. But definitely not the boys my age. They all want to be football players and track stars. Those are the town's heroes. I could never fit in that category." Lukas rubbed his thigh where the leather strap from his prosthetic leg was too snug.

"Most of those boys will end up working in the glass factory. Their high school glory will be a distant memory in a few years, and they'll have little to show for it," Uncle James said cynically. "The key to prosperity is an education."

"That's what my father always says. And I agree with him. I just wish my friends in Beaver Creek felt the same way."

"Lukas, it's quite possible your friends are jealous of your boarding school education and the opportunities it will afford you. You're moving on to bigger and better things, and they're resentful. It's only natural," said Uncle James.

"I guess. Maybe if I were an athlete, at least we'd still have something in common."

"I'll talk to your father about the situation," Aunt Edith interjected. "He'll understand your predicament. You have wonderful friends here who appreciate your unique talents."

"Not everyone accepts me here either. Plenty of kids in the neighborhood make fun of my last name. Frankie Spencer is one of the few who doesn't care that I'm the son of immigrants."

"But isn't it nice to live in a community where brains are valued over brawn—where academic pursuits are encouraged and not ridiculed?" Uncle James asked.

Aunt Edith raised an eyebrow. "Is that so, my former college football star?"

"No one even remembers that I played football. I'm known now for my teaching and writing. And my exceptional wit, of course." Uncle James chuckled.

"I admit that I do like Shadyside," Lukas said as he took another bite of his chocolate eclair, his mood lightening. "How could anyone not want to live in a neighborhood where the houses are works of art and the air is clean?"

"No idea," said Aunt Edith as she shoved a fork into her mouth. "These eclairs are simply delicious."

# *Twenty-Eight*

## POLE

### ABBOTT'S HOLLOW, SEPTEMBER 28, 1917

Pole woke slowly to the painful throb of an enormous headache. He opened his eyes for a split second, relieved to see that his carbide headlamp was still working. Unfortunately, it had been knocked off his head during the roof collapse and was resting several feet away from him. He lay on the cold, hard floor of the tunnel for several minutes, willing himself to move toward the light. He could not do it. The pulsating pain coming from the top of his head coupled with the lower back and leg pain that had been plaguing him all day were more than he could bear. He closed his eyes and wondered if he should pray. His sister, Lily, would certainly be praying if she were in his predicament. Pole doubted there was any point. He was buried deep in the earth, far closer to hell than heaven. He wondered if the devil would appear to collect him and relieve him of his misery.

Sometime later, Pole thought he heard the faint sound of rocks sliding. He forced his eyes open and saw a flicker of light on the wall ahead of him. It was moving closer. Was that

Lucifer? Pole expected the flames surrounding the devil to be much brighter. He closed his eyes, indifferent to his fate.

"Wake up!" a voice shouted. "Are you alive? You're bleedin'!"

Pole felt something nudging him and patting his face. He swatted at the annoying pest.

"You need to get up. The roof's not safe here."

Pole ignored the voice and tried to cover his ears. He felt so dizzy. Suddenly, the throbbing in his head intensified. Was something shaking him?

"Goddamn it! Sorry, I got to do this."

*Slap.*

Pole woke up, startled by a burning, stinging sensation on his right cheek. "What the hell?"

"You need to get up. We've got to get back to the end of Ruthie. Hamish and Gus are waiting there for us."

Pole opened his eyes, squinting against the bright light shining in his face. "Mickey?"

"You got hit in the head real hard. Come on. I'll help you outta here." Mickey pulled Pole to his feet and carried his headlamp for him. "We better not put this back on your head. You got a pretty good gash by the looks of all that blood. You feelin' all right?"

"Not really. My head's poundin', and I'm a little wobbly." Pole touched his right temple, instantly aware of how wet and sticky his face was. "How bad do I look?"

"You're a bloody mess. But that might not mean much. My mama always says head wounds bleed the worst."

"Did you see the water jugs anywhere?" Pole asked, feeling his senses returning. "I was carrying them when I fell. We're going to need 'em."

"Here, you hold your headlamp while I look."

Pole leaned against the wall of the tunnel as Mickey scanned the area with his headlamp, trying to locate their only source of drinking water. For the first time, Pole looked back in the direction of where the roof of the tunnel had caved in. He held up his headlamp and shined it on the massive pile of rock and timber stacked haphazardly just a few feet away. He gasped when he realized how close he had come to being buried under that mountain of rubble. His blood stains were on the rocks an arm's length from where the roof had completely crumbled. He felt lucky to be walking away with only a throbbing headache.

And then a disturbing thought—what happened to Blazovich and Petras? Were they somewhere under that pile of earth? Pole's heart sank. Blazovich's wife had given birth to a premature baby earlier in the week, who was barely clinging to life. Had she lost her husband, too?

"I found the water jugs. They were at least ten feet apart," Mickey said, shaking his head. "Are you crying?"

Pole rubbed at his eyes. "Blazovich and Petras . . . I don't think they made it out."

Mickey's face fell. "You sure? They were pretty far ahead of us. Maybe they made it back to the elevator."

Pole studied the boy's face. He was so young and naive, not having spent nearly enough time in these treacherous mines to become hardened and cynical. The poor kid still had hope. Pole didn't have the heart to tell Mickey the truth.

"You're probably right. They left the area at least five minutes ahead of us. And we were walkin' pretty slow with Gus. I'm sure they're fine," he lied. "At least they can get to the surface and tell the others what happened to us."

"How long do you think before we get help?"

Pole thought of the mine collapse that killed his father in the summer of 1910, only months after they had arrived in Abbott's Hollow. "Not long. Hopefully by tomorrow morning." Another lie.

As Pole followed Mickey to the end of Ruthie Tunnel where they had been blasting all week, he could hear the whinny of a mule.

"Poor Gus is upset. I wish I had some sugar cubes left to give him," Mickey said.

Pole rubbed his head as he hobbled slowly. The mule was the least of his worries. He wondered what condition Hamish was in. His shoulder had been bleeding badly the last time he saw him. Pole wondered how long it had been since the roof collapsed. It felt like hours. He stopped to look at his pocket watch. It was almost seven o'clock.

"There he is. Good to see you alive, laddie. I was worried you didna make it," Hamish said when he saw Pole.

"Just barely. How are you doin'? How's your shoulder?" Pole walked over to the old-timer, who was sitting on the ground, leaning against the face of virgin coal they hadn't yet begun drilling. His work shirt was drenched with blood, as were his pants. He was clutching his side, wincing each time he inhaled. "How deep are your wounds?" Pole leaned over for a closer look. "You didn't break a rib, did you?"

"I mighta. Hurts real bad when I breathe." Hamish grunted. "Doesn't matter though. I can't do anything about it until we get to the surface."

"Maybe we can clean you up a little," Mickey suggested. "See how bad you're hurt."

"Can't do that. We need to save our water for drinkin'. That's the only way to stay alive down here. It'll be days before anyone gets to us—if we're lucky."

"Pole said that help will be here by tomorrow mornin'. Isn't that right?" Mickey said, sounding alarmed. He turned to Pole for reassurance.

Hamish flashed Pole a look of warning.

"I said *hopefully* we'll have help by the morning. It could be a little longer." Pole patted Mickey's back. "Gus sounds like he could use some comforting. Go stroke his muzzle. You know the spot he likes."

Pole sat down on the ground next to Hamish. He watched Mickey carefully approach the whinnying mule standing against the tunnel wall, just far enough away for Pole to have a private conversation with the veteran miner.

"All right, Hamish. Tell me the truth. Are we gettin' outta here?"

"I can't say for certain. We're buried deep. It'll take days for a rescue crew to get through all them rocks and rubble—if the coal company even sends one down here. It might be too risky. In the meantime, we could run out of oxygen—if we don't bleed out first." Hamish looked down at the blood on his shirt.

Pole shuddered. "I thought I wanted you to be honest, but now I think a lie woulda been kinder."

"Sorry, lad. But here's the good news. We'll die of suffocation before we starve. That mule should keep us fed for days."

"You can't be serious. We're not killin' that mule. If Mickey ever makes it out of this mine alive, he'll be scarred for life."

"Didn't I warn that boy not to get too attached to that animal? The mules in this mine are not pets," Hamish said bitterly. "I was trapped underground for five days when the mine collapsed all those years ago. How do you think I survived?"

"You killed a mule?" Pole's eyes widened.

"Nah, I wasn't lucky enough to be trapped with a mule. I ate rats. And so did yer daddy—until he died."

Pole stared at Hamish. "You never told me you were trapped with my pop."

"Gus is doing much better now," Mickey said, sitting down on the ground across from Pole and Hamish, interrupting the heated conversation. "I gave him a drink of my water."

"Don't go givin' all yer water away to that animal. You need to decide right now whose life is more important. Yers or that mule's."

Seeing the look of panic on Mickey's face, Pole quickly intervened. "Mules can go for days without water, Mickey. You need to save what you have left for yourself."

"I just gave him a little. I think he was thirsty from all that whinnying. I'm sure Blazovich and Petras made it up to the surface by now. The mine owners are probably already working on a plan to get us out."

Pole looked over at Hamish, who was getting ready to open his mouth. He elbowed his good arm and gave him the dirtiest look he could muster.

Hamish hesitated a moment before speaking. "Time to turn off the headlamps. We ought to save the carbide for when we really need it."

"Grab your water jug, Mickey, and pick a comfortable spot. It'll be pitch black as soon as these lights go out," Pole said. "I don't want you getting hurt stumbling around in the dark."

"If it's all right, I'm going to sit by Gus," Mickey said.

"Sure, kid. Try to get some sleep," Pole said, trying to sound calm.

The grim reality of their predicament was sinking in, twisting Pole's stomach into an agonizing tangle of knots. He knew a sleepless night lay ahead of him. As he extinguished the flame on his headlamp, he wondered how his poor sister, Lily, was coping with the news of the roof collapse. Would she believe he could've survived? Would anyone? Pole took a deep breath and leaned back against the coal face, trying to conjure a pleasant memory. His restless mind was desperate for a diversion.

# *Twenty-Nine*

## JANOS

### BEAVER CREEK, SEPTEMBER 28, 1917

Janos felt the weight of a dozen stares as he sat across the table from Concetta at the town's only Italian restaurant. He had never invited his business partner to dinner before, but she deserved an evening out after working so hard at the store all week. Sensing that Concetta was also distressed by the prying eyes of their meddlesome neighbors, Janos tried to divert her attention. "Have you and Mrs. Rossi seen any films lately?" he asked as he shoved a meatball into his mouth. "I know you ladies love the nickelodeon."

"We saw *The Immigrant* last week. I didn't like it."

"What's the matter? Don't you like Charlie Chaplin?"

"I did, but now I'm not sure. His film pokes fun at immigrants and makes them look stupid."

"How so?"

"The film is about a bumbling immigrant who gets into all sorts of trouble on a ship to America and then later at a fancy restaurant." Concetta dabbed at her mouth with a napkin. "The poor man looks like a fool at every turn. He eats peas with a knife, for heaven's sake."

"I'm sure the film was meant to be funny, but that sounds mean-spirited. I thought Chaplin was an immigrant."

Concetta nodded. "He's from England."

"England?" Janos laughed. "That hardly qualifies him as an immigrant. He's from an industrialized country where everyone speaks English. Must have been a terribly difficult adjustment for him."

As Janos twirled a few strands of spaghetti around his fork, he wondered why immigrants were always the subject of ridicule. People seemed to take great pleasure in making fun of foreigners' accents, clothing, and customs. Native-born Americans often regarded people like him as dirty and uneducated. Stupid, even. He remembered bitterly the way he had been treated in Riverton, having been called "mill Hunky" more times than he could count. He took a sip of wine, catching a glimpse of the glass factory outside the restaurant's window.

He thought about the progress he had made since leaving Austria-Hungary over seventeen years earlier. Prompted by his brother-in-law's tragic accident, he had immigrated to America with his pregnant wife to help his sister raise her two young boys. It was a decision he never regretted, even though it had resulted in a decade of hard labor in front of a blazing furnace.

Life in Bardejov had been difficult for him and Karina, and they had planned to leave sometime after Sofie was born. Stefan's accident simply expedited their plans. With a child on the way, Janos could no longer tolerate living under the harsh rule of the Hungarian government. Its Magyarization program was cruel, forbidding all ethnic groups living under its rule to speak any language other than Hungarian. Janos would not raise his child in a country where the schools and churches were forbidden to teach the history and language of the Slovak people.

Unlike his classmates, Janos had been one of the lucky few who had learned to read and write in Slovak thanks to the efforts of a Catholic priest, who had taught him in secret. The other children in his village only knew how to speak the language. They learned from their parents in the privacy of their homes—a place where the government could not interfere. However, as most of the adults in the remote village were illiterate, they could not teach their children to read and write in their mother tongue. Janos frequently reminded his children that they were lucky to live in a country where they could speak any language they chose. Ironically, no one in the family spoke much Slovak outside the home anymore. Janos only used it when immigrants came into the store.

"What are you thinking?" Concetta interrupted his ruminating. "You've been staring out the window for a long time."

"I was thinking about how thankful I am to work at the store."

"You don't just work there." Concetta smiled at him, her big, brown eyes exuding warmth and possibly a hint of pride.

Janos's face grew hot. He had always found Concetta attractive, but in the soft glow of the candlelight, she looked rather beautiful. The low light had erased years from her face, making him wonder what she might have looked like as a young girl with jet-black hair. Janos imagined she must have been striking. Unsettled by an unexpected wave of desire, he fought to collect his thoughts. "I was so grateful when Antonio hired me," he stammered. "I expected to work at the glass factory for the rest of my life."

"He needed your knowledge of Slovak and Polish at the store. You attracted many new customers. You grew the business."

"How was everything?" asked a heavy waitress with an Italian accent.

"Very good. Thank you," Janos replied, grateful for the interruption.

"I will bring cannoli for you."

"*Grazie*," Concetta said.

Putting down his fork, Janos eyed his business partner curiously. He was struck by the realization that she was a stranger to him in many ways. The store had always been Antonio's sphere, and Concetta had preferred to stay out of its orbit. She chose to focus her energies on mothering Tony and managing the household. She helped at the store on only the busiest of days when there was barely time to exchange pleasantries and the juiciest morsels of neighborhood gossip. It wasn't until Tony's move to Philadelphia that Concetta had been forced to become Janos's business partner in more than just name. He suddenly wanted to know everything about her. "I should probably know the answer to this question," he began, "but were you and Antonio grocers in Italy? I never asked him what he did before he came to America."

"No. We worked at a vineyard in Tuscany. We fell in love picking grapes." Her smile was bittersweet, fading as she looked down at the red and white checkered table cloth.

"I'm sorry. I didn't mean to upset you."

"Don't apologize. I should be able to talk about Antonio without getting emotional. It's been three years since he passed."

"Some wounds aren't meant to heal." Janos knew how terribly Concetta missed Antonio. The Morettis had enjoyed a marriage built on friendship and trust, rarely trading a harsh word. Janos had envied it, often wishing he had been as lucky in his own marriage. His had ended so disastrously. Pushing the distressing thought from his mind, he turned his attention back to Concetta. "Why did you leave the vineyard? It sounds like a nice place to work."

She nodded. "It was . . . until most of the grapevines were lost to a parasite. Antonio and I tried to find other work, but jobs were scarce due to the droughts. We had no choice but to move to America." She brushed a loose strand of hair away from her face and leaned closer to the table. "What about you, Janos? What did you do before coming to America?"

"I worked at a sawmill."

"And your wife?"

"My wife . . ." Janos fought to catch his breath. He had never discussed Karina with Concetta before. He hadn't shared much about his wife with Antonio either. When his employer had interviewed him over five years ago and asked if he had a family, Janos had simply said that he was the father of two children. When Antonio looked confused, Janos quickly explained that his wife had disappeared and was presumed to be the victim of a tragic accident. Like everyone else who dared ask too many questions, Antonio awkwardly expressed his sympathy and quickly changed the subject.

Janos was surprised Concetta had asked about Karina. Surely her husband had shared his family's tragic story with her. But maybe she had forgotten. Janos closed his eyes as he reached for his wine, hoping it might soothe the ache in his chest. He wondered how the conversation had taken such an unfortunate turn. He suddenly felt a light squeeze on his hand.

"Thank you for dinner, Janos. I haven't been to Luigi's in quite some time."

Relief washing over him, he opened his eyes. "You mastered the art of bookkeeping this week. You deserve a break from cooking."

"It's not much work preparing a meal for one person."

"I guess not," Janos said, noting the sad expression on Concetta's face. "Maybe you could join my family for dinner sometime. Next week, perhaps." He smiled, excited by the prospect. "You could bring a dessert."

Concetta's face lit up. "I could bring cannoli—or maybe a devil's food cake."

"My family will be grateful for any one of your delicious desserts. And for your company, too."

Now Concetta was the one who was blushing. She brushed a few breadcrumbs off the table as the waitress returned with cannoli. As Janos watched her cut the pastry into bite-size pieces, he noticed that her mood seemed lighter, her expression more serene. He was happy his invitation had given her something to look forward to. Perhaps this upcoming dinner might become a regular occurrence. A weekly event, even. As Janos gazed at the lovely woman sitting across from him, he sincerely hoped that would be the case.

## *Thirty*

### SOFIE

#### BEAVER CREEK, SEPTEMBER 29, 1917

Sofie felt ridiculous as she approached the school wearing Marie's gauzy lilac dress. It was several inches too short and far more suitable for a summer wedding than an autumn dance. The fabric was flimsy, and the color not suited to the season. October was only two days away, and Sofie looked like a bridesmaid on her way to a garden reception. She pulled at the dress yet again, hoping to get the hem to fall a little lower than mid-calf. Despite Marie's assurances, she still worried she would be sent home from the dance for showing too much leg.

"It's not too late to turn around. Why don't we go to the nickelodeon instead?" A dark theatre seemed like the only place Sofie might feel comfortable wearing such a dress.

"Don't be silly. I spent almost an hour on my hair," Marie said, patting the dark mound of curls on the top of her head. "Besides, I have to show off this dress. I saved months for it."

Sofie couldn't deny that Marie looked lovely in her new burgundy dress. With her petite frame and her doe-like eyes, she was bound to turn heads that afternoon. Sofie wondered how many broken hearts her friend would leave in her wake. She had a reputation for being fickle, often chasing after boys only to drop them soon after she'd gained their affections. Some thought Marie's behavior cruel, but Sofie knew her friend never meant any harm. It was her gregarious nature and short attention span that were to blame for her reckless ways.

"Now, Sofie," Marie said, clutching her friend's arm. "Promise you won't be a wallflower today. We didn't get dolled up for nothing."

Sofie rolled her eyes.

"Come on. You used to be a fine dancer."

"When?" Sofie looked at her friend sideways.

"When we were little. Don't you remember dancing at all those neighborhood weddings in Riverton?" Marie shook her head. "I haven't seen you dance since . . ."

Sofie studied her friend's face. It was twisted in concentration, her brows furrowed. "Why does it matter? Why are you and my aunt—and even my editor—trying to force me to have fun?" Sofie crossed her arms, her irritation growing. Just the previous afternoon, her editor at the newspaper had ordered her to stop tidying up the office. "Shouldn't you be out shopping with your girlfriends?" he'd asked condescendingly. Sofie did not understand the growing concern about how she spent her time.

Marie suddenly gasped, stopping in the middle of the sidewalk. "Jenny's wedding."

"What?"

"Jenny's wedding," she repeated. "That was the last time you danced."

Sofie clutched her chest as an image so happy—yet so heartbreaking—flashed before her eyes. She was filled with both joy and regret.

*Pole.*

Marie nodded, a sad expression on her face.

"Did I say that aloud?" Sofie turned away, hoping to hide her crimson face.

"Do you think it's a coincidence that the last time you danced was with Pole?" Marie laid a hand on Sofie's shoulder. "The minute he disappeared from your life, so did the joy."

Sofie spun around and glared at her friend. "Stop reading stuff from that crazy German doctor. Not every action has meaning."

"Look, there's Ralph Pulaski," Marie said, quickly changing the subject. "Who's that boy with him?"

"Guess we're going to find out," Sofie grumbled as Marie grabbed her hand and led her toward the blonde boys.

Ralph's cousin Jack turned out to be as reluctant a dancer as Sofie. He had lingered by the punch bowl with her for almost forty-five minutes, chatting about school and then films and then any other topic that might keep him off the dance floor. Marie and Ralph had disappeared into a sea of dancers the minute they'd entered the gymnasium, assuming that Sofie would entertain Jack.

Sofie did not mind the boy's company, as he had turned out to be a bit of novelty. Jack lived on a farm in Indiana County and was full of stories of shearing sheep, taming roosters, and milking cows. He was visiting Ralph and his family for the weekend and had been dragged to the dance, much like Sofie. He seemed to enjoy recounting his barnyard adventures, but there was a hint of sadness in his voice. Sofie had not yet been able to determine why.

"Once I looped that rope around Mabel's belly, she couldn't kick me no more. She still tries on occasion, but her range of motion is shorter. She can't reach me now."

"Doesn't the rope get in the way of milking?" Sofie asked Jack, trying to visualize the anatomy of a female cow.

"Not if you put the rope in front of her udders."

"I'll have to remember that." Sofie nodded as she imagined working on a farm. "It must be nice having fresh milk and eggs whenever you need them. Your mother must do a lot of baking."

Jack's face fell.

"What's wrong?" Sofie worried she had inadvertently stumbled upon the source of his sadness.

"Mama passed away this summer. I'm still havin' a hard time with it." Jack pulled a handkerchief out of his pocket and blew his nose.

"I'm so sorry," Sofie said, surprised that, for once, she was not the object of pity. It was now her turn to provide comfort and ease another's pain. She bit her lip, trying to remember what people had often said to her. "It will get better with time," she blurted. "One day, you'll wake up, and the pain won't be so unbearable."

Jack stared at her. "Sounds like you speak from experience."

Sofie suddenly wished she had a cow nearby to kick her. Why had she given Jack the impression that she understood his grief? She couldn't possibly reveal that her mother had disappeared. That shocking truth always led to uncomfortable questions. Sofie knew her friends and neighbors still whispered behind her back, speculating about the woman shrouded in mystery—the woman whose name no member of the Kovac family could bear to utter. Sofie shuddered. No, she would not share her painful story.

"Haven't we all lost loved ones? Grandparents, aunts, uncles?" Sofie shook her head. "I think we should dance now." She took Jack's hand and pulled him toward the middle of the basketball court.

"But I've never danced with a girl before."

"Well, I haven't danced with a boy since I was ten. Your toes won't be any safer than mine."

"Ten? Isn't that kinda young?"

Sofie thought about her neighbor's wedding all those years ago when her father had suggested that she dance with Pole.

She'd been hesitant at first and embarrassed by the idea of dancing with a boy, but gliding across the floor with her best friend had been easy and natural—just like everything else she and Pole did together. It had been a long time since Sofie had allowed herself to think of her lost friend, and she suddenly felt a familiar ache in her heart. She fought to regain her focus.

"It wasn't a big deal. The boy I danced with was practically my brother."

"That's different now, isn't it?" Jack raised his arms. "Okay. Show me what to do."

Sofie nodded as she grasped Jack's hand and led him in circles around the room. Her classmates were doing the foxtrot, but it was a dance Sofie had never learned. It had become quite popular in recent years when she'd avoided school dances like the plague. Sofie tried to mimic the moves of the girls around her and pretended not to notice when Jack tripped over her feet. The experience was not entirely unpleasant, but Sofie was anxious to return to her place at the punch bowl.

"I can't believe you're dancing."

Sofie looked over her shoulder at Marie, who was grinning from ear to ear.

"We're leaving now."

"Really?" Sofie let go of Jack's hand and turned toward the door. She was surprised Marie had grown bored with the dance, but was relieved nonetheless.

"Ralph wants to go for a walk along the river. My mother knows the dance is ending in an hour, and she expects me to come straight home. If we leave now . . ."

Sofie groaned. She knew exactly what Marie wanted to do.

Sofie and Jack followed closely behind Marie and Ralph, who were strolling arm in arm along the path beside the Allegheny River. The late afternoon sun was warm, but a gentle breeze had begun to blow, making Sofie wish she had brought a sweater.

"We're almost to the old train bridge," Ralph said to Marie. "You want to walk across it?"

"Isn't that a little dangerous?" Sofie asked, catching up to Ralph.

"Not really. It hasn't been used in years. Besides, we'll have a nice view of the river from up there."

Sofie looked back at Jack, who shrugged his shoulders. He wasn't concerned, but then he had probably never seen the structure they were about to cross. The old wooden bridge was not in terrible shape, but it had been abandoned by the glass factory when a more modern steel bridge was constructed closer to the factory's rail yard a few years earlier. The timber bridge was only used now by brave, thrill-seeking teenagers. They dove from it during the spring and early summer when the river was running especially high.

"The bank up to the bridge is steep. I'll climb up first and give you a hand," Ralph said to Marie, who seemed a little too eager to accept his assistance.

Hoping to head off a chivalrous gesture from Jack, Sofie called over her shoulder, "I can manage the hill by myself." She pulled up her dress and dashed up the bank effortlessly.

"You're fast for a girl," Jack said from behind her. "Must be those long legs of yours."

Sofie turned around with a ready glare. "For a girl! What's that supposed to mean?"

"Nothing." Jack smiled apologetically as he caught up to her. "It's pretty up here," he said, his eyes widening as he surveyed the steep river valley. "Especially at this time of year."

"Yes, it's beautiful." Sofie scanned the hillside across the river from town, admiring the red, orange, and yellow leaves awash with the glow of the afternoon sun. She watched as its rays sparkled on the surface of the river, making the waves look as though they carried priceless gems with them downstream. Sofie took a deep breath, inhaling the scent of drying leaves and smoke from a wood-burning fireplace upwind. "Don't you just love autumn?"

Hearing no reply, she turned toward Jack. His face was ashen. "Is something wrong? You look sick."

"I think I got a little dizzy from looking down at the river. We must be forty feet up from the water," he stammered.

"At least. You definitely wouldn't want to fall. It would kill you if the water were running low. Luckily, the river's still high from last weekend's storms."

"That's a relief, I guess." Jack glanced toward the middle of the bridge where Ralph and Marie were locked in a tight embrace, noses only inches apart. He watched as the two kissed, Marie ending the tender moment with a giggle.

Sofie rolled her eyes. "I think we should turn back now."

"Are you sure?" Jack took a step closer, an expectant look on his face.

Sofie studied the blonde boy. He was certainly attractive with his thick, wavy hair and bright blue eyes. And he was tall. It was a nice change to not have to look down at a boy. Sofie even found his barnyard stories and country mannerisms endearing. So why didn't she want him to kiss her?

As Jack leaned toward her, his lips puckered, Sofie felt the urge to flee. "Look at the size of that beaver!" She pointed down at the river's edge.

Jack leaned over the side of the bridge. "Where? I don't see him."

"Damn it!" Sofie grumbled. "He disappeared in the brush." She grabbed Jack's arm and led him back toward the path. "You're pale again. This bridge is no place for you." Satisfied with her diversion, she called over her shoulder, "It's getting late, Marie. Your mother will be sending your brothers to look for you soon."

Sofie smiled when she heard quick footsteps behind her.

# *Thirty-One*

## POLE

### ABBOTT'S HOLLOW, OCTOBER 1, 1917

"It's Monday mornin'. Shouldna we heard some noise by now? Isn't there a rescue crew coming for us?" Mickey asked, a hint of desperation in his voice.

Pole wrapped his arm around the boy lying next to him. He wondered if he should stop checking his pocket watch every time he turned his headlamp on. Mickey had seemed especially upset the previous evening when Pole had announced it was Sunday night. He'd begun spending less time beside Gus and more time with his human companions ever since. "I wish I knew, Mickey."

"It's only been two and a half days," Hamish said. "I wouldn't start worryin' until the fourth or fifth day."

"I'm awful hungry," Mickey whined. "My water's almost gone, too."

"That's why I had you lads piss in my lunch bucket. We can start drinking it soon as our water runs out. We need to kill one or two of them rats today. I heard them over by Gus this mornin'."

Pole trembled. He couldn't believe he was going to spend his last days on Earth drinking piss and eating rats. He had seen a lot of tragedy in his twenty years, but had never imagined his life might come to such a horrific end. When Hamish handed him his lunch bucket on Saturday morning and ordered him to collect the mule's piss, he knew they were in deep.

"I don't think I can drink piss," Mickey said, his voice breaking. "And I can't eat a raw rat either." He started to cry.

Pole hugged Mickey tightly as his chest began to heave, his sobbing growing more intense. He wondered whether God would show them mercy and cut off their oxygen supply. Surely that would be a quick death. But surprisingly, as Pole sat in the quiet stillness of the mine, he continued to detect a slight draft coming from the collapsed end of Ruthie Tunnel. He had mentioned it to Hamish over the weekend, and the two had concluded that the mountain of rubble contained gaps large enough to allow air to flow through. Pole couldn't decide whether that was a blessing or a curse.

Over the past few days, he had considered the agony of a slow death from thirst or starvation and was not sure he could bear it. Fortunately, he had weeks before he would meet that end. Hamish was hell-bent on killing Gus once the supply of rats ran out. The mule's meat would last for a week or longer in the cool temperatures underground.

"Hamish, you never explained how my pop died. Why didn't you tell me you were trapped together?" Pole asked, suddenly remembering what the old-timer had said shortly after the roof collapse on Friday night.

"There was never any sense. It wouldna brought you comfort."

"Why is that?"

"Yer daddy was a real bastart—mean and bitter to the very end. You know how you hear about people softening up at death's door . . . leavin' apologies for their kin?" Hamish asked.

"Sure."

"That wasn't yer daddy. He was gripin' and complainin' up until he took his last breath. He hadn't a drink in over three days—he was mighty crabby. And he was saying such crazy things." Hamish sighed. "I hate to admit it, but I was relieved when he finally passed."

"What did he say?" Pole was desperate to know more about the man who had been such a mystery to him. Even after they'd moved to Abbott's Hollow, his father remained distant, disappearing for days at a time. He rarely showed up to work at the mine, but always seemed to have enough money for booze. He often walked to Portage on Friday nights and caught a train to Johnstown. Pole assumed his father had found himself a nice whorehouse and was spending his weekends there. He never understood how his pop had paid for his wild lifestyle in the last months of his life.

"Come on, Pole. You don't need the details. You already know yer daddy wasn't a good man. Do you need to know any more than that?"

"I'm a grown man now. I want to know what he said."

"Och, damn it! Don't say I didn't warn you." Hamish coughed, wincing as he grabbed his side. "Yer daddy was braggin' about some robbery in that town you came from near Pittsburgh."

"Riverton?"

"Maybe that was it. Anyway, he and his friend got away with a good bit of cash."

"That's not very shocking."

"Well, there's more. He was ramblin' on about how a dying man should probably repent for his sins, but he felt no remorse. He didn't give a damn that the man they robbed got killed."

Pole gasped. "Are you telling me my pop was a murderer?"

"Not in this case. He said the woman who helped him with the robbery did the killin'. Hit the guy over the head, I think.

Yer daddy said the rich bastart deserved what he got, and he never lost any sleep over it. He wondered if that guaranteed him a place in hell."

Suddenly, it all made sense to Pole. That was the reason his father had whisked him away to the Allegheny Mountains all those years ago. He'd been involved in a robbery and had come away with enough cash to pay for booze and whores for months.

"Did my pop ever mention the name of the man who was killed?"

"Nah, just that he was some rich guy who worked at the mill. Some sort of boss. I do remember him describing the curvy blonde who did the killin'. I think she was the man's housekeeper. Yer daddy suspected she was doing more than keeping house."

Pole's empty stomach lurched. Could the curvy blonde have been Mrs. Kovac? Sofie's mother? She had worked for a mill manager, but Pole couldn't remember the man's name. It was lost to him, buried deep within the recesses of his memory, along with everything else he'd chosen to forget about Riverton.

"You all right?" a soft voice whispered in the dark.

It was Mickey. Pole had forgotten about the boy nestled under his armpit. "Sure, kid. Why?"

"You're squeezin' me kinda hard."

Pole suddenly realized he had a firm grip on the boy's arm. His head was spinning, and he had unconsciously grabbed the thing closest to him for support. "I'm sorry . . . but that story," he said breathlessly.

"I told you there was no point in tellin' it," Hamish said.

"Your daddy sounds like a mean man, Pole. You're probably better off without him," Mickey said. "I think my mama was relieved when my daddy disappeared a few months ago. I know I was. Course, he's the reason I'm stuck in this mine."

"No doubt," Hamish said. "Hard to find a man who wants to stick around and take care of his children. Sorry if I upset you, Pole. I thought you knew what kind of man yer daddy was."

Pole took a deep breath and leaned his head back against the coal face. "I've always known who my pop was. I'm just shocked about the woman in the story."

"You know who she was?" Hamish asked excitedly.

"I think it was my best friend's mother. She worked as a housekeeper for a manager at the mill. And I guess she knew my pop well enough to get in on one of his schemes. She once worked at the boarding house where we lived."

"I wonder what happened to her," said Mickey. "If she ever got caught."

"I don't know," Pole said. "I went back to Riverton to find my friend a couple years after my pop moved us here to the mountains. I wanted to tell her I was sorry I couldn't get back to the city for a while—at least not until my sister was older."

"Ah … so it was an old sweetheart you went to find," Hamish said.

Pole felt his cheeks grow hot. He was momentarily grateful to be stuck in the depths of the earth with no sunlight to illuminate his reddening face. He had never considered Sofie a sweetheart. She was only ten years old when he'd known her. But she had been like family to him, as much a sister as Lily now was.

"She wasn't a sweetheart," Pole snapped. He hadn't thought about Sofie in a long time and wasn't sure he wanted to discuss her with a scrappy old Scot and a young kid.

"Didn't mean to ruffle yer feathers, lad. But judgin' by yer reaction, I'd say the lass was important to you. Did you ever find her?" Another painful cough from Hamish.

Pole sighed. "No. I went to her house to see her, but her entire block was burnt to the ground, and her neighbors were gone. I even went by the boarding house where I used to live to see if Sofie left an address with Mrs. Janosik, but she was dead."

"Who's Mrs. Janosik?" Mickey asked.

"She was the owner of the house. If Sofie wanted me to find her, she woulda left word with Mrs. Janosik."

"Maybe she did," Hamish said. "Maybe you got there too late for the woman to tell you anything."

"I don't know. I wrote to Sofie for a whole year after I moved to Abbott's Hollow, and I never heard from her. I wish I knew what happened to her."

"Maybe she moved too—before her block burnt down. Maybe she never got your letters," Mickey said hopefully.

"It doesn't matter now. I'll probably never see her again." Pole closed his eyes. He remembered the last time he saw Sofie. She was standing on her front porch in her nightgown, her long blonde hair in tangles around her face. She was so angry when he told her he had to leave town, but Pole promised he would come back. And Sofie believed him. She'd always trusted him completely.

Pole groaned. He was still haunted by that unkept promise.

"I'm sure you've got someone special waitin' for you to get outta this mine. Maybe a girl in Portage?" Hamish asked. "You're a fine lookin' fella."

"No. Just my little sister."

"Not even that pretty Irish blonde?" asked Mickey. "You know the one who works at the five-and-dime? What's her name?"

"Kathleen. She's fun, that's for sure. But she's not the type I'd like to marry."

"Yeah, I heard she's a little loose," Mickey said.

Pole thought of the few times he had been with Kathleen. She was a wild young girl determined to shed her Irish Catholic roots and rebel against her strict parents. She had a taste for whiskey and enjoyed the company of a wide variety of men. Pole was certain she lacked the decency required to catch a respectable husband, but surprisingly, she didn't seem to care. She was content with her untamed lifestyle and did an impressive job of hiding her adventures from her naive parents.

"Nothing wrong with waitin' for the right girl to come along. When you see her, Pole, you'll know it," Hamish said.

"Now let's quiet down. We need to listen for them rats. When you hear one come near you, smash it with a rock."

"Won't that be hard to do in the dark?" Mickey asked.

"I don't need any light, but you can use one of them headlamps if you like. Hold on, lemme get a match," Hamish mumbled.

Pole listened as Hamish dug through his pockets, his loose change jingling noisily. "I thought we wanted to try and kill a rat or two. Not scare them away."

"You're a scunner, now aren't you?" barked Hamish.

Suddenly, Pole saw a tiny flicker of light burst into a bright flame. The headlamp was lit. It was the first time he had seen his companions' faces in twelve hours or more. Pole was alarmed at how pale Hamish looked.

"I'll hold the headlamp, Hamish. You get some rest. Me and Mickey will hunt rats." Pole took the headlamp from Hamish and studied the old-timer's face. He looked tired and weak. "Mickey, you go sit by Gus. Stay still and pretend like you're sleepin'. Hopefully, one of those rats will get curious and come in real close. And then you can whack it."

Pole watched the boy scramble over to his mule, pausing for a few minutes to whisper into the animal's ear and stroke its muzzle. When Mickey was finally seated on the ground a few feet from Gus, Pole said, "Try to hit the rat square on the head. We don't want a bloody mess. If we get lucky and kill our dinner sooner rather than later, we can sear the meat on the flame of the headlamp. Might make it a little easier goin' down."

"Maybe I can eat a raw rat after all," Mickey said. "We shouldn't waste the carbide on cooking."

"That's the right attitude," Pole said, trying to sound enthusiastic. He wanted to be brave and set a good example for the twelve-year-old, but inside he was quaking with fear. He had serious doubts he would ever escape the carbon tomb encasing him. His life would be cut short, taken before he'd had a chance to fall in love and know when the right girl had come along.

# *Thirty-Two*

## EDITH

### SHADYSIDE, OCTOBER 3, 1917

Edith woke to the sound of her husband's loud snoring. She glanced over at the Tiffany clock on her nightstand and was surprised that it was almost eight o'clock. James had slept late. She leaned over and whispered softly in his ear. "Wake up. It's Wednesday. You have to be at the university in thirty minutes."

"Not today, darling," he mumbled sleepily. "I have a meeting with my publisher."

"Sorry." Edith patted her husband on the shoulder and tucked the heavy eiderdown quilt under his chin. A few days earlier, she had requested that the maid change the bed linens in preparation for the cooler October weather, but wondered if she'd done so prematurely. She had woken several times in the middle of the night, hot and uncomfortable. She had repeatedly pushed the bulky damask quilt toward her husband, who didn't seem to mind the extra warmth.

Edith rose from the bed, pausing for a moment to admire the crimson-colored quilt she had purchased in England a few summers ago. The color was rich and vibrant, a perfect complement to her elaborately carved oak canopy bed. She smiled proudly, certain she had achieved the appropriate look in her Tudor bedroom.

As Edith turned to enter her marble bathroom, she caught a glimpse of herself in the mirror above her dresser. She immediately noticed that the dark shadows had returned to her lower face. Instinctively, her hand went up to finger the stubble growing on her chin and jaw. She sighed gloomily. She would have to shave that morning even though she had just performed the dreaded chore the day before. Was it her imagination, or was her hair growth worsening? It seemed to be coming back much faster than it used to. Edith felt her cheerful mood slip away, despair replacing it.

She shuffled into her bathroom and over to the toilet, pulling up her silk nightgown as she walked. She sat down on the cold wooden seat, pushing her lace knickers down over her knees. As she relieved herself, her eyes traced the swirling gray patterns on the marble floor tiles until suddenly, they were distracted by an unexpected flash of brown. Edith leaned forward and grabbed her knickers. Could it be? She pulled the lacy undergarment up over her knees and examined it closely. There was no mistaking it. A brownish blood stain had marred her perfectly white cotton knickers. It was the most beautiful sight she'd seen in months.

"James!" she shouted. "The herbs worked! The mugwort and pennyroyal—they worked!"

Edith jumped up from the toilet and darted over to the dresser opposite the bathtub. She dug through the top drawer, sifting through piles of cotton, linen, and silk undergarments. After several minutes, she finally found the object she had been seeking hidden at the drawer's bottom—her rarely used sanitary belt. She held it up to the light filtering through the colorful stained glass window. Along with those bright rays of morning sun, hope flooded the room as well.

# *Thirty-Three*

## JANOS

### BEAVER CREEK, OCTOBER 3, 1917

Janos shoved another fork full of devil's food cake into his mouth as he gazed across the dining room table at Concetta. A low moan escaped his lips as he savored the rich, chocolatey dessert. It was the most heavenly chocolate cake he had ever tasted, but he was distracted by a hint of another ingredient, something oddly familiar. "Coffee?" he asked aloud, his mouth still full.

"I wondered whether you'd figure it out. Is it too strong?" Concetta asked.

"Not at all," Janos said, licking some frosting from his lips.

"Where did you find such a recipe?" Anna asked.

Concetta giggled. "It was an accident. I spilled my coffee while I was making the frosting. Almost half my cup went into the mixing bowl. I couldn't possibly throw it out and waste all that sugar." She shook her head.

"Of course not," Anna said. "But it's delicious."

"Thank you."

Janos admired his business partner as she broke into a wide grin. She looked elegant in her navy blue dress and pearl earrings. Her hair was pulled back into a tight bun, revealing her long neck and pretty olive skin. He wondered why he hadn't noticed her beauty until recently.

"Papa, did you hear what I said?"

"What's that, Sofie?" Janos turned toward his daughter, who was seated opposite Concetta. She was staring at him, her eyes narrowed.

"I ran into Mr. Berman today. He said his boss can meet with you next week to discuss the loan."

"What loan?" Anna tilted her head.

Concetta looked up from her dessert plate.

Janos suddenly wished he hadn't dropped by the bank the previous week to inquire about obtaining a loan to buy Concetta's share of the store. After dinner at Luigi's the previous Friday, thoughts of her had been filling his head, not all of them innocent. He was ashamed of imagining Concetta might be something more than a business partner to him, but he was certain he had felt something akin to a spark during their candlelit dinner. He now dreaded the thought of her moving to Philadelphia.

"Janos?" Anna tapped his arm. "Why do you need a loan?"

His throat closing, he took a sip of tea. "I merely wanted to inquire about a loan to buy Concetta's half of the store." He avoided her gaze out of fear his eyes might betray him. "She's thinking of moving to Philadelphia to be near Tony."

"Oh," Sofie said, a smile creeping across her face. "You must miss him terribly."

"I do." Concetta nodded. "But he and Lucia have settled into their new home and seem quite happy with it." She hesitated and put down her fork. "I received news this afternoon that they're expecting their first child. I'm going to be a *nonna*." Concetta beamed.

"Congratulations! You must be so excited," Anna said.

"A grandchild. I'm so happy for you," Janos said, trying to sound cheerful while digesting the bittersweet news. With a grandbaby on the way, there would be little chance of Concetta staying in Beaver Creek. "I'll be sure to meet with the loan officer right away. You'll want to be in Philadelphia as soon as possible."

Concetta pursed her lips. "I still need time to think about this. I'm not comfortable with you taking such a huge financial risk for me, Janos."

"Maybe you could sell your share of the store to someone else," Sofie suggested. "Perhaps that Jewish man who owns the hardware store might be interested."

Janos wished he could elbow his daughter, but she was too far away. Why was she encouraging this move? "Please clear the table, Sofie," he said, hoping to expel her from the conversation.

Concetta stood up. "I've had a lovely evening, but I really must get home. Thank you, Anna and Sofie, for preparing such a wonderful dinner. The chicken was delicious."

"And thank you for bringing the cake." Anna got up from her chair and bent to kiss the petite woman on the cheek. "I'll have to try baking with coffee, but it's so expensive right now."

"Everything's expensive with this damn war," Sofie muttered as she stacked plates. Catching her father's glare, she quickly said, "Sorry about the cursing, Mrs. Moretti."

"I'll grab my coat and walk you home, Concetta."

"No, no, Janos. Sit back down and finish your tea. The walk's not far."

Disappointed, Janos sat down and watched Anna escort Concetta to the front door. He had been a fool for fantasizing about her the last few days. Her heart was in Philadelphia with her son. And the pull of a grandchild was a force with which Janos could not compete. He rested his head on his hand and sighed.

"You and Concetta have been spending a lot of time together lately," Anna said when she returned to the dining room. "Why would you want to get a loan to help her move?"

"I take it you don't approve."

"I think a loan would be better spent on purchasing this house. We've been renting for far too long."

"That's true, I suppose." Janos felt a sharp twinge of guilt.

"Helping Mrs. Moretti move to Philadelphia is the right thing to do," Sofie said as she returned from the kitchen with a cleaning rag. "She should be near her family."

Janos eyed his daughter. "What do you have against Concetta?"

"Nothing. Wouldn't you long to be near me if I moved away?"

Janos took another sip of tea as he stared at the blue butterflies on the green and white floral wallpaper Anna loved so much. It was a distracting pattern, but something he had grown accustomed to. He wondered if he could ever become accustomed to a life without his children. Would he be content traveling across the state to visit them only a few times a year? Probably not. But then again, he only saw Lukas a handful of times during the school year.

"Forgive me for saying this . . ." Anna said hesitantly. "But I think Sofie might be a little jealous of the time you've been spending with Concetta. Since Tony moved away, you've been at the store almost twice as much."

"Is that true, Sofie?" Janos asked.

She sank into the chair beside Anna, but would not meet her father's gaze. "You spend more time with her than your own family. And I've seen the way you look at her."

"Sofie!" Anna scolded her niece.

Janos patted his sister's hand. "It's fine. I admit that I have been spending more time with Concetta lately. I'm sorry if you feel neglected, Sofie." He suddenly understood why his daughter had acted so strangely at the store the previous week and had turned down Concetta's offer of biscotti.

"Sofie, someday your father may meet a special woman and want to remarry. You would be happy for him, wouldn't you?" Anna asked in a softer tone.

Janos felt his face flush. "This is not an appropriate conversation to be having with my seventeen-year-old daughter."

"I don't see why not. I think it's certainly something you can discuss with your older sister, at the very least."

"Please, Anna. Not now." Janos wanted to crawl under the table.

"I will not belabor the point, but it is time you moved on. If not with Concetta, then perhaps with someone else." Anna crossed her arms.

Sofie was suddenly leaning forward, looking as if she wanted to be part of the conversation. Janos glanced at the sideboard and wondered if it would be an inappropriate time to pour himself a glass of whiskey.

"Papa, can we talk? It's about Mama."

Janos flinched. They hadn't spoken of Karina in years. Why would Sofie want to unearth a painful memory long buried? He grasped his tea cup. "What about her?" he said more harshly than he intended.

"We never talk about her disappearance . . . about what may have happened to her," Sofie said solemnly.

Janos's heart ached for his little girl—for the motherless child who had managed an almost believable facade of bravery in the years after her mother's disappearance and her brother's horrific accident. She had been so strong and supportive when he'd come apart after seeing Lukas lying, almost lifeless, in a hospital bed. And then only hours later, he had learned of his wife's unexpected departure from their lives. It was an excruciatingly painful time in his life, one he seldom revisited in his thoughts. *Why bring it up now, Sofie?*

Janos exchanged a worried glance with his sister. "What would you like to discuss? I'm not sure there's much left to be said."

"I've been thinking about Mama a lot lately. I guess it's because I met a boy at the dance who recently lost his mother. It made me think of my own loss. I'm not sure why, but now I want to know why Mama left."

"I think this is a conversation the two of you need to have in private," Anna said. "I'm going to bed."

"You can stay, Aunt Anna," Sofie said. "Maybe you have something to add."

Janos watched his sister lean over to kiss Sofie on the forehead. "Good night, sweet girl," she said as she got up from the table.

As soon as Anna was gone from the room, Janos took a deep breath in preparation for the uncomfortable discussion that lay ahead. "Judging by the word you used, I assume you believe your mother *left* intentionally. You no longer think her disappearance was the result of an accident? You don't believe she was taken against her will?"

Sofie looked down at the cleaning rag in her hand. "Deep down, I've always believed Mama left on her own. I spent a lot of years trying to convince myself otherwise, but I never quite managed it. The only reason I still use the word "disappearance" is to avoid hurting you or embarrassing you—all of us for that matter. Why would I ever want to admit that my mother abandoned me?"

A tear escaped down Sofie's cheek. Janos got up and moved to the empty chair beside her. He put his arm around her and pulled her into his chest.

Sofie rested quietly against her father's chest not more than a minute before looking up. "That's all I have for her, Papa. Just that one tear. I'm done crying for her." She sat up and pushed her hair away from her face. "You know, I used to cry myself to sleep at night in the months after Mama left. I was sleeping with Aunt Anna at the time, and she always told me how sorry she was that I lost my mother. But looking back on it now, I don't think I was crying for Mama. I was crying for you and all the pain she caused you. And for poor Lukas and the leg he lost."

"And for Pole. For the best friend *you* lost." Janos reached for his daughter's hand and squeezed it. He hoped he hadn't been too bold.

The dam broke. Sofie was a river of tears.

"I'm so sorry. We lost so much that summer, didn't we?" Janos rubbed his daughter's back as she buried her face in her hands. He immediately regretted mentioning Pole. He knew how much Sofie had cared about him, but perhaps there was more to the story than he realized.

After a moment of awkward silence, Sofie wiped her eyes and turned to face her father. "Do you remember when the police came to the house that first night Lukas was in the hospital?"

Janos recalled that evening quite well even though he had been reeling from the prospect of losing his son and worrying about the whereabouts of his wife. He had been out of his mind with grief and shock, but resolute in a single purpose. "Unfortunately, I remember that evening like it was yesterday." Janos trembled.

"They wanted to question Mama—to see if she knew anything about Henry Archer's murder."

"But your mother was gone."

"We hadn't seen her since the night before." Sofie shook her head. "And you told me not to tell anyone what Lukas saw at the train station that morning. Remember?"

Janos nodded. He would never forget the panic he had felt soon after Anna had rushed home with news of a murder in Mr. Archer's wealthy neighborhood. He and Sofie had just returned from the hospital and still had no idea where Karina was. She did not know that her son was missing half of his leg and clinging precariously to life. When Sofie had explained shortly after the accident that morning that Lukas was chasing the train because he believed his mother was on it, Janos and Anna had dismissed the notion as nonsense. But once they heard about the murder in Riverton Heights, an incomprehensible suspicion crept in. Had Karina been on the train Lukas was chasing? Had she been escaping the scene of a crime? Regardless of the truth, Janos and Anna knew they needed to cast suspicion away from Karina.

That feat hadn't been terribly difficult. Once the police informed Janos and Anna that Henry Archer was the murder victim, Janos quickly produced a plausible theory. He suggested that whoever was responsible for the mill manager's death must also be responsible for Karina's disappearance. She must have witnessed the crime and suffered a similar fate. When one of the detectives raised an eyebrow, Janos asked how his petite wife could overpower a man like Mr. Archer. He outweighed her by almost a hundred pounds. Besides, such a gruesome act would be grossly out of character for a loving wife and mother. The detectives seemed satisfied with Janos's theory.

"I never understood why you protected her. Aunt Anna, too," Sofie continued. "Did you know that a few days later, when Mama still hadn't turned up, Aunt Anna convinced me that Henry Archer's murderer must have taken Mama. She said that was the only logical explanation for her disappearance—other than an accident."

"Did you believe her?"

"For a little while. I was comforted by the idea that Mama was taken from us. The alternative was too heartbreaking." Sofie lowered her head. "When Lukas came home from the hospital, Aunt Anna persuaded him to believe her theory, too. She told him to never tell anyone he thought Mama was on that train."

Janos had to give his sister credit. She loved his children as if they were her own. She would tell any lie to protect them. "You're practically a grown woman, Sofie. What do you believe now?"

She closed her eyes and exhaled. "I believe Mama was making plans to leave us weeks before she escaped on that train. Her behavior was so odd. She suddenly took an interest in all of us and was loving and kind. I thought it was unusual at the time, but I hoped she'd made the decision to be a better mother."

Janos put a hand to his mouth, attempting to bridle his escaping gasp. He had, at times, suspected that Sofie shared his theory, but had dared not ask. He assumed his daughter must have reached her conclusion slowly, over the course of several years, in the midst of growing up and opening her eyes to the follies of human nature. As for Janos, he'd grasped the truth within hours of learning of Henry Archer's murder. Karina had been acting strange in the weeks leading up to that fateful Saturday morning, declaring her love for him and the children and apologizing for her past transgressions. The last evening the family spent together reading from *The Wizard of Oz* was her final goodbye. And the way Karina made love to him that evening . . . it was unforgettable.

Janos shook his head, trying to erase the painful images. "I had hoped the same thing, but unfortunately, we were wrong. I think your mother made plans to leave town well in advance of that horrible day. I just don't know what her involvement was in Archer's death. Your mother was a troubled woman, but I don't believe she was a murderer."

"She was cruel enough to abandon her husband and children. How do you know what she was capable of?"

Janos looked down at his hands, their powerlessness so apparent. He had failed to see the approaching storm Karina had conjured and failed to protect his children from its wake. He had been under his wife's spell for far too long and had been blind to her true nature. He'd only wanted to see the very best in Karina, even when it was buried deep, under multiple layers of anger and sadness. He didn't board that train, destined for some distant place far from reality, but he was culpable all the same. Janos buried his head in his hands and wept.

"Papa, look at me. Please look at me." Sofie was next to him, her arm wrapped around his shoulder. He had no idea how long he'd been sobbing. He had suppressed his grief for so long, it finally broke free, spewing out of him wildly, uncontrollably. He was embarrassed to break down in front of his daughter, but relieved to be free of his heavy burden.

"You're not to blame, Papa. No one could have predicted what happened. All we ever wanted was to be loved by her. We were so desperate for her affection that we couldn't see what was happening—what she was planning. I understand that now. The only person at fault is Mama."

Janos looked up at his daughter. Her cheeks were streaked with tears, but her face was surprisingly serene.

"None of it matters anymore," she said, shaking her head. "I don't care why Mama left. I don't want to wonder about her intentions. It makes no difference."

Janos gazed deep into his daughter's blue eyes, so clear and unflinching. "Why is that, sweetheart?"

"Because we're better off without her."

Janos was breathless. The truth had knocked the wind out of him. He had often said those very same words to himself over the years and always felt guilty afterward. But there was no denying it. Since he had moved his family to Beaver Creek seven years earlier, they'd been happier than ever before. Shouldering the weight of Karina's dreariness had been exhausting for every one of them. They hadn't realized how taxing the responsibility was until they'd been relieved of it. Janos, especially.

The wounds Karina had inflicted upon her family had taken time to heal and had rendered them all cautious and skeptical. But it was a fair trade. They now lived in a home filled with unconditional love, a place from which no one was plotting an escape. And even Lukas, with his wealthy benefactor and boarding school friends, was always happy to return home to see his family. Perhaps because there was never any doubt that the people he came home to shared an unbreakable bond, strong and resilient like the steel Janos once produced. Formed in the wake of Karina's destruction, it bound them together, making the whole greater than the sum of its parts.

Janos nodded and repeated Sofie's words aloud. "We're better off without her." Only this time, there was no guilt. Karina was gone, never to return. And Janos did not care.

As he took a sip of his lukewarm tea, he realized that his sister had been right. It was time to move on. Time to let go of the past and focus on the future. Janos felt a rush of excitement as he resolved to chart a new course. He had no idea if Concetta shared his feelings, but he was determined to find out. He would reveal what was in his heart and maybe give her a reason to stay in Beaver Creek.

## *Thirty-Four*

# POLE

### ABBOTT'S HOLLOW, OCTOBER 3, 1917

Pole was the stubborn one, the last holdout who refused to drink from the lunch bucket filled with piss. It sat on his lap, the pool of dark yellow liquid completely still and emitting the pungent odor of ammonia. It had been almost two and a half days since he'd had a drop of water. His throat was dry and sticky, and his head ached. There was no doubt he was dehydrated, but he wasn't yet desperate enough to force himself to drink a disgusting concoction of mule and human piss. He took another whiff of the acrid beverage and quickly set it down a few feet away from him.

"I can't do it. I'll take my chances," Pole said. "Maybe I can survive on the juice from the next batch of rats we kill. I'll suck the blood out of their little bodies if I have to."

"The piss doesn't taste too bad if you hold your nose," Mickey said.

Pole looked over at the boy, who was sitting near Gus's rear legs, wearing the only headlamp that had carbide left in it. He had become an expert rat killer over the last two days, bashing two rats over the head with a rock on Monday afternoon. He'd been the first to sample the raw rat meat and had also been eager to wash his kill down with a couple of sips from the piss bucket. Pole was slightly in awe of the young kid, but wondered if he was going through a growth spurt, his hunger pangs louder and more violent than those of a fully-grown man.

"I'll have to try that. Thanks." Pole studied Hamish, who was resting a few feet away. He looked terrible. He'd grown weaker over the past few days, sleeping most of the time and mumbling incoherently when he was awake. Pole had tried several times to examine the old man's wounds while he slept, but he was caked with so much dried blood, it was impossible to see anything. Pole worried that Hamish had broken a few ribs and was bleeding internally. He'd perked up quite a bit on Monday afternoon after eating a whole rat—Mickey and Pole had split the other one—but since then, Hamish had grown quiet and listless.

It was Wednesday evening, and all three miners had agreed it was time to eat again. The two remaining rats lurking around Ruthie Tunnel would make a passable dinner. Hopefully, help would arrive soon, and they would be able to spare Gus. Pole looked at the sluggish mule and wondered how he was faring. The animal had not eaten or sipped a drop of water since Friday—over five days ago. Mickey had offered the mule a sip from the piss bucket earlier in the day, but the poor creature had refused. He, too, would not compromise his standards no matter how unbearable his thirst.

"Look, Mickey!" Pole whispered. "That giant grandaddy rat is creepin' along the wall on the other side of Gus. Get ready."

Pole watched the enormous rat sneak up to the pile of manure behind Gus. It was hungry like the rest of them. Mickey sat motionless, following the rodent's movements with only his eyes. He tightened his grip on the large rock in his lap as the grandaddy rat began poking around the manure pile just two feet away. Pole's shoulders tensed in anticipation as he waited for Mickey to strike the fatal blow. The boy's arm went up slowly.

"Goddamn it," came a loud curse from Hamish as he broke into a coughing fit.

Startled, the rat ran away from the manure pile. Mickey lurched, trying twice to strike it with his rock, but he missed. The rodent panicked, scampering in the direction of Pole, but it soon realized it was heading toward another predator. It quickly changed directions. Acting on pure instinct and primeval hunger, Pole grabbed the rat by its tail. He picked it up and whacked it against the wall of the tunnel.

"Holy shit! We almost lost him," cried Mickey.

Pole studied the limp rat hanging upside down from its tail, the wiry appendage pinched between his thumb and forefinger. It wasn't the first animal he'd killed. He had spent plenty of time hunting deer, rabbit, and turkey in the woods around Abbott's Hollow. He was a pretty good shot and kept his sister and her mother fed better than most of the neighbors. Killing was relatively easy for Pole, but it didn't give him the pleasure that some of the hunters around the patch village derived from it. Hunting wild game was simply a means of survival. But this rat? Pole wasn't certain this poor creature's death was warranted. They had been underground for five full days and hadn't detected any sign that help was on the way. Killing this rat was probably a waste, as they would all be dead soon enough. Pole wondered if he was prolonging their suffering.

"You goin' to skin that rat or stare at it?" Hamish murmured.

His ominous ponderings interrupted, Pole said, "Sorry. I was thinkin'."

"About what?" Mickey asked.

Pole didn't dare poison the boy with his dark thoughts. Mickey had been so brave over the past few days, his hope seeming to grow with every outlandish attempt they made at survival. "I was thinkin' this rat might be the biggest goddamned one I've ever seen. We'll eat him tonight and save the last one for tomorrow or the next day."

"Fine by me. I'm not hungry anymore," Hamish said through labored breaths.

Pole handed the rat to Mickey and walked over to the old-timer, who was motionless, his eyes half open. "Maybe you should have a drink. Hand me that bucket, Mickey."

"No, no. Save it. I'm on my way out." Hamish groaned softly.

Mickey was suddenly at Pole's side with the bucket of piss. "What's he sayin'?"

"I'm dying, lad. Goin' to see my Aggie."

Pole studied the injured man's face in the light of the carbide headlamp Mickey wore. There was no denying it. Hamish looked awful, barely clinging to life. "Are you in pain, Hamish? Is there anything we can do for you?"

"If you get out . . . cash box is under the floor. In the kitchen." Hamish coughed. This time he did not wince or clutch his side.

"Don't you have sons in Johnstown? We can give them your savings."

"They have good mill jobs. You lads need money more'n them. Get away . . . get away from these mines."

Mickey sat down next to Hamish and curled up next to his uninjured side. Pole's eyes watered. "Get some rest," he said, patting the man's shoulder. "You're goin' to be fine. Mickey will keep you warm."

"Don't want to eat any more rats. I'll take some of that mule though." He closed his eyes. "Can't wait to see my Aggie."

Mickey and Pole exchanged worried glances. "He needs to rest. I'll skin the rat while you sit by Hamish. He could use some comforting."

The young boy nodded solemnly.

As Pole pulled out his pocket knife and sank the blade under the rat's skin, he heard a faint noise. "You hear that?"

he asked Mickey, looking in the direction of the collapsed end of Ruthie Tunnel.

He took the carbide lamp from Mickey's head and walked up the tunnel to where he'd been struck by falling debris days earlier. He scanned the pile of rubble, listening for a sound—any sound other than his own breathing.

He stood for several minutes. Nothing. He turned back toward Mickey and Hamish, his head hung low. He called out, "Sorry, kid. I guess I'm imagining things."

And then came the glorious sound of rocks falling. And men calling from the other side.

"We're in here!" Pole shouted, running toward the mound of debris. "We're alive!" Adrenaline coursed through his veins, awakening his senses and giving him a potent boost of energy. "I can work from this side," he yelled as he began picking up jagged chunks of collapsed roof.

"No, don't!" cried a raspy voice from the other side of the tunnel. "Sit tight. We'll come to you. We gotta reinforce the roof."

"Okay, okay," Pole said, trying to calm himself. He noticed Mickey was wrapped around him, hugging him tightly.

"I knew it, Pole. I knew we'd be rescued."

Pole grabbed the boy and held him. His eyes welled with tears as he exhaled deeply, the stress of the last five days escaping him. His tense shoulders finally began to relax, allowing him to stand straighter. He was suddenly a lighter man.

"How many alive in there?" shouted the gruff voice through gaps in the rubble.

"Three men and a mule." Pole looked down at Mickey. "How's Hamish?"

"His breathing's kinda weak."

"We've got one injured," Pole yelled to his rescuers. "How long before we're out?"

"An hour. Maybe two. We'll get you soon as we can."

"Thanks, man. Thanks for comin'," Pole shouted. "Come on, Mickey. Let's go tell Hamish the good news."

Pole walked arm in arm with Mickey back down the tunnel toward Hamish and Gus. When the boy began skipping, Pole happily joined him, humming the tune to "Darktown Strutters Ball." He was brimming with joy, the realization of his awaiting future sinking in. He would get to see his sister again, feel the warmth of the sun on his face, drink a beer. And maybe he would take wild and crazy Kate out for a night of dancing. The possibilities were endless.

As soon as they arrived at the end of Ruthie Tunnel, Mickey ran over to Gus. He stroked the mule's muzzle and whispered the news of their impending rescue into his ear. Pole sat down next to Hamish, who was sleeping against the rock wall. He gave him a gentle nudge.

"Hey, Hamish. We're gettin' out. The rescue crew's coming for us."

There was no response.

Pole studied his friend, who was eerily still. He leaned over and put his ear in front of Hamish's mouth, trying to ascertain whether there was any life left in him. Pole's heart sank. Still holding onto hope, he leaned backward to view the man's chest, searching for a trace of movement, a sign that air was being drawn in and out of his lungs. There was none.

Hamish was gone.

It took almost three hours for the rescue crew to reinforce the tunnel roof and dig Pole and his companions out. When a safe path through the rubble had finally been cleared, a scruffy-looking, stocky man greeted Pole and Mickey.

"It's sure good to see you boys." The man slapped Pole on the back and shook his hand vigorously. He handed him and Mickey fresh jugs of water. "We were afraid we'd be too late. Took too long to get the rescue underway."

As Pole greedily drank the clean, odorless water—a luxury he vowed never to take for granted again—he realized he did not recognize his unshaven rescuer. The man had a weathered appearance as if he'd spent too much time in the elements. Could this sunburnt man be a miner?

"Thanks for gettin' us out," Pole said breathlessly, water dripping down his chin. He looked around the tunnel at the other four rescuers, all of them strangers. "Who are all of you? I've never seen you around the mine."

"I'm Stan Davis," said the scruffy man. "I'm with the United Mine Workers of America. This is our best mine rescue team," he said, motioning to the burly men surrounding him.

"But we're not a union mine," Mickey blurted, confused.

"You are now!" Davis said, grinning like the cat that ate the canary.

"How can that be?" Pole asked.

He remembered the attempts at unionization the miners in Abbott's Hollow had made a few months after the collapse that killed his father in the summer of 1910. Disgruntled and fearful, the men had contacted the United Mine Workers of America to help them negotiate with the coal company for better wages and safer working conditions. The Murphy Brothers Mining Company was small and owned only a few mines. When the workers went out on strike for two weeks, the stubborn Irish brothers—once miners themselves—began evicting families from their company homes and threatened to close the mines permanently. With winter approaching and no other job opportunities in the immediate area, the miners quickly caved and abandoned the idea of unionization. Pole wondered what was different this time.

"Those Murphy brothers like the color green." Davis sniggered. "The war in Europe is causing a serious coal shortage. Prices are on the rise, and your employers don't want to miss out on the chance to fatten their wallets. They recognized the union within a few days of our arrival in town."

"Hold on," said Pole. "I'm not following you. How did you end up in Abbott's Hollow at the same time the coal company was dealing with a collapse?"

"Well, you see, my friend, that's the problem. The coal company wasn't dealing with the collapse." The union man shook his head back in forth in disgust as he spat a wad of chewing tobacco on the ground. "The owners of your mine were going to leave you down here to rot. They were going to close this tunnel and mine around it. They said it was too dangerous to try to get you out. I'd say it was just too expensive for those stingy old men. Anyways, your friends and neighbors didn't like that idea, so they got word to our contact in Portage."

"And the Murphy brothers didn't put up a fight?" Pole asked in disbelief. "They just welcomed the union with open arms?"

"Not exactly. It took a few days to educate them. I told 'em if this war keeps up, we'll have more to worry about than just coal and oil shortages. Uncle Sam's been sending so many of our boys to fight, we're soon going to have labor shortages, too. I asked those old Paddies who would mine the coal then."

"Those greedy bastards," Pole muttered under his breath.

"We got ourselves a union!" Mickey cheered, slapping Pole on the back.

"Well, that's something," Pole said, astonished. "The country had to go to war before we could get a union."

"That's the way it works, boys. Supply and demand. Coal companies all over the state are recognizing the UMWA. For once, labor's got the upper hand. The war effort needs us."

"I'll be damned," Pole said.

"So where's your injured man?" asked Davis.

Pole and Mickey shook their heads, looking at the ground.

"Don't you worry. We'll bring him up and make sure he gets a proper burial. His family will receive a death benefit. So will the families of the two Rusyn miners."

"Blazovich and Petras didn't make it," Mickey whispered.

"I'm afraid not, kid. I haven't seen many mine collapses as bad as this one. You're lucky to be alive." Stan Davis gave Mickey a sideways hug. "Let's get you two up to see the sun—maybe moon by now, I guess." He glanced at his wristwatch. "It's late, but there are probably still people waiting at the mine entrance to see you."

"What day is it anyway?" Pole asked. "Wednesday?"

"It's almost Thursday, October 4th. You're going on your sixth day in this mine. Let's get you outta here," the union man said.

"I'm not leavin' without Gus," Mickey said, crossing his arms.

"We'll take care of him. There's a finc funeral parlor in Portage."

"Gus is the mule," Pole explained. "He's been through hell, too. He deserves a happy retirement."

"He's the property of the mine. The owners won't part with him easily," Davis said.

Pole studied Mickey's face. His joy over being rescued was fading. His sole concern was now the welfare of his best friend. "Bring the mule up," Pole ordered the rescuers. "We'll buy him from the goddamned mine if we have to."

"Really, Pole? You mean it?"

"I sure do."

As Mickey followed the rescuers down the tunnel to retrieve Gus along with Hamish's body, Pole put on a carbide headlamp that someone had handed him. He surveyed what was left of Ruthie Tunnel, memorizing its jagged walls and uneven roof. He never wanted to forget what it felt like to be entombed in that space, helpless and waiting desperately for someone to save him. He vowed never to put himself in such a precarious situation again. He would not be returning to Ruthie Tunnel—or any tunnel for that matter. His mining days were over.

As Pole turned to leave the treacherous mine that had taken the lives of Hamish, Blazovich, Petras, and even his own poor excuse for a father, he managed to muster enough spit in his dry mouth to cast a harsh insult onto the tunnel wall. Watching his saliva trickle down the craggy rocks, he cursed the mine one last time. He even threw in a curse against the devil for good measure, thinking that if a beast such as Lucifer existed, he wouldn't be far from that wretched place.

Pole wondered why Lily wasn't at the mine entrance waiting for him. He scanned the crowd of curious onlookers, hoping to see a flash of his sister's red hair. Where was she? Only moments earlier, the throng of hopeful spectators had erupted into deafening cheers at the sight of Pole and Mickey emerging from the mine with the union's rescue team. The well-meaning patch village residents—and even a few elegantly dressed men and women from far flung places—were overjoyed and genuinely relieved that a couple of men had made it out alive.

As Pole was being patted on the back and hugged by several of his neighbors, he caught sight of a suited man approaching him. He wore a bowler hat and wire-rimmed eyeglasses.

"Excuse me, sir," the man said, offering his hand. "I'm a reporter from the *Johnstown Tribune*. How did you survive underground for over five days?"

Pole scrutinized the thin, fragile-looking man, who displayed no sign of ever having completed a day of manual labor in his entire life. Pole did not know why, but he immediately felt contempt for him. In his most serious tone, he replied, "We ate rats and drank our own piss."

The look on the newspaperman's face was one of utter disgust.

Before the man could say anything else, Pole pushed past him. "If you'll excuse me, I'd like to see my family."

Pole walked over to Mickey, who was chatting animatedly

with his mother and two sisters. "Mickey, I'm goin' to head home to find my sister. I'll catch up with you tomorrow. Stan Davis is going to talk to the Murphy brothers about purchasing Gus for you."

"Your sister's not here?" Mickey asked, surprised by the absence of Pole's only family.

"Bridget's terribly ill," Mickey's mother said in her thick Irish brogue. "She has pneumonia. The doctor doesn't expect her to last through the night."

Pole was speechless. Poor Lily had been dealing with crises on two fronts. "Thanks, ma'am. I need to get home."

Pole pressed through the crowd and hobbled down the dried-up muddy road as fast as his stiff legs could carry him. As he approached his meager one-story shack, he saw the flicker of an oil lamp in the bedroom Lily and her mother shared at the back of the house. He burst through the front door, calling after his sister.

"Lily, I'm home! I made it out!"

The house was eerily quiet, its stillness foreboding. Pole stood silently in the middle of the kitchen for almost a minute before deciding to head to the next-door neighbors'. Clearly his sister was not at home. Just as he turned the knob on the front door, he heard a weak voice behind him.

"She's gone, Pole."

He turned around to find Lily standing in the bedroom doorway, her freckled cheeks streaked with tears. Pole ran to her and wrapped her in his arms. He held his sister close as her chest heaved, the sobs racking her body. When she finally calmed down after several minutes, he led her to the kitchen table and poured her a glass of water.

"When did Bridget pass?"

"Just as you entered the house. The minute you came back, God called her home. He would not take her until he returned you to me."

Pole sighed. Lily believed so strongly in God's protective power over her. He was less convinced. He sat down and stroked her curly red hair. "Did you really believe I was comin' back? You knew I wasn't dead?"

"Of course. I would've felt it if your soul had left this world."

Pole tried to maintain a look of neutrality on his face. His sister's faith was a bit unsettling. He worried that she was in danger of becoming delusional. He could not deny that he'd felt an ominous presence in the darkness of the mine. Whether or not it was the devil, he could not say. But Lily's belief that God had intervened and rescued Pole was a stretch too far. The union deserved the credit for that. Pole wished he could talk some sense into his sister, but now was not the appropriate time.

"I'm sorry you had to deal with your mama's illness all by yourself. I wish I'd been here to help you."

"The doctor from Portage stopped by a few times. The neighbors did what they could. In the end, it was God's will."

Pole squeezed his sister's hand. "It's been a rough week. I'm goin' to clean myself up and get something to eat. We'll handle the funeral arrangements in the morning."

"I'll make you something for dinner. I'm so happy you're home."

Pole kissed his sister on the forehead and headed outside to get the washtub. Bridget was gone. He couldn't believe it. It was a tragic loss, for sure, but it changed everything. Pole really was getting a second chance at life, one he had not imagined when the UMWA pulled him out of the mine. The time had finally come for him to get out of the hollow.

# *Thirty-Five*

## JANOS

### BEAVER CREEK, OCTOBER 20, 1917

"What are you reading now?" Janos asked Concetta as he entered her kitchen after locking up the store. It was the third Saturday in a row that she had invited him for tea and sandwiches following the store's closing at one o'clock. Janos usually ate a late lunch at home on Saturdays, but he was enjoying this new routine. In the two weeks since Concetta had joined his family for dinner, she had seemed increasingly eager to share his company.

"*A Room with a View.* It's a lovely book, but it's making me homesick. The story takes place in Italy." Concetta put down the book and smiled sweetly. "I hope you're hungry. I made egg salad sandwiches and squash caponata." She got up from the quarter sawn oak table Janos had always admired and headed toward the refrigerator, going a few steps out of her way to touch him lightly on the shoulder. "Have a seat," she said.

Janos suddenly felt light-headed. He wasn't certain if Concetta's touch was to blame, or if it was her new fragrance. She normally wore a floral scent, but today, she smelled of citrus and moss. The combination was intoxicating. He quickly sat down, hoping she did not notice he was swaying. "Are you wearing a new perfume?'

"Do you like it? It's called *Chypre de Coty*," Concetta said as she placed a plate full of food in front of him. "I'll have your tea ready in a minute. Just a splash of milk, right?"

Janos nodded. He was flattered by the way Concetta had begun taking care of him. She seemed to be noting all his preferences, making him biscotti without almonds and not drowning his tea with too much milk. Their relationship was evolving and becoming more intimate, but Janos had not yet found the courage to reveal what was in his heart. He had come close several times in recent weeks, but could not bring the words to his lips. Living as a bachelor the past seven years had rendered him pitifully unpracticed in matters of the heart. He wondered if he should simply allow things to progress naturally. After all, Concetta was wearing a new perfume. Was he a fool to presume it was for him?

"*Buon appetito*," she said as she handed him his tea and sat down beside him.

"Thank you, Concetta. You're spoiling me, I'm afraid."

"Don't be silly. It's nice to have someone to cook for. Maybe you can stay for dinner sometime next week. I'll make lasagna."

Janos tried to hide his smile as he took a bite of his sandwich. Unseasoned as he was at courtship, he did not miss the subtle signals Concetta was sending him. He suddenly felt emboldened and eager to share his feelings. His stomach a bundle of knots, he forced himself to finish his sandwich while rehearsing a confession in his head.

"Would you like dessert?" she asked after he took his last bite of caponata.

"Can we talk first?" Janos folded his shaking hands in his lap, hoping to hide them from Concetta.

"Is something wrong?"

He shook his head. "Quite the opposite. I need to tell you something . . . " Janos felt warm, wondering if it would be impolite to ask Concetta to open a window.

She leaned forward, her brows furrowed. "What is it?'

"I didn't go to the bank last week to talk about the loan."

"There's no rush." She waved a hand in the air. "I'm not sure I'm ready to move."

"But there's more." Janos took a deep breath before diving off the cliff. He unclasped his trembling hands and placed one on top of Concetta's. Her skin was smooth and cool to the touch. "I didn't go to the bank because . . . I don't want to buy your share of the store."

"You don't?" she whispered.

Janos squeezed her hand. "I don't want you to move to Philadelphia. I care for you." He leaned closer, caressing her cheek. "More and more each day."

Concetta closed her eyes.

"Am I wrong to think you might feel the same?"

She shook her head.

Without thinking, Janos moved his hand slowly from Concetta's cheek to her chin. He traced her lips with his thumb, reveling in their softness. His desire growing, he leaned forward and gently placed his lips upon hers. He lingered there a moment, hoping she would make the next move. He did not have to wait long. Concetta parted her lips and allowed herself to be swept up in the moment.

Janos could not say how long the kiss lasted. Time seemed to have stopped. It was Concetta who finally pulled away, her face flushed.

"I should probably get dessert," she said, looking away.

"I'm sorry," Janos said. "That was too much too soon, wasn't it?"

"I don't know." She brushed a few strands of hair away from her face. "Maybe."

Janos shook his head. "I'm so ashamed. I've taken advantage of you and our friendship. It will never happen again." He stood up to leave.

Concetta grabbed his arm. "Wait. That's not what I meant. Stay."

He sat down, a bead of sweat dripping from his temple.

"I do care for you, Janos," she said, squaring her shoulders. "But you have to understand . . . until a moment ago, the only man I'd ever kissed was Antonio. I feel so guilty and yet . . ."

He leaned forward, gripping the seat of his chair.

"Strangely excited."

Janos exhaled. "That's good, isn't it?"

She smiled and nodded.

"I understand your hesitation. I haven't had a woman in my life since my wife—" Janos cut himself off. "I don't know the rules of courtship for people our age. I'm not even sure I care to. I only know that the sun shines a little brighter the instant you walk into the room."

Concetta blushed.

Janos reached for her hand. "We don't have to figure this out today."

"Of course not," she said, shaking her head. "But you'll stay for dessert—and maybe try my lasagna next week."

"Absolutely." Janos immediately wondered if he sounded too eager. No matter. A man his age had no time to be coy about his affections. He had never expected another chance at love at the age of forty. He was giddy with the possibilities. And while he knew Concetta was reserved and needed their relationship to evolve slowly, Janos had reason to hope she would eventually want the future he envisioned for them.

# Thirty-Six

## LUKAS

### JOHNSTOWN, OCTOBER 27, 1917

"What do you wanna do now?" Frankie asked Lukas as he shoved another hot dog into his mouth. "We can go to the football game at the high school, or we can see a film at the nickelodeon."

Lukas could barely understand what his friend was saying. Frankie had eaten three hot dogs in the last five minutes, but that hadn't stopped his constant babbling. Ketchup was running down his chin, chunks of food were flying out of his mouth. Lukas wondered what Mrs. Spencer would think, her eldest son displaying such a lack of manners and good breeding in public. He smiled to himself as he imagined the look on the snobby woman's face at seeing her son behave like a common street urchin.

"What's with you today, Frankie? You're eating like a horse."

"No idea. I've been like this all week," he said, wiping his mouth with his shirtsleeve. "Can we stop by the five-and-dime? I could go for a few chocolate bars. Maybe some Necco wafers."

"Halloween is in a few days. You'll be able to steal plenty of candy from the local school kids," Lukas said with a laugh.

"That's not a bad idea. We need to come up with some new pranks to pull this year, too. Greasing doorknobs and knocking over trash cans is getting old. You know, someone once rang our doorbell and threw flour in our butler's face. Maybe we should try that."

Lukas frowned at his friend. "You're going to end up in jail, and your mother will kill you. Forget the pranks. Let's go to the five-and-dime for candy. We can see a film afterward." Lukas hoped he hadn't sounded too pushy, but he wanted to steer Frankie away from the football game. He was not up for the two-mile walk from downtown Johnstown to the local high school's football field. His prosthetic leg had been bothering him all morning. The leather straps were rubbing against his skin more than usual, causing an itchy rash. All he could think about was sitting down.

As they entered the store, Frankie quickly forgot about his craving for candy. Sitting at the lunch counter were three young boys on shiny, red stools with stainless steel bowls of ice cream in front of them. Frankie pulled Lukas toward the lunch counter.

"This sundae is delicious," Frankie said minutes later as he stared at his half-eaten dessert. "But I can't finish it." He put down his spoon and burped loudly.

"Don't make yourself sick." Lukas snatched Frankie's bowl and plunged his spoon into the gooey mixture. "Guess I'll have to finish it for you." He groaned.

"Come on, Kovac! Don't act like you're doing me such a grand favor. I saw you eyeing my sundae as soon as you finished yours. You're as much a pig as I am—you just prefer sweets."

"Well, I'd never eat three hot dogs. You're going to be burping all day, and we'll never meet any girls. They'll be running in the opposite direction once they get a whiff of your dog breath."

"Lukas? Lukas Kovac?"

Someone was tapping Lukas on the shoulder. He turned around to find a large, muscular man staring down at him. He wore the simple clothes of a laborer—brown pants and a blue work shirt. Lukas would have felt threatened by the brawny man if not for his kind face. For some reason, his green eyes looked hauntingly familiar.

"Do I know you?" Lukas asked hesitantly.

"I think you might. Are you Lukas Kovac from Riverton, Pennsylvania? Sofie's younger brother?"

"I am. But I haven't lived in Riverton for years." Lukas studied the man's face. He looked so familiar. His mind worked quickly to connect the dots—to tie the face of this grown man to Riverton and his sister, Sofie. And then, suddenly, he knew. "Oh my God! Pole Stofanik?"

The man grinned from ear to ear as he grabbed Lukas's hand and shook it vigorously.

"What the hell happened to you, Pole? You're enormous! And what are you doing in Johnstown?"

"I could ask the same of you. You've grown up quite a bit, too. How old are you now, Lukas?"

"Fifteen."

"What are you doin' so far from Riverton? Is Sofie here?"

Lukas noticed the way Pole's eyes lit up when he'd said his sister's name. "No. My family lives north of Pittsburgh now. I'm a student at Westmont Academy."

Pole looked confused. He didn't appear to recognize the name of Lukas's school.

"It's a boarding school at the top of the hill. You have to take the incline to get there."

"You go to a boarding school?"

"Yeah, I do." Lukas instantly realized how bizarre his transformation must appear to Pole, who hadn't seen him since he was a boy in a gritty steel town six—maybe seven—years earlier. Judging by his appearance, Lukas guessed Pole's circumstances hadn't changed much. His dirty, callused hands and sturdy arms indicated he performed manual work of some kind.

"Pole, I found a really nice pair of shoes. Can I get them?" A pretty redhead with bright blue eyes approached Pole, carrying a pair of black dress shoes.

"Who's that?" Lukas wanted to know.

"This is my sister, Lily," Pole said, smiling.

Lukas faintly remembered that Pole had a sister. What was the story? He knew Pole had left Riverton around the time of his accident—the same time his mother had disappeared. Lukas winced at the thought. He couldn't think about that time in his life. Revisiting the past was something he rarely allowed himself to do.

"It's nice to meet you, Lily. My name is Lukas. I'm an old friend of your brother's. And this is my friend Frankie," he said as he motioned to the dumb-founded person sitting next to him. Lukas had completely forgotten he was there.

"It's a pleasure to meet you both," the girl said nervously.

"Lily, take those shoes up to the counter and then come back for some ice cream," Pole said. "Maybe Frankie can tell you all about Johnstown while I catch up with Lukas."

When Lily had finally settled in at the counter next to Frankie with a hot fudge sundae, Pole sat down next to Lukas. He patted him playfully on the back. "I can't believe I'm sittin' next to you. I never thought I'd see you again. How's your family? How's Sofie?"

"She's fine. She's a senior in high school. She wants to work for the local newspaper after she graduates next spring."

"Really?"

"She's going to be a writer. She already writes for the *Beaver Creek Dispatch.*"

"Is that the name of the town where you live?"

"Yeah. Beaver Creek. It's about forty miles northeast of Pittsburgh. On the Allegheny River."

Pole nodded. "And how are your parents and your aunt?"

"My father is part-owner of a grocery store, and my aunt takes care of a few boarders. Our house in Beaver Creek is much bigger than the one we had in Riverton."

"And your mother?"

Lukas hesitated. Whenever people asked about his mother, they immediately regretted it. Revealing that his mother had mysteriously disappeared always led to the same reaction. Shock was usually followed by an awkward silence, a curt apology, and a rush to change the subject. Lukas wondered how Pole would react to the news. He was the only person he'd encountered in years who had actually known his mother.

"She disappeared in June of 1910. The same day this happened." Lukas lifted up his right pant leg and waited for a reaction.

Pole was speechless for almost a minute. He then stroked his chin as if trying to work out a riddle. Finally, he spoke. "Christ, Lukas. If I didn't have my sister with me, I'd take you out for a beer. And I thought I'd had my share of misery."

"What happened to you?" Lukas leaned closer.

"I lost my pop in a mining accident that same summer. I've been stuck mining coal in a patch village outside Portage for the past seven years. With my pop dead, I had to provide for my sister and her mother."

"You've been mining coal? That's miserable work from what I hear," Lukas said. "No wonder you look the way you do."

"And how's that?" Pole narrowed his eyes.

"Tough. You look like the last person I'd want to mess with. I mean that as a compliment." Lukas was suddenly nervous. He hoped he hadn't offended Pole.

"Well, I'm done with mining. There was an accident earlier this month—I can't go underground ever again. Me and my sister are catchin' a train for Pittsburgh in an hour. We're leaving these mountains." Pole leaned into Lukas's ear and whispered, "Lily's mother died recently. We're starting over somewhere new."

"Where?"

"I'm not sure. Crazy thing is . . . I was thinking about heading back to Riverton to see if I could track down your sister. I owe her an apology."

"What for?"

"It's a long story." Pole leaned forward to look down the counter at his sister. Seeing she was chatting happily with Frankie, he continued, "You gonna tell me about your leg? And what you're doin' in boarding school? I know your father values education, but how can he afford it?"

Lukas shook his head. "Long story. Go to Beaver Creek to see Sofie, and she'll tell you everything. Just don't ask her about our mother."

"What the hell happened, Lukas? Do you have any idea?"

Lukas had plenty of theories, all of which were too awful and embarrassing to share. He had never even discussed Mama's disappearance with Sofie. Over the years, they had formed an unspoken agreement to continue pretending that their mother had been the victim of a terrible crime. Or a tragic accident. Whatever the reason for Mama's departure, Lukas was sure he'd never find out. He simply plodded on, choosing to forget his painful past and focus instead on the bright future his expensive education would afford him. Except that he would forever have to deal with the irritating reminder of his mother's betrayal attached to his lower right leg.

"I don't know. We haven't seen or heard from her in years. She disappeared the same day that mill manager, Henry Archer, was murdered. My mother was his housekeeper. You remember? The police think his murder and her disappearance are connected."

Pole stared at Lukas. "In what way?"

"They never figured it out. The case is still open." Lukas shrugged and tried to cast off the dark cloud now hovering over him. "How's that sundae, Lily? I hear you've got a long train ride ahead of you. We should head over to the candy aisle and get you some supplies for the trip."

"I'm real glad I ran into you," Pole said as he stood up and slapped Lukas on the back. "I never woulda guessed I'd see you in Johnstown of all places. You think Sofie won't mind seein' me again? You don't think it will be strange?"

Lukas stood up. His eyes were even with Pole's chest. He looked up at the face of his childhood friend, trying to figure out how the teenage boy who had fished and swum with him in the Monongahela River had turned into such an imposing man. Lukas wondered what Sofie would think of him. "She'll be happy to see you. Once you tell her who you are."

"You don't think she'll recognize me? Have I changed that much?"

"Have you looked in the mirror lately?"

"Aren't you a smart ass?" Pole punched Lukas lightly in the chest. "I'm glad that fancy boarding school hasn't ruined your sense of humor. You seem pretty normal, Lukas."

The irony of Pole's statement was not lost on him. All Lukas ever did was try to appear normal to everyone—at school, in Beaver Creek, and in Aunt Edith's Shadyside neighborhood. Unfortunately, he felt that his efforts always fell short. He suddenly wondered if he was being too hard on himself.

"Looks can be deceiving," Frankie chimed in. "I share a room with this kid, and I think he's a bit of a nut. But that's just me." He grinned.

"Shut up, bonehead." Lukas glared at Frankie.

"Lily, we need to be goin' soon if we want to catch that train. Grab a couple chocolate bars and meet me at the register," Pole said.

The pretty redhead got up and waved to Lukas and Frankie. "It was nice meeting you." She skipped off in the direction of the candy aisle.

"All right, Lukas. I guess I'm heading to Beaver Creek to see your sister. You got an address for me?"

"5 Dogwood Avenue. The house is a modest Victorian."

Pole raised an eyebrow. "Okay. I'll try to remember that." He shrugged.

"I told you Lukas is a nut." Frankie laughed. "He's obsessed with architecture."

"Nothin' wrong with that. There are worse things he could be into." Pole smiled warmly at Lukas. "Take care of yourself. Maybe we'll see each other again in Beaver Creek." He extended his hand.

Lukas shook the large, coal-stained hand and looked up at Pole. "I'd like that. I really would."

As Lukas watched Pole turn away from him and head toward the register, he shook his head. He hadn't thought of Pole Stofanik in years. He was a remnant of his former life, the one in which he'd been a carefree kid roaming the streets of a mill town. Lukas's days had been spent causing mischief at school and around the neighborhood or following his sister and her friends to the river. He'd been pretty happy—at least he thought he had—until the day his mother left and caused his horrific accident. Since that fateful day, Lukas's view of Riverton had soured. He now saw everything and everyone associated with that place through a dark lens. But to his surprise, he hadn't felt sad or uncomfortable at seeing Pole. He actually hoped their paths would cross again.

## *Thirty-Seven*

### JANOS

#### BEAVER CREEK, NOVEMBER 11, 1917

Janos groaned as he rose to his feet, screwdriver in hand. He had spent much of his afternoon serving as his sister's handyman and was growing irritated. He had just finished repairing the parlor door, and now Anna was ordering him to tighten the knob on the basement door as well. "You know it's Sunday, don't you?" he said, entering the kitchen. "We can do this another day."

"When? You're always at the store. I would've asked yesterday, but you came home late. Where were you?" Anna asked, smirking.

"Why ask if you already know the answer?" Janos glared at his sister.

She shrugged. "So things are going well between you and Concetta?"

Janos turned away from Anna and knelt down in front of the basement door, hoping to hide his boyish grin. Why was he so embarrassed by his feelings for Concetta? Sooner or later, he would have to make his affections for her public. But it was probably wise to wait until she had fully committed herself to him.

Over the past three weeks, their courtship had progressed, albeit at a slow pace. They'd continued their Saturday lunches together and enjoyed two candlelit dinners. Concetta made no more mention of moving to Philadelphia, but Janos was disappointed that she still hadn't broached the topic of their future together either. Apparently, marriage was not always the foremost thought in a woman's mind, as he'd been led to believe. Concetta seemed perfectly content sharing meals with him and ending the evening with an innocent kiss.

Most of the time, she offered him her cheek. But whenever she'd had a glass or two of wine, she was less restrained and allowed herself to enjoy more passionate advances. During a particularly sensual kiss a few days earlier, Janos had let his hand wander to her bottom. He'd been pleasantly surprised when she did not remove it.

"Janos? You going to answer me?"

He turned around abruptly, sighing. "If I do, will you leave me alone the rest of the afternoon?"

Anna nodded emphatically.

As Janos considered which details he might share with his sister, he heard a forceful knock on the front door. "I'll get it," he said, springing to his feet and bolting down the hall. He was grateful for their visitor's impeccable timing.

Smiling, Janos opened the front door. He gasped as his screwdriver dropped to the floor with a loud thud. His knees buckled.

Anna was instantly at his side, steadying him and pulling him backward. She gave him a reassuring look before addressing the threesome on the porch. "Father Figlar. Sister Agnes. What is this?"

His stomach threatening to unleash its contents, Janos studied the woman propped up between the priest and the nun from Riverton. Her once beautiful blonde hair was frizzy and streaked with gray, her once creamy porcelain complexion deeply lined and sagging. Dressed in a long, black overcoat, she stared blankly at the floorboards.

"Janos. Anna. We're so sorry to show up like this, unannounced. Can we come in?" asked Father Figlar.

"I will not have that woman in my house," Anna hissed.

Completely dumbfounded, Janos stared at the gaunt figure on his front porch. He could not muster a single syllable. An earthquake had struck—the concussion so great, he could not get his bearings or see clearly. He suddenly felt unsteady, swaying back and forth on wobbly legs. The ground was moving beneath his feet. He grasped the door frame for support.

"I got lost on my way home," the woman mumbled in Slovak.

"It's okay, Karina." Sister Agnes patted her back. "You're home now. We've brought you home."

Janos snapped out of his stupor. Words began to flow furiously from his lips. "This is not her home!" he shouted ferociously. "She abandoned her family seven years ago. Get her out of my sight!"

"I'm so sorry, Janos. The situation breaks my heart. I know you and your children have endured unthinkable hardships. But we really must talk," Father Figlar said.

"There's nothing to be said." Anna stepped forward. "If she needs a roof over her head, the church can see to that. Let the nuns have her. Maybe there's still time to save her soul."

"I'm afraid the situation is more complicated than it appears." Father Figlar opened the long overcoat Karina wore, revealing a swollen belly.

"Dear God," Anna said breathlessly.

Janos swallowed the bitter bile in his throat. He clutched his chest as a sharp pain pierced his heart. Rage coursed through his veins, blurring his vision.

"Get that whore away from this house!" Anna shouted as she grabbed her brother and slammed the door closed with her foot. She led him into the dining room where she helped him into a chair and poured him a glass of whiskey.

Janos took two large swigs, grateful for the burning sensation of the liquor in his throat. It temporarily distracted him from the swirling chaos in his mind.

"Are you all right? You were clutching your chest. Should I call the doctor?"

"No, no." He shook his head violently. "Another whiskey." He held up his empty glass.

Anna did as she was told.

Janos took the second glass of whiskey from his sister and downed it in one gulp. He was disoriented and dizzy, but somehow the liquor slowed the spinning room. Anna suddenly came into focus. Her face was ashen.

"Janos . . . I'm so sorry." Tears streamed down her face.

"What do you have to be sorry for? I'm the idiot who married that woman."

Anna took Janos's hand in hers and joined him at the table. She sat quietly, waiting for him to continue.

Janos glanced at his sister, but couldn't think of anything to say. He could only focus on the unsettling image of Karina standing on his front porch. He'd barely recognized her. His once stunning wife was merely a shadow of her former self. She had aged terribly, the deep lines on her face looking more like twenty years' worth instead of seven. What had happened to her?

"Look at me. Please look at me." Anna was shaking him.

"Huh?"

"What are we going to do? We need to talk about this."

"We're not going to do anything. The church can take care of Karina and her baby. She's no longer my responsibility."

"But the child . . ." Anna hesitated. "That baby is the brother or sister of Sofie and Lukas. Does that mean nothing to you?"

Janos grabbed the bottle of whiskey and refilled his glass. He took a sip and then slammed the glass down hard on the table, staining the linens with streaks of amber. Unhappy with the effect of that maneuver, he picked up the glass and threw it against the wall. It shattered into a hundred pieces. That was the release he'd been looking for. Satisfied, he got up from the table and headed for the back door. "I'm the father of Sofie and Lukas. That meant nothing to her," Janos said over his shoulder.

"Where are you going?"

"I don't know."

"Sofie will be back soon. What should I tell her?" Anna asked.

"Nothing—absolutely nothing. Do you understand me?" he snapped.

Anna nodded slowly, fear creeping across her face.

As Janos slammed the door, he felt a twinge of guilt in the midst of his fury. He had never before used a threatening tone with his sister. Goddamn Karina! She was wrecking their lives once again.

# *Thirty-Eight*

## EDITH

### SHADYSIDE, NOVEMBER 11, 1917

Edith stared at the leather-bound calendar in her lap and then turned her gaze back to the mound of mugwort and pennyroyal leaves resting on the side table beside her floral Meissen teacup. It had been almost six weeks since the start of her last monthly flow—forty days to be exact. If she were pregnant, surely she would have had some symptoms by now. Dizziness. Nausea. A headache, perhaps. She would welcome any of those ailments. She pinched a pennyroyal leaf between her thumb and forefinger, wondering whether it was too soon to provoke the flowers again.

"What are you doing, darling?" James looked up from the Confederate soldier's diary he'd been engrossed in the entire afternoon. "You've been staring at that calendar and clump of leaves for almost twenty minutes."

"Has it really been that long?"

James glanced at the rosewood clock on the mantel, a treasure Edith had discovered in an antique store in London. "I suspect it has. What's troubling you?"

Edith sighed. She was growing tired of discussing her

feminine afflictions with her husband. It was demoralizing. But who else would care as much about her innumerable anxieties concerning motherhood? Her cousin Clara had grown exhausted with her constant obsessing years ago and had requested that Edith no longer broach the subject. Poor Clara had suffered several miscarriages of her own and could not bear to hear of her younger cousin's heartbreak. The memories were too painful, she had complained.

Edith studied her husband's concerned face, his sympathetic eyes urging her to allow her confession to flow freely. "I am so conflicted. It's been almost six weeks since my last menses, and I do not feel pregnant. And we were intimate at least a dozen times or more."

"More." James interrupted her, a smirk on his face.

"I can't decide whether to provoke the flowers again or wait a while longer." Edith shook her head fiercely. "The last time I let nature take its course, I didn't have a monthly flow for over six months. How can I get pregnant without one?" She looked down at the calendar in her lap, balling her fists. "I'm almost thirty. Time is running out."

James was instantly out of his armchair and on the velvet sofa beside her, holding her clenched hands in his own. "Calm down, Edith. You need to relax." He looked over at the mound of leaves and frowned. "Those herbs are giving you false hope. You have no proof they induced your last menses. It could have been a coincidence."

Edith wanted to cover her ears, but her husband was holding her hands too tightly. He sounded too skeptical, too rational. Maybe she was a fool for hitching her hopes to those herbs, but she had to place her faith in something. God had certainly not answered her prayers.

James stood up and scooped the mound of leaves into his hand. He strode over to the fireplace and threw them into the flames.

Edith gasped.

"No more herbs, darling. I can't watch you torture yourself any longer." He sat back down on the sofa and held Edith's face in his hands. He kissed her softly on the lips, his mouth lingering on hers for almost a minute. When he pulled away, his eyes were damp.

"I'm taking the spring semester off," he announced. "You and I are heading west."

"What?" Edith wondered if she had inadvertently driven her husband mad with her wild obsessions.

"You need to get out of this house and explore the world. I would suggest Europe, if not for that godforsaken war. California will have to do. Perhaps Wyoming as well. I hear Yellowstone is a fascinating place to visit."

Edith perked up her ears. It had been years since she'd traveled further than New York City or Newport, Rhode Island. Her husband had piqued her curiosity.

"For how long?"

"As long as we want. I can take a leave from the university and start work on another book."

"But what about Lukas? He wants to live with us next summer," Edith protested.

"He can join us in California at the end of the school year. He should see more of the world, too. He can even bring his sister along."

Edith felt a smile creep across her face. James's idea was so exciting. "But what about having a baby?" she whispered.

James squeezed her hand. "It's time to let it go. Time to stop focusing on what you don't have." He leaned back on the sofa, pointing to his chest. "Remember what's already yours."

Edith winced as a sharp pang of guilt pierced her heart. Perhaps she had been spending too much time obsessing over what was missing in her life and had neglected to cherish the blessings right in front of her. She studied James's kind face, his adoring eyes. He would do anything to make her happy. She suddenly realized that her fixation with having a baby was likely making him unhappy. Maybe he had even begun to wonder why he wasn't enough for her. The thought made Edith shudder.

She quickly crawled onto her husband's lap and leaned into his face. "I love you, James. I would follow you to the ends of the earth. A trip to the wild west is exactly what we need." Edith pressed her lips against her husband's, smiling when she felt him squeeze her breast. He was suddenly tugging at her blouse, his tongue exploring her mouth. She didn't care if the servants walked in. They could whisper about her scandalous behavior all they wanted. Edith exhaled deeply, surrendering herself to the moment, allowing James to pull down her knickers. He was going to make love to her on the parlor room sofa in full view of the window overlooking the front lawn, and she did not care who bore witness to the event. She found the idea thrilling. Her preoccupation with her fruitless womb quickly faded away.

## *Thirty-Nine*

# JANOS

### BEAVER CREEK, NOVEMBER 11, 1917

Janos picked up a small, round stone and skipped it across the surface of the river. He had no idea how long he'd been staring at the water. Time seemed to have stopped completely. He was grateful that his head had begun to clear and his heart rate had slowed. He was probably no longer in danger of a heart attack, but he desperately wished he'd brought the bottle of whiskey with him. Getting drunk and passing out on the banks of the river seemed like a good alternative to facing reality.

Janos still could not believe what had happened that afternoon. It was a nightmare come to life. Only he'd never imagined such a situation in his wildest dreams. His deceitful wife had traded her loving husband and beautiful children for a life of lechery. It was impossible to comprehend. Janos shuddered as he imagined the kind of man who could have fathered the child Karina was carrying. What on Earth had she become? How had she fallen so far?

He shook his head and skipped another stone. Was it possible to simply send Karina away and let the church care for her and the baby? Janos would do anything to spare his children the grief of seeing their mother again—especially in her current state. But could he live out the rest of his days in peace, knowing that he'd deprived Sofie and Lukas the opportunity to know their little brother or sister?

Janos thought of his children. He was so proud of who they had become. Despite all that they'd endured, they had grown up to be kind and compassionate people, always sympathetic to the sufferings of those around them. Perhaps their life experiences had given them insight that luckier children—those with stable mothers—lacked. But even without those tumultuous experiences, Sofie and Lukas had always been reflective people. They were always asking questions, trying to understand the world around them. They were incredibly perceptive, seeing things that people twice their age could not.

Janos suddenly wondered if he deserved all the credit for who his children had become. Weren't they half of Karina? She had always been insightful, often seeing the world in ways he could not. She spotted injustices to which he was blind and had a knack for identifying people with dishonorable intentions. She had been the only member of St. Michael's congregation who suspected the butcher's wife was lifting coins out of the collection basket.

It dawned on Janos that perhaps his children had inherited some of Karina's traits, but what they got were better versions of them. Despite her many failings, she had miraculously produced two amazing children.

Karina, the source of his life's greatest miseries, was, remarkably, the source of his greatest joys.

Janos laid his head on the ground, overwhelmed by the revelation. Karina had given him the gift of Sofie and Lukas. What if her baby had the same potential as its siblings? Janos sighed. He was so furious with Karina that he could barely see straight, but he was not the kind of man who would allow his anger to prevent him from doing the right thing. He would not hide the existence of Karina's baby from Sofie and Lukas.

He just needed to figure out a way to tell them. Luckily, Lukas was away at school in Johnstown and wouldn't be back until the holidays. But Sofie? She would be home at any minute. How would she react to her mother's latest betrayal? Janos looked up and searched the cloudless sky. Was he a fool to hope an answer might fall from the heavens? He closed his eyes and prayed.

# *Forty*

## SOFIE

### BEAVER CREEK, NOVEMBER 11, 1917

Sofie peered through the barren trees, focusing on the gray-haired man lying on his back at the edge of the river fifty yards ahead of her. The man looked like her father, but she could not imagine what he would be doing near the river without a fishing pole.

As she neared the sleeping figure, she could see that it was, in fact, Papa. She put down her stringer of fish and left the dirt path, climbing down over the steep bank. Not wanting to startle him, she whispered, "Papa? Papa, wake up." She tapped him lightly on the shoulder.

He jumped up, his eyes open wide. "Sofie! You scared me."

"I'm sorry. Were you looking for me?"

"No, sweetheart. I just went for a walk and needed to rest."

"Are you feeling all right? You look pale."

Papa shook his head as he picked up a stone and cast it into the river. His forehead was creased with worry. "Something happened today." He reached for Sofie's hand and squeezed it. "Please sit. I have some upsetting news."

A chill went through her as she fell to the grass, her knees suddenly weak. Papa's face rarely looked so contorted. The last time he appeared as forlorn was the night of Lukas's accident. Sofie's hand flew to her mouth. "Is Lukas all right?"

"He's fine," Papa said, nodding, running his fingers through his hair. "I fear I'm making this harder." He scraped the heel of his shoe across the stones at the water's edge, trying to remove a clump of mud from it. He finally turned to Sofie after a minute of silence. "*Zlatíčko* . . . your mother came to the house this afternoon."

Sofie stopped breathing.

"Actually, to be precise, Father Figlar and Sister Agnes brought her. She is in poor health. I hardly recognized her."

"What . . . who?" Sofie stammered. She shoved a finger into her right ear, hoping to remove whatever was clogging it. Surely she had misheard her father.

"Your mother needs our help."

There it was again. Papa had said "mother." She hadn't heard wrong. Sofie sprang to her feet, her body rife with adrenaline. "After what she did? She left us! She caused Lukas's accident!" Sofie's rage exploded in one furious breath. "We owe her nothing," she said, shaking her head violently.

"That was my initial reaction, too. But there's more to the story."

"I don't want to hear it." She covered her ears and began to pace. "I don't care. I don't care where she's been or how poor her health is. We talked about this only a few weeks ago . . . we're better off without her." Sofie froze and glared at her father. "I assume you sent her away."

"Your aunt did. She slammed the door in the priest's face."

"Good." Sofie nodded her head so forcefully that a pain shot through the back of her neck. "Well, if that's all, I'm going home to clean my fish." She started up the bank.

Janos leapt to his feet and grabbed his daughter by the arm. "Wait," he pleaded. "You need to hear the rest of the story."

Jerking away, Sofie announced, "I will not hear it. I'm done with that woman." She sprinted up the hill and onto the path. "I thought you were, too," she called over her shoulder.

"She's pregnant!" Papa shouted.

Sofie stopped dead in her tracks. She turned around and looked down over the bank at her father, who was standing with one foot in the river. He had lost his bearings, unaware that his shoe was submerged in the murky water.

"I told you there was more." Papa's arms hung limply at his sides, like earthworms used one too many times for bait. "She's carrying your little brother or sister."

Sofie dropped to her knees on the dirt path. "Why, Papa?" she wailed. "Why can't we just be rid of her?" She buried her face in her skirt and tugged at her hair. She suddenly wanted to rip it all out. "How could she show up with another man's baby? How?" she screamed into her lap.

"I know, sweetheart. It's not fair." Papa was at her side, rubbing her back.

Sofie wept into her skirt, clenching her fists into balls. Her fingernails dug deep into her palms, the throbbing sensation temporarily distracting her from the pain in her chest. As her middle finger pierced the flesh of her right palm, she became vaguely aware of her father's breath against her ear.

"How can I help?"

Sofie looked up through watery eyes. Papa's face was drawn.

"Would you like some time alone?"

She nodded. A hot tear escaped down her cheek.

"It took me a while to calm down. I threw a glass of whiskey at the dining room wall before I stormed out of the house. I ruined your aunt's favorite wallpaper."

"You destroyed her blue butterflies?" Sofie whispered.

"I think so," Papa said, lowering his head. "Take some time to cool off. Skip a few stones into the river. We'll talk more after dinner."

Sofie shifted onto her bottom. As she watched her father walk slowly toward town, she could see the weight of the world on his shoulders. His normally tall, erect frame looked decidedly bent. She cursed her poor excuse for a mother.

Sofie tiptoed across the wooden train bridge, her pockets packed with stones of various shapes and sizes. She planned to launch them into the river and watch them sink helplessly to the bottom. She was hoping that small act of defiance might lessen her fury. However, once she reached the middle of the timber structure, fifty yards from either side of the riverbank, she questioned her judgment.

It had been six weeks since she'd visited the bridge with Marie and the boys from the dance, and the water level had dropped dramatically. There had been heavy rains in the days before her last visit, so the river had been unusually high. But now, with only trace amounts of rain throughout the months of October and early November, the river had become shockingly low. The large, jagged rocks in the riverbed had been revealed, making Sofie uneasy. She wondered how many feet she stood above the river. Sixty? Seventy? She had no idea. She only knew that a fall from the bridge would kill her for sure. She wished there was a railing she could grasp for support.

Sofie eased herself onto the deck of the bridge and allowed her feet to dangle over the side. Gripping the railroad tie on which she was sitting, she peered down at the rocks and the water swirling around them. She swallowed hard as her knees quivered. What had happened to her? She'd never been this fearful of heights. Maybe the trauma of her mother's return had rattled her more than she'd realized.

Before her encounter with her father, Sofie had been in an exceptional mood, feeling satisfied with the day's catch. She'd been eager to get home and help Aunt Anna fry all those fish. She never could have predicted the upheaval awaiting her. Papa's news had shaken her to her core and turned her world upside down. Sofie was disoriented and could no longer find the horizon.

She gritted her teeth as she imagined seeing her mother again. Why had she returned after all these years? Did she really expect her family to forgive her and help her care for another man's baby? Why should they take responsibility for a stranger's bastard?

Trembling, Sofie pulled a stone out of her pocket and hurled it into the river. It fell into the water with a soft *plop*. She cursed and reached into her pocket for a bigger one. This time she flung it toward a group of boulders near the base of one of the bridge's pillars. The stone split into several pieces with a loud *crack*. Still not satisfied, Sofie emptied all the stones from her pockets, launching two at a time against the boulders, each throw more violent than the last.

By the time she was done, Sofie was sweaty and breathing hard. She wiped her face with her forearm and was stunned to find that it was wet. Had she been crying? She hadn't noticed in the middle of her fury. Sofie had never been so angry—not even after the realization all those years ago that her mother had abandoned her family on purpose. And now that wretched woman was back after seven long years, pregnant with another man's baby and expecting help from her husband and children. It was even more infuriating.

Sofie screamed so loud, her throat burned.

There was no way she could ever forgive the woman who had once been her mother. Karina was a selfish, despicable person who deserved no mercy—pregnant or not. And there was no way Sofie would ever want anything to do with her child. She owed as much to that baby as she owed the German Kaiser. She spat into the river. Whatever her father decided to do about Karina and her baby, she would not be a part of it.

## *Forty-One*

## JANOS

### BEAVER CREEK, NOVEMBER 11, 1917

Janos watched Sofie carry her dinner plate into the kitchen where their boarders, Vilium and Marek, were fighting over a piece of pumpkin pie. Sofie had barely eaten anything and hadn't spoken more than a few words at dinner.

"Is she all right?" Anna whispered.

"I don't think so," Janos said. "She's going to need more than a few hours to digest this afternoon's news."

"You seem much calmer now. I'm relieved."

"I'm no less enraged. But I'm putting my anger aside for the sake of that baby."

"What are you going to do? Do you think Father Figlar and Sister Agnes are still in town? Will you try to find them?" Anna asked.

"If I know Father Figlar, he'll stop by again this evening. He doesn't give up easily. I think we should sit and wait." Janos looked down at his own dinner plate. He'd eaten only slightly more than his daughter. He got up from the table and reached for his sister's plate, catching a glimpse of the soggy paper on the wall. "I'll take this into the kitchen, Anna. It's the least I can do for destroying your pretty wall and raising my voice. I'm so sorry."

"Don't worry about it. I actually think you handled the situation quite well. A lesser man would have strangled that woman."

Janos forced a weak smile as he trudged into the kitchen to put the plates beside the sink. Vilium and Marek had disappeared, and Sofie was washing dishes. "Do you feel like talking yet?"

"There's nothing to talk about. I won't have anything to do with Karina or her baby. It's as simple as that," Sofie said defiantly.

Janos was struck by his daughter's tone—and her use of the name "Karina." It was disrespectful for her to refer to her mother by her first name, but he did not reprimand Sofie. Instead, he kissed her on the forehead. "It's possible that Father Figlar may come by again this evening to discuss your mother. I don't know if he'll bring her along, but I wanted to warn you. Would you like to see her?"

"Absolutely not. I'll go upstairs for the rest of the evening as soon as I finish the dishes."

Janos's eyes welled with tears. His poor little girl was suffering once again at the hands of her mother. Their past had somehow caught up to them. Suddenly, he heard a loud knock at the door. "That's probably Father Figlar. You can go, Sofie. We'll worry about the dishes later."

She hurried down the hall and up the stairs as Janos approached the front door. Anna peeked out of the dining room.

"Where's Sofie going?"

"She doesn't want to see her mother."

"I can't blame her." Anna stepped into the hall and stood beside her brother. "Would you like me to get the door?"

Janos shook his head as he stepped toward the front door and opened it. He found exactly what he had been expecting.

For the second time that day, Father Figlar and Sister Agnes stood on his front porch with a weary-looking Karina propped up between them.

"Can we talk?" Father Figlar asked in a low voice.

Janos nodded solemnly as he led the threesome into the parlor. He lowered himself into his favorite chair, watching the priest and nun help Karina onto the sofa. She leaned heavily against Sister Agnes, her eyes closed. "What's wrong with her?" he asked. "Why is she so listless?"

"She's in poor health. She was found wandering your old neighborhood a few nights ago. We have no idea when she arrived in Riverton—only that she was looking for you," Father Figlar said.

"Karina is rather incoherent. Much of what she's said has been confusing. But she believes the baby she's carrying is yours," Sister Agnes said dryly.

Janos could not stifle his snigger. "That would be a miracle, wouldn't it? I haven't seen my wife in over seven years. An immaculate conception, I guess."

"You must find a way to manage your anger, Mr. Kovac," Sister Agnes reprimanded him.

Janos wasn't sure whom he wanted to harm more—his lecherous wife or the sanctimonious nun who had brought her into his peaceful home. He had no idea how to approach the situation without losing composure. He could feel the years of pent-up anger returning, threatening to corrupt his good judgement. He inhaled deeply.

"His anger is valid, Sister Agnes," Father Figlar interrupted the nun. "Obviously, the situation is unpleasant, if not scandalous. But I hoped that as a Christian—and one of the most honorable men I've ever met—you'd be able to care for Karina until the baby is born."

"Why can't the church take care of her?" Anna snapped. "Surely one of the local convents can nurse her back to health."

She scowled at the three intruders on her sofa. "Where's the baby's father?"

"We don't know," the nun said sadly. "We found a ticket stub in Karina's pocket. She boarded a train from Philadelphia last week. That's all she had on her besides a few coins. She didn't even have a suitcase."

"She hasn't been able to tell us much. She's confused. Her ramblings have mostly been about you, Janos, but she did mention someone else," Father Figlar said. "Unfortunately, she grows agitated when we try to press her for more information."

"Who?" Janos wanted to know.

"His name is Victor. We think he's the baby's father," said Sister Agnes.

At the sound of the name, Karina recoiled in fear. She buried her head in the nun's shoulder, pleading, "No, Victor! No! Keep him away!" She pawed at the nun, seemingly trying to find refuge under the woman's habit.

"It's all right, Karina. You're with Janos now. You're safe here with your family." The nun patted her shoulder.

"Do you see why we came to you, Janos? Karina has endured some sort of trauma. Her mind is broken. She needs more help than the church can give her," said the priest.

At the sight of Karina's distress, Janos's anger subsided, if only slightly. He wondered if her current state was the result of an unwanted attack. He suddenly pitied her, but knew she was to blame for her situation. If she hadn't left him in the first place, she wouldn't be in such a terrible mess.

"If she is suffering from some sort of breakdown, then she should be sent to an insane asylum. Isn't that where she would get the best care?" Janos asked.

"I'm afraid not," said Sister Agnes. "Do you not remember the reporting of Nellie Bly?"

"Who?" Janos tilted his head.

The nun shook her head reproachfully. "Nellie Bly exposed

the deplorable conditions inside insane asylums in the late 1880s. She faked insanity in order to be committed to a mental institution in New York City. The world was shocked at her findings."

Anna nodded instantly. "I remember reading about that. The patients were given dirty water and spoiled food. When they were disobedient, buckets of cold water were dumped over their heads."

"Some were even beaten," said Sister Agnes. "An insane asylum is no place to have a baby."

"You're talking about a report that was written almost thirty years ago," Janos said. "Surely there have been improvements."

"Janos, what Karina needs is to be surrounded by familiar faces. She needs the love and care of her family," Father Figlar said gently. "That's her best chance for recovery."

Janos stared across the room at Karina, who appeared to be asleep against the nun's shoulder. He could barely see her belly, still hidden beneath her long overcoat. Sadly, he felt little for her but contempt. He hardly recognized the beautiful woman who had once been his wife. But within that broken body, was an innocent life—a baby who should not be made to suffer the sins of its mother.

"Perhaps once the child arrives, you can find a proper facility to care for Karina long-term—assuming her mind does not recover," the priest added.

"And the baby?" Anna asked.

Father Figlar fixed a sympathetic gaze on Janos. "That will be for you to decide."

Janos swallowed hard. In all his imaginings of Karina's fate, he had never envisioned her turning up on his doorstep in such a pathetic state. He had assumed she'd found a wealthy lover in some far-off city to care for her. She had always been obsessed with the lifestyles of the upper classes. With her humble beginnings, she would never have been able to achieve the status of society wife, but any man would have been proud to have her as a mistress. Karina's beauty had been a prize to be coveted, regardless of one's social class.

But not now. Not this woman. She was wrecked both physically and mentally. And Janos would have to pick up the pieces—if only for the sake of Sofie and Lukas's baby brother or sister. It was a bitter pill to swallow, but he saw no other option. He sighed. "We'll care for Karina until the baby is born."

"And after that?" Anna looked at her brother askance.

"I don't know." Janos shook his head.

"You have time to make arrangements," Father Figlar said. "The doctor who examined Karina thinks the baby is due sometime this winter. Though it is hard to tell, given that she is so gaunt. The child could come sooner."

"The baby might not even survive, considering the condition of its mother," Sister Agnes said.

"We'll do our best to make sure the child has a chance," Anna said. "Karina can stay in my room for the next few months. I will share a room with Sofie."

Janos watched his sister and the nun help Karina to her feet and escort her up the stairs. If it had been any other woman—a stranger even—Janos would have sprung out of his chair and insisted that he carry the poor soul up to the bedroom. But it was Karina. The wounds that had taken so many years to heal were now ripped open and raw. He would have to keep his distance for the time being. He prayed the baby would arrive soon because he had no idea how they would all survive under the same roof.

# Forty-Two

## EDITH

### SHADYSIDE, NOVEMBER 20, 1917

It was barely dawn when Edith's deep slumber was interrupted by a wave of nausea. She opened her eyes and glanced out the window where the darkness of night had turned to a faint gray. Her mouth watered and her head ached. She put her hand on her stomach, sensing it was about to unleash its contents. What had she eaten?

She rushed out of bed and into the bathroom where she fell to her knees in front of the toilet. She lifted the seat and stared into the bowl, its unpleasant odor assaulting her. Edith waited nervously as her stomach churned and her body trembled. She dreaded the act of retching. It was the most disgusting of all bodily functions. Her head hovering above the toilet, her lower body began to heave. A cold sweat formed on her brow as she felt the remnants of the previous evening's dinner travel up her throat and explode into the porcelain bowl. Exhausted, she laid down on the marble floor, grateful for the cool sensation against her head.

"Are you all right? Are you sick?" James was leaning over her, rubbing her back.

Edith could barely lift her head. "I'm terribly ill."

"Do you think it was that strange fish we ate last night?" he asked with a hint of disgust. "I'm done with this rationing business. The cook will be serving only beef and chicken from now on."

Edith shook her head. She had no idea what had brought on this illness, but she hadn't felt this dreadful in years. Not since two summers ago when . . .

"James!" Edith raised her head and struggled to sit up. "Do you think I'm pregnant? Is it possible?"

James lowered himself to the floor with a groan. His heavy frame was quite an encumbrance to his mobility. He came to rest on his knees and reached for his wife's clammy hand. "I thought you were done obsessing about babies."

"I was, but . . . it's been almost seven weeks since I provoked the flowers. This could be morning sickness." Edith's hand went to her belly. "I think I'm pregnant." A rush of emotion overtook her, causing her lip to quiver.

"Slow down, darling. Let's be cautious. I'll call for the doctor as soon as I get you back to bed."

Edith nodded enthusiastically as her husband tried to scoop her off the floor. Unfortunately, lifting his wife from a kneeling position proved too difficult a task. He winced as he struggled to return to his feet with his wife in his arms.

"Enough, James! Put me down. You're going to injure yourself."

"I'm trying to be a good husband." He grunted.

"If I'm pregnant and confined to my room for the next several weeks, I'd prefer that one of us is in good health." Edith chuckled. "Can you imagine both of us stuck in this bedroom all day together?"

"That actually sounds lovely. Although I could return to my own bedroom to convalesce if you'd like." James smiled as he put his wife down on the marble floor and returned to his knees.

"You would miss me terribly." Edith climbed unsteadily to her feet, using her husband's hand for support. She wrapped her arms around him, wedging his head between her breasts. She kissed the top of his head and sighed. "I really do hope I'm carrying your baby. It would be a dream come true."

James looked up at his wife, his blue eyes twinkling.

Edith watched her husband slowly return to his feet, rubbing his knees vigorously during the effort. "That floor is unbelievably hard. After the good doctor examines you, I may have him take a look at my bruising."

As James led her back to bed, Edith felt an incredible lightness. Something stirred deep within her—whether it was indeed a baby or simply hope, she could not be sure. There was nothing in the world she longed for more than a child. She had often contemplated and lamented this great irony of her life. Her family's wealth provided her with all that money could buy—exquisite jewelry, priceless works of art, grand mansions, and the means to travel anywhere in the world. She had a lavish lifestyle to be envied. But no matter how massive her family's fortune, it could not buy her what her heart desired most—a baby of her own. And while she took great comfort and joy in the arms of her loving husband, Edith always felt that a piece of the puzzle was missing. What she needed to fulfill her life's purpose and feel complete in her womanhood was something her body continually deprived her of. Until now. At least that was what she hoped as she laid down and rested her head on her pillow.

# *Forty-Three*

## POLE

### BEAVER CREEK, NOVEMBER 23, 1917

It was a cold and gloomy day, far from what Pole had pictured all the times he'd imagined reuniting with Sofie. He tried hard not to let the weather dampen his spirits as he sat on a train wedged between a desolate hillside and a slow-moving river. He was still not certain he had made the right decision that morning when he'd bought a one-way ticket for himself and his sister to the glass town Sofie now called home. It had been almost a month since he'd seen Lukas, and he was still conflicted about the course of his future. Since their chance encounter, Pole had been excited, but nervous at the prospect of seeing Sofie again—so nervous that he'd hung around Riverton for weeks, killing time doing odd jobs.

Pole felt the bulge in his right front pocket again. He'd never had so much cash. After escaping from the mine, he and Mickey honored Hamish's last wish and took the money hidden beneath the floorboards in his kitchen. Pole had felt guilty about accepting Hamish's sons' inheritance, but he was desperate to get out of Abbott's Hollow. He and Mickey split the five hundred dollars they found and took a few weeks to get their affairs in order before leaving the hollow for good.

Mickey took his mother and two sisters, along with Gus, to Johnstown. He hoped he and his mule might find work on a local farm, while his mother and sisters planned to look for work in the city. Pole, on the other hand, had left the hollow without definite plans. He only knew he wanted to head back to Pittsburgh.

But seeing Lukas had changed everything.

As the train slowed and crossed over the river, Pole was grateful he had some security in his pocket. He was determined to start a new life with his sister and get a decent job, but it put his mind at ease to know he needn't hurry. He could find Sofie, rekindle their friendship, and take some time to figure out if Beaver Creek was a place he and Lily could call home.

"Hey, Lily. Wake up." Pole nudged his sister, who was sleeping against his shoulder. "We're here."

She sat up and swept unruly strands of red curls away from her face, tucking them behind her ears. "That was quick." She peered out the window. "Looks a little nicer than Riverton. Not as much smoke."

Pole stared out the window at the little town situated along the Allegheny River between two steep hillsides. The valley floor it occupied looked almost a mile wide, but it was crammed with so many homes and businesses that structures had been forced to spread up the slope at the far side of town. Pole studied the houses, wondering if any of them had ever slid down the hill during a heavy downpour. He couldn't believe folks would settle on such an incline. And the steps! Who would want to climb all those stairs after a long day's work?

"Yeah. These hills are probably pretty in the summer, but not at this time of year. I don't like lookin' at hillsides full of naked trees and rotting leaves."

"I know it reminds you of the hollow, but at least there's more to do here. Maybe there's a nickelodeon. And some restaurants," Lily said, sounding hopeful.

"We'll check it out. But I'd like to get to Sofie's house straightaway—before I lose my nerve."

Lily put her hand on her brother's knee. "I know it's been a long time, but I'm sure she'll be glad to see you." She winked at him.

As the train screeched to a halt, Pole hoped he hadn't made a huge mistake in coming to Beaver Creek. He prayed Sofie still had a special place in her heart for him and that she could forgive him for not returning to Riverton all those years ago. That broken promise had plagued him for years and torn him apart every time he'd thought of it. It haunted him.

Suddenly, an alarming thought popped into Pole's head. What if Sofie had forgotten about his promise? What if she didn't care anymore? Maybe she had moved on, and his suffering was for nothing.

Pole slapped his forehead. He was driving himself nuts. He took a deep breath, squaring his shoulders. No matter what happened in the next few hours, at least the suspense would finally be over. The knots in his stomach would be gone. He would have the answers to the questions that had been tormenting him for so long.

Pole knocked on the smooth, moss green front door of 5 Dogwood Avenue, his sister at his side. He could not stop his hands from shaking. "Do I look nervous, Lily? 'Cause I feel like my knees are goin' to give out."

Lily pinched him hard in his right side.

"Ouch! Why'd you do that?" he asked, rubbing the area just below his ribs.

"Now you have something else to focus on." She giggled.

As Pole was massaging his side, the front door opened. He swallowed hard. Before him was a tall, blonde girl with eyes the color of a summer sky. Her hair was pulled away from her face, and her dimples were showing even though she wasn't smiling. The youthful face Pole remembered had matured and become more angular. Sofie looked less like her mother now, bearing a closer resemblance to her father and aunt. But she was striking all the same. Pole's knees buckled.

"Can I help you?"

"Sofie . . ." He tried to catch his breath. "You're so grown up." His head spinning, he planted his feet firmly on the porch, trying to remember what he wanted to say. As he focused on Sofie's pretty blue eyes, the words suddenly formed on his lips. "I'm sorry it took me so long to come back."

Through watery eyes, Pole saw recognition on his friend's face.

Sofie's hand went to her heart. "Pole!" she cried. She stumbled onto the front porch and fell into his arms. "I never thought I'd see you again." She heaved deep sobs into his chest.

He wrapped his arms around her and held her as she cried. His entire body tingled as a wave of warmth washed over him. He had finally come to his long journey's end. He'd fulfilled his promise and returned to Sofie. He was overjoyed. Pole glanced at his sister, who was staring at him uncomfortably. Apparently, she hadn't been prepared for Sofie's emotional response.

Finally, Sofie pulled away, wiping at her eyes. "I'm sorry. I don't know what came over me."

"It's fine, Sof." Pole touched her shoulder. "I can't believe you're standin' in front of me after all these years. You're so tall."

"So are you. And wide," she said, smiling. "I didn't recognize you. You've changed quite a bit."

Pole combed his fingers through his hair. "The past seven years haven't been kind to me. I'm sure I look worse for the wear."

"No, no. That's not what I meant. You're just so . . ."

Pole raised an eyebrow as Sofie played nervously with her hands. Her cheeks were turning red. "So what?" he asked, smirking.

"Imposing."

"Imposing? I don't think I've ever been called that before." He chuckled.

"I meant it in a good way. You're a little intimidating, that's all. But your eyes . . . you still have the same kind green eyes," she said, her voice trailing off.

"John Stofanik? It can't be!" Aunt Anna said, appearing in the doorway.

"No, Mrs. Toth. It's Pole. Pole Stofanik." He extended his hand. "It's a pleasure to see you after all these years. And this, here, is my little sister, Lily."

"Oh my! How you've grown!" Aunt Anna tackled Pole with a forceful hug. "And this sweet thing," she said, turning to Lily and stroking her hair. "You've got the prettiest fiery red curls I've ever seen." Aunt Anna glared at Sofie. "Why haven't you invited them in?"

"I'm still trying to get over the shock."

"Come inside out of the cold. I'll make some tea. Sofie, you and Pole can get reacquainted in the parlor. Maybe Lily would like to help me in the kitchen. I hid some cookies in one of the cupboards a few weeks ago, but I can't remember which one."

"I'd be happy to help, ma'am," Lily said cheerfully.

As Aunt Anna led Lily down the hall, Pole took a seat in a worn armchair while Sofie sat across from him on a rose-colored sofa. The pastel hue matched the color of her cheeks. The knots in his stomach tightened. "You have a real nice house. Your brother told me your father owns a grocery store now."

"You saw Lukas?"

"Yeah. That's how I found you. I ran into him in Johnstown. His boarding school is there, isn't it?"

"It is," Sofie said, nodding.

"I've been livin' in a mining village not far from Johnstown for the past seven years. I ran into your brother in a five-and-dime about a month ago. It was so odd. I've wondered for years what happened to you, and then all of a sudden, Lukas was there to point me in the right direction."

"You wondered where I was?"

"Course I did. I promised you I'd come back. I tried to find you." Pole leaned forward and reached for Sofie's hand. When she looked at him uncomfortably, he pulled away. "I'm sorry. I don't know what I'm doin'. The Sofie I have in my head is a young girl who was like family to me—a sister. I need to remind myself that you're a grown woman now. You barely know me."

Sofie's face grew pale. She turned away, wiping at her eyes.

"Maybe I shouldna come. I've upset you."

Sofie sighed heavily and turned back to Pole. "No. I'm happy to see you. It's just . . . you've come at a difficult time."

"Is everything all right? Is something wrong with your father?"

"No, Papa's fine. Well, not really. None of us are." Sofie looked away again, this time biting her lip. She seemed to be trying to muster the courage to say something. She shook her head brusquely. "You tried to find me?"

"I did. When you didn't answer any of the letters I sent, I got worried. I wanted to get back to Riverton right away, but I wasn't able until two summers after I left."

"You wrote me letters?"

"Tons of 'em. I wanted you to know I didn't forget about my promise. My pop was killed in a mine accident shortly after we arrived in Abbott's Hollow. I had to stay there to take care of my sister and her mother."

Sofie grabbed Pole's hand and squeezed it. "I thought you forgot about me."

Her touch sent a bolt of electricity through him. He studied her beautiful face and saw the flicker of light in her eyes that he'd missed for so long.

"We left Riverton not long after you did. I gave all my old neighbors our new address in Beaver Creek. Mrs. Janosik and Father Figlar, too. I hoped they would give it to you if you ever came looking for me."

Pole sighed. "When I got back to Riverton in the summer of 1912, I was too late. Your block had burnt down, and all your neighbors were gone. I even went to the boarding house to see if Mrs. Janosik knew anything, but she was dead." Pole shook his head. "Goddamn it! If only I'd thought of Father Figlar."

"It seems fate was not on our side," Sofie whispered.

"Why the hell did I not think of goin' to the church? How could I forget about Father Figlar? That's my punishment for not being a good Catholic, I guess."

"Stop being so hard on yourself." Sofie stroked Pole's thumb with her own. "You were a young kid carrying the burdens of a grown man." She went silent for a moment. "I'm sorry about your father."

"He wasn't much of a loss. I know that's a terrible thing to say, but I think me and my sister are better off without him."

"I understand," Sofie said. She glanced upward, an anguished look on her face. "You know, I went looking for you, too," she said, turning back to Pole.

"You did?"

"A few years after we moved away, I begged my father to take me back to Riverton to see if we could find out what happened to you. But no one at the boarding house knew who you were, and my old neighborhood was being rebuilt by Russians. We finally saw some of our old neighbors at church, but they hadn't seen you in years."

"If I had just gone to your church, maybe we could've found each other sooner," Pole grumbled.

"It doesn't matter. You're here now." Sofie smiled warmly. "I'm so thankful you ran into Lukas."

"Do you want to tell me what's goin' on with your family? I have a feeling that burst of tears on the front porch wasn't entirely about me. Though I'd like to think so," Pole said with a wink.

"Why don't you talk to Pole?" Aunt Anna said to Sofie as she entered the room carrying a tray of tea and cookies. "It's been almost two weeks. You won't talk to me. You won't talk to your father. It's time you confided in someone."

"That's enough, Aunt Anna," Sofie said gruffly.

"I know you're having a hard time with our predicament, but you can't stay locked in your room forever. Pole, will you please get her to open up to you? If anyone can reach Sofie, I think it's you. God sent you here exactly when she needed you."

"God always has a plan. I've been telling my brother that for years," Lily said as she entered the parlor.

Pole frowned at his sister. "Now's not the time to preach, sis. But I would like to help Sofie any way I can." He got up from his chair and pulled Sofie to her feet. They were still holding hands. "Mrs. Toth, can you save the tea and cookies for later? We're goin' for a walk."

"That sounds like a lovely idea. But make sure to bundle up. Lily can stay here and help me bake. You and your sister will be joining us for dinner, won't you, Pole?" Aunt Anna asked.

"Yes. That would be nice. Thank you."

"Have you found a place to stay yet? I'd offer you a room, but the house is full at the moment. Mrs. Walker has a few spare rooms down the street. I can make the arrangements for you."

"Thanks, Mrs. Toth. That's very kind of you."

"And please stop calling me that. I'm Aunt Anna to you, too." She rushed over and gave Pole another forceful hug. "Seeing you again has made me so happy. What an unexpected gift!"

Pole blushed. Feeling appreciated was a bit foreign to him, but it was a welcome change. As he watched Sofie pull her coat out of the hall closet, he felt completely at peace for the first time in years. She hadn't forgotten him. She had even gone back to Riverton to try to find him. It was more than he had hoped for.

He was so relieved he and Sofie still shared a special connection despite their seven-year separation. He had felt it the moment she'd touched him. Pole suddenly thought of what Hamish had said to him in the mine—that he would know when the right girl had come along. After seeing Sofie's sweet face again and holding her in his arms, he wondered whether he was a fool to think he'd found the right girl.

## *Forty-Four*

# SOFIE

## BEAVER CREEK, NOVEMBER 23, 1917

As Sofie walked the path along the river with Pole, she was overwhelmed with emotion. The upheaval in her life during the past couple of weeks was hard to comprehend. First Karina's return and then Pole's. It was as if her past was coming back to haunt her. The people who'd had such a profound impact on her early childhood and had been inexplicably absent from her life for so long were now back, reopening old wounds. But unlike the wounds her mother had inflicted, the trauma from Pole's absence could be healed. Their friendship could be rekindled. The thought of it was coaxing Sofie out of the dark place she had retreated to since her mother's return.

She fixed her gaze on Pole, who smiled at her sweetly. She couldn't believe the boy she had last seen at the age of nearly thirteen had grown to such an enormous height. He was at least as tall as her six-foot-two-inch father, but much broader with muscular arms and shoulders. Pole was intimidating. But his wavy, brown hair and kind green eyes took Sofie's breath away. She was looking at the same face she had gazed at countless times at the fishing hole. It was simply a more mature, weathered version. She wondered if she should pinch herself to make sure she wasn't dreaming.

"You're so quiet, Sof. What are you thinkin' about?"

Sofie tucked a strand of hair behind her ear, hoping Pole could not read her mind. "Lots of stuff," she said casually. She dared not reveal that she'd been analyzing his physique. "I don't know where to begin."

"Why don't you start with what's going on with your family. Your aunt said you haven't talked to her or your father for weeks. What happened?"

Sofie froze. The thought of talking about her mother made her cringe, but she was tired of suffering in silence. Pole was the only person who had understood her problems with her mother when they were young. If anyone could help, it was him. Without thinking, she grabbed his hand and led him over to a boulder alongside the trail.

"What I'm about to tell you is shocking. I've been too angry to discuss this with Papa and Aunt Anna, but maybe you'll understand. You know what it's like to have a parent you're ashamed of."

Pole's face softened. He squeezed Sofie's hand. "We do have that in common, don't we?"

"I'm not sure how much Lukas told you in Johnstown, but my mother disappeared seven years ago—the same day you left Riverton. It was also the same day the man my mother worked for was murdered." Sofie waited for Pole's reaction. He simply nodded. "I guess my brother mentioned this."

"He did."

"Did he show you his leg?"

Pole nodded again.

"The morning you left Riverton, I went to the train station to see you one last time. But by the time I got there, your train was gone. I was so disappointed . . . but little did I know, the day was about to get worse." Sofie looked down at her hand, intertwined with Pole's.

He leaned forward.

"As I was turning to leave the station, Lukas appeared out of nowhere. He was chasing one of the cars on the train and calling after our mother. He was so close to the tracks." Sofie shook her head. "I tried hard to stop him."

Pole's hand went to his mouth.

"Did Lukas already tell you the story?"

"No, but I think I can guess the ending."

Sofie took a deep breath. "Lukas was certain our mother was in that car and wouldn't stop until he got her attention. He kept trying to jump up and hit the window. On his last attempt, he lost his balance and fell between the platform and the wheels of the train."

"Jesus Christ! That's how he lost his leg?"

Sofie nodded, wiping a tear from her eye. "I didn't want to believe it for a long time—it was too painful—but years ago, I finally accepted that my mother was on that train. She's the reason Lukas lost his leg. She might even be the reason her boss is dead."

"And she's been gone ever since," Pole said mournfully.

"Until two weeks ago."

Pole's eyes widened.

"Father Figlar and that wicked Sister Agnes brought her here. She was found wandering around Riverton looking for us."

"What does she want after all these years?"

"She's pregnant." Sofie could taste the venom on her tongue as she uttered the words. It had been almost two weeks, and her disgust with her mother had not subsided in the least bit. If anything, it had grown. Each and every day she passed by her mother's door, she had to restrain herself from entering the room and strangling her. She had no desire to see her mother or try to make amends. Her only urge was to harm her.

"What the hell?" Pole's jaw was near the ground. "She's not expectin' help from your father after all this time?"

"We don't know what she's expecting. Karina is incoherent. She seems to have lost her mind."

Pole cocked his head to the side. "Are you sure?"

"I haven't seen her myself, but Papa said she's very confused."

"Wait. She's been at your house for two weeks, and you haven't seen her?"

"I refuse to go into her room. She's weak and can't get out of bed. Aunt Anna has been taking care of her."

"What about your father?"

"He's gone into the room a few times, but he comes out looking more distraught than when he went in. He's a fool for taking that woman in. Her presence in the house is making us all crazy."

Sofie thought about the somber mood that had befallen the house since Karina's return. Everyone moped around, incapable of remaining unaffected by the patient in the upstairs bedroom. Avoidance was their only coping mechanism. Papa worked longer hours at the store and hid behind his books when he was at home. Aunt Anna returned to her old habit of hovering over the kitchen stove both day and night, even when she wasn't cooking. And Sofie spent as much time at the newspaper as she possibly could.

Papa and Aunt Anna had tried numerous times to get Sofie to share her feelings about the impossible situation in which they'd found themselves, but she always remained tight-lipped and eager to change the subject. As a result, dinners were terribly awkward and consisted of superficial conversation about the weather and the war. Whenever Papa and Aunt Anna needed to discuss Karina, they retreated to the kitchen and spoke in hushed tones.

"If your mother really has lost her mind, why isn't she in an asylum? And how long will she stay with you?" Pole asked.

"I don't know. I'm not even sure my father knows. Aunt Anna said something about keeping Karina healthy until the baby is born. I have no idea what will happen after that."

Pole looked down at his feet and scratched his head. He remained silent for minutes.

Sofie studied him. She worried her story was too shocking, even by his standards. Her mother had sunk to an unbelievable new low and had brought shame on them all. "Maybe I shouldn't have told you all that. I can't imagine what you must think of my family." She began to whimper softly.

Pole looked up. He wrapped his arm around Sofie, pulling her close beside him. "Aww, Sof. I think the world of your family. I've always admired your father and aunt. Your mother is a bit of a mess—there's no doubt. But your father has always made up for her failings. I'm sure he has a plan to deal with the situation."

In the midst of her turmoil, Sofie found the sensation of Pole's arm around her back soothing. She laid her head on his shoulder and exhaled. She sat motionless for minutes, inhaling his musky scent and feeling the warmth of his breath on her face. She wished she could live in that moment indefinitely. The tumultuous storm that had been whirling inside her for weeks was quieting. She closed her eyes and savored the calm.

"I'm glad you told me everything," Pole whispered. "I know I've been gone a long time, but I'm here now. I'll do anything you need."

Sofie raised her head and met Pole's gaze. There was so much tenderness in his eyes. She suddenly felt a strange tingling in her body, a sensation akin to hunger. Was it desire? She stared at Pole's lips, wondering how they might feel upon hers. Stunned by her inappropriate thoughts, she shook them from her head. Her calm began to dissipate, and the chaos commenced its swirling.

"What is it? What's wrong?"

"I've dreamed about seeing you again for so long. And now that you're here . . ."

"My timing's bad, I know." Pole chuckled.

"You couldn't have picked a worse time to show up." Sofie slapped Pole's leg playfully. "But maybe Aunt Anna was right. You came exactly when I needed you."

"You're the best friend I ever had, Sof. I only wish I'd found you sooner."

Sofie noticed Pole's cheeks were rosy. Whether it was the cold weather or a hint at his emotions, she couldn't be sure. She wondered if he felt the same electricity that was coursing through her. Wrapped in his warm embrace, she was reminded of the indomitable bond she had shared with her childhood friend, their deep affection and devotion to each other. But now those long-buried feelings were accompanied by something new—an unexpected desire for the grown man beside her.

Pole was so foreign yet familiar. So intimidating yet endearing. Sofie was not sure what she felt for her long-lost friend, but was eager to find out. As he helped her to her feet and led her down the path toward town, she stole several glances at his handsome face, focusing on his dark green eyes. She hadn't realized how much she had missed gazing into them. There was no denying that her life was in total disarray, but with Pole at her side, she might regain her bearings and find her way back to the light.

## Forty-Five

# JANOS

## BEAVER CREEK, NOVEMBER 23, 1917

Janos still could not believe his eyes as he studied the young man seated opposite him at the dining room table. Pole bore a striking resemblance to his father, but couldn't have been more different in temperament. Despite the many trials and tribulations of the past seven years, which he had recounted over dinner, he had somehow managed to remain good-natured and kind. His resilience was remarkable. But even more impressive was the miracle he was performing—one that had seemed nearly impossible only a few days ago. Pole was bringing Sofie back to life. The light had returned to her eyes, and she was smiling again.

Whether it was fate or divine intervention, Janos would forever be grateful that Lukas and Pole's paths had crossed in Johnstown. He had often believed that the loss of Pole had taken an even greater toll on Sofie than the loss of her mother. The unanswered questions surrounding his whereabouts had been especially agonizing for her. After their failed attempt to track Pole down in Riverton in the summer of 1913, Sofie had been inconsolable for months, believing she would never see her childhood friend again. Since then, Janos feared there would always be a void in his daughter's heart—one that could only be filled upon Pole's improbable return.

Much to his dismay, Janos had always believed that day would never come. He had never been so thankful for his own miscalculation.

"Dinner was delicious, Aunt Anna. Thank you for invitin' me and Lily. It's been a long time since we've had a home cooked meal," Pole said.

"It's wonderful having you in our home again. It's been too long. And your sister is delightful," Anna said, patting the girl's back.

Janos gazed at the twelve-year-old, who was cozied up next to Anna. The girl had bonded with his sister rather quickly. Lily was likely still reeling from the recent loss of her mother and in need of feminine companionship. Sadly, there seemed to be tragedy in every direction Janos turned. He had always believed his children were unique in their suffering, but Pole and Lily had clearly been dealt their share of devastating blows.

"How long do you intend to stay in Beaver Creek?" Janos asked Pole. "The public school here is very good. Perhaps Lily would like to enroll."

"I've never gone to a real school before," Lily said. "The school in Abbott's Hollow was small, and I didn't go very often." She looked down at her lap.

"If you're worried about being behind in your studies, I would be happy to tutor you. Aunt Anna could help, too," Janos said.

Lilly looked at her brother hopefully.

"We haven't made definite plans yet, Mr. Kovac."

Janos raised an eyebrow at Pole.

"I mean, Janos. It'll take me a while to get used to that." Pole chuckled. "Anyway, Beaver Creek seems like a nice place to live. What are the jobs like at the glass factory?"

"Hot and dirty. But probably not as dirty as mining coal—or as dangerous," Janos replied.

"Yeah. At least I'd be above ground."

"That would certainly be an improvement. But you'll have to make sure you're registered for the draft. The owner of the factory is quite patriotic."

"But I'm only twenty. Have they changed the rules? We didn't get much news about the war in Abbott's Hollow."

"No, Pole. You're safe for now." Sofie sighed with relief. "At least until you turn twenty-one next September."

"You remembered my birthday?" Pole asked, surprised.

"Of course." Sofie smiled coyly.

Janos could not deny that he was enjoying the pleasant exchanges between his daughter and Pole. It was such a relief to see her finally take an interest in a boy. Perhaps he was even witnessing a budding romance.

"Once you're settled at Mrs. Walker's, I'll take you to the factory and introduce you to one of the foremen I'm friendly with," Janos said to Pole. "Hopefully, he'll have a spot for you. And if you think you'd like to stay here indefinitely, Aunt Anna can enroll Lily at the local school."

The girl smiled. "I'd like that very much."

"Well, sis, I think we should probably move on to Mrs. Walker's. It's gettin' late. It's five houses down, right?" Pole asked Anna.

"I can take you to her house," Sofie said, grinning.

"I think Pole will be able to find it," Janos said. "You stay here and help your aunt with the dishes." It pained Janos to see the look of disappointment on his daughter's face, but he needed to speak with her before her mood soured, and she escaped to her room for the night.

"I'll show Lily and Pole to the door then," Sofie said, sounding irritated.

"Thank you again for dinner. It was real nice seein' you after all these years," Pole said as he shook Janos's hand and hugged Anna.

"Since tomorrow's Saturday, I can show you and Lily around town," Sofie said as she walked down the hall with Pole and his sister. "We can even go to the nickelodeon."

As Sofie's voice grew more distant, Janos moved toward his sister. "Did you see how happy Sofie was this evening? She seems to have forgotten about Karina—at least temporarily."

"I forgot about her, too. I need to take her some dinner. I haven't been upstairs since before Pole and Lily showed up."

"I doubt it matters. She does nothing but sleep." Janos was grateful for that small blessing. The few times he had gone into Karina's room during the past two weeks, she'd either been fast asleep or looked like she'd just woken up. She had been groggy and said very little. On one occasion, she actually whispered his name and reached out to him, but luckily, Anna appeared with a tray of food. While Karina was distracted with her dinner, Janos slipped out the door. It was distressing enough to see his former wife with her swollen belly—the evidence of her betrayal growing day by day—but the thought of actually speaking to her was more than he could bear.

"I'll clear the table, Aunt Anna," Sofie said, returning to the dining room.

"Can we talk in the parlor first?" Janos asked his daughter, grateful she had interrupted his thoughts of Karina.

"Sure, I guess."

Once she was seated next to him on the sofa, Janos squeezed her hand. "You seemed happy tonight. I have Pole to thank for that. It's a miracle he ran into Lukas, isn't it?"

"Can you believe how tall he is? He's quite handsome, too."

Janos chuckled. "I suppose he is." Finally, his daughter sounded like a seventeen-year-old. Maybe she was finally ready to tear down the walls she had built around her heart so many years ago. Janos paused to savor the moment before assuming the role of overbearing parent. "Have you told Pole anything about your mother, Sofie?"

Her cheerful expression faded. "I told him everything," she said, biting her lip. "I'm sorry, but Aunt Anna suggested I do it. She said I needed to confide in someone." Her voice began to crack.

"It's fine." Janos patted his daughter's knee. "I trust Pole will keep our secret." He was glad Sofie had finally shared her feelings with someone, but was a little sad she hadn't come to him for comfort.

"He will," she said assuredly. She leaned closer to her father. "What have you told Concetta? I know you two have become close," she said, her voice lowering.

"I told her your aunt is taking care of an old friend who is sick. It was the best story she and I could come up with. We told Vilium and Marek the same lie in case they notice your aunt is sleeping in your room."

"Will you invite Concetta here for Thanksgiving dinner? She shouldn't spend the holiday alone, but what if Karina comes out of her room?"

"We needn't worry about that. Concetta is leaving for Philadelphia in a few days and won't return until mid-December."

Sofie raised an eyebrow. "That's a long trip."

"It is," Janos said, nodding. He was not looking forward to Concetta's departure, but sending her away from Beaver Creek was the easiest way to prevent her from finding out about Karina. Concetta had been surprised when he'd suggested she spend the Thanksgiving holiday with Tony in Philadelphia and even more stunned when he had urged her to stay the entire month of December. She was hesitant to make such a lengthy trip. Janos hated manipulating and lying to Concetta, but knew their romance would come to an abrupt end if she learned of his pregnant wife's return.

"Papa . . ." Sofie said timidly.

Janos noticed the uneasiness in his daughter's eyes.

"Have you sent Lukas any news of Karina? Have you thought about how he's going to react when he comes home next week and finds her here?"

"He's not coming. I got a letter the other day. He's spending Thanksgiving with Edith."

"Oh," Sofie said, disappointed. "I was looking forward to seeing him."

"I know, but it's probably for the best. At least we have another month to figure out how to tell him the news. He won't be home now until Christmas."

"He has more reason to hate Karina than I do," Sofie snapped. "She's the reason he lost his leg."

"Does he believe that? Has he talked to you about his accident?"

"Never. That's strange, isn't it?"

Janos nodded solemnly.

"We've always pretended our mother was the victim of a crime or accident. Lukas never told me whether he believes Karina was on the train that day, but I suspect he does."

"Why is that?"

"Have you ever seen the way he reacts when someone says the word 'mother'? He winces every time. I think he's very bitter about Karina. He just hides it really well. Or . . ." Sofie paused and stared past her father, her face expressionless.

"Or what?"

"He doesn't even realize how deep his resentment is," she whispered.

Janos shuddered. He dreaded the day Lukas would learn about his mother's return. But maybe they would get lucky in the next month. Perhaps Karina would have the baby, recover fully, and be gone before Lukas came home for Christmas. It would be far easier for him to stomach the news of his mother's most recent betrayal if she had already moved on from Beaver Creek. Janos closed his eyes. He wouldn't hold his breath for that miracle.

Satisfied that he had finally been able to have a real conversation with his daughter for the first time in weeks, Janos leaned back in his favorite armchair and prepared to dive into a book. Four sat on the side table, but he wasn't sure which one he was in the mood for.

"Janos," Anna said, entering the parlor with a worried look on her face. "Karina would like to see you."

He stiffened. "What do you mean?"

"Our patient is surprisingly lucid this evening. She's awoken from her stupor," Anna said, shrugging her shoulders.

"What did she say?"

"She said she's feeling better—and I could tell. She sat up in bed and practically inhaled her dinner. She said she wants to talk to you about the baby."

Janos's stomach turned. His luck had run out. Dealing with a weak and disoriented Karina was not pleasant, but it was a better alternative than interacting with her. What could she possibly have to say to him? And would she make any sense?

"What am I supposed to do? March upstairs and pretend that everything's fine?"

"I don't know." Anna shook her head. "This is the first time she's said more than a few words to me. She's been lethargic and confused until today. She actually thanked me for taking care of her."

Janos eyed his sister. "Seriously?"

"Hard to believe, I know. And she wants to know where Sofie and Lukas are."

"My God! What did you tell her?"

"I said they were sleeping."

Janos sighed as he stood up. "I'll be back shortly. Can you make me some tea?"

"Of course. Try to remain calm. Think of the baby she's carrying," Anna said, touching his arm.

Janos climbed the stairs, reciting the Jesus prayer over and over again for comfort. He had hoped for an improvement in Karina's condition for the sake of her baby, but in that moment, he wished she would fall back into her deep slumber. He was terrified at the prospect of speaking to her. He paused at her door and made the sign of the cross before entering the room. "Lord Jesus Christ, Son of God, have mercy on me, a sinner," he whispered one last time as he turned the doorknob.

"Hello, Janos."

Karina sat in bed, propped up by several pillows. She held a brush in her hand, which she quickly placed on the nightstand. She smoothed her frizzy hair with her fingers and looked demurely at Janos. "There are no mirrors in this room. I hope I'm not too unkempt."

Janos studied his wife. The color had returned to her cheeks, and she had put on a little weight. She was still thin, but not as dangerously gaunt as when she had arrived. She looked stronger and more alert. He wondered if she knew where she was.

"You needn't worry about your appearance. You haven't been well, Karina." Janos almost choked as her name left his lips. He was in awe of the fact that he was addressing her directly after all these years. And the irony! How many times had he cursed her name? His hand began to tremble.

"This baby has been much harder on me than Sofie and Lukas. I'm so tired."

Janos stared at his wife's wild hair, hoping to avoid eye contact with her. He wondered what had happened to her beautiful blonde locks. Thirty-five seemed too young an age to be so gray.

"Where are the children? Why haven't they come to see me? I miss Lukas's giggle."

Janos's shoulders tensed. "Karina, do you remember how you got here?"

She shook her head, a forlorn look on her face.

"What do you remember?"

"I got lost on my way home. And no wonder! Our new house is so far from the old one." She fingered the pastel-colored quilt covering her. "I like our new bedroom."

Janos swayed, his terror knocking him off balance. He grabbed the rocking chair for support.

"I've started thinking about baby names. I'd like Mary for a girl—after Mary Pickford, of course. I love her films. And Janos if it's a boy. After his father." Karina smiled at her husband.

Janos cringed. Sister Agnes had mentioned that Karina thought the baby was his, but he assumed she had come to her senses upon emerging from her delirium. *Dear God! She really has lost her mind.*

"Why don't you come over and sit next to me?" Karina asked as she patted the empty space on the bed. "It feels like I haven't seen you in ages."

His head spinning, Janos could not decide how to approach the situation. He didn't want to upset Karina and endanger her baby, but he could not play charades. He could not pretend he had fathered her baby, no matter how beneficial that pretense might be to her wellbeing.

"It seems you're confused, Karina." Janos reluctantly took a step toward her. "But you are right about one thing. We haven't seen each other in ages. Over seven years, to be precise. The baby you're carrying is not mine." Janos swallowed hard. He waited anxiously for his wife's reaction.

Karina's face went blank. She tilted her head to the side and stared at him. "Why would you say something so ridiculous?"

"Because it's the truth."

"How could that be?" she asked, incredulous.

"You left me over seven years ago."

"That's absurd! I'd never do anything so cruel," she said, her voice growing louder with each syllable, her face twisting.

"I know you're having trouble remembering," Janos stammered. "But I haven't seen you in seven years. I am not the father of your baby."

Karina covered her ears and screamed, "Stop it! Stop lying!" She began to rock back and forth. "Stop!" She screeched loud enough to wake the dead. She picked up a book lying on the nightstand and threw it at Janos. It missed his head by a few inches, slamming onto the wall behind him.

Panicked, he rushed over to Karina and grabbed her hands. "Shh. Calm down. Calm down."

"Why are you saying these things?" she wailed. "Why?" She began to sob.

Janos knew she needed comforting, but dared not embrace her. The sensation of her hands in his was disorienting enough. "Why don't you lie down?" he said gently, as he made repeated attempts to nudge Karina onto a pillow. She swatted at him every time.

Suddenly, Anna burst into the room. "What's going on in here?"

Janos had never been so relieved to see his sister. "She's confused. She doesn't remember that she left us."

"I didn't leave you," Karina whined. "I only went to work. I went to Mr. Archer's."

"Is that where you were coming from when you got lost?" Anna asked in a sympathetic tone, as if speaking to a child.

Karina nodded emphatically.

Anna approached the bed and motioned for Janos to get out of her way. She sat down and pulled a vial out of her pocket. "Pour her glass of water," Anna said, pointing to a pitcher resting on the dresser.

Janos did as he was told.

As Karina wiped the tears from her eyes, Anna unscrewed the lid on the vial. She dropped a few white crystals into the glass of water Janos had handed her. She swirled it around for a minute before offering it to Karina. "Drink this. It will help you feel better."

"I'm not thirsty." She crossed her arms.

"It's for the baby. It's medicine to help it grow stronger. You're still too thin."

Karina looked away.

"You want your baby to be healthy, don't you?" Anna chided.

Karina grabbed the glass of water and downed it in one gulp, slamming it on the nightstand when she was finished.

"Good girl. Now get some rest," Anna said, patting her patient's shoulder.

"But what about Janos? Why did he say those horrible things?"

Anna scowled at her brother. She expected him to smooth things over. Janos hated the idea of lying, but seemed to have no other option in that moment. "I'm sorry, Karina. I didn't mean what I said."

She nodded slowly as she sank further into bed. She suddenly looked groggy. Janos turned off the light and slipped out the door with his sister.

"What did you give her?" he asked.

"Veronal. It's a medicine to help her sleep," Anna replied.

"Where did you get it?"

"Dr. Adler left it here the other day. He gives it to his female patients."

"What are we going to do about her? She's convinced the baby is mine. And she doesn't even realize how much time has passed. How is that possible?"

Anna shook her head as she sat down in the only chair in the hallway. She sighed as she took off her right shoe and rubbed her bunion. She massaged her foot for almost a minute before Janos grew irritated.

"Stop that. Stop playing with your foot. We need to figure out what's going on with Karina."

Anna looked up and glared at her brother. "That's what I'm doing."

Janos huffed. "Now you've lost your mind, too." He plopped himself onto the attic steps and buried his face in his hands.

"Her name was Mrs. Horvath." Anna's soft voice broke the silence. "You wouldn't remember her. You were just a baby."

Janos let his hands drop to his sides. His sister's tone had caught his attention.

"She was a lovely woman who lived down the street from us. She taught me how to make lace and Russian honey cake. Her lacework was so exquisite, she sold it in the local general store for a price no one in our neighborhood could afford." Anna sighed. "It was a visit to that store that changed her life forever."

Janos leaned forward. "What happened?"

"Mrs. Horvath took her two-year-old son, Jakub, to the store one day to drop off her lacework. She hadn't planned to stay long, but a businessman from Košice happened to be admiring her pieces in the store as she walked in. He immediately wanted to know if she could create something special for his wife."

Janos wondered how this was relevant, but kept silent as his sister spun her tale.

"It was rare to see such a well-dressed man in our little town, so naturally, Mrs. Horvath gave him her full attention. She spoke with him for several minutes and even took notes on his request. She never noticed that her little boy had left her side."

Janos shuddered. "What happened to him?"

"He wandered out of the store and into the street. He was struck by a team of horses pulling a wagon."

"Dear God!" Janos covered his mouth.

"Thankfully, Mrs. Horvath didn't see it happen. But she was ruined all the same. Her grief broke her. It broke her mind."

"In what way?"

"A few days after Jakub was buried, Mrs. Horvath came to Sunday mass with a baby doll wrapped in a blanket. No one said a word. We were too shocked." Anna shook her head. "The day after that, she was seen shopping with the same doll in a stroller. In a matter of weeks, the town had grown used to seeing Mrs. Horvath nurturing that baby doll and taking it everywhere she went."

"No one tried to talk some sense into her?"

"Our priest tried to intervene on several occasions, but Mrs. Horvath would only become hysterical. She actually slapped him once when he tried to pry the doll from her arms. He eventually gave up and began complimenting her on her baby's outfits. Soon we were all doing it. I can still remember Mama making a fuss about a sailor suit the doll wore one day."

"That story is hard to believe," Janos said, wiping at his eyes.

"And yet it happened."

"Why have you never shared this with me before?"

"Honestly, I haven't thought about Mrs. Horvath in years. But today . . ." Anna got up from her chair and knelt in front of Janos. "I think sometimes a person's suffering is so great that the mind has no choice but to go back to a happier time—to a time before the trauma. The present is just too unbearable."

Janos had never heard such a bizarre story. "Surely this woman had some form of insanity before her son's death."

"Mama always said Mrs. Horvath was the most sensible woman she had ever met."

"But a completely sane person doesn't go mad overnight."

"Sometimes they do, Janos. Sometimes they do," Anna's voice trailed off. "You need look no further than behind that door." She pointed toward Karina's room.

Janos stared at the walnut door that separated him from his wife. Maybe whatever Karina had suffered at the hands of her baby's father had broken her mind. But unlike Mrs. Horvath,

Karina had not been entirely well before her departure from Riverton. He could never put a name to her affliction, but her unpredictable moods had always been troubling.

"So what are we going to do, Anna?"

"We're going to pretend. For the sake of that baby, we will pretend that what Karina says is true. The past seven years never happened."

Struggling to comprehend what he'd just heard, Janos studied his sister's face. Her idea was absurd. But the longer and harder he stared at her, the more stoic and unwavering she appeared. She was determined to do whatever was necessary to ensure Karina delivered a healthy baby. Anna's intentions were noble, but Janos wondered at what cost this charade would come. How sane would he be after weeks—maybe months—of pretending to be a loving husband to his adulterous wife? He dared not predict the outcome of the disaster Karina had created for them, but he was certain it would not be a holy one.

## Forty-Six

### SOFIE

#### BEAVER CREEK, NOVEMBER 24, 1917

Sofie fought to calm her nerves as she stood before the door of Mrs. Walker's home. She had barely slept the night before. Her reunion with Pole had left her excited, unable to slow the torrent of thoughts swirling in her head. Every time she had been on the verge of sleep, Pole's handsome face appeared before her eyes, sending a jolt of electricity through her. Her fingers still tingled, and now her stomach was filled with a swarm of butterflies. As she reached for the brass pineapple door knocker, she wondered if this was the magical feeling Marie gushed about each time she became infatuated with a new boy.

"Good morning, Sof. I heard you comin' up the steps," Pole said, opening Mrs. Walker's front door before she'd had a chance to knock. He was freshly shaven, his wavy, brown hair neatly combed.

"Are you and Lily ready to see Beaver Creek?" Sofie asked, hoping her voice didn't sound too unsteady.

"I am, but my sister's not coming. She's helping Mrs. Walker with her shopping."

Sofie nodded, wondering if Pole had played a role in Lily's absence. Did he want her all to himself? She secretly hoped so. "Let's walk to Main Street first. That's where most of the shops and restaurants are."

"You lead the way. I'll buy you lunch at the end of the tour. We'll be hungry after walkin' around in the cold all morning."

"It won't take long to show you Beaver Creek, but lunch would be nice."

"I told Lily I'd pick her up later so we can go to the nickelodeon. You still wanna come?" Pole asked as he led Sofie down the porch steps, his hand lightly touching the small of her back.

She turned toward his smiling face. His eagerness to spend the day with her was written all over it. "Sure," she said, trying to sound casual.

As they strolled into town, chatting all the way, Sofie noticed that Pole's proximity to her was increasing with each passing minute. They had begun their walk with almost a foot of space between them, but during the course of several stories Pole had recounted about his life in the mountains, he had inched ever closer to her. His arm was now around her back, their coats constantly brushing against each other as they traipsed through the bitter cold. Each time Sofie pointed out a landmark to Pole, he leaned into her face, presumably to hear her better. And each time he did this, she was intoxicated by his heady scent. Pole smelled woodsy like pine or cedar. It was as if he'd been outdoors chopping wood all morning.

Pole exuded a ruggedness and masculinity Sofie was not accustomed to. She noticed the way people on the street regarded him, giving him a wide berth as they passed by. Sofie was not sure why, but she liked being in the company of someone so capable-looking. His imposing presence made her feel protected.

"Do you wanna say hello to your father?" Pole asked as Sofie pointed out the store to him.

"No. That's okay."

"Why not?"

Sofie dared not admit that she preferred having Pole all to herself. Besides, she was still not entirely comfortable watching the way her father now interacted with Concetta. She suspected he was falling in love with his business partner and would be making plans to marry her if not for Karina's shocking return. Sofie cringed as another thought of her mother's betrayal invaded her mind.

"Why do you suddenly look troubled?" Pole asked as he pulled Sofie away from the edge of the sidewalk and led her under the awning of a butcher shop.

"I had an unpleasant thought."

"About what?" He caressed her arm as he stepped closer to her, eliminating the already narrow space between them.

"It's not important," Sofie said, instantly mesmerized by Pole's dark green eyes, their deep color like the thick pine forest she had once discovered while hiking upriver. She wanted to get lost in those eyes, escape to an enchanted place, far from the madness plaguing her family. "It's been too long since you and I spent a day together," she whispered. "Let's not ruin it with talk of sad things."

"We have a lot of lost time to make up." Pole leaned into Sofie's face, pausing when his lips were just inches from hers.

Once again, she found herself wondering how it would feel to have his lips pressed against hers. She trembled as she felt his warm breath against her mouth. Caught between terror and longing, she blurted, "I think we should keep moving. It's cold."

"Are you sure about that, Sof?" Pole smirked.

"I'm not sure about anything anymore." She closed her eyes and exhaled.

"Come on, then." Pole took her hand and led her across the street. "Let's see what's playin' this afternoon at the nickelodeon. I've seen almost every film that's come out in the past month."

"Really?" she asked, recovering her composure.

"Lily's been having a hard time since her mother passed. Seein' shows helps take her mind off her grief. Besides, she deserves a little fun. Before I quit the mines, we hadn't seen a film in years."

"Why is that?"

"The closest theater was in Johnstown. It was an hour's walk just to get to the nearest town where we could catch a train," Pole said, shaking his head.

"I didn't realize you were that isolated."

"Abbott's Hollow isn't a place I'd ever choose to live. I only stayed there for Lily's sake."

"Did you ever think about leaving?"

"All the time. I tried for years to convince Lily's mother to leave, but she wouldn't have it. I had no choice but to wait for the day when my sister was old enough to make her own decisions." Pole went quiet and looked down. "And then Bridget died," he whispered.

Sofie was struck by the somber realization that Pole would not be with her if not for Lily's mother's passing. She scolded herself for seeing the death of a young girl's mother as a blessing in disguise. "Your sister is lucky to have you. You worked in the mines all those years to support her and Bridget. It must have been terribly difficult. You're so brave."

"Not really. Sometimes life doesn't give you a choice. You do what it takes to survive—to protect the people you love. You make sacrifices you never imagined."

Sofie felt so much admiration for Pole. "That accident you described at dinner last night sounded horrifying. I can't believe you were trapped underground for five days."

"Waitin' around to die is the worst torture I can think of. But it gave me plenty of time to think about my life—about the people who matter most to me." Pole leaned into Sofie's ear and whispered, "I thought about you."

Her heart fluttered.

Pole caressed her cheek and turned his attention to the placards on the windows of the nickelodeon. "I wouldn't mind seein' *Coney Island* again. That was a funny film. Hmm, looks like *Cleopatra* is playing, too."

As Pole studied the various placards covered with beautiful movie stars, Sofie gazed at him, aware that her attraction to her childhood friend was growing by the second. A chill went down her spine. Pole's handsome face belonged on a poster, she thought. Maybe a Western.

"What are you looking at?" he asked.

"You. I'm still wondering if this is all a dream."

Pole pinched the back of her hand lightly. "See, Sof. You're awake. I'm really here."

Sofie could not hold back the tear escaping down her cheek. She was so happy to be with Pole again, but her life was in so much turmoil.

He gently wiped her tear away with his thumb, his own eyes starting to water. "It's going to be okay. Things will work out."

"How do you know?" Sofie asked, wondering how Pole had read her thoughts.

"You're a survivor, sweetheart. You're the toughest girl I know. And I'll be by your side, holdin' your hand every step of the way."

With those words, Sofie fell into Pole's arms. She buried her head against his neck, trying to muster the courage to act on the passion he'd ignited within her. She raised her head slowly and met his loving gaze. His green eyes were twinkling, casting a spell over her, urging her to do the unimaginable. She gently pressed her lips against his, delighting in their softness and warmth. Her entire body quivered. She felt Pole's arms tighten around her as he hungrily parted her lips. The sounds on the busy street quickly fell away as Sofie sank deeper and deeper into Pole's strong embrace. She was safe from all the dangers of the world. She was home.

# *Forty-Seven*

## EDITH

### SHADYSIDE, NOVEMBER 29, 1917

Edith lumbered down the mauve carpeted staircase, her ever attentive husband at her side. James had repeatedly tried to convince her to take Thanksgiving dinner in bed, but she was determined to spend the holiday with Lukas no matter how debilitating her nausea. Eight weeks pregnant and vomiting several times per day, nothing could dampen her spirits. She was eager to share her joyous news with Lukas, whom she hadn't seen since late September.

The doctor had confirmed her pregnancy a week earlier, and Edith had been floating on a cloud ever since. Upon hearing the news, she had practically leapt with glee, astonished her prayers had finally been answered. A baby was growing inside her womb, and her love for it was already boundless. Only weeks prior, she'd been examining the possibility that her body was simply not fit to create life. Her dreams of having a child had been growing ever more fragile. And then the most unexpected of miracles occurred.

As her body underwent curious changes, Edith's relationship with her husband evolved as well. She saw it in his eyes, in the adoring way he now looked at her. James had always been a loving husband, constantly doting on her and attending to her every need. But now he regarded her with an extreme reverence, apparently in awe of the wonder taking place within her. He made her feel as if she had a divine purpose.

"Are you sure you're feeling up to this, Edith? Your condition is delicate. Lukas could visit with you in your room."

"Nonsense. I'm fine."

"There would be nothing improper about it, darling. He's practically our son."

"I appreciate your concern, but I feel better than I have in days. I've been sipping tea with ginger all morning."

"If you insist," James said as they reached the foot of the staircase. "Lukas is in the parlor. He's in good spirits. We enjoyed a lovely breakfast this morning and had a long, frank discussion about school."

"Is he still feeling out of place?"

"Quite the contrary. His grades are improving. He's talking of becoming an architect."

"That's splendid! I'm so happy to hear it." Edith quickened her pace toward the parlor.

"Aunt Edith," Lukas said happily as he stood up from his chair and rushed over to greet her. He planted a kiss on her cheek. "Uncle James said you haven't been well."

A smile crept across Edith's face. "Please sit down, Lukas. I have news to tell you. James, will you help me onto the sofa? I'm still feeling rather weak."

"Of course," he replied as he eased his wife onto the green velvet sofa. He plopped down beside her and took her hand, gently placing it on his knee. He winked at Lukas.

"Is everything all right?" Lukas asked. "You're both acting strange. But in a pleasant sort of way."

"Something very unexpected has occurred," Edith said, grinning. "The doctor instructed me not to share my news as it is still early. But you are family, and Uncle James and I would like you to share in our joy."

Lukas smiled knowingly.

"I'm with child! James and I are expecting a baby." Edith clapped her hands with delight. So much for cautious optimism, she thought. No matter the risk, she intended to relish every moment of this blessed experience.

"Congratulations. I'm happy for you both."

"We've hoped and prayed for this miracle for a very long time," Edith explained. "It has been a long journey with unspeakable heartbreak, but our time has finally come."

Lukas nodded in earnest. "The little guy will be lucky to have you as parents."

"Or little gal." James chuckled. "I simply cannot wait to spoil her."

"We will be infinitely happy no matter what blessing the Lord bestows upon us. This child will be loved like no other," Edith gushed. Her heart rejoiced at seeing the excitement on the faces of her husband and adopted nephew. Though Lukas was of no blood relation and had not come into her life until the age of eight, she loved him as if she had borne him herself. She celebrated his successes and grieved his heartaches. She obsessed about his future and vowed to do anything necessary for the sake of his happiness. Lukas was hers in every way that mattered. He would truly be a big brother to her baby.

"I don't care whether the baby is a boy or girl," Lukas said. "It will be fun to have a little one to chase around the house."

"It certainly will be," James agreed.

"Uncle James tells me that school is going well for you, Lukas. Your outlook has improved since our last visit?" Edith asked.

"It has. I've been studying more. I've decided to focus on my future instead of worrying about whether I belong."

Edith smiled proudly as James squeezed her hand. "That's wonderful news. But I'm curious as to what has brought on this change."

"I don't know," Lukas said, shaking his head. "I ran into an old friend from Riverton last month. He's been mining coal for the past several years. Maybe seeing him made me realize how lucky I am—how much worse my life could have turned out."

Edith nodded. "That's very insightful."

"Look at that! Our boy is growing up. He's becoming a mature adult. Perhaps he would like a scotch after dinner," James teased.

"Let's not get ahead of ourselves, dear husband." Edith elbowed James in the ribs. "Now, Lukas, I hope your father wasn't too disappointed that you're not spending Thanksgiving with him."

"I don't think so. I wrote him that I'm putting more effort into my studies. I explained that I only had enough time to visit Shadyside over the short holiday weekend. At least I'll see him at Christmas."

"You certainly will. But you must stop here for a day or two before you take the train up to Beaver Creek. We're on the way."

"Of course, Aunt Edith. I always enjoy your home during the holidays. No one has a prettier tree than you."

"This is your home, too. I wish you'd start thinking of it that way."

"I'll try."

Suddenly, Edith heard a low growl beside her. "Dear God, was that you?" She glared at her husband.

"Forgive me. It seems my stomach has no sense of propriety," James said, rubbing his midsection. "Dinner should be ready by now, shouldn't it?"

Lukas laughed. "I'll go check with the cook. We can't have Uncle James starving on Thanksgiving."

"Let me do it, Lukas. That's not the duty of a guest," James said as he leaned forward to stand.

"No, no," Edith scolded her husband. "I just instructed Lukas to think of this house as his own. It is quite proper that he address the staff. Now go on," she said, motioning Lukas down the hall.

As Edith watched Lukas set off toward the kitchen, she melted into the sofa, lulled by a quiet feeling of contentment. Having finally been granted some serenity, she realized how troubled she had been in recent months—maybe even years—about her struggle to have a baby. Her long-fought battles with her mysterious ailments had been taxing enough, but her heart-breaking attempts to bear a child had chipped away at her soul. The constant disappointment had been agonizing.

None of it mattered now. She was finally at peace. She closed her eyes and caressed her belly, imagining what her beautiful baby might look like. Would it have James's striking blue eyes? His blonde hair? Or maybe her own dark locks? She sighed. It did not matter whom the baby resembled. Edith only knew that her little son or daughter would bring indescribable, delirious joy into their lives.

# *Forty-Eight*

## JANOS

### BEAVER CREEK, DECEMBER 15, 1917

Janos glanced up at the clock on the train station's platform, a single snowflake landing on his cheek. The sky had been gray for days, threatening to deliver the season's first snowfall, but the smattering of flurries floating down around him was a feeble attempt at best. It was mid-December, and they had yet to receive any measurable snow. The weather had certainly been cold enough, but there hadn't been any precipitation for weeks. The entire fall season had been unusually dry, and the river, now frozen over, was the lowest he had seen it in years.

Janos had been pacing the platform like a nervous cat for almost twenty minutes. He'd arrived at the station fifteen minutes in advance of Concetta's train, and now it was five minutes overdue. He had missed her terribly over the last three weeks, but had been grateful for the respite from his constant lying. He was shocked at how adept he'd become at deception, telling untruths with as much ease as his wife once had. As soon as his ordeal with Karina was over, Janos intended to head straight to confession. He hated the manipulative person she had forced him to become.

At least he'd been lucky in recent weeks, seeing Karina only once on most days. With her pregnancy advancing, her growing belly had made it impossible for her to escape her confinement in Anna's room. After the night she had awoken from her stupor a few weeks earlier, Janos had feared her condition would continue to improve and that she would soon be wandering around the house or even the neighborhood. Thankfully, that nightmare had not come to life.

Karina was now well enough to flip through magazines between her many naps, but was too weak to get out of bed to seek him out. She had no choice but to wait for him to pop into her room for a few minutes after dinner each night. As for the absence of the children, Janos had explained to Karina that they were both confined to their rooms with the chicken pox. Unfortunately, that lie would not remain viable for long.

His legs growing tired from pacing, Janos was relieved when he finally heard the shrill whistle of a train. He ran his fingers through his hair, hoping Concetta would not find him too disheveled. The stress of the last month was taking its toll. The clumps of hair clogging the bathroom sink each morning had grown more copious.

"Janos!" Concetta rushed toward him the second she disembarked from the train. She looked lovely in her red wool coat and matching hat, the vibrant color a perfect complement to her chestnut eyes. She kissed him on the cheek and took a step backward to survey him. "Have you lost weight? You look thin."

"Do I?" he asked coolly, knowing full well he had punched a new hole in his leather belt the previous week to accommodate his shrinking waist. "How was your trip? You must be starving after the long journey. Should we go to Luigi's for an early dinner?"

"I'd rather eat at home. We can grab a few cans of soup from the store." She studied him. "But maybe we should go out for dinner. You look like you haven't been eating well. Are you ill?" She stood on her toes to touch his forehead.

Once Concetta was finished gauging Janos's temperature, he took her hand and led her toward the porter, who was unloading the baggage from the railcar. "Let's find your suitcase and get you home. I want to hear all about Philadelphia."

After Concetta had recounted her visit with Tony over canned chicken noodle soup and an entire loaf of French bread, she placed a bowl of stewed peaches on the table. The scent of cinnamon and brown sugar made Janos's mouth water. He marveled at how she managed to make a meal of canned goods taste like she had been slaving in the kitchen all day. He wondered what it would be like to come home to such an accomplished cook every night.

"It sounds like Tony and Lucia are doing well in Philadelphia. It must put your mind at ease to know they have Lucia's parents and sisters living nearby," Janos said, lifting a spoonful of peaches to his mouth.

"Yes, the baby will have plenty of cousins to play with when he gets older."

"I'm happy you had a pleasant trip," Janos said, wondering when Concetta might broach the subject of moving again. She had been glowing the entire time she'd discussed her son and his in-laws. Janos worried his dreams of a life with Concetta were slipping away.

"I miss Tony already, but it's comforting to know he is surrounded by good people. He has the large Italian family that Antonio and I were never able to give him."

"You must want to join him as soon as possible," Janos said, trying to sound supportive.

Concetta looked up from her bowl of peaches. "Did I give you that impression?"

"Your face lights up every time you speak of Tony. It's only natural that you'd want to be nearer to him."

Concetta bit her lip. "Tony said something similar about the way I look when I speak of you." She turned away, presumably to hide her reddening face. She remained silent for a moment and then turned to meet Janos's gaze. "I don't want to move."

"You don't?"

"I adore my son and his new family, but I could never make a home in Philadelphia. It's too crowded."

Janos almost fell out of his chair.

"I want to be where you are. I think it's time we discuss our future," she said, stroking his hand.

Janos's heart raced. Concetta's words were music to his ears, but he was in no position to discuss the future—not while his pregnant wife was still sleeping across the hall from him. He clutched his chest.

"Are you okay?"

He reached for his water. "I think I'm choking on a peach." He drained the entire glass in one gulp and then dabbed at his watery eyes with a napkin. When he had recovered, Janos saw that Concetta was staring at him.

"I think I know what's wrong. You've changed your mind about me, haven't you?" She pulled her hand away from him. "That's why you tried to convince me to stay in Philadelphia for over a month."

Janos sat paralyzed and speechless. For a split second, he wondered if this was the right course of action. Should he break things off with Concetta until he was finally rid of Karina?

Concetta got up and began clearing the dishes. "I'm a grown woman. I can handle the truth. You don't have to let me down easy, Janos." She slammed the dishes into the sink. "You can see yourself out."

Panicked, Janos sprang to his feet. He was behind Concetta in the blink of an eye, his arms wrapped around her, his mouth against her ear. "I want to be with you. More than you know." He kissed her cheek softly. "I just need time to sort things out."

"What things?" She turned around, her brown eyes damp with emotion.

Janos's mind raced to invent a lie. Desperate, he blurted the first name that entered his mind. "Sofie."

Concetta tilted her head.

"She's jealous of the time I've been spending with you and . . . I don't think she's ready for me to marry again." Janos exhaled, realizing there was some truth to what he had said.

"Oh," she said, sounding relieved.

"We need to give her a chance to warm up to the idea of you and me. Perhaps it's best if we continue spending our time together at your house and avoid my family for the time being."

Concetta frowned. "If you think it's best."

"Let me work on Sofie for a few weeks. Maybe we can share our intentions with her later in the winter."

Her eyes widened.

"Maybe I'm underestimating my daughter." Janos kissed Concetta's forehead. "Perhaps it won't take so long." The truth was he had no idea how long it would take to sort things out—to be rid of Karina. As Janos pulled Concetta into his chest, he allowed himself a moment to fantasize about what a future with her might look like. But being a cautious man, he did not lose himself in that reverie for too long. He understood the obstacles standing in his way and knew his odds at overcoming them were dismal.

# Forty-Nine

## POLE

### BEAVER CREEK, DECEMBER 15, 1917

Pole gazed at Sofie as she sipped her tea across the dining room table from him. She looked so pretty with her hair pulled away from her face. A few strands had escaped the loose braid at the back of her neck, but the effect was flattering. The wavy, blonde locks framed her face and drew attention to her sky-blue eyes. Pole was staring at her, but did not care if she noticed. Sofie had caught him gazing at her several times over the past three weeks and had simply returned his dreamy look. Sometimes they just sat in silence, holding hands and studying each other's faces, awed by the fact that they were breathing the same air. The unknown distance between them had vanished, the misery of their separation now a memory. The world had somehow righted itself. Pole and Sofie were together again.

"How was work today? Is it getting any better?" Sofie asked, looking up from her tea cup.

"Still hot as hell. I can't wait to move up and get away from the furnaces."

Being new to the industry, Pole had been offered a position at one of the glass factory's furnaces, working alongside Eastern European immigrants. His job was to oversee the melting of sand, limestone, and soda ash into glass in a furnace heated up to 2800°F. The work was scorching hot and miserable. But the foreman had promised him that his assignment was temporary, and he'd soon be moving up to the casting and rolling room. If he was successful and caught on quickly, he might become a foreman one day. Pole was assured there were plenty of opportunities for native-born, English-speaking workers.

"I get nervous thinking about you working in front of a furnace. It reminds me of when Papa worked at the mill," Sofie said, shaking her head.

"It's only temporary. I'll be a foreman before you know it." Pole reached across the table and caressed Sofie's hand. "You worry too much. Always have."

"Some habits are hard to break, I guess."

Pole picked up Sofie's hand and kissed it. "Where's your family? It's quiet for a Saturday afternoon."

"Papa's picking Concetta up from the train station, and Aunt Anna's at the neighbor's baking cookies."

Suddenly, Pole heard shouting from upstairs.

"Anna!" the voice bellowed. "Anna! I need you!"

Sofie shot a panicked look at Pole. "What should we do?"

"Go see what she needs."

"I can't do that. She still thinks I'm ten."

"Are you serious? I thought your father woulda marched you into her room by now. Karina needs to see that you're all grown-up. She needs to know the truth."

"She doesn't care about the truth. She's stuck in 1910. And Papa and Aunt Anna won't correct her because they don't want her to get hysterical. They say it's for the sake of the baby." Sofie rolled her eyes.

"Anna! Where are you?" the voice shouted even louder. The hollering was followed by a thundering crash. Something had hit the floor.

"Christ! I'll go up." Pole sprang to his feet and ran toward the staircase. He knocked only once before bursting into Karina's bedroom. He was not prepared for what he saw. The nightstand had been knocked over, and a glass pitcher had shattered. The floor was covered in water and shards of glass. But that was not the most troubling aspect of the scene. Karina was sitting in bed, the quilt peeled away from her, her nightgown hiked up past her knees. Her swollen belly and breasts protruded from the thin fabric. Pole immediately looked away. He was not sure if he was more distressed by her scantily-clad pregnant body or the haggard appearance of her once beautiful face. She looked weathered, the cruelty of the years scars on her face.

"It's okay, Mrs. Kovac. Aunt Anna will be here shortly to tidy up." Pole turned back toward the door.

"John Stofanik! What the hell are you doing here?" Karina asked, the venom in her voice palpable.

Pole sheepishly turned toward her as she drew the quilt over her belly. "I'm not John. I'm his son, Pole."

"What sort of game are we playing today? You think I don't recognize you?"

"I'm sorry ma'am, but you're confused. I'll go find Aunt Anna for you." Pole hoped to escape the room without incident. There was a wildness in the woman's eyes that made him uneasy.

"You will not. Pull that rocking chair close to the bed." Karina motioned for Pole to sit down and then wiped her brow with the back of her hand. She sighed loudly, as if irritated by his presence. "Seeing you . . ." her voice trailed off.

Unable to hear her low whisper, Pole said, "I'm sorry. What was that?"

Karina's eyes bored into Pole's. "Seeing you is troubling!"

She practically spat the words at him. She began muttering to herself in Slovak.

Pole reluctantly took a seat, unable to take his eyes off Sofie's mother. She was talking to herself and growing more agitated by the second. He could barely understand a word she said, her speech was so rapid and his knowledge of Slovak nothing but a long, distant memory. She closed her eyes and shook her head violently, as if to erase an unpleasant image from it. Karina was struggling, and Pole sat paralyzed, unsure of what to do.

*Maybe she really has lost her mind.* He had been doubting her memory loss was genuine, given what he knew about her involvement in the robbery and murder of her employer. When Hamish had told him the story behind his pop's abrupt escape from Riverton, Pole's opinion of Mrs. Kovac had changed dramatically. He now believed she was capable of anything. Faking amnesia certainly wouldn't be beneath a woman able to commit murder. But the disturbing behavior Pole was witnessing made him think otherwise. Perhaps Karina's torment was real. Without thinking, he reached out and stroked her hand.

"Calm down now," Pole said reassuringly. "It's all right."

Karina stiffened at his touch. A crazed look overtook her face as she seized Pole's wrist and dug her nails into his flesh. "I know why. I know why I'm bothered by the sight of you."

His arm burning, Pole's first instinct was to pull away. But he was afraid of provoking the woman's ire any further. She looked deranged and full of hate. He tried to remain calm. "I told you, Mrs. Kovac, I'm not who you think. I'm Pole Stofanik. I'm not my father."

"Enough already!" She clutched his wrist tighter. Blood began to trickle down Pole's forearm. "You're the reason I had to leave. You weren't supposed to be at Henry's."

Pole steadied himself. He wasn't sure he wanted to hear anymore, but he wondered if playing along might be worthwhile.

Maybe he could get the final pieces of the puzzle of Sofie's mother's disappearance.

"I wasn't?" Pole asked innocently.

"Stop playing dumb. Pavol was supposed to do it himself. Payback for what happened to his brother."

Pole nodded slowly, now eager to hear more. "And?"

"And you messed it up!" Karina rubbed her temples. "My head hurts," she whined, sliding further into the bed and pulling the quilt up under her chin.

Worried that she was about to lose her train of thought, Pole leaned forward. "How did I screw up?" he asked, lowering his voice to make it sound more like his father's.

Karina cocked her head to the side. "When did you learn to speak proper English? And where's your accent?" She eyed him suspiciously, an eyebrow raised.

Pole rushed to invent an excuse. "I've been takin' classes."

Karina sneered. "You in a classroom! Now that would be a sight." She studied Pole's face, her eyes squinted in concentration.

"What's wrong?"

"You don't look the same. You don't sound the same either. But you're still a rotten son of a bitch! Now get out!" she screamed.

Pole jumped up and bolted for the door. "I'm sorry. I'm sorry I upset you," he stammered, looking back one last time at the unhinged woman. He regretted that he'd entered her room. That he'd shown her his face. If Karina wasn't insane, she was the best actress he had ever seen.

"What happened to you?" Sofie's eyes grew wide as Pole entered the dining room. "You're bleeding," she said, looking down at his arm. "And I heard screaming."

"Your mother thought I was my pop. She was pretty upset at the sight of me."

"Why?"

Pole shook his head. Could he tell Sofie what he knew about her mother's involvement in her employer's murder? He certainly didn't have all the pieces of the puzzle, but he now knew enough to assume that Karina and Pavol had been part of a scheme to get revenge on Henry Archer. Pole just wasn't sure how his pop had gotten involved and why Karina said he was the reason she had to leave town. And why did she care about the death of Tomas Tomicek anyway? Had she even known him? Pole scratched his head. The details were sketchy, but it looked like what Hamish had told him in the mine was true. Sofie's mother was indeed the curvy blonde who killed Henry Archer.

"Pole? Did you hear me?" Sofie was standing next to him, dabbing the scratches on his forearm with a dish towel. "Why would she be upset by seeing your father?"

Pole studied Sofie's beautiful face. She had been through so much in her seventeen years. Would knowing the truth about her mother ease or add to her burden? He was not yet ready to make that determination. "I don't know, Sof. Your mother isn't well. We shouldn't take anything she says or does too seriously."

Sofie nodded.

Pole stroked the back of her head. "You should probably go get your aunt. I think Karina was tryin' to get herself some water when she knocked over the nightstand."

"Okay. I'll be back shortly."

As Sofie rushed out the door, Pole opened up the sideboard and poured himself a glass of whiskey. He downed it in one gulp and then poured himself another. He wondered how many drinks he needed to forget what he knew about Karina. He didn't want to be the one to tell Sofie that her mother was far more twisted than anyone could have imagined.

# *Fifty*

## JANOS

### BEAVER CREEK, DECEMBER 19, 1917

Janos scolded himself as he trudged home in the dark, wishing he had worn more layers. The snow was falling steadily now and quickly accumulating on the ground. He suspected there were already six inches of fluffy white powder on the sidewalk in front of him. The wind had picked up dramatically over the course of the afternoon, its powerful gusts blowing and drifting snow throughout the neighborhood. Janos pulled the collar of his coat up around his face, hoping to shield his stinging cheeks from the bitter cold. He looked forward to the warm meal and hot cup of tea that would surely be waiting for him on the dining room table.

As he entered the house, Janos was surprised to find no sign of life in the parlor, kitchen, or dining room. There was nothing on the stove or in the oven, and the table had not been set. Where was everyone? He turned around and headed toward the staircase when he heard loud moaning coming from above.

Had Karina's labor begun?

Janos froze, unsure of what to do. Unlike her previous births, he had no place by his wife's side. Her wellbeing was of no concern to him, her child of no relation. He did not wish Karina ill, but had no want of updates from the doctor or midwife. He was not worried about the intensity of her pain, nor did he feel compelled to enter her room to provide comfort. Janos simply wanted to be anywhere but under that roof. He stepped toward the front door, wondering how long it would take him to return to the store in the growing blizzard. Perhaps Concetta and Mrs. Rossi would not mind if he joined them for dinner.

"Papa! Where are you going?" Sofie shouted, quickly descending the staircase.

His daughter had caught him in the act of escaping. Janos turned around slowly, his head hung low. "I'm not needed here. I'll spend the night at the store."

"You can't do that. Aunt Anna can't deliver the baby on her own."

"You think I'm going to help?" he asked, stunned by the ridiculous assumption Sofie had made. He hadn't assisted in the birthing of his own two children. Was he to help bring a stranger's baby into the world?

"Dr. Adler's not here yet, and the blizzard is getting worse. What if he doesn't make it?"

"Your aunt has helped deliver many babies. She'll show you what to do."

"You don't understand, Papa." Sofie's voice began to crack. "I can't go in there. I won't."

The panic in his daughter's voice was palpable. Janos reached out and patted her arm. Suddenly, more moans came from above. Only this time, they were lengthier and more anguished. The labor was progressing.

Sofie looked up at the ceiling, her face growing paler by the second.

"What would you have me do? Enter that room and witness my wife—who abandoned me—give birth to another man's child? Have I not been punished enough?"

Sofie's face fell. Janos feared his tone had been too rough.

"I need a hand up here!" Anna appeared at the top of the stairs, her face drenched in sweat. Her gray hair was unkempt and falling out of the bun at the back of her head. "Will neither of you help me?"

Karina's moans evolved into screams. Janos shuddered when he thought he heard her calling his name. "Are none of the neighbor ladies available to help? Aren't there any midwives around?" he asked desperately.

"Aunt Anna is afraid they will gossip. Karina keeps asking for you—she wants to see her baby's father," Sofie said.

Janos grabbed the newel post for support. "Dear God. Who can we trust? What about Mrs. Walker?"

"She's feeding our boarders," Anna replied, wincing at another of Karina's screams. "I sent Vilium and Marek over there for dinner. She's also got to feed Lily—and Pole if he ever makes it home from work in this storm."

Janos and Sofie exchanged hopeful looks, seeming to read the other's mind. "Lily!" they both shouted.

"I'll get her. I know we can trust her." Sofie ran to the closet and quickly put on her coat and hat.

"Be careful. It's treacherous out there," Janos warned his daughter.

"I'll be back before you know it. I'm only going halfway down the block."

Suddenly, Karina's wailing rose to a crescendo. Janos cringed at the sound.

"I've got to get back in there. If that baby comes in the next five minutes, Janos, you'll have no choice but to help me," Anna said sternly. "If something goes wrong, I'll need an extra pair of hands—assuming I can even figure out what to do. Goddamn this miserable storm! And goddamn that slow-moving Dr. Adler!"

*Goddamn Karina.* Janos cursed her for the millionth time that month. As his sister returned to his wife's side, he grabbed the half empty bottle of whiskey from the sideboard. He held it up to his face, wondering who had drunk it. He'd bought it less than a week ago. He shrugged and took it to the basement along with a dusty, unopened bottle of Scotch he had found at the back of the cabinet.

Hoping to find refuge from the sound of Karina's relentless screaming, Janos closed the basement door and descended the steps. The boiler would surely drown out the commotion coming from two floors above him. As he neared the nook below the staircase, he grabbed a blanket from a mountainous pile of dirty laundry Anna must have forgotten about and placed it between himself and the dirt floor covered in coal dust. As Janos sipped his whiskey, the sound of the hissing boiler filling his ears, he closed his eyes and imagined he was somewhere else. He tried to conjure a happy memory to distract himself from his aching heart.

He thought of Sofie and Lukas. He saw the chubby, sweet faces of a seven-year-old and a five-year-old wandering the banks of the Monongahela River on a warm summer's day. They were chasing a swarm of butterflies, laughing and giggling as they flapped their arms, trying to mimic the colorfully winged creatures. Janos's heart had filled with joy that day, watching his children, so full of innocence and curiosity. He held tight to that image as he finished the bottle of whiskey and opened the scotch.

"Papa. Wake up."

Someone was shaking him. He opened his eyes to a spinning room. Sofie's face was a blur.

"Did you drink all this?" she asked, holding up two bottles of liquor. "You reek."

Janos tried to focus on his daughter. His head was throbbing, and his stomach felt like it was about to rebel. He stared at the bottles Sofie held in her hands. The whiskey was gone, but thankfully, it looked like he had only drunk a quarter of the Scotch.

"We were worried sick about you. We thought you went out into the blizzard. I only came down here to put more coal in the boiler."

"Sorry. I wanted a quiet place to rest. What time is it?"

"Almost eleven."

"And Karina?" Janos asked, not sure he wanted to know the answer.

"She gave birth to a healthy baby girl. Lily helped Aunt Anna with the delivery, and Dr. Adler got here twenty minutes after."

Janos sighed. "That's a relief."

Sofie looked down at the floor. She made swirls in the dirt with the tip of her shoe. "What will you do now that the baby's here?" she whispered.

"I don't know. I have no more answers than the day your mother arrived."

Sofie sighed. "Lukas will be home for Christmas in a few days. I'm worried about how he's going to react to the situation."

"Me, too," Janos said, rising to his feet. As he felt the full weight of his body upon his wobbly legs, a sense of dread washed over him. His time to come up with a plan to deal with Karina was running out. Her baby had arrived healthy—his and Anna's goal had been achieved. There was now little reason for his wife to remain under his roof. The longer she stayed, the greater the chance that she would never leave.

Reluctant to abandon his refuge beside the hissing boiler, Janos forced himself to climb the stairs with his daughter. He tried to weigh his options, but his mind was still too foggy with drink. Perhaps a solution would appear to him in the morning light, once the storm had cleared. All he knew in that moment of drunkenness was that he would not allow Karina to ruin his happiness with Concetta. She would not destroy his life a second time.

# *Fifty-One*

## EDITH

### SHADYSIDE, DECEMBER 20, 1917

Edith woke to the sensation of something warm running down her leg. She had slept so soundly through the night, she wondered if she'd lost control of her bladder. That happened to pregnant women sometimes, didn't it? She slid her hand under the sheets and felt the dampness between her legs. She stiffened. She quickly withdrew her hand from under the bedding and examined the sticky liquid. It trickled down her fingers. Trembling, she prayed to God and all of his angels as she pulled back the heavy eiderdown quilt and peered beneath it.

It was everywhere. On the sheets, on the blanket, all over her nightgown. Blood. It was the same crimson hue of the quilt she so cherished.

"No!" Edith shouted. "No! Not again!" she screamed so loud that her throat burned. She beat the mattress ferociously until she was nearly out of breath. She then ripped the quilt and sheets from the bed and threw them onto the floor. "Burn it! Burn all of it!" she yelled, tearing at her nightgown. The blood-soaked garment clung to her body, deepening her fury.

Suddenly, James was in the doorway, his face white with fear. "Edith!" he cried, rushing toward her. "I've got you. I've got you."

Edith collapsed into her husband's arms, allowing him to scoop her up and carry her into the bathroom. As he gently placed her in the bathtub, she seized his wrist. "Get it all. Get every last bit of it out of this house."

"Get what, darling? What?" James asked in desperation.

"Red. The color red," she growled as her head rolled to the side, darkness consuming her.

## Fifty-Two

## SOFIE

### BEAVER CREEK, DECEMBER 22, 1917

"Where's Lily? I thought she was helping you with dinner," Sofie asked as she entered the kitchen.

"She was, but she went upstairs to check on your mother and the baby. She can't seem to keep her hands off that child," Aunt Anna said, stirring a pot of stew.

Sofie nodded. She had never been particularly interested in babies—at least not in the way Lily was. She felt guilty that she still hadn't held her baby sister, but feared her acceptance of Karina's baby might be viewed by her father as a betrayal. When Aunt Anna had brought the baby downstairs the morning after the blizzard, only Pole and Lily had fussed over her. Sofie and her father had simply glanced at little Mary, thankful she had been born healthy and not at all surprised that she'd inherited her mother's blue eyes.

Pole had a keen interest in the baby, and it had caught Sofie off guard. He seemed to be in awe of Mary, constantly competing with his sister for time to rock her and gaze at her tiny face. He had even snatched the baby from Lily's arms on one occasion when he thought his sister wasn't holding her correctly. Sofie never imagined a burly coal miner would be so enamored with an infant. She had also not expected to be so jealous of the attention Pole gave it.

"Will it ever end?" Papa muttered from the dining room, interrupting Sofie's thoughts.

She glanced through the doorway at her father, who seemed to be talking to a pile of invoices. The entire dining room table was covered with stacks of paperwork.

"What are you doin' here?" Sofie suddenly heard Pole say from the parlor. Had someone knocked on the front door? Curious, she left the kitchen and rushed down the hall.

"Sofie!" Lukas said happily as he embraced his sister. "I see you and Pole found each other." He winked at her.

"We did. Thanks to you," Pole said, shaking his hand.

"Are you staying here at the house?"

"No. Me and Lily are staying with Mrs. Walker."

"You're early." Papa said nervously as he entered the room and hugged his son. "We weren't expecting you until Christmas Eve."

"Aren't you happy to see me? I haven't been home since the end of summer." Lukas chuckled as he slapped his father playfully on the back.

"Of course, I am." Papa forced a smile. "But I thought you were going to see your aunt Edith for a few days."

Lukas's smile disappeared. "I got a telegram yesterday. She's ill and not feeling up to visitors."

"Is it serious? Edith always has time for you," Papa said.

Lukas shook his head and went silent for a moment. "She's had a difficult week . . . but the doctor expects her to make a full recovery."

"We'll have to send her a card or some flowers," Sofie suggested. She had always resented Mrs. Harford for stealing her brother from them, but she could not deny that the heiress had been good to him.

"You look different, Lukas. Did you change your hair? Or maybe you gained some weight. You look chubby," Sofie said as she poked her brother in the stomach.

"You're one to talk. Looks like you spent more than five minutes on your hair and outfit for a change. Who are you trying to impress?" Lukas laughed, looking at Pole.

Sofie resisted the urge to punch her brother and quickly turned toward the kitchen to hide her reddening face. "I'll get you some hot tea, dear brother," she said in her most sarcastic tone.

"I've already got it." Aunt Anna entered the parlor with a pot of tea and a tray of walnut and poppyseed *koláče* she had baked in preparation for Christmas. "It's almost dinner time, but a few sweets won't hurt." Aunt Anna handed Sofie the tray so she could hug Lukas. "I missed you so much."

"I missed you, too," he replied, kissing his aunt on the cheek.

"We're going to take turns holding the baby. Do you understand now, Pole?"

Horrified, Sofie turned around to see Lily coming down the stairs with Mary in her arms.

"Her tummy's nice and full, and she's sleeping peacefully. It might be a good time for you to finally hold her, Sofie." Lily stopped dead in her tracks when she caught sight of Lukas.

"Hi, Lily. Do you remember me from the five-and-dime?" he asked. "Are you babysitting?"

The color drained from Lily's face. "Sort of."

Sofie's eyes darted around the room. Papa, Aunt Anna, and Pole looked even paler than Lily. She stared at her father questioningly, wondering if this was the moment he would break the news to Lukas. She had hoped for more time to enjoy her brother's homecoming before things got unpleasant.

Papa cleared his throat. "Lily has quite a way with babies. She told me the other day that she's thinking of becoming a midwife."

"Let's all sit and have some tea," Aunt Anna said. "Pole, can you bring in one of the chairs from the dining room?"

"Yes, ma'am." Pole gently caressed the small of Sofie's back as he slid by her. When he returned to the room, he leaned close to her ear and whispered, "Try to look calm." He then grabbed her hand and led her over to the empty armchair next to her father. He placed the dining room chair next to hers and sat on it, never letting go of her hand.

Lukas, Aunt Anna, and Lily had all settled on the sofa and were already sipping tea and selecting cookies from the tray. Sofie tried to relax as her father and aunt interrogated Lukas about school and his grades in particular. He replied pleasantly, pausing occasionally to stroke the cheek of the baby Lily held in her arms. He, too, seemed enchanted by little Mary. As Lukas began the story of a Halloween prank gone terribly awry, Sofie finally felt herself relax. The sound of her brother's voice was comforting, his animated gestures heartening. The people she loved most in the world were finally together in the same room, and Sofie was grateful. She turned to smile at Pole, but was startled by the tension in his jaw. His gaze was fixed on the staircase. From Sofie's vantage point, she could not see what was troubling him.

It only took seconds. She saw the pair of feet descending the staircase.

Pole sprang out of his chair and rushed up the stairs to cut Karina off. Sofie looked over at her brother, who hadn't seemed to notice the movement. He was bent over the baby, tickling her chin.

"Get away from me, John!" Karina shouted. "Get out of my way!"

Everyone looked up. Sofie felt her heart pounding in her ears. There was no hiding the truth now.

"Janos! Why is John Stofanik lurking around our house? And why haven't the children come to meet their baby sister?" Karina marched down the stairs past Pole and stomped into the parlor. "Who are these people?" she asked, pointing at Sofie and Lukas.

Sofie could not believe her eyes. It was the first glimpse

she'd had of her mother since she invaded their home over a month ago. Karina looked like a woman possessed. Her grizzled hair lay in tangles, the shadows under her eyes so dark, they looked like bruises. The gauntness of her face accentuated its deep lines, making her look haggard. The sight of Karina made Sofie's eyes burn. What had happened to the unforgettable beauty who was once her mother?

Sofie slowly moved her head in the direction of her brother, not certain she wanted to witness his reaction. He sat paralyzed, his jaw practically on the floor, his eyes narrowing.

"Mama?" he whispered.

Karina tilted her head as she eyed Lukas. She bit her lip in concentration, seeming to work out a riddle. "What did you call me?"

Lukas looked sideways at Papa, then at Sofie, his brows deeply furrowed. "What's she doing here? What happened to her?" he stammered. "Is this *her* baby?" He pointed at Mary, quickly sliding away in revulsion.

Papa stood and squared his shoulders. "This is not the way we wanted you to find out, Lukas. I'm terribly sorry. It's a long, sad story."

Lukas leapt to his feet. "I have a sad story, too, don't I, Papa? Don't we all?" His eyes bored into Sofie's and then Aunt Anna's. His wild gaze came to rest on his father. "How could you let her into this house? What's she doing here after all this time?" he shouted. "Seven years!" He shook his head furiously. Lukas lunged toward Karina and pulled up his right pant leg. "Look at what you did. Look at my sad story!" he screamed just inches from her face. "I lost my leg because of you. Because you left us." His face burned red with rage.

Pole grabbed Lukas and pulled him away from his mother. "That's enough, Lukas. That's enough."

Lukas swatted at Pole repeatedly, forcing him to tighten his grip. He continued to struggle for what seemed like minutes, but quickly realized his efforts were futile. He was no match for Pole's massive frame.

In between sobs, Sofie noticed a striking change in Karina's demeanor. Her lip quivered as she inched toward Lukas, her arms outstretched. She reached for his cheek.

"Lukas, my baby," she whispered. "What happened to my little boy?" Tears streamed down her face.

His own face wet with emotion, Papa approached Karina and gently placed his hands on her shoulders. "I've tried to tell you, Karina. So many times. Lukas and Sofie are all grown up. They're not children anymore."

For the first time, Karina focused on Sofie. Her hand went to her mouth. "The blonde hair . . . I should have known," she whispered. "She's so pretty," Karina said in awe. "And this one?" She pointed at Pole.

"This is Pole Stofanik. Not John. He was killed in a mining accident several years ago," Papa said.

Karina nodded slowly as she surveyed the room. The picture was becoming clearer now. "The baby!" she gasped, gripping her husband's shirt. "You said she's not yours."

"No. No, she's not," Papa said sadly, shaking his head.

"Oh, God!" Karina doubled over. "I remember," she cried through labored breaths. "I remember. It's Victor's!"

Sofie watched in horror as her mother collapsed onto the floor, wailing and clawing at her scalp. She writhed like a wounded animal, her savage cries threatening to shake the house from its foundation. Sofie trembled with fear. She had never seen a more tormented soul. Her first instinct was to run to her mother's side and comfort her, but her legs refused to move. Sofie was frozen and on the verge of tipping over. An ice sculpture about to shatter into a million pieces. Suddenly, Aunt Anna was at her side, steadying her, whispering words of comfort into her ear.

In the midst of the turmoil, Sofie detected motion to her right. She turned her head and caught a glimpse of Pole. He was pulling Lukas tight to his chest and turning him away from his mother's suffering. He wrapped his arm around Lukas's head, covering his ears, shielding him from the deafening screams.

His eyes half closed, Papa bent down and scooped Karina off the floor. He cradled her in his arms, rocking her and whispering in her ear. Her sobbing gradually subsided. But as Papa began to climb the stairs, Karina's crying was replaced by something puzzling and no less troubling.

"I didn't want to leave. I didn't want to. I was going to stay," Sofie heard her mother whine. Then the wailing resumed.

# *Fifty-Three*

## JANOS

### BEAVER CREEK, DECEMBER 22, 1917

Fighting back tears and biting his quivering lip, Janos gently laid Karina on the bed. He pulled the hem of her nightgown down over her knees and covered her with the quilt. "Calm down. You're safe. You're safe now," he whispered in Slovak as he stroked her hair.

"Please, Janos," she begged in between cries. "Don't leave me." She reached up to pull him onto the bed.

Janos took hold of her hands and squeezed them. "I'll stay. I promise. But let me get you some water. Your throat is probably sore."

Like a sick child desperate for comfort, Karina nodded her head eagerly. Her face grew more sullen as Janos moved toward the door.

"I'll be right back," he said, grabbing the empty glass resting on the dresser. He took it into the bathroom and filled it halfway to the top. He pulled the vial of Veronal out of the medicine cabinet and poured a few crystals into the glass. He returned to the bedroom and sat down on the bed next to Karina.

"Drink this," he instructed his wife, wondering how quickly the medicine would take effect. He wasn't certain he had given her the correct dose.

Karina contained her crying long enough to drain the glass.

"You should get some sleep. You'll feel better in the morning." Janos patted her shoulder.

"Will you hold me? I'm so scared. Please hold me," Karina pleaded through shuddering breaths.

Janos could not stand the sight of his wife's anguished face. Against his better judgment, he pulled her into his arms and held her as she cried. She was a child again, unable to calm down after a tantrum, gasping for air in between sobs. But sadly, Janos understood Karina's fit was not brought on by childish concerns.

"Shh. I've got you. You're safe." Janos no longer felt disoriented or repulsed by the woman in his arms. She was broken and in desperate need of compassion. He would never forget the harm she had inflicted on him and his children, but he was beginning to see that Karina deserved his forgiveness. Her agony upon remembering the identity of her baby's father spoke volumes. It was clear she had already suffered for her sins at the hands of this *Victor* person. No matter her crimes, Janos had never wished such a severe punishment for her. He had never wished for her to be driven to madness.

Janos was also beginning to realize how blind he had been to the true nature of his wife's suffering throughout the course of their marriage. He had lived in a constant state of denial, making excuses for her strange behavior. Perhaps he should have sought the advice of a doctor all those years ago after Sofie was born. Karina's disinterest in her baby and constant weeping were troubling, but everyone said it would pass. Anna assured him that it would. And his sister had been right—at least for a time. But Karina's sadness returned, and her mood swings became more unpredictable. She withdrew from her family and allowed her dark moods to consume her.

Janos had ignored the warning signs and failed to recognize that his wife's symptoms pointed to a larger problem. He understood that now. But unfortunately, whatever she had endured during her seven-year absence had completely robbed her of her sanity. He feared she was now beyond saving. He pulled his wife tighter to his chest and buried his head in her hair. It still smelled of rosewater. As he caressed her cheek, he wondered if the Karina of his youth was still in that body somewhere, buried beneath layers of sorrow and anger. And unspeakable trauma. Could she be coaxed out?

Janos did not know the answer, but he had to try. He had to give his children a chance to love their mother. They deserved a chance to know the woman he'd fallen in love with almost two decades ago. He missed her desperately. As his eyes filled with more tears, he vowed to seek out as many doctors as necessary to repair his wife's broken mind. He would even ask Edith Harford for help. She had plenty of connections, and her pockets were deep.

Janos knew there was no way to turn back time. The ending to his and Karina's love story had already been written. But he would do his best to restore his wife's health. Not for his own sake, but for hers and that of her children. Sofie, Lukas, and baby Mary needed the love of a mother. Janos hoped there was a doctor somewhere who could help his family find the path to redemption.

"Janos? Are you crying?" Karina's sleepy voice interrupted his thoughts.

"No," he said, wiping the tears from his cheeks. "Try to get some sleep." He kissed her on the forehead and laid her back down on the bed.

"Don't be sad," she whispered. "We have three children now. Three beautiful children."

"Yes, Karina. They are beautiful." Like their mother once was, he lamented to himself.

As he sat on the edge of the bed, waiting for his wife to fall asleep, Janos closed his eyes. The image of a stunning, seventeen-year-old blonde appeared before him. Her eyes were the color of the sky, and her smile was bright. She'd dropped her suitcase in the middle of the road, and Janos was helping her collect its contents. As they both reached for the same sweater, their hands touched and their eyes met. Janos trembled, certain that the earth had moved.

Despite all that had happened since, he did not regret meeting that enchanting beauty in the middle of a dirt road.

## *Fifty-Four*

# LUKAS

### BEAVER CREEK, DECEMBER 23, 1917

Lukas fought to maintain his balance as he stumbled through the snow, his head throbbing, his insides in the midst of a rebellion. He had already stopped twice to vomit into a snowbank. Unfortunately, the fistfuls of powder he'd shoved into his mouth had not done much to remove the bitter taste lingering on his tongue. He hoped some tea and toast might do the trick.

His walk home from Charlie's house was taking forever. Snow was beginning to fall, and his coat and shoes were getting wet. He pulled up his sleeve and glanced at his wristwatch. Was it just before six or seven? He could barely make out the hands. It was a moonless night, and his arm refused to stay still.

Lukas was not used to drinking whiskey, but all he had wanted to do after seeing his mother the night before was forget. He needed to purge himself of what he'd seen, what he'd heard, and most importantly, what he'd felt. The shock at seeing her had shaken him. He had fled the house and escaped into town, ending up in front of the nickelodeon with a few acquaintances from his old school. They weren't really friends—just some football players who used to tease him about his wooden leg. But when Lukas offered to pay for their admission to see a film, they were suddenly his new best buddies.

They had gone to a diner after the movie, and then Teddy suggested they go to a saloon after he'd caught a glimpse of the thick wad of cash in Lukas's wallet. It seemed like a good idea at the time, especially since the saloon was owned by Teddy's uncle. They could sit in the back of the room and drink as much as they wanted, and no one would bother them. How badly Lukas wished someone had kicked them out.

Lukas had no idea how much he'd drunk or how he had ended up on the floor of Charlie's bedroom. He was the nicest of the three boys, so maybe he had taken pity on him. He might have felt guilty if the kid who had bought his dinner and drinks froze to death in a snowbank. He probably didn't have any idea where Lukas lived either.

All Lukas knew was that he felt like shit and that his wallet was empty. He trudged toward home, grateful it was a Sunday and everyone in his house would be asleep. As he neared Dogwood Avenue, he stopped dead in his tracks, almost certain he had seen a shadowy figure descend the front steps of his house. He rubbed his eyes. Was his mind playing tricks on him? Was he still drunk? He shook his head, trying to clear the fog. He squinted harder at the porch, but this time he was sure he saw movement. The figure was now on the sidewalk, making its way down the street.

Curious, Lukas quickened his pace. He wondered why any member of his family would be roaming around the neighborhood at this hour. Maybe one of the boarders had to work a Sunday shift. But if so, he was headed in the wrong direction. It looked like this person was headed for the river. Unable to quell his curiosity, Lukas followed several yards behind.

As he pursued the mysterious figure onto the path along the river, he began to wonder if it was Sofie. Were she and

Pole meeting in secret in the woods? He knew many of his classmates met girls in strange places for the purposes of bush-whacking, as they liked to call it. Lukas cringed. He didn't want to witness any part of that. He'd had enough trauma in the past twelve hours. He turned to head home, but the distinct cry of a baby sent a shot of adrenaline through him.

Was that his mother's baby? And who was wandering around with her in the cold? Lukas closed the gap between himself and the darkly cloaked figure, finally catching up to it at the old wooden train bridge. The pitch blackness of the sky had turned a dark gray, and he could make out the outline of the bridge as well as the shape of a person crossing it. The baby's cries were much louder now.

Horrified, he shouted, "Stop! That bridge isn't safe!"

The figure ignored him. It continued to move further across the deck.

All of Lukas's senses were suddenly heightened. He scrambled up the bank, then paused at the beginning of the bridge. Afraid to go any further, he yelled, "Stop! It's too icy." He tried not to look down at the frozen river below.

The person finally turned around at the sound of his voice. It was his mother.

Lukas gasped. What on Earth was she doing? "Come back. Come back to me," he pleaded. "I'll take you home."

"Leave me alone! I'm taking a walk with my baby." She continued her journey.

"Mama! It's Lukas. Please stop. It's not safe here." He tried to sound calm so as not to scare his mother, but she showed no sign of having heard him. As the baby's cries grew louder, his mother began to sing a lullaby. "Jesus Christ!" Lukas muttered under his breath.

As he gingerly stepped forward, he was surprised to find that the bridge was not as icy as he had feared. The freshly fallen snow was providing some traction. As he slowly made his way toward the middle of the structure, the baby grew quiet. His mother didn't seem to notice when he was only a few feet from her. She was looking down at her baby.

"Will you come home with me? Please, Mama."

She looked up abruptly. "Do I know you?" she asked, her tone hostile.

"It's Lukas. Your son."

"My son is only eight."

"We can talk about it when we get home. Just come with me." Lukas offered his hand.

"Absolutely not. Now get away from me." She took a step backward.

The sky was brightening, and Lukas could see how perilously close his mother was to the edge of the bridge. He dared not make a move. He didn't want to frighten her and cause her to slip. His panic rising, his mind raced to find a way to get her to safety. But his head hurt, and he couldn't think clearly. He blurted, "I know you don't recognize me—it's been seven years. But I really am your son. My birthday is January 15th, my eyes are green, and I once put a frog in Aunt Anna's tea pot. She almost boiled it."

His mother's eyes grew wide.

"And I used to love *The Wizard of Oz*. How's that? Do you believe me now?"

She stared at him, her face expressionless.

"Can we go now?" Lukas's fear was quickly being replaced by impatience. He was cold, dizzy, and tired of playing games. He took a step forward and reached out to his mother. He could now see that the baby was attached to her breast.

She swatted at him.

"Why'd you do that? Can you at least give me the baby?"

"No!" she shouted. "Someone, help me! He's trying to steal my baby!" Without thinking, Lukas lunged at his mother, snatching the baby from her breast. He grabbed hold of her coat with his free hand and tried to pull her toward him, but he was met with a flurry of fists. He stumbled backward. The forceful blows were too much for his wooden leg. As he fought to regain his balance, he felt the burning sensation of fingernails tearing at his cheek. Lukas hadn't expected such a visceral reaction from his mother. Suddenly, and without warning, an inexplicable surge of energy coursed through him. He rose to his full height and extended his arm to shield his face from further damage.

A shrill scream pierced the silent forest. When Lukas lowered his arm, his mother was in the air, falling backward off the bridge, plummeting toward the frozen river. There was no time to react.

"Lukas!" a deep voice shouted.

Disoriented, he turned toward the sound of his name.

Pole was rushing toward him with a rifle and a limp rabbit in his hand. "Jesus Christ! What the hell happened?"

Lukas's knees buckled. "She fell. Oh, my God! Mama fell!" His hand flew to his mouth.

Pole peered over the side of the bridge and put his hands on Lukas's shoulders. "Are you sure? Are you sure that's what happened?" Pole was shaking him.

Lukas nodded.

"You didn't push her?"

"No! I would never. I was trying to pull her away from the edge, but she wouldn't stop hitting me. She wouldn't stop clawing at me. I was so scared she'd drop the baby," Lukas said, gasping for air.

*Why can't I breathe? Why is the world spinning? And why does Pole think I pushed her?*

Pole put an arm around Lukas and led him and the baby back across the bridge to solid ground. "Sit here, Lukas. Take it easy for a minute."

Lukas saw Pole's mouth moving rapidly, but couldn't make out the words. His friend's face was blurry. Distorted. The back of Lukas's head was suddenly cold. Was that snow? He turned his head to the side and buried his burning cheek in the fluffy, white powder. Ahh, relief. Now if only the throbbing in his head would go away.

# *Fifty-Five*

## POLE

### BEAVER CREEK, DECEMBER 23, 1917

As Pole slipped through the front door with the baby in one arm and Lukas sagging against his side, he silently prayed for strength. The entire walk home from the train bridge was a complete blur. He had been so focused on trying to find a way to deliver the heartbreaking news to Sofie and her family. He and Lukas had remained at the scene of the accident and had spoken to the police at length. They'd left Karina in the care of the coroner, who had assured them that he would take great care in delivering her body to the town's only funeral parlor.

Pole could hear Janos, Sofie, and Aunt Anna in the dining room speaking in hushed tones. He immediately wondered if the news had already reached them. As he entered the room with the baby in his arms, they all fell silent.

"What are you doing with Mary?" Sofie asked, a puzzled look on her face. "We thought she was asleep upstairs with Karina."

"No one checked on her this mornin'?" he asked.

"No. After what happened last night, we figured it was best to let her and the baby sleep late. We haven't heard a peep out of them," Aunt Anna replied. "And where have you been, Lukas? What happened to your face?" she asked as soon as she saw the scratches on her nephew's cheek.

Lukas sank into a chair and held his head in his hands.

"What's wrong? What happened?" Janos asked, tension in his voice.

Pole took a deep breath as he pulled Mary tighter to his chest. "There's been an accident. Karina left the house before dawn with the baby. She must've been confused again. Lukas found her at the train bridge and tried to get her to come home, but she refused. She didn't recognize him." Pole hesitated. The faces around the table were hanging on his every word. His mouth froze up, unable to form the words.

"And?" Janos asked, his voice breaking.

"Karina fell off the bridge."

Pole's heart ached as he watched Sofie and Janos's faces twist with grief. Sofie reached out to touch her father's shoulder as his head fell toward the table under the weight of his sorrow. He began to cry. Sofie turned her face to hide behind a wall of thick, blonde hair. She made no sound, but the subtle movement of her shoulders gave away her crying. Pole knew she was hurting, even if she didn't want to show it.

Only Aunt Anna remained stoic. The only indication that she had processed the news was in the way she gripped her tea cup. She seemed to be holding onto it for support as she looked from her brother to her niece and nephew.

"The coroner is taking care of—" Pole broke off. "I'll stop by the funeral parlor tomorrow mornin' and make arrangements."

"That's very kind of you," Aunt Anna said softly.

Pole looked around the room at the people he had come to think of as family. Every one of them was either grief-stricken or in shock. Maybe both. How had things gone so terribly wrong? Karina did not deserve this tragic end to her life, no matter her sins. And now Pole was left wondering if her death relieved him of his duty to tell her family what he knew about her disappearance all those years ago.

For weeks, the burden of his knowledge had become increasingly difficult to bear. He debated telling Sofie about her mother's involvement in Henry Archer's murder almost daily. But telling her the truth was a double-edged sword. Sofie might be relieved to know that her mother only left her family because she was fleeing the police. But on the other hand, she would learn that her mother was a murderer.

And if Pole were to tell the truth, he certainly couldn't leave out the details about his pop's involvement in the debacle. Karina claimed *he* was the reason she had to leave town.

Pole had been so conflicted about the situation, he'd consulted a priest in the local Catholic church's confessional. He changed the names of all the people in the story, of course, and poured out his soul in the hopes that a man of the cloth might shed some light on his predicament. But unfortunately, Pole had left the church more confused than ever. The priest had instructed him to recite ten Hail Marys and five Our Fathers. Pole cursed the old codger on his way out of the church, wondering why he'd wasted his time.

As tragic as it was, maybe Karina's death gave Pole an out. Many months from now, her crimes would not matter. They would all grieve her loss and find a way to move forward with their lives. Her sins would be buried with her.

But more troubling now was the image of Lukas pushing his mother off the train bridge.

Pole shook his head, trying to erase the ridiculous notion from his mind. It was dark, he told himself. He was at least fifty yards away when he saw the boy with his arm extended toward his mother. The snow was falling steadily and had reduced visibility. Could anyone see clearly under those conditions?

Pole sighed heavily. He gazed at Mary's sweet face as he assured himself that Lukas had merely been protecting himself and an innocent baby from a deranged woman. There was no other logical explanation.

As Pole stroked Mary's cheek, she opened her pretty blue eyes, sending a rush of emotion through him. He stumbled into a chair as he fought the urge to cry. He did not succeed. As the tears rolled down his face, he prayed for Karina's tortured soul, hoping she would find the peace in heaven that she had been denied on earth.

## *Fifty-Six*

### SOFIE

#### BEAVER CREEK, DECEMBER 23, 1917

Her eyes heavy with sleep, Sofie inhaled the musky scent of Pole's aftershave as she lay nestled against his chest on the parlor sofa. She felt comforted by his familiar aroma, the warmth of his muscular body pressing against hers. She was not sure how long she had slept, only that she must have cried herself into a deep slumber. As she buried her head further into Pole's chest, praying the rest of her nap might be dreamless, she heard her father whispering nearby. Sofie could have sworn he'd said her name. She had no wish to return to a full state of wakefulness—the reality of the past twenty-four hours was too much to bear. But Papa had said Sofie and Mary's name in the same breath. What was he talking about?

Not wanting to interrupt the conversation, Sofie lay quietly against Pole, focusing on the voices around her.

"Do you really think she's ready to take on that kind of responsibility, Janos? She hasn't even graduated from high school yet," Aunt Anna said. "She wants to continue working for the paper."

"I know. I know," Papa said, the frustration in his voice palpable. "But what are we to do? We can't send Sofie and

Lukas's baby sister to an orphanage. She needs to grow up around family."

"That's a lot to ask of her. It might be different if she were married and ready to start a family of her own."

Pole suddenly shifted beneath Sofie. She felt his chest rise and fall. And then a slight quiver. "Mr. Kovac," he said, his voice cracking. "Maybe . . . maybe marriage isn't that far off. For Sofie, I mean." He coughed nervously.

Sofie's ears perked up. What were they all proposing? What was *he* proposing? Her heart raced. She quickly debated whether to speak up or continue eavesdropping. She willed herself to calm down and listen further.

"What do you mean?" Papa asked Pole.

"Well . . . I care about Sofie an awful lot." Pole paused to clear his throat, then crossed his legs. "I was hoping we might marry someday . . . but with everything that's happened, maybe the time is now."

"Oh my," Aunt Anna whispered.

"I love Sofie," Pole said, sounding more confident with each word. "And little Mary is an angel. I'd be honored to take care of them both."

Sofie could no longer contain the torrent of emotions whirling inside her. She bolted upright, startling her father, aunt, and Pole.

"How long have you been listening?" Pole asked, his face beet red.

"Long enough. I can't believe you're all making plans without me—as if I don't have a say in the matter. And, Papa . . ." Sofie glared at her father. "What makes you think I want to raise Karina's baby? Have you lost your mind, too?"

"Sofie! That's enough! That is the last time you will refer to your mother as 'Karina.'"

"Why are you defending her, Papa? What's changed?" Sofie stammered, wounded by her father's tone.

"Everything. Absolutely everything." He shook his head before burying it in his hands.

Sofie turned around to face Pole, who seemed to be holding his breath. She then turned to Aunt Anna, desperate for an explanation. Her aunt stared at her blankly, looking tired and short on sleep.

Suddenly, Papa raised his head. "I barely slept last night. I was haunted by your mother's agony at remembering the identity of Mary's father—this *Victor* person."

Sofie noticed her father had practically snarled as he'd said the man's name.

"I don't want to imagine what he did to her. It's too painful. But I fear I am partly to blame." He shook his head again—violently this time, as if trying to erase an unpleasant thought. "If only I'd seen the warning signs. If I'd taken her to the right doctor …"

"What are you talking about?" Sofie asked, trying to make sense of her father's ramblings.

"I finally figured it out last night . . . what I couldn't see while she was still living with us. Your mother was not well, Sofie. She hadn't been well for a very long time. Not since—"

"Before Sofie was born," Aunt Anna interrupted her brother.

Sofie and her father turned toward her aunt.

"Yes," Papa said, nodding. "The mood swings, the erratic behavior—they all started after Sofie was born. She became so distant. So detached." He looked down at his lap.

"So it's my fault my mother was such a troubled woman," Sofie said bitterly, knowing her insinuation was childish.

"No, sweetheart," Aunt Anna said. "Not you, but maybe the pregnancy. Childbirth can wreak havoc on a woman's body. Sometimes her mind, too. It's possible that the pregnancy triggered something."

"We may never understand the extent of your mother's suffering, but I will forever regret that I failed to recognize it in time to help her. Maybe she wouldn't have left us. She wouldn't have fallen victim to this stranger, and she'd still be alive." A fresh stream of tears flowed down Papa's cheeks. "I wish I'd done more."

"Don't you dare blame yourself, Janos," Aunt Anna scolded her brother. "Karina lost her mind because of what Victor did to her. He's to blame for her death. The problems she had during your marriage have nothing to do with her forgetting the past seven years. She was clearly traumatized in some way."

Sofie got up and knelt before her father. She took his hands in hers. "I'm sorry, Papa. I'm sorry you feel responsible. But even if you'd taken Mama to a doctor, it might not have made a difference. She still might have left us." Sofie turned to her aunt. "I would like to believe that a mental illness was the reason Mama was so neglectful when I was little. Maybe she wasn't as cold as I thought."

Papa stroked Sofie's hair. "We'll never get all the answers, *zlatíčko.* The only thing I know for certain is that your mother loved you. Despite all her failings, she loved you and Lukas. All of us."

Sofie trembled. She was overwhelmed by her father's confirmation of what she had always hoped to be true, what she'd often doubted in the years since her mother's disappearance. Her heart heavy with sorrow, she laid her head on her father's knees and wept.

"My poor, sweet girl." Papa placed his hand on Sofie's shoulder. "It's time to let go of the past. Let go of the anger. Hold onto the happy memories."

Sofie sniffled as she looked up at her father, nodding slowly. "I loved her, too, Papa. I was just so hurt after she left. I pushed my feelings way down deep inside me and covered them up with anger. Hating her was easier."

Papa kissed Sofie's forehead. "We can honor your mother by taking care of her baby. Say you'll raise Mary." Papa looked past her and smiled. "Pole will make a fine husband."

Sofie met her father's eyes. A glimmer of hope shined through his sad expression. She turned to Pole, who was looking at her expectantly. She took a deep breath before rising to her feet to disappoint everyone.

"I'm so sorry, but I can't." As Pole's face fell, Sofie rushed to his side and grabbed his hand. "You mean the world to me, Pole. I never want to be separated from you again." She caressed his cheek lovingly, hoping her touch would communicate what she was too embarrassed to say in front of her family. "But I'm not ready to be a wife or mother."

Pole nodded as he squeezed Sofie's hand.

She leaned closer and whispered, "Someday I will be. I hope you'll still be around."

Pole raised Sofie's hand to his lips and kissed it. "I'm not goin' anywhere, Sof."

A shiver went down Sofie's spine. Pole's love for her was written all over his face. It was in the tender tone he used when he spoke, in the gentle way he had kissed her hand. Sofie wanted to tell Pole that she loved him, too—that she had for as long as she could remember. But her declaration deserved a more perfect moment. She needed to be free from the heavy cloud of grief threatening to swallow her. She needed to reveal what was in her heart when she felt lighter and more hopeful. She prayed that moment would not elude her for too long.

"I need to check on Lukas," Aunt Anna said suddenly. "He was so distraught when I put him to bed. I gave him some Veronal to help him sleep."

"He's still in shock. He needs some time to process what's happened. We all do," Papa said, his voice unsteady. He rubbed his temple. "Maybe Mrs. Harford can be of some help. Perhaps she can take him on another trip and distract him for a while."

Sofie tilted her head. The solution was so obvious. "I know what we need to do."

# *Fifty-Seven*

## JANOS

### BEAVER CREEK, DECEMBER 23, 1917

The sun was setting as Janos climbed the steps to Concetta's front porch. He rarely entered her house this way, as he was used to slipping in and out of her kitchen through the door inside the store. But it was Sunday, and the store was closed. Concetta would not be expecting him. He had turned down her invitation to Sunday dinner the day before, thinking he would use his only day off to travel to a convent in Pittsburgh to see if the nuns might assume responsibility for Karina and her baby. Janos now understood the cruelty of that plan.

He wiped a tear from his cheek, wishing there was a way to rewrite the past, to create a happier ending for Karina. His heart ached at the thought of Sofie and Lukas grieving the loss of their mother a second time. How he longed to turn back the hands of time and remove a link from the dreadful chain of events that had led to this inconceivable suffering. He sighed, wondering why grief made sane men wish the impossible.

"What are you doing here?"

Startled, Janos turned around to find Concetta coming up the sidewalk, a covered plate in her hand. "I came to see you," he said.

"Your timing is perfect. Mrs. Rossi and I were baking all afternoon. I made you some *pizzelles* and *ricciarelli*." She grabbed Janos's hand as she climbed the steps. "Come inside. We'll have dessert before dinner," she said with a wink.

Janos followed Concetta into the house and helped her remove her coat. She had traces of flour on her burgundy skirt and a smudge of almond paste on the front of her white shirt. Without thinking, he took her face in his hands. "Do you have any idea how special you are to me?"

She smiled. The color of her cheeks was now the same shade as her skirt.

"Can we go into the parlor for a minute?" Janos asked, a lump forming in his throat.

"What's wrong?"

"I haven't been honest with you for quite some time."

Concetta's eyes widened.

"Please, come," Janos said, leading her to the sofa and sitting down next to her. "Before I begin, I want you to know that I care very deeply for you." He shook his head, knowing those words did not ring true enough. "No, Concetta," he said, squaring his shoulders. "I love you."

Her hand flew to her mouth.

"I only pray that you can find it in your heart to forgive me."

Janos took a deep breath in preparation for the emotional conversation that lay ahead. He sensed the coming moments would be pivotal. They would determine the course of his future, for better or worse. As he met Concetta's gaze, he saw both fear and sympathy in her lovely brown eyes. She squeezed his hand, a subtle sign of encouragement.

The confession suddenly flowed from Janos's lips, like a dam released one too many days after a torrential storm. The flood was fast and furious, its effects momentous. Through intermittent sobs, Janos revealed the identity of the guest who had been staying at his home, the existence of her newborn baby, and the tragic end his wife had met at dawn of that same day. He even recounted Lukas's heartbreaking reunion with his mother the night before. As the details streamed out of him, Janos feared that the truth, like a raging river, would carve out a new landscape and change the world as they knew it.

When he reached his story's end, he wiped his eyes and focused on Concetta. He had been so caught up in the emotion of his tale that he had barely made eye contact with her. Or perhaps it was shame that had caused him to avert his gaze so many times. He studied her face and was surprised to find it streaked with tears. He caressed her cheek. Had he broken her heart with his betrayal?

"I'm so sorry I lied."

"Don't apologize," Concetta whispered. "You've suffered more than enough." She shook her head. "My heart aches for all of you." She wrapped her arms around Janos and buried her face in his chest.

He exhaled, relieved to be free of his lies. He leaned back on the sofa, pulling Concetta with him. They sat in silence for several minutes, taking refuge in each other's arms.

"I hope your feelings for me haven't changed," Janos whispered as he stroked Concetta's hair.

She lifted her head to meet his eyes. A tear escaped down her cheek.

Janos held his breath. Had he lost her forever?

Concetta leaned into his face, nodding. "I love you more than yesterday. More than I ever thought possible." She pressed her lips against his. "You are an even better man than I imagined."

A wave of warmth washed over Janos. The ache in his heart abated.

# Fifty-Eight

## EDITH

### SHADYSIDE, DECEMBER 24, 1917

Edith sat in the parlor admiring her ten-foot-tall Christmas tree adorned with gold and silver ornaments. She was surprised by the elegance of the new metallic theme and rather enjoyed the way the light reflected off the dozens of shiny bulbs and baubles hung on the Douglas Fir. Green and red decorations were so prosaic anyway. So commonplace. She was not an ordinary woman. An average tree would no longer do in her home.

As she gazed out the window at the blaze on her front lawn, she was struck by the strange beauty of the scene. The enormous pile of draperies, bedding, linens, and clothing stacked atop her red chaise lounge and four red-patterned armchairs had created an impressive fire. The flames shot as high as the second story of her home. And the ashes. Their beauty was mystifying. They fell gently from the sky amidst the fluffy, white snowflakes, their contrast stark yet strangely wondrous.

The dark against the light. The delicate interplay of these two forces was fascinating. Their constant struggle brought balance to the world.

Edith was stunned by the profundity of her thoughts. The light and the dark, she mused. One could not exist without the other. They occupied separate spaces in the universe, taking turns at dominance. When joy was at its zenith, illuminating the world, the threat of darkness was ever present. It waited in the shadows for an opportunity to conquer the light. To resume its rule.

And this time, its destruction had been all too thorough. Edith stroked her empty womb, fighting back tears. The salty taste of blood was on her lips. She'd bit herself too hard this time.

"Edith, darling, lunch is almost ready. Will you please join me in the dining room?" James asked as he entered the parlor, reaching for his wife's hand.

"Did Shannon get rid of that dreadful Christmas china with the red poinsettias?"

"Yes. She put it away."

Edith balled her fist. "Tell her to collect every last piece and add them to the fire."

"I'm worried about you." James said, lowering his voice. "It's Christmas Eve, and we have a wretched bonfire in our front yard. I can't imagine what the neighbors must think." He hesitated. "Your behavior is growing more peculiar. Some might even call it frightening."

"Who said that? Was it my cousin Clara? She's always sticking her nose where it doesn't belong."

"No. Let me rephrase. *I* am frightened by your behavior. You are not well, Edith." James peered out the window at the blaze and frowned. "Look at our lawn! It should be a delightful, wintry scene with all this snow. Instead, it's been marred by ashes."

Edith studied the dark circle surrounding the fire. The ashes extended at least a dozen feet in every direction, blackening the snow. Further out, ash was sprinkled arbitrarily, creating ominous patterns in varying shades of gray. She nodded. "Yes.

Your pure white snow has been ruined—like so many other things as of late."

James squinted in the direction of the front gate. "Who's that?" he said to no one in particular.

Curious, Edith leaned forward. She could see a man coming up the walk, but could not determine his identity. He was bundled up in a heavy coat, the collar pulled up high over his ears.

"Is that Lukas?" James asked.

Edith stood up. "I cannot see him in this state," she said, fingering the stubble on her chin. "I'm going upstairs. Tell him I'm not ready for visitors."

"Since when is Lukas a visitor? He's family. He's our son," James said, his voice breaking.

As Edith climbed the first few stairs, she heard the squeak of the doorknob. She quickened her pace.

"Lukas?" she heard her husband say. "What are you doing here?"

Edith paused at the top of the stairs, eager to know what had brought Lukas to the house on Christmas Eve. He was supposed to be spending the holiday with his family.

"I need to speak with you and Aunt Edith. It's very important."

"Is everything all right?" James asked. "Have you been crying?"

Edith rushed down the stairs. "What's wrong? What's happened?" She put her arms around Lukas, who was standing in the foyer shivering. His entire body was covered with snow, his dark blonde hair now white. "Where's your hat?"

"The wind took it. I couldn't chase it because I was carrying this." He opened his coat to reveal a tiny baby wrapped in a pink, fuzzy blanket.

Edith gasped. "Who is this?"

"Her name is Mary. She's an orphan in need of a home. Her mother died only yesterday."

Edith leaned closer to the little angel. She was sleeping peacefully, unaware of the strangers admiring her sweet face.

"Who was her mother? Are you in a position to offer her to us?" James asked, his tone both skeptical and eager.

Lukas nodded as a tear rolled down his cheek. "Her mother was . . ."

Edith caressed his arm, waiting for him to finish his sentence. He shook his head, the grief apparently still too raw. "You can tell us when you're ready." She kissed his cheek and rested her head against his shoulder.

"Her mother was someone I loved very much," Lukas whispered suddenly. "She'd been gone from my life for so long, I'd forgotten how much she meant to me." After a quiet moment, he asked, "Would you like to hold her, Aunt Edith? Would you like to hold my baby sister?"

Comprehension dawned on Edith. She turned to James, who was nodding his encouragement, his blue eyes twinkling.

As Lukas placed baby Mary in her arms, Edith felt the warmth of the sun upon her face. Its bright rays had somehow pierced through the storm clouds and penetrated the stained glass window above them. She smiled. The light had returned to vanquish the darkness.

# Author's Note

*Beneath the Veil of Smoke and Ash* was inspired by my research into my family's genealogy and my interest in the history and culture of Pennsylvania. In the summer of 2012, I asked my ninety-year-old grandmother a few questions about her childhood and was presented with a scrapbook and several shoeboxes of old photos. I'm not sure why Grandma Pearl had never shown me these treasures until the final months of her life, but I am grateful nonetheless. She opened up to me that day about her childhood and showed me pictures of her Lithuanian parents as well as her Slovak in-laws. She recalled the days of running moonshine for her mother during the Prohibition era and mentioned a young Polish friend of hers who went by the name of *Pole*. I was fascinated by Grandma Pearl's stories, but even more captivated by the images of my great-grandparents who arrived in America at the turn of the twentieth century to work in the steel mills of Pittsburgh. I wondered what they were like and what sort of challenges they might have faced. These imaginings inspired me to write the story of the Kovac family.

While the characters in my novel are fictional, the world they live in is not. I read several books about Pennsylvania's steel and coal mining industries in the early twentieth century as well as excerpts from *The Pittsburgh Survey*, a sociological study conducted from 1907-1908, which chronicled the living conditions of immigrant families. Thanks to YouTube, I was able to watch silent films of steelworkers and coal miners performing hazardous work during the 1910s and 1920s. And during a visit to the Tour-Ed Mine and Museum in Tarentum, Pennsylvania, my father shared memories of his thirty years of coal mining with me as we stumbled through dark tunnels 160 feet below ground. It was extremely important to me to provide historically accurate descriptions of both the steel mill and coal mine as well as the towns that were built around them. Also important to the telling of this story was an authentic portrayal of the attitudes of both workers and companies like the US Steel Corporation toward unionization. I hope my efforts have been successful.

Residents of Western Pennsylvania may be wondering why I created the fictional towns of Riverton, Abbott's Hollow, and Beaver Creek. The answer is that I simply wanted to give myself more freedom to write the Kovacs' story, though I have left clues that point to the inspiration for these settings. I should also mention that Westmont Academy, the boarding school Lukas attends in Johnstown, is also a figment of my imagination, created for the purpose of reuniting Pole and Lukas in Central Pennsylvania.

Because Karina is so central to the story of the Kovac family, it is important to address her mental illness. Most readers probably recognize that Karina suffers from depression during the first part of the book, but they may not realize that her illness was triggered by the birth of her first child. It may sound strange, given that Sofie is ten years old, but there is an explanation.

According to the American Psychological Association, anxiety and depression are common complications of childbirth, affecting as many as one in seven new moms. Fortunately, the majority of these cases improve quickly with time and proper treatment. But for roughly 38 percent of women diagnosed with postpartum depression, the condition becomes lifelong.

Factors that affect the probability that the disease will persist include a woman's sensitivity to the hormonal shifts of pregnancy as well as the time it takes to diagnose and treat her condition. Environmental stressors like financial hardship, a traumatic birth experience, and the lack of a support system can play a role as well. And, of course, some women may be genetically predisposed to depression and other mood disorders. For these women, the shift in hormones during pregnancy and childbirth trigger a condition that has not yet surfaced. A psychiatrist I spoke with likened this phenomenon to a tulip bulb under the earth's surface waiting for the right conditions to bloom. As for Karina's depression, I'll let readers make their own conclusions about why it persisted.

When Karina returns to her family after her seven-year absence, she is also suffering from dissociative amnesia. This mental disorder occurs when a person blocks out certain information, usually associated with a stressful or traumatic event. The individual is unable to remember important personal information and may suffer memory loss spanning months or even years. In some cases, only the memories involving the traumatic event are blocked. People with this disorder may or may not be aware of their memory loss and may appear confused.

As for Edith, she suffers from polycystic ovary syndrome (PCOS). It's a hormonal disorder common among women of reproductive age. It can affect a woman's ability to have a child as it stops her periods or makes them difficult to predict. PCOS can also cause acne, weight gain, unwanted body and facial hair, and a deep voice due to the excess of male hormones associated with this condition. Because of the hormonal imbalance in women with PCOS, their ovaries may develop numerous small collections of fluid and fail to regularly release eggs. Polycystic ovary syndrome is one of the leading causes of female infertility, affecting as many as one in ten American women of childbearing age (ages fifteen to fifty).

On a final note, I would simply like to share that the writing of the Kovacs' story impacted my life in unexpected ways. I set out to recreate the world of my great-grandparents and gain a deeper understanding of American labor history and mental illness, but never imagined I would come away with such a profound appreciation for the human condition.

／

# Acknowledgments

I have so many people to thank for guiding me along the path to publication. I am extremely grateful for the editorial expertise of Kathryn Johnson. Her insights helped me make significant improvements to the early drafts of my novel. Jane Friedman, Arielle Eckstut, and David Henry Sterry were instrumental in helping me revise my opening chapters. They also provided sage advice about the querying process and the publishing industry in general. I can't recommend their services enough.

Very critical to my writing process was the arsenal of family and friends who were willing to read my novel and provide feedback. I am grateful to my parents, Joe and Linda Pasterick, as well as my friends, Melissa Whitlinger, Marcy Bradley, Alicia Kavulic, and Ulrike Bussmann, for their honest assessments and enthusiastic support. My writer friends, Jennifer Jabaley, Christy Maguire, and Elizabeth Conte Torphy, provided invaluable critiques as well as sympathy and humor when my journey got bumpy.

I owe a special thanks to my dear friend, Stacy Riggle El Sabbagh, whose belief in this novel never wavered. She was the ultimate cheerleader and even went so far as to recruit her colleagues at Pittsburgh Public Schools to serve as beta readers for me. The feedback I received from Stacy and her coworkers,

John Masilunas, Andrea Harhai, David and Colleen Pilarski, Kathleen Hammer, Jackie Kimmel, and Ron Stein, was essential to the final round of revisions to my novel.

I would like to thank Professor Michael Kopanic, Jr. of the University of Maryland Global Campus for reviewing the final version of my manuscript and providing many helpful suggestions relating to Slovak culture and the history of Western Pennsylvania. I am also grateful to Professor Marcela Michalkova of the University of Pittsburgh for her assistance with the Slovak language.

I am so happy I found a home for my novel at She Writes Press. Brooke Warner, Shannon Green, Julie Metz, and the entire team have been a dream to work with. Crystal Patriarche, Tabitha Bailey, and Hanna Lindsley at BookSparks have also been amazing. Their publicity services far exceeded my expectations.

I would like to thank my husband, Jon, for reading every draft of this novel and believing so fiercely in my writing. I couldn't ask for a more supportive partner. And last, but certainly not least, I am grateful to my children, Ethan and Morgan, who endured years of me bouncing story ideas off them on the way to soccer practice. I hope they will read this novel someday and be proud of their Slovak and Lithuanian heritage.

## *Questions for Discussion*

1. Karina is especially vulnerable as an attractive young woman working in the home of a bachelor with a prominent position at the Riverton mill. Should she have quit her job instead of submitting to Henry's sexual advances? Would she have been less susceptible to her employer's abuses had she not been an immigrant?
2. At the end of the first chapter, Karina has a flashback of being groped by drunks at the boarding house. Compare the behavior of these immigrants to that of Henry Archer. Given the scarce employment opportunities for a woman of Karina's status and means as well as the lack of legal recourse for sexual harassment and assault during the early twentieth century, what could Karina have done to stop these abuses?
3. Janos's work at the steel mill is incredibly dangerous and has taken a terrible toll on his health. Were you surprised by the deplorable working conditions at the mill? Did anyone in your family immigrate to America to work in the steel industry?
4. Sofie is an anxious ten-year-old who worries about her father dying in an accident at the mill. She resents her neglectful mother and wonders why she never pays her any attention. In what ways has the outside world impacted

Sofie's family dynamics? How have Janos and Karina contributed to Sofie's unhappiness? What role does Pole play in Sofie's life?

5. Karina's relationship with her family is complicated. She loves her husband and children, but rarely shows it. She is fixated on her family's lack of money and status and is overburdened by her affair with her employer. What impact does Karina's depression have on her interactions with her family? How does it affect her decision making, especially as it relates to Henry and her plot to escape Riverton?
6. Janos is often frustrated and hurt by Karina's unpredictable behavior. He resents the fact that she neglects him and the children and wants a more intimate relationship with her. When talking about moving to the glass town, he tells Karina, "Once we get away from Riverton, we can forget about the past and wipe the slate clean. We'll build a new life for our family" (p. 104). Do you think Janos suspects Karina has been unfaithful? Is he a fool to want to start over with her?
7. Karina and Henry are both ambitious and desperate to escape Riverton. Their actions are often motivated by their deep desire for upward mobility. Compare and contrast these two characters. Does Henry deserve Karina's wrath when he ditches her for Edith? Is his ending satisfying, given that his negligence led to the death of Tomas Tomicek? If Henry hadn't abruptly ended their relationship, would Karina have gone through with her plans to leave Riverton with him, or would she have chosen to stay with Janos and her children?
8. Seven years after leaving Riverton with his father, Pole is stuck in the mountains of Central Pennsylvania, mining coal to support his sister, Lily, and her mother. Were you surprised by the descriptions of life in the patch village and the ways the miners were exploited by the coal company?

Did anyone in your family immigrate to America to work in the coal industry?

9. Since Karina's disappearance, Janos, Sofie, and Lukas have moved on with their lives and are doing quite well in Beaver Creek and Johnstown. Discuss the ways their lives have improved in the past seven years. Are they better off without Karina? In what ways has Karina's disappearance traumatized the family? Is she to blame for the loss of Lukas's leg?
10. Edith suffers from a mysterious medical condition, which is interfering with her ability to have a baby. Were you able to diagnose her without googling her symptoms? Were you surprised that Edith became Lukas's benefactor after the train accident? How has her infertility impacted her relationship with her husband, James, and with Lukas?
11. When Pole is trapped in the coal mine for five days, he is forced to consider his mortality and weighs the option of a slow and painful death versus drinking piss and eating raw rats—or possibly even Gus—in order to survive. How would you cope if you were in Pole's situation?
12. After seven long years, Karina returns to her family pregnant and on the verge of insanity. What do you think happened to her? What role do you think Victor played in her absence and trauma? Do you agree with Janos's decision to care for Karina until her baby is born?
13. When Sofie and Pole reunite after their seven-year separation, they quickly rekindle their friendship, and a romance blossoms. Why do you think Sofie opens her heart to Pole, given that she had absolutely no interest in boys prior to Pole's arrival? What is so special about their relationship?
14. Janos has fallen in love with Concetta and desperately wants a future with her, but Karina's unexpected return jeopardizes his plans. Should Janos have been honest with Concetta about the situation with Karina instead of trying

to hide it from her? How does Janos's relationship with Concetta compare to his marriage with Karina?

15. Edith is overjoyed to learn that she is pregnant, but utterly devastated when she loses the baby. When she discovers blood all over her nightgown and bedding, she instructs James, "Get every last bit of it out of this house. . . . Red. The color red" (p. 335). What do you think of her reaction to her miscarriage and her behavior in the weeks that follow? Is she losing her mind?
16. Lukas follows his mother across the icy train bridge because he fears for her safety as well as baby Mary's. When Karina refuses to take Lukas's hand and becomes defensive, a struggle ensues, and Karina falls off the bridge. Do you think Karina's death was an accident, or do you think Lukas pushed her?
17. Do you think Karina got the ending she deserved, or was she a victim of her mental illness and society? Does Janos deserve any blame for not recognizing Karina's suffering before she left Riverton? Do you feel sympathy for Karina? If not, why?
18. What do you think happens to Janos and Concetta after the story ends? What about Sofie and Pole? Will Pole tell Sofie what he knows about Karina and her role in Henry Archer's death? Will Edith, James, and baby Mary have a happy life together? Will Lukas blame himself for his mother's death, or will he move on and make peace with his troubled past?

## About the Author

A native of Western Pennsylvania, Tammy Pasterick grew up in a family of steelworkers, coal miners, and Eastern European immigrants. She began her career as an investigator with the National Labor Relations Board and later worked as a paralegal and German teacher. She holds degrees in labor and industrial relations from Penn State University and German language and literature from the University of Delaware. She currently lives on Maryland's Eastern Shore with her husband, two children, and chocolate Labrador retriever. *Beneath the Veil of Smoke and Ash* is her first novel.

## SELECTED TITLES FROM SHE WRITES PRESS

She Writes Press is an independent publishing company founded to serve women writers everywhere. Visit us at www.shewritespress.com.

*The Mill of Lost Dreams* by Lori Rohda. $16.95, 978-1-63152-719-7. Three immigrant families and one eleven-year-old orphan risk everything to find a better life in the textile mills of Fall River, Massachusetts—and learn what happens to those whose dreams of a better life are irreversibly and unexpectedly lost.

*Wolf Den Hollow* by Donna Murray. $16.95, 978-1-63152-765-4. When Sila, a beautiful Cherokee teenager, flees her alcoholic and abusive husband in the dead of winter, she finds herself knocking on the door of a mill office, desperate for work—and meets the handsome Charley Barclay, the owner. Despite the fact that they have virtually nothing in common and thirty years between them, a spark ignites.

*Eliza Waite* by Ashley Sweeney. $16.95, 978-1-63152-058-7. When Eliza Waite chooses to leave a stagnant life in rural Washington State and join the masses traveling north to Alaska in 1898 during the tumultuous Klondike Gold Rush, she encounters challenges and successes in both business and love.

*The Vintner's Daughter* by Kristen Harnisch. $16.95, 978-163152-929-0. Set against the sweeping canvas of French and California vineyard life in the late 1890s, this is the compelling tale of one woman's struggle to reclaim her family's Loire Valley vineyard—and her life.

*Lum* by Libby Ware. $16.95, 978-1-63152-003-7. In Depression-era Appalachia, an intersex woman without a home of her own plays the role of maiden aunt to her relatives—until an unexpected series of events gives her the opportunity to change her fate.